"Have you seen this volcano goddess?" Dina asked.

"I've seen her hair," Saurage said. "And it's like yours."

She laughed. The conversation wafted her home, to a London ballroom, to a dandy whispering witty comments in her ear. The captain moved with agility, despite his size. The eyes of the company were on them.

"You dance well," she said when next they came together.

"So do you. We shall share the evening."

"My aunt and uncle have ordered me to spread my attentions amongst the men."

"And Captain Savage may have only one dance?" he asked.

His use of the forbidden name caused a quiver in the muscles of Dina's legs, but she kept her face emotionless. "How did you know?"

"Aunts and uncles always warn against me. Act as a stallion, you're treated as a stallion, not a gelding."

"You know they call you Savage?"

"I not only know—I enjoy it…!"

Dear Reader,

When we ran our first March Madness promotion in 1992, we had no idea that we would get such a wonderful response. Our springtime showcase of brand-new authors has been so successful that we've continued to seek out talented new writers and introduce them into the field of historical romance. During our yearly search, my editors and I have the unique opportunity of reading hundreds of manuscripts from unpublished authors, and we'd like to take this time to thank all of you who have given us the chance to review your work.

Rae Muir's exciting debut novel, *The Pearl Stallion*, features an unlikely romance between the infamous Captain Savage and the penniless Lady Endine, who stows away on his ship to escape marriage to a horrible man.

And be sure to keep an eye out for our other three titles. *Warrior's Deception* by Diana Hall, a medieval novel about a marriage based on lies. *Fool's Paradise* by Tori Phillips, the charming tale of a noblewoman and the jester who becomes her protector. And *Western Rose* by Lynna Banning, the story of a rancher and a schoolteacher who must work out their differences before they accept their love.

Four new talents, four great stories from Harlequin Historicals. Don't miss a single one!

Sincerely,

Tracy Farrell
Senior Editor

RAE MUIR

The Pearl Stallion

Harlequin Books

TORONTO • NEW YORK • LONDON
AMSTERDAM • PARIS • SYDNEY • HAMBURG
STOCKHOLM • ATHENS • TOKYO • MILAN
MADRID • WARSAW • BUDAPEST • AUCKLAND

ISBN 0-373-28908-1

THE PEARL STALLION

This edition published by arrangement with Harlequin Books S.A.

Printed in U.S.A.

Books by Rae Muir

Harlequin Historicals

The Pearl Stallion #308

RAE MUIR

lives in a cabin in California's High Sierra, a mile from an abandoned gold mine. She is, by training, a historian, but finds it difficult to fit into the academic mold, since her imagination inevitably inserts fictional characters into actual events. She has been a newspaper reporter, wrote and edited educational materials, researched eighteenth-century Scottish history, ran a fossil business and raised three children in her spare time.

She loves the Sierra Nevada, Hawaii, Oxford and San Francisco. Her favorite mode of travel is by car, and she stops at every historical marker.

For Kate, Cynthia, Mia and Karla

Chapter One

Dina leaned back in her hammock chair, surprised that the list of things she hated about Calcutta had reached no more than nineteen. Number one was, of course, the heat. Perhaps she might record that twice, bring the condemnations to a round twenty.

No, she had been here less than a fortnight. Another unpleasantness was bound to surface within the next few days. Unless she could find her way onto a ship, sail back to England. How had she, Lady Endine Wilmount, the reigning beauty of three London seasons, ended up in India with the "fishing fleet" to find a husband?

Drops of perspiration ran down her neck, tickling her. How could human beings live in this heat? Ten days in Calcutta, and she was exhausted.

A husband, Uncle George had insisted last night. Both she and Emily were expected to gain a proposal within the next three months. Dina groaned. If she had wanted a husband, she would have accepted Viscount Wolfe, or Lord Randolph Porter.

"The *Pearl Stallion* is in port," said a man's voice close by. Dina sprang from the hammock chair, scrambled into the thicket of vines hanging from the banyan tree. She did not recognize the voice beyond the hedge.

"Damn! He'd been gone so long I'd... I'd hoped he'd dropped off the face of the earth." Dina recognized the voice of her uncle George.

What was her uncle doing in the garden in the heat of the afternoon and with a visitor? And what would he do if he found her, clad only in her shift and a scant silk dressing gown?

"If he sailed over the edge of the earth," said the unknown with amusement, "we'd never find out where he goes."

"Another prosperous voyage for the bastard?" her uncle asked in a voice thick with envy.

"More than before. An absolute treasure of silk and tea in the hold. Gossip says the ballast is crates of antique porcelain."

Uncle George groaned. "We must find out how he does it. Then, when there's money enough to lease a ship—"

"You'll never have money enough if you keep buying carriages and other fripperies," the other man said chidingly.

He must be someone with power and prestige, Dina decided, for her uncle did not protest either the tone or the rebuke.

"My wife. . . ." Uncle George sighed. "Does he know? Any sign that he knows our little scheme?" he whispered.

"That I cannot say," said the stranger lightly. "And it does little good to worry over what we cannot know."

"Damn! How can such a man have Lord Mornington's favor? His behavior should exclude him from polite society, even here in Calcutta. I wish him in hell!"

Dina was struck by the depth of the violence in her uncle's speech. He'd been raised a Quaker, like his brother and sister, like her own mother. But while other members of the family had clung to the faith, her uncle had obviously rejected it, abandoned it on the English shore when he took ship for India.

The two men approached so near that Dina held her breath. Sweat poured from her face in the tropical heat; she dared not move her hand to wipe her forehead, for fear she would rustle the leaves and betray her presence in the dead calm of the afternoon.

"Something must be done to get him out of India," her uncle stated. "You have the ear of the governor-general. Convince him to cancel his license..."

"One of their most profitable captains?" the unknown asked sardonically.

"They could deprive him of his ship."

"He owns the *Pearl Stallion.* Remember, he has influence with the Company directors. The Honorable Anson Saurage may be a plague for certain people in Calcutta, but he *is* the son of an earl. Your envy and fear are too obvious. We'll work against him quietly. Lord Mornington will not be governor-general forever."

Uncle George cursed.

"And," continued the stranger, "as I understand, his brother has no children. A fall from a horse, a summer fever, and your Captain Savage would be a peer. He may be secretive about his trading routes, and short-tempered when concerned about his ship, he may be a suspicious sort who is a threat to, uh...some people...but he's no fool, and his memory is long. He'll recollect everyone in India who called him Captain Savage, and his revenge could be dreadful."

"Damn, him!" repeated her uncle.

Saurage. The family name of the Earls of Valmont. Dina had danced with the present earl, flirted with him, for who would not want to be a countess? If only she'd had a decent portion, perhaps right now she'd be the countess of Valmont, instead of an impoverished chit, two-and-twenty years old, looking to the women-hungry men of India to get a proposal. But she'd not been able to compete with the extravagant dowry of Miss Amelia Strawn, and Miss Strawn was now the Lady Valmont. Dina nearly echoed her uncle's curses as she considered her fate.

Would she have accepted Valmont if he asked her to be his wife? Or would she have turned him down, as she had turned down a crowd of London dandies whose names she could not recall in this squalid, humid furnace.

More crunching gravel, and Dina sensed the two men were standing very close together. "Do you think he knows?" her uncle whispered.

"You keep asking me questions I cannot possibly answer. How much Lieutenant Becker suspected when he left the shipyard last year, I can't say. Did he acquaint Saurage with his suspicions? Who knows?"

"If Saurage suspected irregularities at the shipyard, he'd have gone to Mornington, wouldn't you think?" Uncle George asked desperately.

The stranger laughed. "Mason, you'll exhaust yourself. Such mental exercise isn't good in this heat. If Becker comes to the shipyard, I'll try to sound him out, both on our private matter and on where the *Pearl Stallion* traded. How does Saurage turn a cargo of pig iron, cotton and tin pots into one of silk and tea?"

"Letting Lieutenant Becker glimpse the shipyard ledgers was foolish," snapped Uncle George. "And letting him get wind of the bargain with the Dutchman...."

"Mr. Mason," said the stranger arrogantly, "may I remind you of your position."

"Sorry. Terribly sorry." Her uncle's tone, and the crunch of gravel, told Dina he was bobbing his head, shuffling his feet. "I'd counted on the *Pearl Stallion* going to the bottom in a storm. I'd prayed for it.... Now I must warn Mrs. Mason that the man's in town. Do you suppose he will be at the ball tonight?"

"I shouldn't think he'd miss it. He's fond of dancing and gone a year, he must be straining for company."

"My two nieces are here, hardly a fortnight in Calcutta. They must be warned to be circumspect." The men turned, and the sound of their feet on the gravel died away. Their voices dwindled to faint wisps of sound.

Dina crept around the waist-high bushes, staying well out of sight, then dashed for the portal leading to the rooms she shared with Cousin Emily.

She passed the open door of her uncle's study. His spyglass stood upright on his desk, like a great column. Dina leaned into the room and snatched up the glass. She climbed the ladder into the second story of the bungalow, an attic under the thatched roof. The small, low-ceilinged room concentrated the heat; her lungs ached with every breath.

An unglazed window overlooked the dun-colored Hooghly and the ships at anchor there. Dina knelt, brought the glass to her eye. The bare masts and busy decks of the East Indiamen sprang into close range, as if she might reach out and touch them. She studied one ship after another. A dark hull, smaller, sharper, than the Indiamen, with three raked masts. She halted the sweep of the glass and moved back to the stranger.

At this distance she could not read the names, but with this ship there was no doubt. The sleek hull was black, unrelieved by any white gun ports or red stripes. The figurehead stood out like a gull in a flock of crows. Even at this distance she could see the flowing mane, the wild head, of a proud stallion, glistening in the sun, as if carved from some precious gem.

The *Pearl Stallion.*

Small landing craft surrounded it. Bales and chests swung off the deck into the launches, lifted by lines dangling from the yardarms.

She moved the glass back to the *Morgan Castle,* the ship that had carried her to India. Nearly six months she had spent in its dreary confines and the sight of the ship brought quivers of memory. The storm in the Atlantic, days of noise and being tossed about, her sea chest broken free from its restraints, thundering from side to side in the cabin, threatening to break her leg if she so much as stepped from her bunk.

And the awful mornings when the female passengers were kept below, out of sight but not out of hearing of the punishments conducted above. Once she had glimpsed a sailor as he was hustled to the surgeon, his back harried into a bloody mass. She shivered. She would go on just one more ship, the one that would carry her back to England.

She closed her eyes and forced herself to think of London, cool, foggy London. A ballroom, filled with light, reflections of the candles in the jewels of the women and on the gold braid of uniforms.

It was too hot to concentrate on anything. But she had to concentrate, to plan how to get out of this hell. She'd seen the range of the cemetery. Half of the young men and women who came to India died within five years.

Marriage. She'd have to pick very carefully, some officer or company secretary who was close to the end of his contract, who would soon have a furlough in England. Then, once in England, she'd refuse to come back. She'd live in dingy rooms in a country town before she'd return to India. Less than a hundred pounds a year. That was all she had from the money her grandmother had left.

Dina pushed the damp tendrils of hair off her neck and forehead. Considering the heat, she was fortunate that short hair was in fashion. Some men had objected when women cropped their hair, but Lord Valmont had admired her curls.

Of all the men she'd dallied with in London, she'd found Lord Valmont one of the most attractive. He was delicate almost to the point of frailty. Such a man might be dominated by his wife. She'd have to put up with his marital demands, of course. She presumed he was strong enough for that. But otherwise, the wife of a man like Valmont could live her own life.

She tried to imagine Lord Valmont as the captain of a ship in the East India trade. Ridiculous! But his brother was the captain of that black hull in the harbor. Perhaps he had officers who did the real work while he sat in his cabin, taking his snuff with a perfectly bent wrist.

Trade? Would a Saurage engage in trade? If he did, he destroyed any credibility with the *ton*. But she presumed a captain could disengage himself from the business. Certainly there was some officer who bargained with the natives of the Spice Islands and Canton, leaving the captain to receive dignitaries in his elegantly appointed cabin.

She sat up, suddenly inspired. Captain Saurage's ship had just come from China. Would he now go on to England? She lay down, her head swarming with plans. She'd find out if Captain Saurage had a wife. If not, she'd overawe him with her attentions, and when the *Pearl Stallion* weighed anchor, she'd be aboard. It was not a brilliant match, marrying a younger son who had, perhaps, fallen into trade. But if her uncle's remarks were true, Saurage had grown rich in the China trade. And in India she might do so much worse. He was absolutely second best, but a second-best earl's son was better than the second-best son of a clerk.

She clenched her jaw so tightly her teeth hurt. The daughter of the earl of Cairnlea, sunk so low! Better that she harness herself to the brother of an earl, even if he had shamed the family by sailing to China and hawking tin pans. Her heart pounded when she thought of what even a weak husband could—would—ask of her. She closed her eyes and forced herself to relax, made her breath come slowly and evenly. It would not do to get upset. She had a plan. Tonight, at the ball, she would begin the capture of Captain Saurage's heart.

Dina crept down the stairs and peered into Emily's room. Her cousin was sound asleep under her mosquito bar, placidly unaware that she was the cause of Dina's distress. Because Emily had not found a husband and was almost thirty years old, because Dina had fallen into the care of Emily's pious father, who disapproved of bright London life on principle, Dina had been forced to accompany her cousin to India. Uncle Leonard threatened to cut off her allowance if she did not go.

Dina went to her own room, threw herself onto her bed and closed her eyes. She must consider how to charm Saurage.

The corridor was cold, the stone floor beneath her feet uneven. She should not be here, but Carlton had dared her to explore the upper floors of the castle. She did not fear old Lord Moreton, their host. But her father had forbid den her to leave the confines of the nursery, which was so unfair, because she was twelve years old and should have some of the freedoms her brother enjoyed.

A scream rose to a peak, then cut off. She stood paralyzed. Carlton had teased her about the ghosts who walked these corriders. But surely ghosts walked only at night.

She turned, trembling, retracing her steps. By the time she reached the gray stone arch at the end of the corridor, she was running.

Another scream forced her to turn before she dashed down the stairs. She recognized the shift-clad body that stumbled into the hall, the man close behind who tripped the woman with his stick.

Dina clasped her hands tightly over her mouth, watched the fair body writhe under the blows of the heavy cane, and listened to her mother's screams.

She sat up in bed, her hands tangled in the mosquito netting, her heart in her throat. She was not at Moreton, her mother was ten years dead, and her father had shot himself in the woods of Ratherton, the day after the estate was sold to settle his and Carlton's gambling debts. Carlton was months in his grave, his neck broken when his horse balked at a gate and catapulted him into a tree. The family line was cut off, Ratherton gone.

"I'm going to find a husband to take me back to England," she whispered to herself with determination. "He will not be like Father. He will not be like Father."

Dina found her aunt and uncle on the veranda, already dressed for the evening. Uncle George, restricted by his high starched collar, turned his whole body in her direction as she came out the door.

"Quite beautiful." He nodded. "You London ladies know how to carry off in style." The barest hint of sarcasm tinted the words, enough to let Dina know she had not been complimented.

"I'm not in style," she protested. "This dress was made more than a year ago."

"It's quite au courant for India," said Aunt Lily. "Is Emily ready?"

"Nearly so. She overslept in this heat." Uncle George laughed as heartily as his tight neckcloth allowed.

"It isn't hot yet. It's only February. The summer is two or three months away. You'll soon learn to deal with the climate. The first few months...." Emily's plump figure appeared in the doorway, cutting off George's lecture.

"Please sit down," said Aunt Lily. "There's something we must discuss. I believe you should tell them, George."

Uncle George cleared his throat and looked into the garden. He blushed, his prudish nature clearly upset by what he must say. Dina stifled a giggle.

"A man has come to town," he said finally, in anticlimax. Dina shifted restlessly. Why doesn't he just come right out and tell us why we must avoid Captain Saurage? she thought.

"Who?" asked Emily innocently.

"A gentleman... No, he is no gentleman, even though he was nobly born. If you can call the mating of a peer with a chambermaid noble."

That wasn't possible. As Dina recalled, Lord Valmont's mother had been the daughter of a marquis. Aunt Lily took over the narration.

"The *Pearl Stallion* came into port early this morning. Anson Saurage is her captain. You'll be introduced, but you must be no more than polite to him. If he asks for a dance, you may accept, for he's a man of some importance, the brother of an earl who has the ear of Lord Mornington. If he requests you as a partner more than once, you must decline. Say you cannot disappoint the other men, which is true, for there are few single girls in Calcutta this year."

"What has given him such bad tone in Calcutta?" Dina asked wryly. "The behavior and antecedents of many of the men I've met here are somewhat questionable, yet you've not warned us against them."

"He's . . . he's different," stammered her uncle. "He makes no secret of his...rather, he flaunts his...excesses."

"So being secret about sin cancels its sting?" she asked archly.

"It's the air Savage carries about, his open disdain for any sort of regulation. You'll recognize it when you see him," her uncle said sharply.

"Savage, you say? I thought his name was Saurage," Dina remarked sweetly. "Perhaps I'm mistaken." She made no effort to keep the mockery out of her voice, and expected a harsh retort from her uncle. Instead, he gulped at being caught in the gaffe.

"A slip of the tongue," he said with false lightness. "It's what the rough men on the docks call him."

"Is he related to the Oxfordshire Saurages?" asked Dina quietly, knowing full well he was.

"Yes," said her aunt shortly. "And a disgrace I'm sure they think him, although I don't know that any are left except his brother, the earl. Perhaps you've heard of him. Lord Valmont?"

"I've met him," said Dina proudly.

"You have?" gasped Emily, her moon-face agog. "How am I to come off well at this ball, when you've flitted about London for years and can mention hundreds of people whose names are in the prints?"

"What good did those years do me?" Dina asked bitterly. "You'll show up much better than I." Her reputation as a jilt had followed her to India, she was sure.

"I'm glad you're accepting the consequences of your unproductive life and perhaps considering making amends," said Uncle George. "If, in that time, you had perfected the talents expected of an honest woman, you would not find yourself in this situation. As things stand, you don't have the skills to fill even the post of governess."

Dina gritted her teeth, tried in vain to find some hurtful remark she could direct at her uncle.

"Lieutenant Benjamin Mark has inquired about the two of you," Aunt Lily said. "You'll find him a sweet boy, probably a bit young for you, Emily, but of an age for Dina."

"Is he the one with the spots?" asked Dina.

"Time will, I'm sure, ease the affliction. And we must always look beyond spots and try to see the true character of those we meet. A man with spots on his reputation is so much worse than one with spots on his face."

"Are you referring to Captain Saurage?" asked Dina, adding honey to her voice.

"Yes," said her uncle forcefully. "How many times must I warn you? You are to have nothing to do with him beyond the barest courtesies."

"What are the limits? May he kiss my hand, or must I pretend I'm burdened with my fan and bouquet and not give him the opportunity?"

Aunt Lily opened her mouth, but Uncle George intervened.

"You forget yourself, Lady Endine." He never used her title except when he was angry. "You spent three seasons in London. You must know how to stay on the edge of courtesy without offering encouragement, for Leonard says you rejected innumerable proposals from men of good station. I said one dance, if he asks. Come. The landau is being brought around."

The ballroom was overcrowded and disastrously hot. Dina eyed the mass of uniforms and dark coats, searching for a slight, fair-haired man who might be the savage captain. She saw no one who resembled Lord Valmont. The music began, a minuet, but she hung back near the door, under a flapping punkah cloth. The temperature was no lower, but at least the air moved.

The crowd parted to permit entry to a massively built man. He towered over every other person in the room. His long dark hair was pulled back from his face and bound into a pigtail with a silk casing, sailor-fashion. He walked in the rolling gait of a man not long off a ship. She would have taken him for a common seaman, except that he was impeccably dressed in the London style of 1800 or 1801, four or five years ago. His cravat was perhaps not high enough, but the coat fit his body perfectly. Buff pantaloons outlined his powerful legs so precisely they would have drawn approving eyes from the London dandies. No woolen pads augmented those sturdy calves. She saw the muscles move beneath the silk stockings when he mounted the final stair.

He was dark, not just his hair and eyes, but his skin also, as brown as a native. But the overwhelming impression was of size. A giant of a man.

She stared at this amazing specter like a half-witted girl, then gasped and opened her fan when she realized that the stranger's eyes, sharp, impenetrable, were upon her. She lifted her fan to shield her face, but found it impossible to break from his gaze. He radiated a heat no punkah cloth could dispel. Aunt Lily bustled to her side.

"I shall introduce you," she said under her breath. "Captain the Honorable Anson Saurage." Her voice splintered with disapproval. "My niece, Lady Endine Wilmount."

Chapter Two

Dina's fan dropped from her nerveless fingers and hung by the silken cord over her wrist. He could not possibly be the brother of that delicate peer she'd known in London! His hand reached for hers even before she made the offer. He grasped her fingers, then turned her hand over and placed his lips suggestively on her palm. The heat remained even after his mouth had been withdrawn.

"May I ask, with your permission, Madame Mason—" he bowed to Aunt Lily "—for the next dance with this charming lady?"

He led her to the floor and took his place facing her in the line of dancers. He advanced gracefully and bowed as she curtsied. She made the first turn on his arm.

"Your hair is the color of Pele's," he said.

"Whose?" she asked, startled that his opening remark made no sense whatsoever.

"The volcano goddess of the Sandwich Islands. Pele. Her hair is golden, with tints of red."

"How do you know?" she asked in amusement. "Have you seen this goddess?"

"I've seen her hair," he said. "And it's like yours."

Dina laughed. The conversation wafted her home, to a London ballroom, to a dandy whispering witty comments in her ear. Saurage moved with agility, despite his size. The eyes of the company were on him, and thus upon her.

"You dance well," she said when next they came together.

"So do you. We shall share the evening."

"My aunt and uncle have ordered me to spread my attentions amongst the men."

"And Captain Savage may have only one dance?" he asked.

His use of the forbidden name caused a quiver in the muscles of her legs, but she kept her face emotionless.

"How did you know?"

"Aunts and uncles always warn against me. Act as a stallion, you're treated as a stallion, not a gelding."

"You know they call you Savage?"

"I not only know, I enjoy it. Saurage is French, came over with the Conqueror. Savage, with honest English accents, better describes my character." He grinned. "The blood of the noble Saurages runs very thinly in my veins."

"How are you a savage?" she asked lightly, teasingly.

He did not answer immediately; the figures of the dance separated them, and several moments passed before she was again on his arm.

"I will not be patronized," he said seriously. "Those who wrong me, I destroy. They may suppose they're safe, but my revenge is simply delayed, not forgotten."

"You frighten me," she said prettily, trying to return the conversation to a lightness appropriate to the ballroom.

"I should."

The music came to a halt. She tried to read the depths of his obscure black eyes. His eyebrows met above his nose, defining his darkness. Dina stepped back, frightened by the raw power of him, then remembered there was something she must learn.

"Tell me, Captain, are you married?"

He laughed deeply, from his chest, from his very gut. "Yes. To the *Pearl Stallion.*"

"I saw her today. She's beautiful."

"Would you be afraid to come into her, below decks, with me, alone?" he asked, his dark eyes narrowed.

"Yes, I would be afraid," Dina said honestly. "But I would come if I had the chance."

"You're different, Lady Endine," he said.

The orchestra struck a chord to indicate the beginning of the next dance. He bowed and held out his hand. For an instant, she hesitated; a nerve deep within her vibrated with anxiety. Then she took his hand and curtsied.

Through the glove, his hand was hard, like that of a working man. He was more than a head taller than she, and she was tall for a woman. He studied her openly, both face and body. With most men, her nervous panic came only at the very end of the courtship, when the offer of marriage was made. Then she always said no, frightened of the harm that came to a woman possessed by any man. With Saurage, the quake of fear was instantaneous. After just a few minutes in his company, she found herself ready to scuttle off. There was nothing of the dandy about him, no surface pretense to disguise the underlying sensuality.

"Thank you, Lady Endine," he said graciously at the end of the measure. "Why are you in India?" The question, so blunt, caught her off guard.

"Why is any single woman in India?" she snapped. "To find a husband. That's the only reason any sane woman would come to this snake pit."

He laughed so loudly heads turned in their direction. Aunt Lily, her face pale and drawn, made fluttering gestures, indicating that Dina had spent enough time with the bold captain.

"I like honest women."

"You do?"

"Yes. There's some natural honesty about you. May I have the next dance?"

"You may ask," she said playfully, "but I'll deny you, because I need to step out and breathe open air. And find a cup of punch."

"Then let me be your escort." She took his elbow and lifted her head, directing a simpering smile at Aunt Lily. She struggled to keep the smile in place as she walked with

Saurage across the ballroom. Her face must not for one instant reflect her trepidation, the tightness in her chest. She tried not to think of what this man would ask of her. A proposal of marriage, then the dark demands. And he was so huge!

No matter what he was, or how he behaved, he was an earl's son, and the best man available in India. How soon would his ship be ready to leave? No time for a leisurely courtship, like the ones she had allowed in London. She would have to imitate the women of the *ton* who set out to get the men they wanted.

Saurage fought the crowd around a punch bowl on the veranda. She spread her fan across the lower part of her face. When he was quite close to her, she lowered the fan, revealing her slightly parted lips, the tip of her tongue just visible. She took the cup from his hand, smiled what she hoped was a seductive smile, maintaining the hint of tongue. That was how Lady Snowe greeted a man in her salon. And she was always surrounded with men.

The dark thatch of hair above his eyes rose and separated. He downed his cup of punch in one gulp, moved his lips in a slow mimicry of her own gesture. She answered with a smile and a more obvious thrust of her tongue.

"Shall we rejoin the dance?" he asked in a low voice.

"Most certainly!" She must flaunt the forbidden captain before Uncle George. She took his arm. He pulled her hand through his elbow, covered it with his left hand. His fingers curled under hers, gently scratched her palm, frightening her. She'd never flirted so openly, nor had she ever dallied with such an unconventional man. But so long as they stayed in public, nothing untoward could happen. All she had to do was avoid a lone embrace in the garden. No, she'd have to risk even that. That was when the proposal would come.

In the line of the dance, she passed from man to man, then came back to Captain Saurage, linked her hand with his arm to dash beneath the raised arms of the company. She pouted her lips slightly, dropped her eyes. When next she met his gaze, he smiled broadly and the brows rose even higher. They joined the line of couples, their hands raised together in the arch, his thumbs pressed suggestively into her palms.

"We should meet soon," he whispered in her ear as they turned. "Someplace with less crowd and noise. More intimate."

"Yes," she breathed.

As she made her promenade about him, she saw her uncle, his face dark with anger. Her heart lifted in delight and her feet barely touched the floor. She'd managed to make her uncle furious. Perhaps he would send her home! She had wrapped Captain Saurage around her little finger. Savage indeed! At the end of the dance she spread her fan across her mouth, then hooked her little finger around the edge and moved it in a tiny gesture of invitation. The tame Savage grinned at her. She lifted her head in triumph, but shivered at the chill that snaked up her spine and settled at the base of her skull.

Dina sat on the edge of her bed, brushing her hair, considering her success. She relished the memory of her uncle's livid face as they had ridden home from the ball. Her aunt had scolded her over the breakfast table. Dina's only regret was that her behavior had dimmed Emily's triumph. Mr. Porter, a sober Quaker gentleman who worked at Government House, had asked to call upon her.

Captain Saurage was arrogant, full of pride, and she was going to get him. No other man in Calcutta could touch him, for looks, for grace, for connections, possibly for wealth. Through him, she would get back to England. She hated his massive physical presence, the smoldering domination of his personality, but that would have to be borne with. Any husband would have to be borne with.

Her thoughts were interrupted by a servant at the door.

"Mr. Mason is home and requests the presence of the ladies."

Her uncle being home in the middle of the day was not surprising. All Calcutta shut down in the afternoon heat.

But wanting to see the ladies? Well, she'd expected a sharp lecture. If she was to make Uncle George angry enough to send her home, she must continue the needling.

Emily and Aunt Lily sat with Uncle George on the veranda. Obviously, they were to bear witness to her shame. Perhaps her uncle intended to send her home immediately. She took a deep breath and schooled herself to look terribly unhappy when he told her he had arranged her passage.

"Sit down," he said genially. "Sit down. I have received great news, and we all must share it together."

Had Mr. Porter already asked for Emily?

"This morning an invitation was delivered to me at the rooms...uh, the shipyard administrative building." His chest bulged like a pouter pigeon's; Dina had never seen his head so high.

"Lady Margaret, whose husband, Sir Hall Allinson, is secretary for the Marine Department, has asked us to dine."

"George!" exclaimed Aunt Lily, clasping her hands to her chest. "How thrilling! At last, in the very highest company..."

"I believe," continued her uncle, "that it is to Lady Endine that we owe this invitation." There was no mockery in his voice when he said her name. "The secretary cannot ignore the presence in Calcutta of the daughter of Lord Cairnlea." Dina had never seen Uncle George's eyes so bright, his shoulders so square. Through her, he was achieving what her father had been unwilling to give his brothers-in-law: entrée to the highest social circles.

Dina smoothed her white muslin as she stepped from the carriage. The frock had been designed to fall from a band of Persian turquoises just beneath her breasts, but Uncle Leonard had kept all that remained of her jewelry in England. She had to make do with a blue silk ribbon, tied in back with long streamers to move against her hips when she walked. Her hair was dressed with matching ribbons.

A cluster of men and women stood in a shady room of the secretary's house. Wide doorways opened onto broad verandas, and near each opening a punkah slave crouched, pulling over and over again on the rope that set the overhead cloth to flapping. Lady Margaret herself took the awed family under her wing and led them into the recesses of the huge room.

"You, of course, are acquainted with Captain Freemantle," she said, steering them to a tall, angular gentleman in a gold-laced coat.

"He's a nephew of Lord Belleview," Lady Margaret whispered in Dina's ear.

The captain blanched, but he controlled the emotion quickly. His face relaxed into studied indifference, but Dina knew he was shocked to find her aunt and uncle advanced to his social milieu.

"You haven't met my nieces," said Uncle George. "The Lady Endine Wilmount, Captain Freemantle. Miss Emily Mason." Uncle George shoved them both toward the captain, who bowed over their hands.

"Welcome to Calcutta," he said.

There was something about the careful modulation of his words... Dina examined him more closely.

"Captain Freemantle is head of the shipyard," explained Uncle George.

"The shipyard!" Dina exclaimed. "And do you enjoy your work?" she asked, so that she might hear him speak again. Captain Freemantle turned his shoulder to the rest of the family and addressed only Dina.

"Yes. I have been in charge for a year and a half. Since the death of Captain Tuttle of Coromandel fever."

There was no doubt. This was the man who had visited her uncle in the garden a few days ago.

"And do you have plans to return to England?" Dina asked quite casually. It was absolutely essential to get this bit of information before she wasted any time on a man.

"No. In India, the ambitious have room to expand. Look at what the Wellesleys have accomplished."

He touched her shoulder lightly and shifted her around so that the rest of the family was looking at his back. The snub was so blatant, Dina warmed with embarrassment. She glanced across the room, searching for someone she knew. Captain Saurage stood in one of the wide doorways. His body filled the opening, and for a moment she had the sensation of being trapped.

Lady Margaret materialized at her side. "Captain Saurage will escort you into dinner, my dear," she said. Dina enjoyed a brief glimpse of her aunt and uncle, their faces pale in shock.

"You have met Captain Saurage, I believe," said Lady Margaret archly.

"Yes. At a ball. He's an excellent dancer."

"He's an excellent man...in many ways," whispered Lady Margaret. "I'm sure you've discovered that already."

Lady Margaret abandoned her in front of Saurage. Dina extended her hand. He kissed her lightly on the knuckles, but his fingers held the hand too tightly.

From somewhere in the depths of the room she heard Lady Allinson's fluting voice: "But it is a matter of *rank*, you must understand."

Dina laughed.

"I'm glad I find you in good humor. What is worthy of your laughter?" Saurage asked with great formality.

"My uncle was so thrilled by this invitation, but he doesn't like the result. Hostesses in Calcutta are as much slaves to precedence as any in London. Whenever the two of us are present, we'll be seated together. The son of an earl, the daughter of an earl."

"Will you find it distasteful?" he asked quietly.

"Not at all," she protested. She raised her fan, then lowered it slowly so that he alone saw her open mouth. She ran her tongue along her upper lip suggestively, twice. He led her into the dining room and helped her to her chair. His fingers touched her bare shoulders, and lingered there a moment longer than necessary.

"You are beautiful today, Lady Endine," he said. "As beautiful as Lady Snowe, who some in England think has no equal. You're a bit taller than she, but in generality of figure, perhaps the same. It's difficult to tell with women, until the fabric and the accoutrements are stripped away."

Dina stiffened in her chair, then forced herself to relax. It was precisely the sort of innuendo a man would utter in the presence of a woman he found interesting.

"So it is with men, also," she said lightly. "The skill of hosiers with padding has led many a woman into unwanted intimacy with a man of skinny shanks."

"And have you appraised mine?" he asked with a sidelong glance.

"They have passed judgment," she whispered.

"You have experience in judging?"

"Three seasons in London. Even the best attempts of Wilson's tailors have failed to fool me."

He leaned toward her, and their shoulders touched. His left hand slid across her thigh beneath the heavy damask.

"Have you met our host, Sir Hall?" he asked. The nearness of his mouth caused curls to move on her forehead. He leaned in front of her to make the introduction. His hand tightened upon her thigh; the muscles of her leg tensed, and she suppressed a gasp of panic. His fingers relaxed their hold, but still lay upon her leg.

"How have you been keeping yourself amused, Lady Endine?"

"We've driven in the evening," she said with studied evenness, while her leg quivered beneath his hand. "And I must rest a great deal, for I'm unaccustomed to the heat."

"It's well for the ladies to rest in the daytime, to prepare for the night's activities," he said mischievously. His fingers moved slightly. Her thighs prickled. "Have you had many opportunities to meet Calcutta's gentlemen? All would be interested in making your acquaintance."

Would a touch of jealously help the courtship along?

"I've met many men here," she said with a toss of her curls, "each more fascinating than the last."

His fingers tightened. She sat straight and stiff, not daring to look at him. In London, when this happened, she gently removed the offending hand as a quiet reprimand. But this man must ask her to marry him, and do so quickly, before he sailed away. She must give him far more latitude than she'd allowed any suitor in London.

The footman leaned over her shoulder; the hand withdrew. Hot curries, others cool, with the flavor of coconut. Saurage's hand returned, higher on her thigh, and her body jerked involuntarily, reacting to him. She snatched a glass of wine and swallowed most of it in one gulp.

She paid almost no attention to the food set before her. The footman filled her glass anew, and she drank with abandon, hoping an abundance of wine would blot out the anxiety seizing her body. She heaved a sigh of relief when Lady Margaret signaled that the ladies would retire.

She led them to refreshing rooms where large china basins had been filled with perfumed water. Servants stood by with soft washing cloths and thick towels. Maids materialized and renewed their mistresses' wilted curls. Dina touched her temples and her wrists with a damp cloth, but resisted the impulse to plunge her face into the chilled water. It would feel delicious to blot out the dizziness that came from too much wine. But to yield to the temptation would cause damage, and would reveal that she, her aunt and her cousin had no maid, but helped one another in dressing.

"There's someone who would like to meet you," murmured Lady Margaret in Dina's ear. "Come with me."

Her hostess led her from the room, down a dark, cool corridor, up a twisting staircase with latticed and carved banisters. A candle burned on a low table in the center of a broad veranda, the flame reflected in tall bronze jars. A many-armed idol stood between her and the candle, and in the flickering light the sinuous arms seemed to move. She gasped at an unmistakable movement in the shadows, then covered her mouth in embarrassment. A slave sat inconspicuously against the wall, pulling on a rope that moved a silken punkah cloth. Dina breathed again, ashamed of her fright, then followed Lady Margaret across the veranda.

As her eyes grew accustomed to the dim light, she perceived the outlines of a couch, partially obscured by fragile, almost transparent silver draperies. She stepped forward, peered into the deeper shadows beyond the broad eaves, where the tops of gray-green trees shone in the starlight. She turned to inquire of Lady Margaret who wished to meet her in this strange place, but her hostess had vanished. She stood alone.

"Hello?" she begged hesitantly. She was no longer sure where in the shadows the spiral staircase lay. An arm circled her waist, one she'd known before, embracing her as part of the dance. He spun her to face him.

"At last we are alone," he said. He swallowed her startled cry. His hand, behind her head, forced her into a moist, repugnant joining. His tongue thrust into her. She struggled to deny him, but his lips overpowered hers, parting them to accommodate his invasion.

Chapter Three

Saurage's mouth freed her, but Dina could neither speak nor cry out. She dragged air, heavy with the fragrance of sandalwood, into her deprived lungs. She gasped and coughed as he led her to the silver-shrouded couch, her weakened hands struggling vainly against him.

"An hour, I'm afraid, is all we have tonight. But this is just the beginning." His hands encompassed the mounds of her breasts, caressed them through the muslin. "Beautiful. No modiste's foolery here," he said, pleased.

Dina twisted in his grasp, managed to take one unrestricted breath, and released it in a shriek of consummate terror. One of his hands covered her mouth, his lips pressed close to her ear.

"Don't pretend fright," he murmured. "I'm not like other men here, who find pleasure in pretending rape. Continue your inventive flirtations. I like willing and aggressive women."

His broad hand covered not only her mouth, but her nose, as well. She was suffocating, and her head spun with fright and the effects of the wine. She twisted under the weight of his hand, then sank her teeth into the fleshy pad at the base of his thumb. He wrenched his hand away, giving her the chance to slip away, dash across the room, heedless of the direction she took. His hand caught hers, pulled her back.

"No!" she screamed.

"No?" he asked. "No? It was you who began this flirtation, my lady. How did you expect it to end?"

"Not this," she begged. "Not this. Please, not this."

"Every gesture at the ball was made to rouse me, and tonight you reacted well to my hand where no lady would tolerate it. I went to great pains to arrange this meeting, and I don't appreciate being denied."

"Arrange?" she gasped.

"Of course. I asked you at the ball, did you want me to fix a more private meeting for us, and you agreed. Your stupid aunt and uncle are occupied below. Now is our time."

"You . . . the invitation!" she gasped.

"Naturally. At my request. You didn't think Lady Margaret looked forward to the pleasure of your aunt's company over the coffeepot, did you?"

There was no possible reply. She closed her eyes, shuddered, pressed her clenched fists against her mouth, wondering to what disaster she had led herself.

"May I ask you—" his voice was sarcastic "—if this isn't what you had in mind, what did you hope to achieve?"

"Marry!" she gasped into her knuckles. "You to ask to marry me!"

He grabbed her shoulder and spun her to face him. A breeze drifted across the veranda, moved the candle flame. The shadows of his face danced with devilish amusement.

"Marry?" he asked in astonishment. "You know very little of me, do you?" He pulled her against his body, so that she felt the lines of its power. Streaks of phosphorescent energy flashed into the hidden corners of her being. "You might know me completely. Tonight . . . While my ship is refitted, at my house to share days and nights of desire."

"Marry," she whispered. "Will you marry me?"

"No, little lady. I'll not marry any woman who finds it necessary to come to India to find a husband. When I return to England, I'll find a wife among the daughters of the merchants, some woman who brings gold to my purse, as well as her warm pocket to my bed. I do not propose marriage to penniless ladies of the *bon ton*. But a mistress . . ."

"I cannot!" she gasped. "I must marry—get out of Calcutta. You seemed the best man about."

He let her go, laughing and she staggered away from him, but found no stairs, only a carved screen. She felt the tracery with her fingers—a bas-relief of a man. The carving was obscene. A jutting male organ, the smooth thighs of the female lover. She jerked her hand away.

"I don't know whether or not I should feel flattered," he said lazily behind her. "Being the best in this herd of swine is a small compliment."

She heard the soft sweep of his feet on the grass matting, the dreadful sound of him, like thunder, coming to reclaim her. He was toying with her, letting her think she might get away before he dragged her into renewed embraces. How many times would he impose the terror before— His heat proclaimed his nearness. She backed against the screen. The light played upon the iridescence of his silk coat, an aura across his shoulders. The *Pearl Stallion*. It was not just the ship. It was the man, as well.

"Do you wish to leave?" he asked, unexpectedly gentle.

"Yes," she gasped, nearly sobbing with relief.

"You shall go now," he continued. "I find no pleasure in forcing a woman. But a word of advice. Stop flirting, if you don't intend to carry through. Every man in Calcutta sees your beauty, and not all will be willing to end such a meeting harmlessly. Even I have my limits. Stay away from me, and if we appear in the same room, cast down your eyes modestly."

He led her into the shadows, behind another screen. "Wait here," he said. Dina wrapped her arms about her shoulders, not daring to touch the screen, for fear of what erotica she might discover. He returned with the candle. Not three feet from where she stood was the elegant tracery of the banister.

"Careful on the stairs," he said. Dina fled down the narrow treads. A light appeared, Lady Margaret lifting the shutter on a silver lantern. She spoke sharply, and a servant appeared.

"She'll help you straighten your dress and hair," she said kindly. "Tell your guardians we had a charming private conversation. That will account for your absence. No one below heard you scream, for there is musical entertainment, and we are some distance from the drawing room."

"How could you?" Dina choked out the words. "You're no better than a procuress."

Lady Margaret sneered. "You'll learn our Calcutta ways, my dear. You should have given yourself to him. Captain Saurage is most entertaining." Dina drew back in horror. This woman had heard everything they had said.

"A pity you're so shy," she continued, "although some men welcome innocence. Let me know if any of the men below take your fancy, and I'll arrange a meeting. But only when you're ready to be sensible about the matter."

"I want to go home," Dina said, then clasped her hand over her mouth to stifle sudden, involuntary sobs. Lady Margaret stepped back, openly surprised.

"Really, my dear, it is of no great consequence, what they ask of you. These men give their ladies magnificent gifts, and you would be living in a proper house, not that thatched hovel your uncle provides."

She vanished majestically up the stairs. Giggles and laughter floated down as she greeted the captain. They ridiculed her virginity, her fear. She trembled as the servant pressed and rearranged her crumpled ribbons. She followed the silent figure down dreamlike corridors, stood outside the drawing room, adjusting her mind to the tinkle of the pianoforte. She feared that everyone in the room would see the turmoil still churning her body. A soft touch on the back of her hand made her jump.

"Please, Lady Endine," said Captain Freemantle, "Won't you take my chair?"

"Thank you," she said gratefully.

He stood beside her until the performance was finished. He offered his arm to lead her to the refreshments.

"I have little opportunity to meet women as beautiful as you," he murmured. "May I call upon you?"

"What?" she asked, her whirling mind aware that Freemantle had asked a question.

"May I visit you at your uncle's house?"

"Yes, of course," she said, then realized she spoke without thought. Anyone, anyone at all might court her. Anyone who might stand between her and the horror she had met upstairs.

Savage hung over the railing, watching how the *Pearl Stallion* reacted to the winch pulling her into the dock. He hated the moment when the ship was landbound, when he was banished to a house ashore. Hated it, except that he'd have a woman or two to still the storm in his loins.

He'd thought he had found his temporary companion at the ball, but she had proved to be a disappointment. Flirting as if she knew how to pleasure a man, then leaving him hurting. He cursed Lady Endine, but at the same time he felt dreadfully sorry for her. Three seasons in London, and she thought she knew enough to cope with Calcutta society.

He wondered for a moment what man among them would vanquish her defenses. Lady Margaret and Sir Hall would arrange it very soon, and the poor little stick would scream her lungs out while one of the rakes of Calcutta... He shuddered, then pretended he had simply shrugged his shoulders, uncaring of her plight.

She should get herself a husband as quickly as possible. Before she ended up a fancy woman for the crowd that clustered about Sir Hall. Before the whole house of cards Freemantle and Mason had constructed in the shipyard tumbled, taking her down with them.

He felt sorry for her, and had to admit that part of that emotion stemmed from the guilt flickering around his heart. He'd not treated her well. But great heavens! How was he to have known?

"She started the flirtation," he said aloud, justifying his behavior. He turned aside angrily. Why should he be wasting time even thinking of her?

The iron wheels of the carriage rumbled over the paving stones. Dina kept her parasol placed so that her face was shaded. If she was not careful, her skin would become disgracefully dark.

"It is a sign of Captain Freemantle's interest that he has asked us to the shipyard," said Aunt Lily significantly.

Captain Freemantle joined them at the gate. Aunt Lily insisted upon moving next to Emily so that he might sit next to Dina. Dina pressed herself against the side of the carriage to put space between them. When Freemantle twisted in the seat to point out some feature of the yard, she twisted away from him to keep the space wide. For two evenings running he had visited her. The Masons had left them alone on the veranda after coffee. But she couldn't marry Captain Freemantle. He planned to stay in India.

"These are the warehouses," he said. "When I assumed command of the shipyard, they were in great confusion, but now, when an item is requested, I can direct my workers to it instantly."

Dina made the mistake of turning to see the warehouses. His green eyes fastened on hers, and she read the determination in their smiling depths. She turned her head, searching frantically for something to distract him.

"What's in those barrels, Captain?" she asked foolishly.

"Beef," he said. "They're destined for a ship just now being refitted and restocked."

Dina inclined her parasol so that he could not see her face. The carriage turned a corner. Carefully tended lawns and gardens stretched from the drive to the river, and at the upper end stood a white, two-story bungalow. She exclaimed her appreciation.

"You like it?" asked Freemantle.

"It's beautiful," she said honestly. "One of the most beautiful prospects I've seen in India." A peacock and peahen marched across the trimmed lawn, as if on cue. Dina would have watched them, but for Freemantle's hand, which crept across the seat toward hers.

"This is the home furnished for the captain of the dockyard as part of the emoluments of the position. I have not occupied it, for it seemed foolish, living alone, to go to the expense of maintaining the large number of servants such an establishment demands. When I marry, of course, it will be opened, the house to which I'll bring my wife."

The message could not have been clearer. He leaned toward her, his green eyes peering under the parasol with a suggestive smile. He was offering himself. She could have this beautiful house, in return for giving herself to him and staying in India.

"There are no furnishings, naturally, but you might tour the interior. Or shall we go to find the punch bowl?"

"I'm quite thirsty," she answered, her voice choked.

The administrative building was in the center of the vast acreage of the shipyard, a two-story building of whitewashed stone with a veranda shading it on all sides. Freemantle led the women to the second-story veranda, to the side that overlooked a wide enclosed parade ground.

"Go find Mr. Mason," he said to a servant. "Ask him to join us. You have a chance to see a fine sight," he said to Mrs. Mason.

Dina studied the dusty yard and could see nothing special about the place. Perhaps the shipyard boasted a band that would serenade them while they drank punch. The thought of a group of musicians laboring in the broiling sun did not please her. A plank gate opened, and twenty or twenty-five men in ragged lines marched into the courtyard. Two men, stripped to the waist, were dragged forward, their upraised arms bound to tripods of thick poles. She clenched a hand on her chest, pressing wrinkles into the damp cotton.

"Good morning, Mason." It was Captain Freemantle's voice, next to her, though sounding as if it came from a great distance. "The refreshments are on their way, and we have entertainment. I hope the ladies enjoy the spectacle."

Servants appeared with a bowl of chilled punch, plates of small cakes. Dina wrenched her eyes from the scene below. Unbelievably, a large piece of ice floated in the punch. The servant stood before her with a tray. Dina's stiff hands could barely grasp the cup, which was slippery with condensation. She looked at her aunt, who stared without concern—with curiosity, in fact—at the preparations below.

"They are thieves?" she asked.

"The worst kind of thieves, Mrs. Mason. They took supplies intended for our brave sailors and sold them for their own gain."

"What do they intend to do?" asked Emily fearfully.

"I've ordered all thieves to be flogged," said Freemantle proudly. "Fifty lashes each. Softness with these people only leads to further trouble."

Dina's feet burned with her need to flee. She looked over her shoulder, but the door into the shadowy interior was blocked by her uncle. He stared nonchalantly into the courtyard. Captain Freemantle raised his hand.

The thud of the cat-o'-nine-tails, and the scream, came together. Dina tightened her hands around the cool cup, held it against her temple and closed her eyes to shut out the horror. Nothing could eliminate the sound. Her mouth was desert-dry, but her throat closed against refreshment. She forced her eyes open, to look not at the writhing man, but at her companions. Was she the only one whose flesh crawled?

Emily's eyes were wide, and her chin was trembling. Her chubby hands clasped her knees. But she watched. Aunt Lily observed the proceedings with fearful approval, nodding with each blow. Dina did not turn far enough to see her uncle, but she glimpsed Captain Freemantle. He smiled, and the triumph on his face sickened her.

"Does it upset you, my lady?" he asked lightly.

"Yes," she whispered. "It is barbaric!"

"No. They are barbarians, and this is all they understand. Look, Lady Endine. This is what keeps you safe in your lovely bungalow."

Uncle George's bungalow? Or the bungalow where Freemantle would take her as his wife? Dina jumped to her feet. She pushed past her uncle, but Freemantle's arm caught hers before she gained the safety of the building. He forced her to turn with him and face the courtyard. The bound man hung limp, his cries reduced to dreadful moans.

"You shall become accustomed to India," he said quietly in her ear. "It's a cruel place, but rewarding for brave men and women."

Dina closed her eyes against the horror. Something was cool and wet in her hand. She still grasped the cup of punch. She twisted in Freemantle's arms, flung the punch into his gloating face, and in the confusion dived into the dim room beyond the door.

Her eyes, accustomed to the bright sunlight of the quadrangle, failed her. She stumbled on the corner of a rug, and the floor rushed up to meet her. She pulled herself into a ball, her arms over her head to blot out the renewed screams. Freemantle's arms were about her, drawing her to him as he knelt on the floor beside her.

"My dear, my dear..." he protested. "I'm doing this for you. Don't you understand. We shall live here, in the shipyard, and all the men must have it beat into them that no misbehavior will be tolerated."

She slithered out from under his arm, regained her feet, ran through door after door and found herself on the opposite veranda. In the crystal distance, a ship rested in the dock. It was black, except for the glowing figurehead of a wild stallion. She reached out to touch it before she fainted.

Dina lay under her netting, twisting in the moist sheets. Her mind shot from one vision to another, from Freemantle's glow of pleasure as the men were flogged to his vicious philosophy, which would control her life in that charming white bungalow. And now the invitation from Lady Margaret. The thick white paper lay on her desk, shining in the dim light.

> You must visit us on Friday, for there are several people you should meet. The carriage shall call for you. Plan for the entire day, for we have a collection of carvings you will enjoy. You saw but a hint of what we possess when you joined us for dinner.
>
> I understand completely that young ladies fresh from England may not appreciate Indian art, but after a day of exposure, I'm sure you will begin to understand its fascination.

Dina sprang out of bed and paced the short distance from the wall to the door leading onto the veranda, ignoring the beetles that scuttled away from her bare feet. Her eyes burned from shedding inexhaustible tears. She must get away from this dreadful place, back to England, before she went mad. She would swallow her pride and go into service. Why shouldn't she become a governess? She knew mathematics, and geography, and history. She knew French and Italian, and could read a bit of Russian. Her sewing was amateurish, and she had never been interested in mastering the pianoforte, but these things could be learned, if one was determined.

She'd find a way to get on a ship. She could support herself. She need never marry. She need never subject herself to the demands of a man, to the heartless cruelty of a man.

She was still awake when dawn came, when she heard Emily stirring.

"Get up, lazybones," Emily said gaily from the door. "We're going to work on our costumes for the ragpicker's ball, remember?"

"I'm not going," Dina said flatly.

"But, Dina! *Everyone* comes! That's where we'll meet the secretaries, and the councilmen. The generals!"

"Is that why you've put off Mr. Porter?" asked Dina crossly. "Hoping you'll meet someone higher on the ladder at the ragpicker's ball?"

"Well," said Emily shyly, "a girl can dream."

Dina looked up from her book; a bird had chattered unexpectedly in the night garden. A rap at the door. Who would be calling, at this hour, on the evening of the ragpicker's ball?

She was alone in the house with the servants, for she refused to face Captain Freemantle, whose proposal of marriage she intended to reject, or Lady Margaret and Sir Hall, whose invitation she had turned down. The carriage had departed more than an hour ago, carrying her uncle, dressed as a common seaman, her aunt, a flower seller, and Emily, a sober milkmaid.

"Lady," said the manservant at the door. "A gentleman to see you. Captain Saurage."

Saurage! What could he want? Had he changed his mind? Dared she trust him? She considered her alternatives: Captain Freemantle. The Allinsons.

"Come with me," she ordered the servant, "And stay with me."

Saurage waited in the small entry garden, two other men in the shadows behind him. He wore a white shirt, open at the neck, and the loose canvas trousers of a sailor, much the same as the clothes her uncle had worn to the ball. But on Saurage, it did not have the appearance of a costume.

"Lady Endine, may I give you some advice?"

"I thought you didn't wish to see me again."

"I feel compelled to speak to you once more. May I introduce my friends?" She nodded.

"Dr. Charles Hampton," he said, gesturing toward the sailor on his right. "Surgeon of the *Pearl Stallion.* First lieutenant of the *Pearl Stallion,*" continued Saurage, gesturing to the second man, "Mr. Becker. These gentlemen are here as witnesses, in case I've been observed calling upon you. They can testify that nothing untoward happened between us."

"What do you want of me?" she asked quietly, making sure she stood between Saurage and the door, so that she might run into the safety of the house.

"I wish to warn you, Lady Endine. Get out of your uncle's house. Find a man to marry and leave this house, and warn your cousin that she should do likewise."

"Why?" she exploded.

"Your uncle, together with the superintendent of the shipyard—"

"Captain Freemantle?"

"Captain Freemantle . . . will be involved in a scandal. I cannot say when—next week, next year—but any connection with them will destroy your chances at an honorable proposal."

"How dare you accuse my uncle—?"

"Do you think your uncle can afford a carriage on his salary?" he asked sardonically. "You're more innocent than I thought. Find someone to marry, and get away."

"Why are you telling me this?" she cried.

"Because, for some ridiculous reason, I feel sorry for you, Lady Endine. You're a foolish beauty who thinks London prepared you for Calcutta. The elite will thrust you away once they've ravished you. They will offer no protection when your uncle's scheme collapses."

He spun on his heel, gestured for the two men to follow him, and disappeared out the gate leading to the street.

Chapter Four

"Captain Freemantle is here," announced Emily, leaning into Dina's room. "Uncle says for you to come." She giggled. "I'm sure he's going to ask for your hand. Imagine, only a month in Calcutta and already you have a gentleman closeted with Uncle."

Dina dressed carefully, trying to postpone the meeting she dreaded. Her uncle would be violently angry when she refused the captain, but refuse him she must. Saurage's words haunted her. Scandal... ravishment... She paced herself as she walked the length of the corridor, taking slow, silent steps.

"Tomorrow," said Freemantle's voice.

She stopped, frozen. Did he want the wedding to be so soon? What about the banns?

"Saurage has said nothing to Lord Mornington," Uncle George said weakly. "He suspects nothing, and is leaving."

"Or perhaps he has informed Lord Mornington, and the governor-general is waiting for him to leave, waiting for us to feel secure," offered Freemantle. "Then, when we least suspect, at some moment when the evidence would be most difficult to hide..." Dina imagined Freemantle drawing a finger across his throat.

"You're sure he's leaving?" asked her uncle fearfully.

"He's requested a pilot. The waterfront gossip says the Savage is sailing with the first land breeze, and the gossip must be right, for he filled with water today."

"Thank God!" breathed her uncle. "It seems certain, then."

"One of the men I punished escaped, and I've learned he went on board the *Pearl Stallion.*" Freemantle continued. "I can't imagine the poor heathen knows anything, he wouldn't understand ledgers if he saw them, but Saurage taking him on is suspicious."

"Yes, yes. But tomorrow he'll be gone, and he's said nothing to Lord Mornington." Relief was palpable in her uncle's voice. "I hope the next typhoon takes him down."

"I, too, hope he never returns."

Her uncle mumbled words she could not understand.

"My dear Mason, that would be *unethical,* for a captain in charge of the shipyard. . . ." The threat behind Freemantle's words brought bumps of fright to Dina's arms. He laughed wickedly. Uncle George laughed more nervously.

"The lower tier of his water barrels . . ." Freemantle whispered slowly, so quietly she barely heard the words. The rest of his statement was lost. Dina turned and fled to her own room.

"Emily!" she called out, making her voice sound distressed, choked. She pushed a finger down her throat until she gagged; she leaned over the washbasin and mimed retching.

"What?" asked Emily from the door.

"Get a servant. I'm ill."

Emily's arm weighed on her shoulder. "What's wrong?"

"I don't know," she said thickly, then retched again.

"I'll get Aunt Lily," said Emily hastily.

The two women and a servant put her to bed. She didn't have to pretend to be sweating and feverish. She'd been damp with perspiration ever since the *Morgan Castle* had sailed into the Hooghly, and the mere thought of Freemantle as her husband made her shiver with despair. She panted weakly on the pillow, hoping her face was pale.

"Did you see Uncle?" asked Emily.

"I intended to see him, but was seized in the corridor with terrible cramps. Please send him my apologies. And Captain Freemantle," she added weakly.

A servant was set to fanning her. Dina pretended to fall asleep, but her mind raced. By feigning illness, she might avoid Captain Freemantle's proposal for a day, as well as postponing Lady Margaret's insistent invitations, but for how long could she maintain the pretense?

Savage had once held her in his power, and had refused to hurt her. He had warned her of Uncle George and Freemantle's illegal activities at the shipyard. The conversation between her uncle and Freemantle confirmed his words. Savage was the only man in Calcutta who showed the slightest bit of concern for her welfare.

The plan blossomed, fully formed, in her mind. All she needed was pluck and luck, and she would be on a ship bound for home. Captain Freemantle would be left behind. Sir Hall and Lady Margaret and their vicious friends would be left unsatisfied.

She made herself lie still and rest until twilight. She heard the clink of teacups on the veranda. She crept across the hall and found the cupboard where her uncle kept his clothes. The sailor's costume was on the floor, unwashed. The trousers and shirt smelled of tobacco and sweat. She clutched them under her arm, moved noiselessly back to her own room, where she hid them under the bed. She lifted the latch on the door leading to the veranda, so that it would be free when night fell. Next, she made a bundle, using a large silk scarf she had purchased in the bazaar during the first days of her stay in Calcutta. Two dresses were all she allowed herself, along with a shift, extra stockings and a shawl. She shoved the bundle under the bed, too. Finally, she stretched out under the mosquito netting, calmed her irregular breathing and pounding heart, but did not sleep.

"I believe it is simply excitement," she heard her uncle say in the hall. "She must know Captain Freemantle intends to speak to her of marriage. He asked me, and I agreed."

"I hope it isn't the fever the Lambert children had." Her aunt's voice was tight with worry. Dina hoped she was not so concerned that she would check on her during the night.

When the house grew silent, she dressed slowly to avoid making any sound. The trousers were too large, and she had to pin folds in the cloth to tighten the waist. The door to the veranda creaked, so she opened it inch by inch, allowing the hinges to rest after each fractional movement, until it was just wide enough to slip through. Then she eased it shut with equal deliberation. The banyan tree abutted the wall of the garden. It was easy to lift herself into the sturdy branches, drop the bundle over the wall, then follow it into the dusty street.

The sluggish water of the Hooghly reflected the light of a declining moon. There was no mistaking the activity around the *Pearl Stallion*. The sight of the ship reminded her of the man. *It makes no difference what he does to me,* she thought with resignation. *I must get away from here, and he at least will be kind.*

A native boat touched the shore, where lanterns illuminated huge piles of oranges, mangoes and pineapples. Dina pointed to the *Pearl Stallion,* held out the few coins she possessed, cursing herself for having wasted her allowance on the silk scarf. She did not know the worth of the coins, whether they were enough to pay the boat fare. She held her breath while the men counted and exhaled with relief when they got back into the boat and beckoned for her to join them. They pulled with easy strokes to where a launch lay beside the ship. A huge net of fruit was being lifted onto the deck. While the backs of the sailors were turned, she slid onto the launch. No one said a thing as she climbed the steep side of the *Pearl Stallion,* following a sailor who was disentangling one of the heaving ropes.

The lanterns on deck made pools of light, but they also created deep shadows. Dina grasped two small bags of fruit in her arms and headed for the only place that might offer a hiding spot: the main cabins behind the mizzenmast, the officer's cabins. A native clad as a sailor stood by the hatch.

"For the captain-sahib?" he asked. She nodded, not daring to speak, for fear she would betray her sex.

Lanternlight seeped into the cabin from the companionway, and threads of moonlight came through the wide stern windows and the skylight. There must be someplace here to hide, someplace where she would not be found until the ship was safely away from Calcutta, on its way to England. She pushed the bags of fruit under a table.

The ship swayed gently. A beam of moonlight crossed a door. She opened it slowly, waited until her eyes became accustomed to the darkness. It was a sleeping cabin, lighted only by a small skylight. She stood stock-still, listening for the sound of breathing, then cursed the delay her foolishness had caused. None of the officers would be asleep on the night they planned to sail.

She ran her hands across the bulkheads, touched the rough texture of a curtain. Behind it hung men's clothing—coats, trousers, the slick surfaces of oilskins. She stooped. The curtain went all the way to the deck. Behind was a small space where she might hide. She put the bundle behind her head so that she could lean more comfortably into the tight corner formed by the bunk and the curtained wall. Nothing to do but wait.

She wondered whose room she was in. The smell of the coats seeped downward and told her. She had danced with that odor, been embraced by an arm that radiated that smell. The scent of him—his tobacco, his sweat, his soap—mingled with the stink of the Hooghly's dirty waters.

When he found her, what would he do? Perhaps she should search for someplace else to hide. Here, on this bunk, he could do what he had planned to accomplish in the private of Sir Hall's veranda. No one would come to her rescue. A captain was king on his ship. The officers could not object; in fact, they would be duty bound, if she escaped his clutches, to return her to her tormentor. Could she stand it, the six-month journey back to England, being made to serve Saurage? It would not be worse than Freemantle, or what Sir Hall intends, she told herself sternly.

The ship swung at its moorings. A command above her head ordered the launch away, and a muttered almost-cheer formed a background chorus. Bare feet pattered overhead. Blocks rattled, and then came a chanting from far away. The click of ratchets echoed through the ship as the anchor came up. A cheer, louder now, and the vessel moved.

Dina sat very still, waiting for him to enter the cabin. But a captain would not come to his cabin until his ship was safely out to sea. It might be hours before they cleared the Hooghly. She relaxed. She'd found the best possible place to hide. Until, of course, he came. She closed her eyes.

When she opened her eyes, the cabin was dimly illuminated by dawn filtering through the open skylight. The ship moved slowly, with very little roll, so they must still be in the estuary.

"Well, Hampton," said Savage's voice, so close overhead she jumped. "We're off again. How does it feel?"

"Excellent. I'm not fond of Calcutta, you know that."

"How many in the sick bay?"

"Only two. Knocked on the head in a fight ashore, but neither will be abed long. Nothing serious."

"The man Radgni?"

"I have him on light duty. He can't lift until the tendons of his back are healed, so I put him to guarding the hatch aft, watching who and what came down last night. Freemantle's man knows how to swing a cat. Another ten lashes and the man would have been crippled for life."

"No fevers aboard?"

"No, thank God! I'll feel better when we're in colder waters. The Indian fevers can't follow us there."

"And when we're in colder waters," said Savage in his sardonic way, "you'll be speaking with great nostalgia of the pleasures of the tropical sea. You're a strange sailor, Charles, never satisfied with the place where you are."

"That's what makes me a good sailor," retorted Hampton. "I'm always anxious to put water under the keel and go somewhere else."

"How will that fit in with the beauty waiting in Charleston?" teased Savage.

"Age should settle my spirit, don't you think?"

The ship rose, and in a single instant changed from a level, passive thing, to an active participant in the ever-moving sea. The first waves of the Bay of Bengal lifted the bow. Rapid commands overhead brought the pattering of a hundred feet. The ship responded, pressed forward against the waves. The humming of wind in the rigging vibrated throughout the ship, through the sturdy pillars of the frame, the lighter wood of the bulkheads.

"Mr. Lightner," said Savage, "set a course for the strait."

Footfalls now in the main cabin. The table, Dina thought, where I hid the fruit. It's the chart table. The navigator has come to the chart table to set the course. What will he think if he finds the bags of fruit?

Savage laughed overhead. It was a great celebratory laugh of pleasure. Dina's heart lightened a bit at the sound. He would be kind to her. And he would take her back to England. As if to reassure her, a sunbeam came through the skylight. Dina stretched out her cramped legs and waited. She would have an instant of warning when he opened the door.

"Topgallants, Mr. Becker," Savage called, above her. At that moment, the door opened. She pulled herself into a tight ball. Who could it be? A servant? The curtain lifted. The eyes that met hers were startled and frightened, as her own must be. The sailor was barefoot; his hand was extended to remove one of the coats from a peg. He backed away, the arm still out straight toward her. The curtain dropped, his footsteps hurried to the door, pounded on the companionway, then overhead.

"Captain, please, there's something wrong," she heard him say in breathless tones.

"Wrong, Kranz?"

"A stowaway, Captain, in your cabin."

"Damn those Indians," said Savage. Dina lifted the drapery and crawled from beneath it. She had crouched for so long, her legs were cramped and she could not gain her feet. She pulled herself erect by gripping the edge of the bunk, but it wavered beneath her hands, swinging on ropes from the overhead beams.

The door flew open under the blow of an angry fist. His brows knit together in a dark slash above his eyes. He stared down at her with those opaque eyes and the thick, dark brows lifted. Dina collapsed to the deck, her legs in agonizing pain.

"Please, Captain, please!"

"You?" he blurted out.

"You told me the truth," she said weakly, "about my uncle. About Freemantle. Take me to England with you. I'll do anything, but don't send me back."

"England?" he repeated stupidly.

"Anything you want, I'll do," she repeated, meaning every word. "Just take me to England."

Savage reached out his hand, grasped her shoulder, pulled her to her feet, then pushed her onto the bunk. *Now it comes,* she thought. *Will he do it in front of his servant?* He waved the sailor out of the cabin and closed the door.

"How did you get here?" he asked sternly.

"I came out with some natives last night. I just climbed on board. The sailors were loading things."

"There was a guard at the aft hatch."

"A native. I was carrying fruit. He said something about them being for the captain and let me by."

"Radgni."

"Pardon me?"

"The Indian on sentry duty. He didn't know you were not part of the crew. And his mind may still be in confusion from the flogging he received from Freemantle's toady. The day you sat by and drank iced punch and watched two men tortured." He snarled with disapproval.

"Don't remind me," she begged. "I've been sick for days with the memory."

"Why are you here?"

"I overheard my uncle and Captain Freemantle. They said you were leaving. They're happy to see you go, because they're afraid of you."

"They have reason to be. Did they say anything specific?"

Dina thought back to the conversation of the afternoon before. " 'The affair,' they called it. They're afraid you'll go to the governor-general."

"Why should that bring you here? You yourself, as the beautiful daughter of the Earl of Cairnlea, have access to Sir Hall, and eventually the governor-general. You might suggest an audit of the shipyard. And if you were to marry an officer... you most certainly have met someone by now who'll marry you."

"Freemantle was going to speak to my uncle for me. I didn't know how long I could hold out. Please, please, I want to see England again, even if I must scrub floors or serve at table. I'll do anything!" she cried. "Believe me, you may do anything you wish!"

"We're not bound for England."

She stared at him in disbelief. The assumption had been so long in her mind, she could not dismiss it.

"Where?"

"The Pacific. Beyond that, I'll not say. The first India-bound ship we spy, I'll put you aboard her. There's no room on the *Pearl Stallion* for a woman." She covered her ears with her hands to shut out the harshness of his voice.

"Don't send me back," she begged. "My uncle will force me to marry Captain Freemantle."

"You had choices once, Lady Endine. Even in India you have some choices, for I doubt your uncle will drag you to the church in chains. Now you're under my command, and you have none. You'll return to Calcutta."

* * *

Dina curled on the bunk in the tiny cabin and listened to the rain beat over her head. Four days out of Calcutta, and not one day without constant squalls, drenching rain, sudden roaring winds that laid the *Pearl Stallion* on her beam-ends. The sailors had had no rest at all, but turned out day and night to adjust the sails in the violent periodic storms. She had heard the shouts of the officers, the falls of booted and bare feet on the deck, the thunderous crack when a sail split, the groans of the helmsman as he struggled to keep the ship before the wind.

An officer—a lieutenant, she believed—had given up his cabin so that she might have privacy. A sailor had shoved her into the narrow box—four feet by six feet by five feet high—saying, "Captain says you're to stay here."

Nothing since but meals of fruit and cold meat, with a little bread, brought by the captain's man, Kranz. The door had been hooked back to give her light and air. Occasionally a sailor passed by, but never did eyes stray through that opening to remark upon her presence, let alone stare at her.

She felt one great blessing. She was cool. So cool she'd put the checked shirt on over her dress and wrapped herself in the shawl and the silk scarf. She might be in England, in some tiny country cottage. Except that even the meanest cottage would have a fire on a hearth, and windows from which she could view the sweep of the storms over the rolling fields.

The storm eased, the pounding rain ceased within a few seconds. Another lull, during which the crew would prepare the ship for the next gale. It was in these periods of quiescence she waited with dread for the cry of "Sail ho!" As soon as they met another ship, she would be bundled aboard it, to be taken in disgrace back to her uncle in Calcutta. Back to Captain Freemantle. What would they do to her to make her agree to the marriage? Or would her reputation be so blackened by this escapade that Freemantle would withdraw his proposal? She smiled at the possibility.

Booted footsteps on the companionway. She'd grown accustomed to the pattern of their sound, fading aft to the main cabin. Perhaps he's forgotten I'm aboard. The footsteps came toward her door.

"Lady Endine?"

She jumped off the bunk at the sound of Saurage's voice, tried to stand up, and struck her head on the deck beams. Even she was too tall for the restricted space below decks.

"Would you please join me in the aft cabin?" he asked. Why did he make it a question? It was an order. She had no choice. He'd told her so.

She followed him through the labyrinth of timbering, into the cabin, with its spread of stern windows. Through them she saw the wake of the *Pearl Stallion,* a white streak on the surface of the sea, quickly eradicated by the tossing waves. Was another ship in sight? He gestured toward the padded bench under the windows.

"Sit down." He perched upon a stool in front of the table on the forward bulkhead. Beneath the table were rolls of paper in cubbyholes. The ship's maps and charts.

"I'm sorry you've been imprisoned so long without exercise, but the weather has been unsuitable for a lady to be on deck."

"I understand."

"Thank you. I hadn't imagined you'd be my guest for so long, but the winds have driven us from the normal lanes of shipping. In two days we'll be among the Andaman Islands, then into the Strait of Malacca, where we'll most certainly find East Indiamen bound home from China."

Dina bowed her head and pressed her spine against the frame of the window. Her hands clenched at the edges of the silk scarf and drew it about her as a token of protection.

"Is that where you're bound? Malacca?"

"There, and beyond. The Strait of Malacca is the gateway to the China Sea and, farther east, the Pacific."

"You sail to China?"

"Where I trade is my concern. You're heading back without the information many would like to know. Did your uncle send you aboard to find out?"

"No. He doesn't know I'm here. Please, sir," she whispered into the folds of the silk. "Please, don't send me back."

"Don't send you back?" he exclaimed. "Pray, what am I to do with you on this ship? Carpenter's mate, perhaps?" His sarcasm made Dina drop her head even lower. "Are you skilled enough with the needle to be the sailmaker's assistant?"

She shook her head without meeting his eyes, but a surge of anger drove her to lift her head.

"You warned me against Freemantle, and my uncle, yet will send me back to them without any thought of what will happen to me!" she cried.

"I risked a great deal to warn you. I told you, find a man to marry you. Perhaps on the East Indiaman you'll meet a man who'll be flattered to have a connection to a noble house, even if the title is dead and the lands gone."

"What if I don't wish to marry? Is how I feel of no account to you?"

"My duty is to this ship, this crew, and to the Company. If you have no inclination to marry, you should have made plans for your life before you were forced to come to India and fall under the control of your uncle."

"It never occurred to me..." she mused.

"What never occurred to you?"

"That I'd not be taken care of. That I should have to make my own way. My brother refused to discuss family matters with me—I mean the state of the family fortune. The estate had been sold, I knew that, but several thousand pounds came from the sale, and I presumed..." She stopped, unable to confess the dreadful situation of the Wilmount family to a stranger.

"You presumed the money was there, invested for you?"

"Yes."

"And it was not?"

"It paid my father's and my brother's debts. They spent many hours each day at their club."

He laughed at her earnest confession. "And the estate honored their vowels, is that it?"

"Yes. And when Carlton was killed, I found he'd been living on money borrowed from friends. There was nothing left but his debts, and a very small inheritance I had from grandmother, which he'd not been able to touch. Less than a hundred pounds a year, not enough to live on..."

"If one intends to make a mark in the season, certainly not enough. But there are families in your sweet remembered England who live on less than a shilling a week. They'd sneer at your distress that you have only one hundred pounds a year."

"Less than a hundred pounds," she reiterated. His bitter laugh cut her short. Kranz bustled in, pulled a folding table into position before the window seats.

"Your dinner, sir," he said. "Cook finally got a fire going, so it's hot food today."

"Thank you, Kranz. This is the Lady Endine Wilmount. She will dine with me today."

"Very good, sir." He inclined his head far enough that it might be considered a bow.

Dinner consisted of boiled beef, rice, and more of the same fruits she'd been eating for the past four days. Dina looked around the table; no condiments, except for a mustard pot. Drink was watered rum. So this was how he intended to treat her!

"On the *Morgan Castle* I was admitted to the captain's table, and we had some luxuries. I see you do not share the captain's stores with your guests," she said tightly, meaning to shame him.

"There are no captain's stores on the *Pearl Stallion*, nor special food for the other officers." When she jerked her head up, he grinned at her confusion. "Every man on this ship eats the same food. I believe it makes the officers more careful in the purchase of stores, to know they'll be eating what they send into the hold."

Dina shrank against the frame of the window, aware that her barbed accusation had sprung back upon her without touching him. There was another point, however. She waited until they had both eaten, then looked at him pointedly. "The poor native who failed to stop me when I came below. How many lashes did he receive in punishment?"

"None. There's no cat aboard the *Pearl Stallion,* except for the one who catches rats in the hold."

"You don't flog?" she asked in amazement.

"No. It solves no problems, and creates many."

"But how can you make your crew behave?"

"My crew shares in the profits of the voyage. They receive no wages. If there's a loss, they get nothing. If there's fantastic gain, they go ashore with gold in their pockets. They agree to abide by ship's discipline, or they're put ashore."

"But you take the bulk of the profits, certainly."

"I own the ship. It's my savings invested, my money that supplies the food and keeps the masts seated on the keelson. But the lowest of my crew, when we came into Calcutta, received more money than an able seaman could expect to make in ten voyages on other East Indiamen. Everyone on this ship shares, both in hardships and in gain. It's a peaceful ship, and I have no trouble getting the best of crews."

"If your system works so well, why don't other captains do as you do?" she asked, curiosity overcoming her distrust of him.

"Most captains are afraid to try anything new. Men have been flogged since the Romans pushed galleys into the sea. Flogging must be, therefore, absolutely necessary. Captains trained in that way fail to see that men react better to praise than to blame. The cat-o'-nine-tails is an instrument of torture that should have disappeared with the rule of barons and lairds."

He pushed the table away from the bench and rose to go, stooping beneath the upper deck.

"Tomorrow we'll sail into the Andaman Sea. Within a day or two we'll find the ship to take you home. In the meantime, you may spend your days here or in your cabin, whichever you find more comfortable. When the seas have calmed, you may come on deck to walk for an hour."

Chapter Five

Dina studied the two dresses she had so hurriedly stuffed into her bundle. Both were designed for sturdiness, not style. How was she going to tempt a man into marriage dressed like this? That was what she would do on the Indiaman. If the captain was married, she would go after the first lieutenant. One of the men on that as-yet-unknown ship would propose to her before they sailed into the Hooghly.

Could a Company officer get free passage back to England for his wife? She'd never thought to find out what perquisites went with Company service. Where in England could she survive on less than a hundred pounds a year? If she married a lieutenant, she couldn't expect any support from his meager wages. She hated the thought of being far from London, but anyplace would be better than Calcutta. Any man would be better than Freemantle.

The *Pearl Stallion* danced over the swells of the tropical sea, pressed into the waves, then rose joyfully over them. Dina went to the main cabin to look out the windows. Overhead she heard the voices of the watch officers. A clearing throat quite close by warned her of a new presence. Dr. Hampton, bent beneath the beams, came into the cabin.

"The captain says you may come on deck for one hour, if you should be pleased to."

Hampton had clear blue eyes beneath tumbled brown hair. She hadn't thought about Hampton. Would he marry her?

"Thank you, Dr. Hampton." She gestured for him to sit on the bench beside her.

"Tell me, you have known Captain Saurage for a long time?"

"No, not for long. Less than four years. We met in Baltimore, when he waited there for the ship to be completed."

"America?"

"The British may rule the seas, but the Americans build the best ships. Particularly for the Pacific trade."

Dina refused to be diverted from her inquiry.

"But the two of you, you're friends?"

"Of course."

"Could you please ask of him, I beg of you, not to send me back to Calcutta? If a friend of his spoke on my behalf, perhaps he would understand...."

"Lady Endine, no women are allowed on the *Pearl Stallion*, except as temporary visitors. And then only at the captain's pleasure."

"In port, the sailors bring their—"

"No. This ship has no sailors' doxies aboard in port. That's only for ships whose captains dare not let their men ashore. It's condoned by captains who are sure their men will run away."

"And Captain Sav—Saurage is sure his men will not?"

"Yes. And you may call him Savage. He rather takes pride in the name."

"Doctor, you're bound by oath to help all human beings who come under your care, are you not?"

"Absolutely. But you don't seem ill, Lady Endine. Not even seasick. May I compliment you on your firm stomach?"

"It's not my stomach that needs help. Captain Savage is determined to send me back to Calcutta. My uncle will force me into a terrible marriage with Captain Freemantle." She saw an expression of shock cross the man's eyes, and felt the first warm glow of hope. He'd help her.

"Some man must marry me quickly and help me get to England, or I'll die in India. Would you marry me, Doctor, to save my life?"

He shifted his weight on the bench and cleared his throat. "I'm very sorry, Lady Endine. You do me a great honor. But I'm engaged to a young lady of Charleston, South Carolina, who will—within the year, I hope—become my wife."

Her heart congealed. She covered her face with her hands in embarrassment.

"I'm deeply sorry for you, Lady Endine, but I also love Miss Hawkins beyond words to describe. I've sailed on the *Pearl Stallion* for three years to make the fortune necessary to build my hospital in Charleston. On our return from this voyage, Miss Hawkins will be waiting in Calcutta, with Captain Hawkins and Mrs. Hawkins. We'll be wed, and I'll journey home on their ship, with my new wife."

"How is it," she asked bitterly, "that your future father-in-law sees no difficulty in having women aboard his ship, but Captain Savage sees us only as...problems?"

"You must bear with the captain, my dear," he said quietly, touching her arm. "He's a great, good man, but he's been deeply hurt in life. He's young, and still believes in revenge."

Dina raised her brimming eyes to him.

"You don't?"

"No. Revenge is a double-edged sword, and it cuts both ways. The party who feels wronged finds himself wounded, possibly even more deeply than the one who wronged him."

"He hates me."

"No, not you. The world you stand for. The world that treated him like a pariah. Were you there, when he walked the streets of London?"

"No."

"He came home a sailor, an officer, and thought to take his place in society."

"The *ton* ridicules younger sons who must depend upon trade for their income. I know. I heard the gibes directed at merchants for years."

"Then you, of all people, should understand him." He shifted his weight. "Is it a beautiful world, London? I've never been there."

"London is beautiful, not to look at so much as to just be in. The most wonderful place in the world, I believe."

"And you wish you'd never left?"

"I do indeed. I wish I'd accepted one of the proposals of marriage offered me. I rejected six."

"So, there's one man who stands in your memory." Dr. Hampton smiled. "Perhaps he'll wait for your return."

"No. What I mean is, one would have been as good as another."

"You regret you didn't take a man you didn't love to be your husband?" he asked, looking surprised. "A marriage without love would seem to have little to recommend it."

"I've seen very little about love to recommend it. I believe it's but a silly dream for silly young girls. If I'd only known to what end I'd come..."

"If we all had foreknowledge, we would avoid many a trap. But life runs only in one direction. I'll speak to the captain about your difficulty, as a medical man is bound to do, but I cannot change his mind in this matter, I fear." He rose to go. "You should take some exercise. It would clear your head and help you decide on the future. The sea as it is today, warm and delightful, always convinces me the days ahead will be equally wonderful. Would you care to accompany me?" He offered his arm, and she accepted it.

The sea and the wind, as he had promised, welcomed her with good tidings. She released the silk scarf from her head and let the breeze play through her short hair. They walked together on the quarterdeck. How unfortunate for her that this man was promised to someone else.

A man in a worn blue coat was turning the glass in the binnacle.

"You remember Lieutenant Becker," said the doctor.

The lieutenant bowed deeply, then turned his eyes to the ship, studying the set of the sails. The doctor guided her to the stern.

"Lieutenant Becker is one who has also suffered at the hands of Captain Freemantle. He was assigned to the shipyard and immediately suspected irregularities. Freemantle threatened to turn the accusations against him. He resigned and joined us on our last voyage."

Dina turned to stare at the officer, curious about a man ruined by Freemantle. Becker was tall, graying, older than either Savage or Dr. Hampton. He had grown gray in the service of the Company, and Freemantle had ruined him. What would Freemantle do to a wife, to a woman who depended upon him totally?

"I must find a man to marry me," she said, then looked with horror into Dr. Hampton's face when she realized she had, indeed, spoken the words aloud.

"Why, Lady Endine? Isn't it possible for you to find some method to support yourself without sacrificing your life to a man you not only don't love, but one you hardly know? Many women in my country make their own way until they marry."

"I have few skills. I doubt I could find clients for lessons in flirting."

"Many American women make their way with the needle, or the spinning wheel—"

"Ha!" she exclaimed loudly.

"You think it would be perhaps lowering yourself to take on..."

"I never learned these things. My education was terribly impractical."

"Perhaps you could learn."

Dina stared over the stern of the ship. Would going into service lower her any more than marriage to Freemantle? Good God! To what depths might Calcutta pull her? If she could only sew, she might get a position as governess with some good family in India. They might overlook her deficiencies on the pianoforte. Savage intended to send her back to Calcutta, but did that mean she had to yield herself gracefully to her uncle's domination? Perhaps Captain Savage or this American gentleman would loan her a few rupees, so that she could live until she found a position.

Perhaps her uncle need never learn she was back in town, or at least not until she had attached herself to one of the powerful families, a family who would protect her. A vision of Sir Hall's veranda rose in her mind, and she wondered which of those powerful men she could trust.

"Is there anyone on board," she asked sweetly, "who is skilled with a needle and might teach me sewing?"

The sailmaker's assistant sat on the deck of the main cabin, his legs crossed, patiently instructing Lady Endine Wilmount in the use of needle and "palm." Captain Savage watched for a few moments from the shadow of the passageway, pleased by the humble demeanor and studious attention.

"What are we making?" she asked.

"Your ditty bag," was the reply. "Captain says you came aboard without a ditty bag."

Savage could see from Dina's puzzled face that this remark meant absolutely nothing to her. At least she was keeping busy and not bothering him with suggestions for the cook or crew discipline.

"What's your name?" she asked of the man sitting before her.

"Crook, my lady,"

"Have you sailed with the captain before?"

"Aye, my lady. Three voyages. Almost three years."

"And where do you go, you and the *Pearl Stallion?*"

Savage tensed. Someday, just in this way, at a casual question from a beautiful woman, his secret would be out.

"That, my lady, is not something we ever say," Crook said politely.

Savage relaxed, smiled, and went up on deck. Hampton walked toward him, and Savage knew immediately he was her messenger, armed with another plea for mercy and a berth on the *Pearl Stallion.* He glanced significantly at the open skylight and guided Hampton forward until he was sure they were out of her hearing.

"The lady is terrified at being sent back," began Hampton.

"Of course she is. She's entangled herself in a web spun by a great spider—perhaps two, if you count her uncle."

"But the web is not of her making, and the entanglement is quite by accident. Couldn't we leave her with some English trader at some port? Malacca, perhaps?"

"What would her situation be in such a foreign place? No, it's better she take her chances in Calcutta, rather than risk being dragged into the harem of an island raja. Her hair makes her worth a fortune." There was something about the reflection of the sun on the sea in the middle distance that reminded him of her hair.

"She fears she'll be forced into marriage. She's a fine woman, Anson." Savage knew the use of his private name signaled an appeal to his friendship, not a suggestion from the ship's surgeon to the captain. "She should be given a chance to meet many men, find one she loves."

Savage laughed wildly, without meaning to.

"Her? Love? What she loves lies clinking in the pocket. You Americans are sentimental to the extreme. She's not married because no man with wealth enough and position sufficiently exalted ever asked for her. She took the chance that she had another year or two to make up her mind. She gambled wrongly. Now she must take the first man she can tempt, suffer her uncle's wrath, or accept being bedded by Freemantle."

Hampton hammered the railing with the heel of his hand. "My God, what would he do to a woman?"

"It does not bear thinking of, does it?"

Hampton pounced on the words, as Savage had known he would.

"So, what can we do?"

"We're outward bound, Charles, and the voyage will be a long one." He hoped that settled the conversation. Hampton turned to face him sternly, and he knew his words had not settled a thing.

"Do you have friends in Calcutta who would honor a recommendation from you? Someone who would protect her?" asked Hampton. "You're well acquainted with Lady Margaret Allinson."

Savage made a little humming sound between his teeth by way of answer.

"She might provide shelter to Lady Endine?"

"Possibly," said Savage. "Or force her into something worse than marriage." He'd been uneasy ever since he had pulled her, struggling, to the silver-curtained couch. It was an uneasiness that flowed from guilt. The mention of Lady Margaret brought it cascading over him again. He was the instrument of her introduction to Lady Margaret.

"Thank you, Anson. It would ease my mind greatly if some arrangement—"

"Why should you be concerned?" Savage asked, turning around, for he'd already started back to the quarterdeck.

"I'm a physician."

"She's not ill, is she?" he asked fearfully. Or pregnant, he thought with distaste. By one of those foul men.

"No, but she's been close to corruption, and if I can spare her being drawn into that, it's my responsibility."

"Pass the word for Mr. Becker," ordered Savage as he took his position behind the steersman. He hated to disturb Becker's rest, for he'd been on deck much of the past four days, and now, with the cursed woman in his cabin, he had to snatch what sleep he could in a hammock swung next to the navigator's. No more than three minutes passed before Becker's head poked through the hatch.

"Aye, aye, Captain," he said with naval formality, saluting. Savage worried that the man's bent shoulders might indicate a melancholia of mind, then decided it was the natural result of being tall and growing old on a ship. *That's how I'll look in twenty years if I stay in this life.*

"How does she handle, do you think?"

"A bit by the stern, I believe, sir."

"Any recommendation? You know the loading of her."

"We could shift the water barrels, sir, a portion of them, perhaps, and bring cargo aft, which is lighter, sir."

"See to it, Mr. Becker."

"Aye, aye, sir."

The noise from the companionway was strange. Thumps punctuated by feminine shrieks and masculine oaths, each followed by "Begging Your Ladyship's pardon." Savage strode to the hatch and leaned over the opening. His stowaway was fighting to get on deck, but was held back by Crook, who had been warned to guard against such an eventuality.

"Lady Endine!" Savage roared. "You're not to come on deck without permission. *My* permission. Get into your cabin."

"The water!" she shrieked, leaning over her captor's shoulder and stretching out her neck to see him on the deck. She looked a bit like a goose trying to flee the butcher.

"He said he did something to your water! Freemantle!"

Savage stared at her for a long moment. Her feet did not touch the deck. She balanced on the sailor's shoulder, her hands waving, her feet kicking to find something solid.

"Get up here and report," he snarled.

She stumbled onto the deck. He hoped Crook hadn't left any bruises that might convict him of mishandling her when he got her transshipped. God in Heaven, where were all the East Indiamen?

"What's all this?" he asked harshly, trying not to be moved by the breeze in her golden hair and the way her dress molded to her body on the windward side.

"Freemantle and my uncle!" she gasped. "When I heard them talking, they spoke of you never coming back to Calcutta!"

"And?" He could not choke out further words. His chest heaved with fear. The supplies from the shipyard? Had Becker checked the beef barrels carefully? And the bread?

"Captain Freemantle whispered something. All I heard was 'The lower tier of the water barrels.'" As an afterthought, she added, "sir," and he, even in the midst of his fear, was forced to smile at her attempt at seagoing etiquette. He led her to the railing, where they could stand side by side and he needn't look directly at her.

"What else did he say?"

"Nothing I can remember for certain. Only that they hate you so, for fear you know something. And because you're growing rich and will go home a nabob."

"What did they do to the water barrels?"

"I don't know. Freemantle spoke very quietly. I couldn't hear. I was frightened, for he was going to ask for my hand, and Uncle agreed to the marriage."

"How did you avoid them?" he asked sardonically, to cover up the fact that he might swim in her blue eyes.

"I pretended to be sick. Then I went into Uncle's room and found the costume he'd worn to the ragpicker's ball, and when everyone was asleep I climbed over the garden wall. You know the rest."

"When you return to Calcutta, you'll carry a letter to the governor-general. You will also tell him what you know. Before we sailed, I suggested to the secretary for the marine, Sir Hall, that something is amiss in the shipyard, but you'll take proof with you, a sample of whatever we find in the lower tier of barrels. I'll also inform the governor-general that he must protect you, for if Captain Freemantle thinks you threaten him, your kinship to George Mason does not shield you. He might insist on marrying you, because a wife cannot testify against her husband."

She gasped, and her hands flew to her face. It took all his strength not to put his arms around her.

* * *

Dina secured a lanyard around one leg of the chart table and punched a hook securely through a piece of canvas. She studied the edges she must sew together to form the canvas into a cylinder. Crook had damned the first flat seam she'd sewn; he'd mocked it as poorer than any he'd seen done by a ten-year-old cabin boy and ordered her to do it again, properly.

The leather sling about her right hand was uncomfortable, but Crook insisted a palm was necessary to push the needle through the canvas in the proper fashion. She struggled with the awkward equipment, but persevered. It might not be the type of sewing she'd be required to do as a governess, but it was sewing.

And won't my young charges be impressed when I can teach them to make a real sailor's ditty bag?

Voices came through the skylight, talking in the incomprehensible jargon used only on board ships.

"Pardon, lass," said Mr. Lightner, the navigator, as he came into the cabin. "Must set new bearings."

"Bearings to where?" she asked as she slipped the line from the table leg.

"Ten Degree Channel," he replied, weighting a chart to lie flat with an assortment of dividers and rulers, and a spool of twine he took from her supplies on the floor. She stepped back, but watched the procedure curiously.

"Why now?" she asked. "The day's half-gone. Shouldn't this have been done at sunup, when the day began?"

"First good view of the sun in days, lass. And the day on shipboard starts at noon. Shooting the sun, always at noon. That gives us our position." He bent over the chart. "Six plus naught is six, times nine is sixty-three . . ."

"Fifty-four," said Dina automatically.

"What?" asked Mr. Lightner, raising his head. "I'll be pleased, lass, if you'd quiet yourself and let me get ahead with me work."

Dina backed toward the stern windows. She'd interfered with the workings of the ship, exactly as Captain Savage said women were likely to do. Mr. Lightner reapplied his chalk to the slate.

"Six plus naught is six, times nine is sixty-three." He marked a spot on the charts and laid down the parallel rulers while muttering numbers to himself.

"Course nor', ten degrees east," he muttered, and started out the door.

"Mr. Lightner," Dina protested. "Six times nine is not sixty-three. It's fifty-four." All she got in reply was a look of withering scorn.

"Never did know a lass who learned the rule of nine properly," he said, dismissing her with a tone of pity. "I'd appreciate you not bothering me in the performance of me duties."

Dina stood quietly, bent under the deck, moving her fingers against her thigh to double-check her figuring.

Where might this idiot head them? Couldn't the captain find better crew than this? But she was a woman, and she was not to interfere with the operation of the ship. If this is any example of the wisdom of sailors, she thought bitterly, they should let a few women aboard. No wonder the East India Company loses ships every year, tossed upon rocks no one thought were near, shores supposedly tens of miles distant.

She heard Mr. Lightner's voice on the deck overhead. "Course nor', ten degrees east."

"Course nor', ten degrees east," repeated Mr. Becker.

Booted footsteps on the deck, to the aft hatch, down the stairs. Dina busied herself reattaching the lanyard to the leg of the chart table, then sat down on the floor to resume her work.

"Do you really believe six times nine is fifty-four?" asked a voice from the door. Dina looked up to see Savage's massive body. He completely blocked the opening, particularly since he had to stoop beneath the upper deck beam. The sight of him from this angle shadowed her mind, for it showed exactly how much bigger he was than she.

"Yes. I'm quite certain it is."

"And you're correct. The damned fool will have us crashing ashore on the Andamans. And he came to me highly recommended. Thank heavens the skylight was open and I heard what was going on down here." He pulled out the chart, rubbed out the position Lightner had marked, then sat on the stool to refigure. Dina hastily began detaching her work from the table leg.

"Don't interrupt your work," he said negligently, waving a hand toward her. "I'll not be long."

He marked the new position, stood up, stepped over the taut line stretching from the table to the sewing. The full canvas trousers did not display his powerful legs the way pantaloons and hose did, but her body remembered the flex of his muscles. The memory flashed hot.

"East, ten degrees north," said Savage's voice from overhead. "Mr. Lightner, take care on your figures."

"My figures were right, sir," he protested. "This course will put us on the rocks north of the Nicobars."

"You must restudy the rule of nine, Mr. Lightner. The lady below knows it better than you."

"You must not pay heed to a lass, sir. Women can't go past the rule of three. I know, for I once was tutor to the family of the laird of—"

"Obviously not the family of Lord Cairnlea, for his daughter knows the rule of nine."

Mr. Lightner stomped off the quarterdeck. She'd made an enemy, thought Dina. She should never have been so bold as to correct the master, for navigation seemed to be his job. But if she had not, they might have crashed into the Andamans, whatever they were. Strange that the sea should be so full of small things one had never heard of. Sailors had to be wise to keep on the water and not run onto rocks and islands. And in some way, at each noon, they could look at the sun and do some figuring, and then put a dot on a map which marks exactly where the ship lies.

She peered at the chart on the table. It was empty of all but the tiniest of islands, no land that could possibly be seen in any direction, yet there was the dot Captain Savage had placed upon the paper. It marked the precise point of water where the *Pearl Stallion* floated, this exact, ever-changing square mile of sea.

She was still studying the miracle when Mr. Lightner came in and, without looking at her, set about straightening and rearranging the rolled charts in the cubbyholes below the table. Dina lowered her eyes to her sewing and concentrated on making the stitches even.

"What charts!" snarled Lightner. "Never find our way with such charts." He threw one on the floor. "Not even in the king's English, and he expects the right course every time with such charts. And lasses with foolish sewing getting in the way and interrupting a man's work."

Dina dropped her canvas and quickly slipped the lanyard from the leg of the table. She backed to the stern windows. A pitch of the ship sent one of the discarded charts rolling to her feet. She stooped, picked it up and unrolled it.

"Pribylov, Unalasha, Yakutat, Pavlovsk," She pronounced the names out loud from the difficult Russian script.

"Mr. Lightner," said a dark voice from the doorway. "Lady Endine is in possession of the main cabin at this time. Sorting the charts can be done when she's not here."

"Russian America," Dina said quietly, lifting her eyes to the captain.

"What?" he snapped, genuine alarm showing on his face.

"Russian America. That's where you're going. To Russian America."

He crossed the cabin in two strides, snatched the chart from her hands.

"How do you know? This chart isn't even in English."

"I know a bit of Russian. The daughter of the Russian ambassador...she was often at country homes, and we amused ourselves on rainy afternoons..." Dina let her voice die. His eyes, normally so unintelligible, shone with anger. His full mouth was thin, drawn back in disgust and rage.

"Good God!" he shouted at the man. "You ham-fingered, muddle-headed rogue!" Lightner fled before the captain's fury, leaving Dina to face the entire flood. She retreated to the bench before the windows, but did not sit down. She would face him standing, or at least standing as much as was possible in the low cabin.

But as he advanced, eyes like lightning flashes, she slumped on the bench in terror. She had learned his secret. What would he do now? There might be no cat aboard, but a man could punish a woman in a way so much worse.

"Go to your cabin!" he snarled. He turned and jammed the chart back into the cubbyhole, crumpling its end with the force of his thrust.

Chapter Six

Savage watched carefully as the block and tackle was strung from the yardarm and the first of the water barrels was lifted from the hold. Strong arms rolled the barrel into the scuppers and started the bung. The crew stepped back, grimacing at the stench of the water.

"Every barrel from the lower tier on deck and dumped," Savage ordered.

He watched until he was certain everything was well under control. He allowed himself a glance at the shoreline, less than a quarter mile away. From here he could see a flash of tumbling water high on the hill, the only hint of the existence of the stream where he would fill his barrels with fresh water.

The cove where the *Pearl Stallion* anchored was breathless. The crew had towed her in toward the shore, exhausted by the equatorial heat as they struggled at the oars. The lady below must be dying in that close, unventilated cabin. He could let her on deck, now that he'd decided her fate. He clenched his teeth, dreading a new confrontation with her. Her deep blue eyes, when he angrily snatched the Russian chart from her hands, had been clouded by tears. She'd been so frightened she actually shrank before him. That was how she must have been in the dim veranda, if he'd been able to see her clearly. If he'd taken the trouble to even look. He must not frighten her again. He felt too much guilt when he did.

"Kranz," he said as his steward hove into view. "Bring the lady on deck, aft, so she'll be out of the way."

Her gown was soaked with perspiration and clung to her, revealing her figure in a most disturbing fashion, drawing his eyes. She ignored him and looked around at the enclosing landscape, at the activity amidships.

"Where are we?" she asked.

"Sumatra. We're ridding ourselves of Freemantle's poison and refilling with fresh water."

"What did he put in the barrels?"

"Water straight from the Hooghly. Stinking water full of unspeakable filth. If we'd come to it in midocean, we'd have died of thirst, or dysentery, or something worse."

Dina stared at the jungle landscape. Sweat formed on her brow and ran down her face, coming together at the point of her chin. Her face did not have the oval beauty demanded by fashion. It was triangular. No, the shape of a heart. Her golden hair was dark with sweat. Her blue eyes reflected the sky and the calm harbor. He tried to tell himself that kindness and caring came from dark eyes—at least that had been his experience—but her eyes fascinated him, and he found it hard not to look into them. He waited for her to ask what he intended to do with her, but she seemed more interested in her surroundings than in her personal fate.

"Why is the ship surrounded with this netting?" She leaned over the rail and fingered the net, which hung in loose swags.

"Boarding netting. In these waters we must be on the lookout for pirates."

"Pirates? Seriously?"

"The Malay pirates have seized more than one ship this year and murdered its crew. Haven't you ever considered why Indiamen carry cannon?"

"I presumed so that, in case they met a French warship, they might defend themselves."

"It would be a very small French warship that couldn't overpower the guns of an East Indiaman. No, the cannon are designed to drive off a pirate who comes very close and tries to board. The pirate does not intend to sink his prey but to capture it. He wants the ship and its cargo, and doesn't want to be bothered with the men who sail it. They come to a very nasty end."

And the women an even nastier one, he thought, but did not say so. She'd be worth a fortune to an East Indies pirate.

"Have you finished your ditty bag?" he asked, to change the subject.

"Yes. Crook praises it as the best he's seen for a beginner."

"So I've heard. Now you can start on your seabag."

"Why should I want a seabag?"

"To hold your clothing."

"The bits of clothing I have fit in the ditty bag."

"I'm giving you several yards of light canvas for trousers, and enough cotton to make four shirts. And wool for a coat. You'll need warm things in a few weeks, when we broach the northern ocean."

She turned to him, her blue eyes and her mouth wide in astonishment. "I can go with you?" she asked in amazement.

"I have little choice. You know our destination, and the moment you're back in Calcutta and start talking, the news will spread. I don't need the competition of hordes of East Indiamen. The Boston ships are bad enough. You go along."

"Thank you," she breathed with relief. "Thank you."

"It is I who should be thanking you," he said gruffly and hated that his tone made him seem ungrateful. "The water..."

"You, or Mr. Becker, or someone else would surely have discovered the cheat before it became a matter of thirst," she said confidently.

"Who's to say?" he shrugged. "Perhaps when the barrels were shifted. But you saved us the discovery before i was too late. Do you wish to know the rules of your life on board the *Pearl Stallion?*"

"Rules?"

"Of course. I can't let a woman run loose on the ship. You'd soon find that not all the men have notions of honor where women are concerned."

"And you do?" she asked doubtfully.

He glared at her, resenting the insult. She dropped her eyes in the face of his anger. By God, he'd not taken her maidenhead when he had the chance. He'd restrained himself at a moment when his whole body was tuned to be inside a woman. He'd taken the risk to warn her about Freemantle and Mason. The woman had no sense of gratitude at all!

"You'll be restricted to your cabin, which Mr. Becker has graciously ceded to you."

"No!" she cried. "You can put me wherever—"

"Another cabin is being rigged for him farther forward. He is one of your defenders, Lady Endine. When confronted with the facts, he grew quite pale and voiced alarm at what Captain Freemantle might do to you. He was quite willing to sacrifice his cabin."

"Thank him for me."

"I'll do that.

"You'll dine with me in the main cabin, which will save Kranz the trouble of serving two meals. Except when I have the other officers with me. Then you'll dine in your cabin. When there's no ship's business in the main cabin, you may sit there. I'll open my library to you, but I'm afraid you'll find it very limited.

"When the weather's fine, you'll be allowed on the deck for one hour each day to get exercise. I hope you understand the reasons for these restrictions."

"Not really. I should like to spend more time here, on deck, and if you would trust me..."

"I can trust you, but the effect you have upon the men is disturbing to discipline. Already, for every man on this ship, the body of a woman is nothing but a pleasant memory, and shall be only a memory until we're months across the sea. The men may find women among the natives of Russian America, but more probably they'll have to wait until we anchor in the Sandwich Islands before they can fully satisfy their urges. You're a woman, and some of the crew wish to use you as a woman."

"They've asked you?" She clutched at the railing and shrank from him. He couldn't see her eyes, but knew they must be clouded with fright, as they had been when faced with his anger.

"No. But the inclination is obvious." Why shouldn't the crew want her? He struggled against the impulse to drop his eyes to her hips, where the damp muslin plastered against her form.

"But I'll see you daily," she said.

Could she read his mind?

"It's my policy that officers and men share everything on this ship, both hardships and good times. If I were to relieve myself in you, every man would have the right to demand his turn. I doubt that even the most skilled whore of London's streets would want to service nearly sixty men."

He watched her body shrink until she was a damp hunchback tucked against the railing. Periodically, over the past few days, he had seen more confidence, the flashing woman of the ballroom. Creeping aboard the *Pearl Stallion* had not been the act of a coward. But mention of sex turned her into the terror-filled child he'd encountered at the Allinsons. The memory of what he had thought to do there burdened him every time he came close to her, every time her body tensed, expectant of violence.

"Do you agree to these rules?"

"What choice do I have? You yourself told me I no longer had a choice, nothing to do but obey you."

"I'm glad the message sank in. It will be a new experience for you, to obey a man, will it not?" She nodded miserably. He hoped she was not crying, but he couldn't tell, for she had averted her face.

"Obedience will be good practice for my future, I'm sure," she finally replied.

"Your future? You've made a decision?"

"I'll try to get a position as a governess. With some wealthy family bound back to England."

"After a year on a ship, in the company of fifty-some men, I doubt your reputation will recommend you to many wealthy families." He didn't even try to keep the sarcasm out of his voice. Her innocence was truly amazing. "The officers and crew of the *Pearl Stallion* may leave your virginity intact, but few shore dwellers will believe they did."

"What am I to do?" she asked in sudden terror.

"Keep at your needle and palm," he said. "Perhaps you could set yourself up as a sailmaker." He enjoyed her consternation, for the mobility of her anxious face kept his eyes focused upward, away from the shape of her body. "Or perhaps you could make shirts and trousers for sailors. You'll get practice by making your own wardrobe."

"Couldn't I make myself gowns, to be more respectably clad?"

"And cold. Remember, we're going to the North Pacific. Trousers and shirts."

"Yes, sir."

He had not intended to reduce her to this drooping, frightened flesh. He'd said all this very badly, obviously. The flashing eyes of the ballroom flirt were dulled, the graceful hands were in tight fists on her chest. She'd begged to be allowed to stay, but she had not considered the consequences of being on a ship full of men armed with carnal desires. He thought of Hampton's suggestion. Leave her behind in one of the ports of the Spice Islands. His eyes slid unwillingly away from her face, to the body defined just sufficiently to rouse him. The thought of that body in the grasp of one of the island rulers made him slightly ill.

"I've ordered the crew to call you 'Lady Endine.' Some of the Americans resisted the title, but I assured them it was of no more significance than calling the lieutenant 'Mister.'"

"Would you please tell them I prefer to be called Dina? My friends call me Dina."

"And we're friends?"

"I think we must be, if we're to be together all the way across the Pacific."

Dina lay awake in the oppressive darkness of her cabin. The bunk rode easily on knotted lines strung through hooks in the beams. It lifted only slightly in the swells of the Strait of Malacca. She could not sleep for the heat, and for wondering if her newly granted wish was what she truly desired.

She had not thought two steps ahead in this matter. Analyzing her life, she realized she had never thought two steps ahead in anything. Each rejected marriage proposal had been made with the expectation that a better one, or at least another one, would present itself at the next ball. There had been no hurry, for life was bound to trail along much as it had in the past. Life with Carlton had been so much fun, a lively serial of weeks at country houses and months in London. Even in January or February, long before the season began, London was better than being stuck in the country.

Now she was beyond the provinces, with fewer prospects for a proposal than in the poor society of Calcutta. She'd reached the absolute nadir for a woman. Only Mr. Hampton and the captain could seriously be considered as marriage partners. And Mr. Hampton was in love with some colonial child, and Captain Savage did not want a human wife.

His name is Saurage, she corrected herself. But more and more she thought of him as Savage. Not just in name, but also in spirit. A noble savage, who was kind to her while at the same time he terrified her. He had reduced her to total obedience, limited her domain to a cabin hardly big enough for a single step. The main cabin was only slightly more spacious, and available only when it was not needed by someone else. The deck of the ship, perpetually crowded with men working at one thing and another, was open to her only with the captain's permission. Everything with the Savage's permission.

A year on the *Pearl Stallion.* At least ten months. She moaned.

A shout, and the patter of bare feet overhead. Some adjusting of the sails, probably.

Ten months or a year of this, and she would go mad. The captain's library contained four books on navigation, two books about India, one book about China, and Gibbon's *Decline and Fall of the Roman Empire.* A survey of the sea chests of all the officers and men had produced not one novel.

From the deck came louder shouts, and the clash of steel, a sound unlike anything she'd heard since she'd come aboard. Then came a pounding knock at the door. "My lady!"

She unbarred the door and opened it a crack.

"You're to go to the orlop! Captain's orders!" Crook's thick arm shoved the door open. "Come quick! Pirates!"

"Let me dress," she begged.

She pulled on trousers and a shirt, the closest things at hand. No boots, no cap, for he tugged at her arm. He led her down the ladders to the lower deck. By the light of swinging lanterns she saw a makeshift operating table created by pulling sea chests together. Dr. Hampton crouched at the bottom of the ladder, gazing up toward the deck, twenty feet above.

"Don't worry, my lady, they shan't get aboard. Just precautions," said Crook.

"Where's Billy?" someone shouted close to her ear. She winced at the noise. Just then the thunder of guns on the upper deck shook the entire ship and reduced her to startled jelly.

"In here, my lady," said Crook, holding back a curtain to reveal a hammock slung between two timbers.

"Where's Billy?" The voice was even louder. "He's to carry powder."

"I don't know. Captain said for me to bring her down. Said nothing about Billy."

"Heaving timbers, man! There's but one more shot for every gun unless the powder's carried up." Dina turned from the insecure nest that had been fashioned for her.

"I can carry it. Where do I go?"

"To each gun. But you must take off your boots. No boots in the magazine."

"I'm barefoot."

"Good." He dived into a hole in the deck, seemed to disappear like a gnome sinking into the soil, then pushed up heavy cylinders of fabric.

"The captain will not like this," said Crook. "She's to stay here, on the orlop deck."

"The captain will not like the guns running out of powder," said he of the loud voice from the hole in the deck.

Dina grasped the rope handle of the wooden tub. She could barely lift it, let alone carry it unaided up the ladders between the orlop and the upper deck. The man saw her problem and took some of the dark cylinders out of the tub.

"That's more a ladylike load, my lady."

Another roar of guns overhead.

"Now run like the wind, my lady. When Billy comes, you can turn it over to him."

She trailed the tub up the ladders, through the aft hatchway. Radgni guarded the hatch, a long pike in his hands. He looked at her with surprise, opened his mouth to object, then simply pointed to the starboard cannon. In a few seconds her tub was empty, and she ran for the hatch. She was on the ladders when the guns roared and she realized they must be out of powder for the next firing.

"How close are the pirates?" she gasped as the tub was filled for a second time.

"Coming from behind one of the islands," said the man. "Go!"

The tub was heavier this time. She hefted it with both hands and let her bare feet grasp the flat rungs, forced the muscles of her thighs and calves alone to lift her up the ladder. Men were waiting at the hatch and grabbed the powder from the tub before she had ever set foot on the deck. On the way back down, she met a young sailor carrying a tub. Billy, perhaps.

When she arrived on the orlop, nothing was said about her resting, so she began her trip upward again. She had to step aside to let two men by. They were carrying a third man.

"What happened?"

"Gun recoil. Over his foot."

Dina looked down. The foot looked strangely flat. She gagged and ran the rest of the way to the deck. What was happening? What was happening? Where were these pirates, except off somewhere to starboard? Billy shot past her, sliding down the ladders, his tub thumping behind him.

The men who grabbed the powder came from the left, not the right. She had no idea who should have it and decided it was not her task to stop the grasping hands. She tried to imitate Billy in his fast descent, but ended up tumbling and barely catching herself. The tub went clattering down to the orlop. By the time she had descended to meet it, and dodged Billy on his run upward, it was filled.

Dina lost track of how many times she climbed up to the deck, slid back to the orlop. Billy, she realized, was making two trips to her one.

"They're trying to board!" gasped Billy. Dina stood still, separating the sounds of guns from the screams and shouts of men. A roar directly over her head startled her into a hurried descent.

"Now's the important time, miss," said the man pulling powder from the magazine. "Grape into their boats. Haul away."

Billy was already beside her with his empty tub. He grabbed her filled one and sped up the ladders, giving her an extra few seconds of rest. Dina picked up the tub he had abandoned and followed him, exhausted. Her chest ached from her inability to draw one calm breath.

Guns were firing singly now; she heaved herself up the ladder. Billy grabbed the tub from her hands and thrust the empty one at her, nearly sending her tumbling backward down the ladder. Her hands shot out, and she saved herself, despite the tub, which pressed at her feet. Billy had already disappeared into the haze above.

The cheering began faintly when she descended the final ladder, then turned into a torrent of sound that flowed even into the orlop. Billy hung on the ladder, yelling, and the man on Dr. Hampton's makeshift medical table cheered, as well.

"What's happening?" she cried.

"They've cut off, the cowardly coves!" yelled Billy.

"They're gone?" she asked.

"Yes," said the man crawling from the magazine. "Pirates don't want to spill their own blood. If someone's ready for them, they slip away and wait for easier prey."

Dina lifted the curtain concealing the tiny spot that was to have been her refuge during the attack. She thought about climbing into the hammock, but the effort seemed too great. She dropped to her knees beneath it. Her chest heaved from the unaccustomed exercise. How long since she'd been taken from her cabin? Half an hour? An hour?

"How bad?" said Savage's voice, only a foot or two away.

"Lyon's foot, I don't know," Hampton replied. "We'll try to save it. Scraggs, just a knock on the head. He'll be right tomorrow. Are they gone for good, or just discouraged for the moment?"

"Two of their boats were swept with grape. I don't think they'll be back anytime soon. And tomorrow, if the wind holds, we'll put this pirate nest behind us."

Light flooded around Dina.

"How fares the ship's lady?" asked Savage, the curtain in his uplifted hand. He laughed as he looked down at her, kneeling on the floor.

"At your prayers when in peril of your life," he said. "A worthy position, although not one any man aboard can assume, or we should certainly all be dead."

"Nay, sir," said the man who was carefully cleaning every grain of spilled powder from around the magazine entrance. "The lady carried powder, along with Billy."

The hand that reached down and grasped her shoulder was surprisingly gentle, for she knew the strength of the arm that commanded it.

"Why kneeling, then, Lady Dina?" he asked gently. "Hurt?"

"No. I was going to the hammock, but I was simply too...too tired." She leaned into his arm involuntarily. "I've never worked so hard in my life. How long did I run up and down those ladders with that heavy tub?"

"Ten minutes, perhaps. It didn't take us very long to make those cowards scamper away."

"Ten minutes?" she said, unbelieving. "I thought it was an hour."

"No. Ten minutes. Perhaps less. Come. I'll have some tea brought to the cabin."

"Tea? I didn't think you had such luxury aboard."

"Oh, yes. For those times when we need to calm ourselves, take a few moments to think. I believe this is one of those times."

He led the way out of the orlop, almost pulling her up the ladder, then up the companionway to the deck.

"There," he said, pointing. "The pirates were hiding behind those small islands, but we've sailed here before and know the trick. So the lookouts kept a very close watch, and the pirates' boats were hardly away from their shelter before we spotted them."

Dina drew away from the circle of his arm and leaned against the railing. What would her friends in London think of her life now? Carrying powder for cannons to resist pirates? Facing a year aboard a ship with more than fifty men and a captain called Savage? She tried to think back a year, to form some idea of how long it would be.

What had she been doing a year ago? The beginning of the season in London, only a few weeks of life remaining for Carlton. Both she and her brother had flitted about town as if their time there would last forever.

"The tea is in the main cabin," said Kranz, behind their backs. Savage led her down the companionway.

"No one I know in London will believe these things," she said, almost to herself, once she was seated on the bench beneath the stern windows.

"You'll have great stories to amuse the gentlemen at the salons when you return," he said.

"No one will believe me. I'll get a reputation for lying, as well as for being a loose woman."

"You should keep a diary."

"It would be amusing to keep a journal, but I neglected to put paper and ink in my bundle when I left my uncle's so hastily. I had my mind on other things."

"I should think the threat of a marriage to Freemantle would focus a young lady's mind fiercely," he said casually. "Your forgetfulness would be natural."

"Why did you want me below, in the orlop?" she asked. "I would have been safe in my cabin."

"The orlop would have been the safest place if the pirates boarded. And if they had seized the ship—" he hesitated, then spoke again, looking directly in her eyes "—Dr. Hampton had orders to kill you."

Chapter Seven

Dina braced herself against the *Pearl Stallion*'s plunge without thinking. Her whole body moved automatically—tight against the bench under the stern windows when the bow rose, her foot against the chart table when it dropped.

She tried to concentrate on *The American Practical Navigator,* by Nathaniel Bowditch of Massachusetts, but the shriek of the wind in the rigging was barely muffled by the deck above her head. The noise of the ship, the timbers working against one another in the violent sea, roused fears that the vessel would break apart in the North Pacific. No one would ever know what had happened to the *Pearl Stallion* and the souls aboard her. Her skin crawled when she thought of her uncle's prayers that the ship might sink.

She had examined the chart and seen the expanse of water. No land, nothing, within thousands of miles. The *Pearl Stallion* was hove to in that empty part of the globe, a scrap of sail keeping her bow to the wind. The horrible lurching of the ship could be borne with; the eternal wet from the sea leaking through the active boards might be guarded against; but the noise, days on end of noise, strained her to the edge of insanity. An hour, half an hour, of silence, and she might grasp normalcy. But nothing she or the captain or any of the crew could do would bring that silence.

She tried to blot out the roar by concentrating upon the book. "Plane sailing is the art of navigating a ship upon principles deduced from the supposition of the earth's being an extended plane, on which the meridians are all parallel to each other."

It would be easier to understand if she could jot down notes in the blank book Savage had given her. But the violent rolls of the ship made pen and ink unthinkable.

Savage was in the cabin without her having heard his steps in the companionway. She got to her feet, balanced there long enough to grab the oilskins as he stripped them from his body. She hung them over a tub to drip. Kranz was in sick bay. He'd overbalanced in the hatchway on the second day of the storm, and he had a great lump on his head.

Savage smiled at her, and she took heart from his good humor. She would ask him.

"I should like to go on deck."

"No. The helmsmen are tied to the wheel because the deck's so often awash." He smiled again. "In a few hours."

"Why not now? A few hours will make little difference."

"The storm's passing."

"How can you tell?"

"Don't you hear the sound of the wind in the rigging? It's dropped two full tones in the past hour."

"I hadn't noticed," she confessed.

"You must learn to notice these things if you hope to be a navigator." He looked at the book on the cushions, dropped to the deck, and braced himself against the bench. "Come. Join me. Standing's no pleasure for anyone in this sea."

"I doubt I'll ever learn navigation," she said, gratefully curling up against the bench, making sure several inches separated her knees from his. "I don't understand the moons of Jupiter."

"No need to. We have chronometers now, which tell us the time in Greenwich. Perhaps tomorrow the sun will let us mark our position. We're bound to be closer to North America, for the storm and the current are pushing us in that direction."

The door opened to admit a sailor carrying a basket.

"Food, sir," he said shortly, keeping his feet with insolent ease, looking down at them without surprise, as if it were normal to find the captain sprawled on the deck of the main cabin, next to a lady.

"Thanks, Benning. Tell Cook we may be able to have a fire in a few hours."

"Aye, aye, sir."

The sailor rolled out the door. Savage took a jug from the basket, pulled out the cork, took a long pull, then wiped the top with a damp handkerchief he extracted from his pocket. He handed it to her. She sipped the watered rum, which tasted slightly of lemon. Savage watched her. He lay relaxed against the bench, still smiling, and as always, his stare made her uneasy. Lately a flutter had invaded her stomach whenever they were near one another.

"Why do you do this?" she asked suddenly, emboldened by his smile and relaxed posture.

"What?" he asked, looking around to spot the action to which she referred.

"Sail to Russian America. Sail anyplace, for that matter. The life's hard. And frightening."

"To get rich."

"But there's just as much chance your ship will go to the bottom and you'll never be heard from again."

"No, with my ship and my crew, there's a better chance of a prosperous voyage. This blow has frightened you?"

"Yes. When I sailed to India, we were in a storm in the South Atlantic. But then I at least had Emily to cling to. Here I must maintain my own spirits, without help."

"We've been lucky. No typhoon in the China Sea. And this is but a passing summer storm, a few winds sneaking out of the northern sea past their season."

He opened the basket and offered her cold pork and biscuit. The fresh fruit the sailors had loaded in Calcutta was but a pleasant, regretted memory.

"What will we find in Russian America?"

"A friendly welcome at Pavlovsk, for the war in Europe has kept Russian ships from visiting regularly. They're learning to depend upon us, rather than their own countrymen."

"And you'll sell them the cargo...whatever it is you've got stowed below."

"You'll see when we arrive. Wool and cotton, pig iron, pots and pans, knives, powder, shot. And brandy, although these Russians prefer their own spirits, vodka."

"And you'll trade for—?" she asked boldly. He'd not been so open with her since Kranz had found her in his cabin.

"Furs. Fox, seal, wolf and bear. If we're lucky, sea otter. You must have a sea-otter pelt to take back to England to trim a cape. Would you like a bearskin for your bunk?"

The offer took her aback, and the mention of her bed roused anew the tingle he so often engendered within her. "I...I...I..." she stammered.

"We'll be bound for the Sandwich Islands to replenish our provisions once the trading's done in Pavlovsk. You wouldn't get much good from a bearskin in those waters."

"I suppose not," she said, finding it more comfortable to agree with him, no matter what he said.

"The Russians once had two settlements to call upon, but the southern one, on the island of Sitka, was destroyed."

"A mutiny?"

"No, not exactly. The natives in neighboring villages attacked the fort when most of the men were absent."

"The natives aren't pacified?" she asked, in no little panic.

"Not in the south. And Baranov insists he must have a settlement in the south to show the Russian flag. The Spanish and Americans push at his borders."

"Baranov?"

"Aleksandr Baranov. The lord of Russian America. The governor. You'll meet him. I know of no other woman, English or American, who has visited his realm, so you'll be confused with compliments, not to mention the rough attentions of his hunters. But don't expect to join in the feasting. The Russians have primitive arrangements at meals. Respectable women eat separately."

"How Oriental," she exclaimed. "I'd thought, from the Russian ambassador's daughter, they'd given up such odd customs."

"In the west, perhaps, around Saint Petersburg, where everyone tries so hard to be French. But the Russians in America are old-fashioned."

"So I'll be condemned to stay on the ship?"

"No. Baranov's lady will entertain you, I'm sure."

"I look forward to being on land again, even for a few hours. Being able to walk without wondering where my foot might go. Having fruit and vegetables..."

"Don't expect much in the way of fresh food in Pavlovsk, particularly this early in the season. They live on fish and seal meat. Bread is a luxury, and tea a drink for exceptional celebrations."

He laughed at her, and she knew her face had betrayed her disappointment. She'd been dreaming of buns with butter, and muffins to be toasted at the fire.

"And in the Sandwich Islands?" she asked.

"Perhaps we can get bread there from a whaling ship, made from what the Americans call corn flour, which is Indian maize. The natives eat a fermented paste made from a root. That serves for bread."

She made a face and he laughed at her, with that full laughter that rose from his gut. Deep inside, she shivered from the impact of the sound, a quivering that pressed on her heart and increased its beating. The sensation recalled, to a faint degree, the reaction of her body when he had forced her against him.

He looked directly at her, so she twisted away, pretending she wanted to see the condition of the sea out the small area of the stern windows not covered by deadlights. His eyes were not opaque, as she had always supposed, but glowing, with a depth she had not noticed before. Something within them was ripe and full, and if she allowed herself...

She cast about for something to say.

"Thank you for allowing me to attend the noon observations."

"You thanked me before. Does it mean so much?"

"It's easier to understand, seeing how a sextant is used, instead of just reading it in a book."

"Would you like to try it yourself, when the sun comes out once more?"

She turned to him without thinking, was seized by the unusual softness in his dark, rugged face.

"I should like to very much—if Mr. Lightner would not take it as an affront, that is."

"Mr. Lightner will do as I tell him. This is his first voyage on the *Pearl Stallion,* and it will be his last. He's not only incompetent, but old-fashioned in his ways. He's tied to the navigators of the past, who had the disagreeable habit of keeping their knowledge secret. They claimed it prevented mutiny that the hands were mystified by the chart and sextant. But I've always believed it was nothing but the jealousy of men who want to retain their power. Mr. Bowditch—" he gestured toward the book on the bench "—has gone a long way toward ending that closeness. Anyone with a mathematical bent who can read can now learn to navigate a ship."

"I don't wish to offend Mr. Lightner. If you show favor toward me, it may give him... notions... and he could spread rumors to make the men discontented." Her face warmed at her own oblique reference to her gender, and to the act that a man forced upon a woman. Savage was already sitting too near, and the unusual casualness of the conversation created tiny spikes of alarm in her brain.

"Mr. Lightner is not in any position to spread rumors about you. The entire crew knows what six times nine is now, and is not likely to forget it. Haven't you heard what they mutter when he announces our location at noon?"

She nodded.

"'Belike the Lady Dina should be a-checkin' of 'is figurin','" he said, imitating the accents of the forecastle. "He's not popular with the crew."

"But if he should say..." She stopped, unable to complete the sentence.

"That I have bedded you?"

She nodded, keeping her eyes on her dirty trousers. She hadn't changed since the storm had begun.

"Why should they believe him? A secret of that magnitude would be devilish hard to keep secure on board a ship of this size."

She said nothing, simply kept her hot face down.

"We'll say no more about it, and when the sun graces us with his presence, you'll have your first chance with a sextant. Crook says you're gaining well with the needle. He praised your decorative skills."

His finger caught her beneath the chin, and he lifted her head. She drew back, fearful he might try to kiss her, fearful of that moist, open, penetrating kiss.

"Come, come... We'll never say anything again that suggests the differences of Adam from Eve, remarks that reduce you to the melancholy of a frightened child. I find you more likable as a curious woman. What have you done to gain the respect of the indomitable Crook?"

"I pulled threads of different colors from my silk scarf, and embroidered a pillow for my bed. Crook gave me oakum to stuff it. It has flowers and what's supposed to be a nightingale, but I'm afraid it has more the look of an owl."

"Then say it's an owl, and have done with it."

She laughed, and was delighted at how wonderful it felt to let the ripples of happiness overtake her tense body.

"I hadn't thought of that!"

"I canna concentrate with the lass on deck," said Lightner. "She will have to take her exercise at some other time."

"She's here at noon because she's going to learn to use a sextant."

Lightner snorted. "A female's na strong enough to use a sextant. 'Tis not kind to have her made a fool of before the whole crew."

Dina feared he was speaking the truth. When she made her appearance on the quarterdeck at noon, almost the entire crew had found some vital task in the rigging. Every one of these jobs seemed to require that the worker face the exact spot where she stood.

Besides Savage and Lightner, Mr. Becker stood by with his sextant, plus two young men she knew as Mr. Barber and Mr. Loti. Barber was no more than fourteen or fifteen and was English. Loti was a bit older, she thought, and was a native of the South Seas. The two boys seemed to fill the positions of lesser lieutenants or midshipmen, but she was uncertain what they actually did. Dr. Hampton leaned against the mizzenmast and took no part in the mathematical exercises, but the very fact of his presence weighed upon her. Everyone wanted to see her make a fool of herself.

Savage gestured for her to join him. She stood no closer than was necessary, but he moved against her and put the sextant in her hands. It was heavy, and for a moment she thought perhaps Lightner was right. A woman didn't have the strength for this.

"When the sun is at its zenith," he explained, "we measure the distance it is above the horizon. Look through the eyepiece."

She held the instrument, her muscles protesting at the awkward position and the need to stay completely still upon the moving deck of the ship.

"The horizon keeps moving."

"Of course it does. The only completely accurate measurements are made on dry land. On ship you make several observations, then average them. What do you have, Becker?"

She did not join in the exchange of information until Savage asked her to report. Lightner eyed her mockingly from under his lowered lids, the corners of his mouth turned down.

"I shall go figure the position," he said shortly.

"Let Lady Dina do it," said Savage pleasantly. "Good practice for her."

"*Ladies* do not do such work," said Lightner, putting stress upon the first word.

"They do when it's necessary," said Savage, "just as they make their own clothes when there's no dressmaker about."

"There's no necessity for her to bother with the charts and position," protested Lightner. "Plenty of men about who can do that."

"Go," ordered Savage, and Dina fled to the main cabin. She spread out the chart, figured the position using the tables in the navigator's books, writing with chalk on a slate. She made a light pencil mark at the point on the chart where she had fixed their position.

"Captain said I was to check you," said Lightner haughtily as he entered the cabin. Dina stepped away from the chart table, watched the man painstakingly refigure every step of her calculations. Once she saw him count on his fingers to check the result of his multiplication. He said nothing, but simply darkened the dot she'd made upon the chart.

"I was right?" she asked faintly.

"In the maths, yes," he said sarcastically. "But what will the men think of such unladylike behavior? I would look to the lock on your cabin door, if I was to be you. Unless—" his voice had dropped to a whisper "—you are unladylike in those matters, too."

He tried to smile a friendly smile; it became a grimace.

"When a woman raises doubts about her womanhood in the way of learning, men suppose she's a tart in the other thing, as well."

"Some men," she said quietly.

"You had best leave this alone, before some decide what you are." He went out of the cabin quickly, before she had a chance to reply.

She had an enemy now, and on such a small ship, an enemy could build trouble. She had almost no contact with the crew in the forecastle, while Lightner might speak to them freely, talk against her. How long before two or three of the more gullible sailors believed his lies and tried to waylay her, or get into her cabin?

She wished her cabin had a skylight, so that the officers on the deck would hear her if she cried out for help. She must spend as much time as possible in the main cabin, which was too public for an assault, besides not being the normal haunt of the crew. Or on deck, where no man would even think of approaching her.

Two days passed, with nothing except Lightner's disapproving glances on the deck, and his curt warnings whenever they were in the main cabin alone, after the observations had been taken. The weather turned warm following the storm; each day she gained Savage's permission to sit on deck and write in her diary.

On the fourth day, when she came onto the quarterdeck carrying Savage's sextant, the number of crew members in the rigging had dropped considerably, as the spectacle of a woman on deck at noon had grown commonplace.

There was scarcely any darkness at all now. The sun shone weakly, from near the horizon, even at ten o'clock at night. Dina found she got less and less sleep as her hours of reading or sewing were extended. It was quite late that night when she finally went to her cabin.

The tiny space was pitch-black. The lantern, a candle in a tin sleeve, that normally hung from the deck beams, had gone out. She used the dim light from the lantern outside the door to search for a flint and steel. She took the lantern down and busied herself relighting it.

The instant her back was turned, she felt the pressure of another body, heard the slam of the door. The cabin became a dark cell. Dina managed only one strangled cry before a hand covered her mouth. Whoever was in the cabin with her was very large, and for an instant she supposed it was Savage, finally come to take her. She twisted her hands against a bare chest, the skin smooth and almost hairless. She knew the mat on Savage's chest, having watched him strip off a soaking shirt. One of the crewmen had given in to his lusts. There was no room to struggle, even if she could have resisted the bulging muscles.

"Still," said a voice she didn't know. "You witch. You not stop, I kill."

Witch? She twisted her head, but could not free her mouth from the rough hand.

"You stop?" the voice questioned.

Dina nodded her head as vigorously as she could in his tight grip. She'd stop doing anything to escape him.

"Give me black marks," the voice ordered. The hand released her, shoved her away so violently she fell across her bunk and struck her head on the bulkhead on the other side. Stars exploded behind her eyes. What remained of her mind thought vaguely, *Black marks,* but couldn't conceive what the man might mean.

Light glowed, but this time it was real, not the effect of a blow on the head. The sailor had managed to light the lantern. She saw a dark face, dark chest and dark hands holding the lantern aloft. He was nearly doubled up in the narrow space.

"Give black marks me," he demanded again.

"I don't know what you mean," she whispered, blinking her eyes to bring the world back into focus.

"Black marks make so," he said. He made a loose fist and moved it up and down, as if he were writing. "Make sick."

"They make who sick? I don't understand."

"Me."

"You!" She thought for a moment, trying to clear her mind. What did writing have to do with this man and his health? The man tightened his face, and wrinkles formed across his cheeks. He seemed to be searching for words. From his broad features and stalwart build, she presumed he was from one of the Pacific islands.

"You witch. Make sick, black marks. Bad witch."

"Who said the black marks would make you sick?" she asked with a sinking feeling.

"Give bad marks me or die me. Not, I kill witch, take."

"Kill me?" she whispered through stiff lips. "How?"

He clasped his hands about her head and bent it back. Then, just as she felt the strain on her neck, he released her.

"Die fast," he said with satisfaction. Dina leaned against the bulkhead, gasping, placed her hands about her neck to ascertain that she was still whole. She pointed to the ditty bag hanging at the head of her bunk. She had unraveled the threads of the raw edge of canvas at the top of the bag, then retied them in an elaborate pattern, adding more colorful threads from the silk scarf so that almost the entire bag was covered with a decorative fringe. The man looked at the bag and drew back as much as he could in the space. He grabbed her hand, raised it to indicate that she should take the bag from the hook.

Dina looked at the colored designs with new eyes. Did this man think the bag itself was some kind of magic? She lifted it from the hook, and he pressed himself against the door, avoiding any possibility of being touched. His eyes fixed upon the bag, and she grew braver, seeing his fright. He was as scared as she, but for different reasons.

"Who said the black marks are magic?" she asked, in as calm a voice as she could command.

"Small man say lassie, not Lady Dina."

Lightner, naturally. He was one of the few Scots on board, and he persistently called her "the lassie." She nodded her head with new understanding. Lightner was not going to destroy her by telling the crew she slept with the captain. It had not entered her mind that Lightner might play upon the ignorance of one of the men, convince him that she was evil and have her killed.

"He makes black marks himself," she protested. "Are they bad? Do they make people sick?"

"Small man say bad lassie make black marks, not man."

She thrust her hand into the bag, and the man gasped. She hadn't thought he could withdraw more, but when she pulled the book from the bag, he seemed to sink into the door.

"Who are you?" she asked. "What's your name?"

"Charley. Cap'n fo'top."

She thought back to those days when the crew lined up for inspection or Sunday services. The very tall, broad brown man who stood at the head of a group of sailors. She waved the book around. His eyes widened.

"This book is a record of the voyage. The captain keeps such a book. The log. Do you know about the log?"

Charley nodded.

"Is the log evil? Does it make you sick?"

"No. That cap'n's thing. Cap'n man. Lassie witch."

"Mr. Lightner said I was a witch?" He nodded, keeping his eyes on the book.

"What else did Mr. Lightner say?" The man looked thoughtful for several moments, and Dina decided he was putting his thoughts into English.

"Lassie make black marks, evil, make sick me. Hate me."

"I hate you?"

"Yes."

"I don't even know you. Why should I hate you?"

"You make bad..." he raised his hands, as if holding a sextant. "Ship on rocks. Witch," he said finally, as if that explained everything.

"I'm a witch and make the noon observations go wrong. So we don't know where we are and will run onto rocks?"

Charley nodded vigorously.

"And what else did he say?" she asked, now able to be stern and commanding. Charley could certainly kill her, but not so long as she kept him at bay with the magic of her book and by talking.

"Witch be..." He made a gesture of finality with his hands, chopping downward, as if cutting something off. "Witch be—" he repeated the gesture "—if Charley..."

With a look of inspiration he unbuttoned the front flap of his canvas trousers. Now it was Dina's turn to draw back, scramble into the corner where the bunk met the wall of the ship. He withdrew his flaccid organ, mimed the thrust of sex. He laughed.

"No." He shook his head widely, smiling, as if to still her alarm. "Small man lie." He pointed a finger at his chest, began rebuttoning his trousers. "Live place..."

"Your home? Where you come from?" she suggested.

"Home," he repeated. "Kill bad lassie." He thrust his hips forward several times and laughed. "Fun, not fo' witch." He made the cutting motion with his hand and shook his head.

Dina watched him carefully while she considered the broken English and the gestures. Where he came from, bad women were killed. Lightner had told him he could disarm the witch by forcing her to have sex, but Charley knew better.

"Mr. Lightner lied about how to get rid of a witch?" she inquired. Charley clearly didn't understand the question, and he leaned toward her. Dina raised the book as protection, and he withdrew.

"Small man," she said, and Charley nodded. "Said fun will end the evil?" Charley laughed and nodded. He would have rocked back and forth with his mirth, if there had been room.

"Small man... fool."

"If he's a fool, maybe he's wrong about the black marks. Maybe small man bad."

This disturbed Charley. He twisted his lips and opened and closed his mouth.

"Black marks," she said soothingly, "let me talk to people far away." Charley plainly didn't believe this, and he frowned at her.

"The black marks are a way of talking that lasts forever. Using the black marks, I can talk to people after I'm dead."

Charley drew back against the door again. I shouldn't have said that, Dina thought. That really does sound like magic, very powerful magic.

"The captain makes marks in the log, so when he gets home, people who have not sailed on the *Pearl Stallion* can look at the black marks and know exactly where she went."

Charley's face showed his doubt. She opened the book at random, and for a moment she thought Charley was going to flee, for his hands snatched at the lowered bar on the door.

"Wait," she begged, laying her hand on his. "Look at the black marks. They won't hurt you."

Charley regarded the book from the corner of his eye, as a man might look at a group of people he suspected were talking about him.

"This says—" she pointed at each word individually "—'In the night pirates attacked the *Pearl Stallion,* but were driven away. Captain Saurage said it took only ten minutes, but it seemed like hours. I was exhausted by—' "

"Pirates," exclaimed Charley suddenly. He extended his arm stiffly. "Boom. Die."

"You worked one of the guns?"

"Gun me." He nodded, then thudded a fist against his chest.

Dina pointed at the next line and shoved the book toward Charley. He gazed at the thing warily, but did not withdraw in fright. "These words say, 'The men at the guns used grapeshot and—' "

"Grapeshot," he said, smiling and nodding.

"That word right there." She pointed. "That black mark says 'grapeshot.' " Charley grew brave enough to lean toward the book and examine where her finger lay.

"Black marks talk?" asked Charley dubiously.

"They talk to someone who knows how to read." She dug into the ditty bag in sudden inspiration, but her efforts caused Charlie to shrink away from her again. She drew the cork from the bottle of ink, looked at the point of her quill to see if she could write without sharpening it.

"Look," she commanded imperiously. "I'm going to write 'Tonight Charley, the captain of the foretop, came to see me because he had been told that writing was magic that would make him sick.' " She pointed to the word. "That's your name. 'Charley.' And that means 'sick.' "

Instead of being pleased, he looked even more frightened than before.

"Charley, black marks," he whispered. He gestured toward the book and repeated fearfully, "Charley, black marks." He clasped his hands together, and she saw the individual strength of each finger. She could almost feel them gripping her head, forcing it back, until the ultimate snap came.

"I can make anyone's name in my book," she said hastily. She wrote "Saurage." "That's the captain's name. Saurage. The captain gave me the book. Do you think he would have given it to me if I could do evil with it? Send the ship onto the rocks? Make his crew sick? The captain loves his ship and loves his men."

"Cap'n good," agreed Charley.

"And he gave me the book to make black marks in." She mimed Savage handing her the book, then became herself, nodding and thanking the captain, patting the book. This amazed Charley, and he turned himself around to sit next to her on the bunk. Dina shrank away from him in an automatic reflex, then realized she must continue her show of strength to keep the upper hand. Charley still might kill her, but he didn't think it necessary to rape her. She took his hand and laid it upon the book. He stared at her, eyes wide, but didn't withdraw his hand.

"See. The book doesn't make you sick. The black marks are not bad. They are talking."

"Talk," he repeated, perhaps to give himself courage. He spread his fingers, then traced the lines of writing across the page. "No hear talk me," he said.

"It is silent talking. No noise. You hear the talking up here," she said, tapping her head.

"No hear talk me," he said again.

"You have to learn to hear the talking of the black marks," she said, laughing inwardly at her descent into Charley's version of English. "Would you like to learn?"

Charley's face showed he didn't understand her.

"Me make you hear talking?" she questioned. He shook his head.

"Mr. Lightner can hear the black marks talk, and so can the captain and Mr. Becker. And Mr. Barber and Mr. Loti."

"Loti?" he asked in amazement. "Loti same me, not same live place."

"And Loti has learned to read. Can hear the black marks talk," she said lamely, to make sure he understood.

Charley sat beside her, his face down, so she could not decipher his expression. His hands twisted between his massive thighs.

"Black marks talk me?" he whispered. "Lassie make talk me?"

"Yes. I can teach you. I'll show you how to write and to read. To make the marks and to hear them talk."

"Big man me, hear talk," he concluded.

"Yes. You'll be a very big man at your home if you can hear the black marks talk."

She was prepared for a smile of delight, a nod of pleased agreement. Charley slid off the edge of the bunk and, in the minuscule clear space of the cabin prostrated himself before her. He said words she did not understand, words in his own language. There was no mistaking their tone of adoration and awe.

Chapter Eight

Dina hesitated several times before she gathered her courage and knocked on the door to the captain's cabin. Throughout the day she'd intended to approach him, but now she could delay no longer. The long northern twilight seeped through the stern windows. Tomorrow she had to give Charley a definite answer, and she couldn't proceed without Savage's permission. Teaching one of the crew members to read and write might have consequences she didn't understand.

"Yes," said the deep voice beyond the door. She lifted the latch, stood as erect as possible, and faced Savage.

"May I please speak to you, sir? . . ."

He sat at his desk, which was really a flat board on hinges, with chains to keep it level when it was lowered from its storage position against the bulkhead.

"Yes," he said. He laid down his quill and stood up. "We'd best speak in the main cabin."

She nodded gratefully. With Lightner active among the crew, it was best they not give any substance to gossip. He sat on the bench, but she remained standing, as a good crew member should do when addressing the captain.

"Last night Charley, the captain of the foretop, talked to me," she began. She had to be very careful, so that she wouldn't betray the way their conversation had started. She didn't want Charley to get into trouble because he had been duped by Lightner.

"Yes."

"He's mystified by writing. He saw me writing in my journal on the deck, and he thought it was some kind of magic."

"Not an uncommon idea among the primitives," he agreed. "In fact, not uncommon among the illiterate of England."

"He'd like to learn to read and write, and I told him I'd teach him if... if you don't object."

"Why should I object?" he asked, puzzled. "And sit down, for heaven's sake." She dropped onto the bench, but not beside him.

"I wasn't sure how you felt about the... lower orders learning to read."

"Charley isn't of the lower orders. His father is a chief on his island. Enforces the law, makes the important decisions, but not a king, because the people can get rid of him if he isn't doing a good job. Charley's on the ship to gain prestige—he wants to succeed his father, but since a son doesn't automatically follow his father as chief, he has to establish himself as a powerful man in his own right."

Dina's heart pounded. She'd been much closer to death last night than she thought. Charley, as the chief's son, had probably considered it his duty to rid the ship of the "witch."

"Then you'd have no objections?" she said weakly, and hoped he didn't interpret her breathlessness as due to his presence beside her.

"None, so long as it doesn't interfere with his work. Where are you going to get pen and paper for this project?"

"I hadn't thought that far," she admitted. I've never looked ahead, she told herself. I've got to start considering things beyond tomorrow.

"There isn't supply enough on board to run a school. You'll have to think of something to substitute for normal writing instruments."

"I'm not running a school," she corrected him. "Just Charley."

"About half the crew's illiterate, or knows very little more than how to write their names. New Englanders and Scots usually know how to read and write. Englishmen and the natives don't. Once they see that you're willing to teach them, they'll descend upon you like locusts on a wheat field. Are you ready for a class made up of fifteen or twenty grown men?"

"If they're well behaved, I shouldn't mind at all, and everyone in the crew seems to be very cooperative, so I shouldn't expect any trouble."

"Cooperation is one of my rules. Cooperate, or find yourself another ship." He lifted a foot, examined the side of his boot. It was a casual gesture, but she saw the thin pinch of his mouth and knew he was not calm at all. "How did Charley come to speak to you?" he asked sharply.

Dina searched her mind hurriedly without finding a suitable response.

"He has no business in any part of the ship where you're allowed, not your cabin, or this one. Have you been wandering and getting yourself into trouble?" The last words were said so tightly she barely understood them. His eyes narrowed as he turned his attention from his boot to her.

"No, I've stayed exactly where you said I should. I'd rather not say more, for I don't want to get Charley into trouble."

"How?" he said through clenched teeth, facing her fully, closing the distance between them. Dina backed away.

"He came to my cabin." Savage's hand shot out and grasped her upper arm.

"To ask you to teach him to read and write?" he asked mockingly, his face inches from her own.

"Yes," she lied, turning her head to avoid the sight of him.

Savage stood up, stooped, his mass looming over her. His large hands rested on her shoulders, a weight that pressed her down into a posture of humiliation.

"Look at me," he ordered. Dina raised her eyes to his and shivered at what she saw. He was capable of anything, was as likely as Charley to murder her. More likely.

"I'm the captain of this ship," he snarled. "When something goes wrong, I'm expected to know what's going on so, I can change it, or fix it. I don't like secrets and I don't like being lied to." The pressure of his fingers seemed to part the flesh from her bones. "Every man in the crew knows better than to lie to me, but you haven't learned yet, have you? Why did Charley come to your cabin?" The pain shot from her shoulders to her arms, but she was afraid to cry out, afraid to object, for if he released her shoulders he could strike her.

"Why was he in your cabin?" he asked, each word distinct, like a stone dropping on a hard floor. "Have you decided to take up a new vocation, to make some extra money?" His voice sank to a whisper, so low it would not carry through the skylight to the deck. "Have you overcome your aversion to the beast in men, or is that aversion just to me? Come. Tell me. You might as well confess it straight out, for I can make you tell me and I won't hesitate to do what's necessary." He laughed, it was not his normal full-bodied laugh, but a hollow, fearsome threat.

"In two minutes you'll be willing to swear that Charley met you on the moon, anything to make me stop what I'll be doing to you."

Dina opened her mouth, but nothing came out except a thin cry of terror. She shook her head in desperate confusion, only half understanding what she was denying. Savage's hands tightened, and he lifted her bodily. She cried out in fear and pain when he thrust her down on the deck. Her legs collapsed, so that she was not kneeling, but prostrate before him. Charley's deep bow had conveyed thanks and adoration; this was completely different. Savage was exercising his brutal dominance. Her chest tightened at the thought of what he might make her do. He was a cruel, despicable monster. She shoved suddenly against his strength.

"I hate you!" she screamed.

His hands wrenched her about, flung her full-length on the deck.

"Tell me!" he shouted.

She pushed herself up on her hands, made herself look into his dark visage.

"I'll tell," she said quietly. He picked her up. She hung in his hands like a rag doll.

"Don't hurt me, please," she said in a flat voice.

He pushed her onto the bench.

"Don't you ever make me do this again," he snarled. "You tell me everything that happens on this ship. Here there's no privacy. When I ask, you tell. What happened in your cabin? Why did he come?"

"To kill me," she said simply, then realized that was a very bad beginning. "Mr. Lightner convinced him I was a witch, and where Charley comes from, they kill witches. He showed me how they did it, by breaking the woman's neck."

"Christ almighty!" He dropped next to her on the bench, the change in him so complete that she felt as if light from a noon sun filled the cabin.

"Tell me everything. I may hang Lightner."

"No, no!" Dina gasped, fearing the return of his violent mood. "You've got to understand. Lightner's afraid I'll take his work from him. I've made him look like a fool in front of the men, even though I never intended to do anything of the sort, and—"

"He is a fool, and unwilling to admit when he's wrong. You had nothing to do with it. You simply showed yourself to be wiser than he."

She had to keep him talking about Lightner. Her shoulders felt as if they'd been caught in a vise. She had to keep him talking, or the violence might return. "Why did you hire him?"

"My old master, Folkstone, left the ship in Canton."

"And you had to find someone in Calcutta to replace him?"

"Yes, and rather quickly. And Lightner had known Becker when they'd served together several years ago on a voyage to Canton. I took him on at Becker's recommendation, and now Becker's very contrite about the outcome. I've tried to reassure him that our first impression of people is very often wrong. Tell me the rest. Why did Charley come to your cabin?"

Dina disciplined her mind until it was cleared of everything but the memories of that half hour with Charley. She tried to duplicate his halting speech, replicate his gestures. She lowered both her voice and her eyes when she explained Charley's amusement at Lightner's belief that sex would disarm a witch's power.

"He laughed?" asked Savage.

"Yes. He thought it very funny, and he said Lightner was a fool for thinking such a thing. He called . . . he called it 'fun,' and showed me it wasn't something a man did with a witch." Savage bent over, pressed his knuckles against his forehead and began to laugh. It began in his chest, then shook his entire body. He rocked back and forth. Dina wasn't sure what she had said that was so funny. Perhaps he was laughing at her, the way he had laughed with Lady Margaret at her expense. She sat still, burying her emotions, waiting for his mirth to subside.

"How did he show you?" he gasped.

"Do I have to tell you that?" she begged.

"Yes."

"He opened his trousers and moved his hips," she whispered through stiff lips.

He roared with delight. "Heaven's thunder, how I'd like to have seen this interview." Dina glanced toward the skylight. It was open only an inch or two, but that was far enough that an eavesdropper on deck could hear every word.

"And in the end, Charley asked you to teach him to read and write?"

"Yes. After he understood that Mr. Loti could read and write, and that you'd given me my journal. He refused to believe that you'd do anything to harm the ship. Why did you laugh?" she asked daringly.

"I was just imagining, if carnal connections were the cure for witchcraft, how the accusations would fly. Every time a ship came into port, the number of witches would multiply by the hundreds. The skies would be darkened with broomsticks, and black cats would overwhelm the town."

Dina spun out of control in the vortex of his changeable moods. She couldn't control her own nervous giggles, which set Savage laughing again. An unexpected roll of the ship sent his body against hers. When he pulled away, her hand was in his. He drew it to his mouth and kissed it gently.

"I'm sorry I hurt you," he said softly, so quietly that she sensed more than heard the words. The tone of his voice, the roughness of the hand clasping hers, brought an end to the emotional whirlwind. Her eyes filled, and she felt the path of a tear as it slid down her cheek.

"I'll not keep secrets from you, I promise. I thought I was protecting Charley. From now on I'll try to consider the difficulty of your position," she whispered. "I'll tell you everything you want to know."

"Is that promise to the captain or to a friend?"

Dina shook her head, unable to say more. She lowered her head until her disordered hair touched her knees. His hand gripped hers tightly, and she did not try to withdraw from the touch. He dominated her completely, but was it as friend or captain? Never in her life had she felt so totally surrounded by the power of one man, except for that terrifying time when she feared her father had seen her at the head of the stairs.

"My promise is to the captain of the *Pearl Stallion,*" she finally said. "You hold the safety of all of us in your hands, and I particularly owe you my life. Dr. Hampton said you wouldn't leave me behind in Sumatra."

"No, I would not."

"You could have, and not given me another thought."

"I could have left you behind, but I'd have lived with the guilt of that act for the rest of my life. When a man does a great wrong, particularly to a woman, he may think the whole affair will eventually disappear into the silence of the past. But beyond that wall of silence, the storm of protest never stops. Then he does things to block out the noise, and creates more evil. In the end, an avenger appears, condemns him to a hell composed of nothing but that roar, eternally."

"How do you know?"

"I sprang from a man who did this."

Dina recalled her uncle's remark about the chambermaid who had birthed this man. "Your father?"

"Yes."

Dina waited for the rest, wondering at the intimate path the conversation had so suddenly taken, surprised at her own serenity as the warmth of him spread through her palm, her hand, her arm, penetrated her chest and her heart.

"My father got a child upon a chambermaid, a tall, dark wench who caught his eye when she came into his house when she was only four and ten years old. He would have exiled her to the hovel from which she'd come, except that a fever swept the neighborhood, killed his beautiful young wife and reduced the son she'd borne him to an emaciated skeleton no one thought would live. He looked at the girl's swollen belly, swept her off to London, where he had the ceremony performed that made the child legitimate. He didn't consider that the ceremony also made the tall, ignorant girl a countess."

He sat upright and stared straight ahead. The only thing tying her to his solemn speech was the tight grip of his fingers. She shook her head at the contrast between the gentleman speaking now and the out-of-control brute of a few moments before.

"He took the girl back to his ancestral home just a few days before she bore him a son, in a room close to the one where the blond child of his first wife lay dying. He praised his new wife and saw nothing but wonder in the strong son she gave him. He lavished gifts upon her and pledged his love. He lay with her and got another child upon her.

"It might have gone on thus, except there was a nurse who adored the first son, who was so devoted that she bound the tiny body to her own, breathed her own life into him. As the months passed, and the child recovered, my father saw less to recommend the clumsy, dark boy and his plain, uncouth mother. In the frail blond boy he saw the features of his first wife, and his memory re-created her a saint. His love for the servant girl could not survive the rebirth into life of his first son.

"He took the eldest boy to London, leaving his unwanted wife in a cottage on the estate. There she bore him a daughter, my sister. We seldom saw our father, but try as he might, he could not shut us away in another world. The three of us hovered at the edge of his life. Because of the ceremony, he could not remarry. He tried to have the marriage annulled, but the clergyman who had performed the wedding had become a bishop, and stood in the way of what he considered to be a crime.

"My father could not make us disappear, so he treated us with greater and greater disdain. When I was ten, my mother died. He came to see to the disposal of the children, who reminded him of the wrong done their mother. His glee at my mother's death sickened me, made me hate him. He informed me I was to go into an East Indiaman as a midshipman. My sister was sent to live with a community of religious women.

"Twelve years later, he died, a drunken sot. I believe he used the wine and brandy to silence the blast that stormed in his mind. I saw him once more, when I came back to England a lieutenant, highly recommended to assume command of a ship, although I was but twenty years old. I thought, as the son of an earl, I could enjoy a turn through London's season. The ladies of the *ton* sneered at my poverty, at my occupation. My father and brother snubbed me. My brother, an insignificant fop, my father, a drunken gambler, and they thought it beneath them to have anything to do with someone who participated in trade." His voice descended to a harsh snarl.

"I went to my father's house, made him see me. I discovered the abject state of the family fortunes, and I vowed I'd return to England a nabob, that he would touch none of my money until he and my brother crawled in apology at what had been done."

He covered his eyes with his free hand and bent nearly double, as if the recollection caused an agony within him. Then he straightened up, released Dina's hand and turned to her.

"If I'd left you behind, twenty years from now I'd live in constant fear that a dark young man, conceived upon you in the cruelty of a harem, would come to me, to take revenge upon me for the wrong done his mother. You would be confined in silence, far away, but the screams of your accusations would deafen me."

"Is that why you didn't rape me when you had the chance?" she asked.

"Yes. To do that sort of violence to a woman diminishes a man. Even sending you back to Calcutta, as I intended to do, made me most uncomfortable."

"You didn't show it at the time," she said sardonically, and felt a jolt of fear at her daring.

He accepted the rebuke with a sober nod. "I have a responsibility to my ship and to my crew. That duty overrides every other. And—" he grinned slyly "—I believed that any young lady with the courage and cleverness to stow away on a ship had the talent to avoid a marriage she didn't particularly desire."

"Perhaps I might have, but I didn't believe it then. And there were other things urging me to escape in any way I could."

"More than the marriage to Freemantle?"

"Yes. I'd been invited to the Allinson house. Lady Margaret wanted me to meet some friends. I declined the invitation, but she was insistent."

"I thought that's what would come," he said, nodding. "Nearly every attractive young woman who comes to Calcutta is drawn into their circle. Most women don't seem to mind it, once they've settled into the routine of it. The morals of Calcutta always seem a bit strange to newcomers from England."

"Morals?" she asked in astonishment. "I saw nothing moral about their lives at all."

"There are strict rules to Calcutta society, just as there are in England. A beautiful young woman is passed from man to man for a period, until her condition is beyond concealment. Then she's married off, sometimes to a man of the inner circle, if one has taken a particular interest in her, but that's infrequent. More usually, it's to a ship captain who is often away on long voyages, one who wishes to rise in the graces of the Company."

"And he lets the disgusting business continue?"

"I said, a man who wants to gain power in the Company. The woman's children are something of a miscellany, but eventually she's the wife of a man of consequence and has a secure position. Unless, of course, her husband dies, and she's left with her random collection of children and no one who cares if she lives or dies."

"Would they have forced me?" she asked faintly. "If I didn't want to do this, would Sir Hall have made me?"

"Perhaps not Sir Hall, but there are some who would enjoy exactly that. Lady Margaret takes pleasure in deciding which man should first have a woman. She's rather in charge of finding young women, in the way the head wife of a raja finds nubile girls to fill her lord's harem."

"And everyone accepts this terrible thing?" she cried.

"Not everyone. But you must remember, many of the men are single, and there's a lack of beautiful, accomplished women. And not all young women take such a moral stance as you. Many enjoy the freedom of their position, not too firmly tied to husband and home, and emerge with wealth and power. A woman's greatest misfortune is the failure to conceive a child, for then there's no need to find her a husband, and no end except a decline in the rank of the men she serves."

Dina shuddered. "And that's what you thought of me? When I flirted with you at the ball?"

"Of course. I thought you'd already been inducted into the system. You should feel flattered by the assumption, for only the most beautiful of the girls who come are invited in. Your cousin Emily hasn't the slightest chance."

"Thank heavens," she said sincerely. "And I thank you most heartily for saving me from the clutches of Lady Margaret."

"I've done nothing of the kind. We'll eventually return to Calcutta, and you'll be thrust back into that society. Don't reject it out of hand. Some women find it very profitable, and a way to gain a husband of some prominence in India."

"I don't intend to stay in India," she said firmly.

"After a year on the *Pearl Stallion,* you may find yourself with no other choice. You begged to stay aboard, but staying destroys your reputation—no honorable man will have you. You have no money or title to overcome that disability. Think carefully before you deny these men your body. It may be the only chance you have left. And a woman of your imagination might find it an interesting, challenging life."

Dina's stomach turned over, and sweat stood out on her forehead, despite the chilly air. She wanted to strike out at him for this appalling statement, yet her hands were frozen, chained by the truth he had laid before her, horrid, yet beautiful in its symmetry, like a multi-colored snake. She drew back from the serpent, but found its coils fastened to her heart, burrowing into her brain.

She had not escaped, and Savage offered her no consolation that she ever might. She would be back, climbing the stairway with Lady Margaret, being led to another man who wished to make her acquaintance.

"Is there anything else you must tell me about Charley, before I give you permission to make a scholar of him?" he asked gently. She realized he wanted to take her mind away from the distant future, make her focus on the next few days.

"It's not inevitable," he said, his voice intertwining with the vile images swimming in her mind. "You're a strong woman. You can create futures of your own making, perhaps. I'll give you all the help I can."

"Will you marry me?" she asked in desperation.

"No. I told you long ago, I'm married to the *Pearl Stallion*. She's the road to my fulfillment. Through her, I return to England wealthy, rich enough for revenge. My father escaped me by dying in a haze of drink, but my brother will feel it. He'll beg for money, for loans, and I'll brush him away as I now brush a fly from my knee. And if his weak loins beget a son, I'll humble the child the way I was humbled. The women of the *ton* will parade their daughters before me, my wealth blotting out my mother's name. I'll let them make fools of themselves, lead them into traps that destroy them. Then I'll walk away, the proposal they expect unmade. They will be ruined."

Dina shrank from him. "I'm one of those women," she said weakly.

"I know." The words were so flat, she could not abstract any meaning from them.

"How can you even consider doing this?" she asked sternly. "You parade your virtue in not harming me, claim you fear being overwhelmed by guilt if you hurt a woman. But you're ready to consider the destruction of these women, who you don't know. Won't their fate haunt you?"

"It's totally different," he said. "I'll but offer an opening to ambitious chits, women controlled by greed, who deserve what comes to them. Their destruction will flow from their own acts, not mine."

Dina shook her head in disagreement, but he paid no heed.

"Now," he said, putting an end to the personal conversation, assuming his tone of command. "Did anything else happen between you and Charley? The whole truth."

"Something else happened, just before he left, and I don't understand what it means." Savage looked at her expectantly. "He knelt at my feet—more than knelt, crouched down before me—and said things in a language I don't know. I suppose the language of his home. I felt...I felt as if I were some pagan goddess, and he worshiped me."

"One never knows with these islanders," said Savage casually. "We have little knowledge of their rituals and religions. I told you once your hair was that of Pele."

"Yes," she said anxiously, waiting for him to reveal his thoughts.

"Perhaps Charley noticed the same thing. I can't remember if she's a goddess of his island or not. Now I must get back to work." He dismissed her with a wave of his fingers.

Dina sat for a few minutes in the main cabin, then, when Kranz appeared to light a lantern, fled to the privacy of her tiny space. A lantern already hung above her bunk. She lifted her hands to extinguish it, felt pain in her shoulders. She peeled back her shirt and discovered the marks of his fingers upon her skin.

She blew out the lantern and curled up upon her bunk fully clothed. The bruises were only one part of the injury he had done her. Verbally, Savage had pummeled her, beaten her, then tumbled her into a deep hole, leaving her to make the steep climb out by herself.

She hated him, yet the clasp of his hand had been comforting. She loathed his domination of her, yet wanted to crawl more completely under the protection of his strength. She despised his vicious nature, which could plan revenge upon a child not yet born, upon women who had nothing to do with his rejection except by the class to which they belonged, yet she longed to comfort him for the brutality that had been visited upon him in his childhood.

She tossed on her bunk and wept in frustration. She had no way to combat him. He was indeed a savage, prone to rapid changes in temperament, changes that came and went like the wind. She was caught in his strange designs of morality. He would not rape her, but would turn her over to Sir Hall and his minions for an even worse ravishment. He would not abandon her in Sumatra, but he would let her make her own way in Calcutta, encourage her to become the strumpet of calculating men.

If they landed on one of these strange Pacific islands, would he object if a chief who resembled Charley demanded her as a sacrifice to some pagan god? The fact that she could not answer the question made her fear him even more.

She escaped into sleep, but the retreat proved illusory.

She followed Lady Margaret up the latticed stairs. She cried out, begged not to be forced to do the things awaiting her beyond the screen, but her feet were controlled by something outside herself, and she had no choice but to follow.

The carvings moved, came alive, and she was surrounded by demons possessing many arms, all holding her, all touching her in abominable ways. One had Charley's broad face, and he smiled at her shrieks as her clothing melted away. "Witch, me kill," he said pleasantly.

The demons became men, dressed in buff pantaloons. They surrounded her and paid no attention to her cries or the pain that convulsed her. Over her supine body they discussed the latest style in neckcloths in London. She knew she should be listening, remembering, because if she did not know the things they told her, she'd not have the baby they demanded, and this humiliation would be inflicted upon her again and again.

She lay upon the floor, her body frozen in agony. A huge figure towered over her, no longer Charley, but Savage, holding a raised cane in one hand. She awaited the blow, paralyzed. All she could do was scream and scream....

"Dina!"

He held her, and she couldn't fight her way free. Her hands were tangled in his heavy chest hair, the way a fly becomes entangled in a spider's web.

"Dina! What's wrong?"

Light streamed through the open door of her cabin, and strong arms embraced her.

"Dina, it's nothing. It was a nightmare."

She writhed in his arms, determined to avoid the final, horrid embrace, then saw Kranz standing in the doorway, a raised lantern in his hand. She cried out in terror at his threatening pose. The sound brought her wide awake. In the yellow light, her patterned ditty bag hung above her head, the pegs on the bulkhead held her clothes. She sank against Savage, raised her arms and wrapped them about his neck. She cuddled against his body.

"Nothing's wrong, Dina," he whispered in her ear. For a moment, his body twisted away from her. "That's all, Kranz. You can go," he said loudly.

The yellow light disappeared, and nothing remained but the comfort of his voice, the warmth of his body, and the gentle touch of his hands on her face. She moved her legs and found them whole, though an icy, devouring pain was left behind from the dream.

"I'm cold," she whispered. The chill of the short night had penetrated her clothes. Even her bones felt cold. He pulled her against his warmth, found a blanket with one hand and clumsily wrapped it about her. The nightmare began to disintegrate, but the more despicable parts of it stayed clear and whole.

"Please don't hurt me," she begged. "I'll do anything you want, tell you anything, but please don't hurt me again."

"Is that what the dream was about? I was hurting you?"

"Yes. Partly," she added honestly.

"What was I doing?"

"A cane. You were going to beat me with a cane, and I was already terribly hurt and couldn't move."

His hand caressed her hair, brushed it back from her face. He kissed her gently on the forehead.

"What had I done to hurt you so terribly?" he whispered, and the pain in his voice struck deeply into her heart.

"Nothing. It was other men who hurt me, but I knew what you planned to do would be even worse. And then Charley was going to kill me."

He rocked back and forth, cradling her as if she were a baby. He hummed a rough tune under his breath, as if calling up some long-forgotten gentleness.

"Forgive me, Dina," he said simply. "Please forgive me."

Chapter Nine

Savage walked onto the twilight deck, into the cold, clinging fog. The sailors at the pump were ready; he turned around slowly under the stinging jet of icy water. Kranz stood by with his dressing gown, wrapped it around his dripping body when he signaled that he'd had enough. Once back in his cabin, he dismissed the servant.

"I'll get dressed by myself," he said.

Instead of finding his clothes, he sat heavily on the edge of his bunk. He'd have given anything, his entire fortune, to erase what had happened last night. The memory of how he had grasped her, intentionally causing her pain, forcing her to her knees before him—the memory grated across his brain like the burn of a rope on an unprotected hand.

He'd justified his action by pretending he had to know what had passed between her and Charley, but he knew the truth, and the truth was more jarring than the icy shower he'd just endured.

When had he started to love her?

He'd wanted her from the beginning, of course, but that had been lust of the most depraved kind. The lust that came from long weeks of continence, lust finally set free on shore, visited upon the first woman who caught his eye.

His lust had prevented him leaving her in Sumatra, because he couldn't stand the idea of her in the service of some dark sultan. Now he'd come close to beating her because of Charley's visit to her cabin. His innocent visit. Or had it been?

He'd not slept at all, and Dina's account of her conversation with Charley no longer made much sense to him. But it had been innocent in terms of sexual favors, of that he was certain. He moaned at the thought that he must do something about Lightner. The man's inept plotting had almost caused a murder. If Charley had broken Dina's neck, he, the captain, would have had no choice but to hang Charley. One broken neck, a second broken neck in consequence. If it had come to that, would Charley, in the babbling incoherence of anticipated death, have said enough to implicate Lightner, and would there have been a second body at the yardarm? Or would the man behind the whole thing have gone free, unconvicted of Dina's murder?

He shuddered at the thought of Dina's slender white body being dropped over the side, into the cold North Pacific. He had to protect her, now and until he no longer loved her. In the next eight months, she'd do something so infuriating that his love would evaporate and he'd feel no compunction about leaving her in the cesspool of Calcutta.

The thought of Allinson and his friends having their way with her caused him to break out in a sweat that made his recent shower useless. How long did love last? Would it survive until they sailed into the Hooghly, so that he'd be forced to defend and care for her even then?

He'd send her home, which is what he should have done to begin with. Could he stand to do it while he still loved her? To part from her, when he desired her so fully?

He closed his eyes and imagined bringing her to him slowly, not as in the clumsy attack he'd initiated in Calcutta. This morning, after the nightmare, she'd put her arms about his neck and let him touch her face and hair. She had curled against him in the way a woman does after passion, waiting to see if her man will rise to please her again. He imagined how she would touch him, once she'd overcome her fright and shyness.

He opened his eyes and found himself alone in his cabin, hard as a marlin spike—and no use for it, nothing at all. He took several deep breaths and began to dress. It was an impossible dream, and he made himself face that fact. If he should take her, he would violate the implied agreement between himself and fifty men. They shared everything—the cold, the food, the storms, the heat. They even shared the torture residing in their bodies, bodies longing for the touch of a woman.

For an instant he cursed her presence, but then he remembered that six times nine wasn't sixty-three. Someone else would have caught the error, he told himself, but deep inside he wasn't totally sure, and the thought of the *Pearl Stallion* broken upon rocks, awash in a turbulent sea, made him tremble.

Soon they'd be in Pavlovsk. He'd find himself a chubby northern woman, if any had come south this summer to join in the hunting. All his present difficulties would dissolve after he'd exhausted himself sexually. The thought made him more confident. He dressed to go back on deck. Once in Russian America, the entire crew would have a chance to soak up the pleasures of the shore. Then to the Sandwich Islands to restock with provisions. He forced himself to recall the women of the Sandwich Islands. Then Canton. Then Calcutta, again.

What will I do in Calcutta? What if I still love her? What if I can't bear to turn her over to Hall Allinson? Or send her back to England?

"I can't think of that," he whispered to himself. *That's at least six months in the future. Right now I must think of meeting Baranov and getting the best trade out of him I can. Make sure he gives me something besides fox and seal. A good percentage of sea otter.*

Think of that chubby northern woman, he ordered himself sternly, shifting his hand, a little uncertainly, to touch the still-firm erection. He thought of a woman in bed. His imagination conjured up a body, not chubby and brown, but slender, tall and fair.

"Land ho!" came the call through the skylight, as if in answer to his predicament.

He shrugged on his blue coat, the only thing about his dress that distinguished him from the crew. The rush of bare feet overhead sounded like a sweep of rain. It was always the same, this dash of men to the deck when the cry of "Land ho!" reverberated through the ship.

Dina stood outside her cabin, waiting for him. "Please, may I come up on deck?"

"There's nothing to be seen from the deck yet," he explained. "The call came from the maintop."

Her expression was so pleading, he reconsidered his answer. He hadn't said no. It would not be a retreat from an order if he allowed her to come. He had a great deal of repairing to do between them, and he might as well start today.

"You may come."

"Thank you," she said without smiling.

"Wear something warm. It's damp."

She's a woman worth loving, he thought as he left the muggy confines of the cabins and lifted himself onto the deck. And that look of a beaten dog is your fault, and yours to change.

"Who called?" he asked Mr. Barber, who was on the quarterdeck at the moment.

"Charley, from the foretop."

"Tell him to come here and report to me." Barber looked at him quizzically. Savage knew he expected some explanation for this unusual procedure, but he gave him none. Barber hesitated only an extra second or two before hailing the foretop and demanding Charley's presence.

Someone was sure to have overheard him shouting at Dina last night, he thought, and Charley was going to be scared half out of his wits. He watched Charley's slow descent from the top, his plodding walk aft, past the helmsman. Savage turned away, as if the man's approach were the most ordinary thing in the world. Lightner stood at the railing, staring in the direction where the land hovered beyond the horizon. His tanned skin was stretched taut across his cheekbones, and his jaw worked nervously.

Charley lifted his hand to his forehead as a token of respect, but showed no indication that he feared his captain. Charley was the only person on board who could look him straight in the eye, and the only man who even approached him in height. On second glance, Savage decided that Charley had the advantage on him. Not by much, half an inch perhaps, but certainly the islander was taller.

"What do you see?" he asked, pointing toward the horizon.

"Dark." The word was followed by an up-and-down gesture that Savage presumed meant hills or mountains. "Far, far," continued Charley, making the gesture again. "White."

"Mountains with snow in the distance, dark hills closer," Savage said, interpreting. Charley nodded. There was an imperceptible turn of the entire crew toward the aft hatch; Savage knew what was happening. He didn't have to glance in that direction to know that the golden head had appeared, that Dina had come on deck.

"Charley, Lady Dina tells me you would like to learn to read and write." For the first time, Charley dropped his eyes. "She may tutor you. But there's no pen or ink or paper aboard for you to use. You may go to the carpenter and request a bit of smooth board and tell the cook he's to give you a supply of charred sticks that you can use as pencils." Charley bobbed, smiling. Savage presumed he understood only about half of what he was saying.

"If there are other men who would like to learn, they must wait until she has made some progress with you. You asked first."

Charley not only bowed, but tugged on his forelock in imitation of the groveling ways of the English lower class. It distressed Savage to see the highborn islander imitating his inferiors.

"The proper response to a request granted, Charley, is a bow. And you say, 'Thank you.' "

"Thank you," repeated Charley.

"Go back to the foretop and report anything new you see."

Savage walked casually to the railing and pretended he was looking for the first hint of the horizon. Lightner's hands clenched at his side, the knuckles white. Dina's face showed a wash of relief, of gratitude. He moved closer to Lightner.

"I do not often hang men on this ship, but it is not unknown," he muttered from the corner of his mouth. He was pleased to see sweat on the navigator's brow.

Two hours later, a dark line stretched low on the northern horizon, and above it towered white peaks, like cumulus clouds drawn together into some unusual formation. Half the crew hung in the rigging, but their interest was not confined to the distant view. They watched two heads bent over the head of a cask, one dark, one golden. Charley's blunt finger followed the vertical row of letters Dina had traced on one page of her journal. The men turned away and pretended not to see the fair hand guiding the brown one holding the charred stick, writing approximations of letters on the surface of a smooth board.

Savage made sure he didn't look in that direction at all.

Much to Dina's disappointment, the *Pearl Stallion* ran along the coast for two days. The darkly forested hills were often out of sight below the horizon. She had expected to come within sight of land and then proceed into harbor. But it was only on the third morning that the ship, under scant sail, before a brisk breeze, entered a channel between mountains green-black with towering trees. Nothing gave any indication of civilization. They might well have been the first humans ever to venture into this inlet.

Her interest in the somber landscape was distracted by the fact that Charley, within three days, had not only learned all his letters, but had progressed to combining them into words. She wrote English words he knew on the board, showed him how to pronounce them. Somehow she had to expand his knowledge of English, or his reading would be worthless. Someone approached the spot on deck where they worked. Dr. Hampton squatted down next to the cask.

"I thought this might help you," he said, placing a book next to the makeshift slate. "You left in a hurry and probably forgot yours, Lady Dina." It was a Bible with a limp leather cover.

Charley scrambled to his feet and bowed. "Thank you," he said. He clasped the volume in his hands without lifting it from the top of the cask, as if he expected reading skill to spring from the book, through his hands, into his brain. "God book you?" he asked.

"Yes," said Dr. Hampton, "I hope you find it instructive. I won't keep you from your learning any longer."

As he walked away, Dina opened the cover.

To my darling Charles, may God keep you safe while we are parted, Your Sweetheart, Laura.

She scrambled to her feet and called in the direction of the doctor's vanishing back. "Dr. Hampton, this was given to you by your intended. We can't possibly use it. I can't guarantee it won't be damaged."

Hampton turned, but didn't retrace his steps.

"She would be very pleased that I gave it away in such a good cause."

Dina looked at the inscription soberly. How long ago had his Laura written those tender words? Three or four years? Did she still love him, after all this time? Hampton claimed he still loved her, and would marry her on his return to Calcutta. Dina muttered a brief prayer that the doctor would not be disappointed, that this woman had not let love disappear, or, worse, turn to hate.

"Pavlovsk!" someone shouted. The crew rushed to find a vantage point from which to observe the Russian city.

Dina scrambled upon the cask that had so recently been her school room, then sagged in disappointment.

Pavlovsk was a huddled village of wooden buildings, some large, some small, but all of a color to sink into the gray background. Two spires rose from one of the larger structures, each topped with a cross. The only startling thing about the town was the heaving black mass along the waterfront, a cluster of people that, from this distance, seemed to be a single organic unit, ebbing and flowing, undulating, growing and shrinking. A few strange boats put out from shore, boats that the rowers seemed to wear, rather than occupy. A faint cheering came across the water, answered by a hoarse cheer from the ship.

"Break out the flag, Mr. Becker," said Savage, and the British colors soared to the head of the mizzenmast.

Dina squinted her eyes, strained to see if there were any women among the crowd. She looked forward to meeting Madame Baranov. She wished she had her uncle's glass so that she could observe the crowd as individuals. So far, everyone she saw seemed to be a native. Not one person wore European dress.

A hook of land created a sheltered bay, and here the *Pearl Stallion* dropped anchor. The sailors eagerly swung one of the ship's boats over the side. Savage, now in a coat trimmed with gold braid, waited until the sailors had taken their places at the oars.

"We shall have a great banquet tonight," he said before he went over the side. He glanced around the crew until he found the cook. "Start preparing our contributions, and Mr. Becker, make sure a cask of brandy is available to be brought ashore."

"What do you think of Russian America?" asked a voice at Dina's side. She turned to face Dr. Hampton.

"Not a city at all, is it? A village, not any larger than Woodstock or Burford. Perhaps smaller."

"You're disappointed?"

"Yes. I'd hoped to spend some time ashore, perhaps find someone to make me new gowns. I'm tired of dressing like a sailor. But the only clothing I see here are skins and furs."

"Perhaps in the Sandwich Islands," he suggested. "English and American sailors gather there. And the climate's so warm that skins and furs are unsuitable."

An hour, then two hours, passed, and a disagreeable sharp wind swept across the small harbor. Dina went to her cabin and stretched out on her bunk. At least this was as far east as they would go. She remembered her journal, sat up and began writing out her first impressions of Pavlovsk.

The noise of the returning boat sounded throughout the ship, but did not interrupt her writing. Savage would tell her when and if she might go ashore, and there were several hours of the day left before an evening celebration would commence. She was so certain she would not be bothered that the knock at her door made her jump.

"My lady, the captain wishes to see you in the main cabin."

Dina ran her hands over her hair, corked the ink bottle and wrapped her bedraggled shawl around her shoulders. They still ached from Savage's angry grip, and when she twisted her head she could see the dark bruises he'd left behind. Since that night, she had been polite to him, given him the attention the captain deserved, but she avoided any closer contact. All she had to do was live through the stay here, the voyage to the islands, to Canton, to Calcutta. She would strike up a closer friendship with Dr. Hampton, and spend her time on deck with the sailors who wanted her to teach them.

The main cabin was, to her surprise, crowded. Every officer was present, as well as Dr. Hampton and Mr. Lightner. Some stood, others sat on the bench under the windows or on stools or casks and crates, obviously brought in for the meeting. Those sitting got to their feet when she entered, or rather stood as much as they were able. She thought they looked like a flock of wet, bedraggled chickens, bent over to avoid the force of a storm.

"Here, Lady Dina," said Savage, indicating a vacant place on the bench next to him. She obeyed his summons, restraining her impulse to laugh at this congregation of fowls, and sat down, and the assemblage followed suit.

"How much Russian do you understand, Lady Dina?" asked Savage. She looked at him in astonishment, then in alarm, for his shoulders sagged and his eyes were wary.

"Very little, I'm afraid. I can tell a lady her dress is very beautiful, and say good-morning and good-evening. I can read a bit more than I can speak."

He shook his head in disappointment. "Do you suppose you could talk to these people? I've always spoken German with Baranov, but he's not here. He's at Sitka."

"Sitka!" exclaimed Hampton. "They've retaken Sitka?"

"Yes, after a rather heated battle, I gather, although there's no one here who understands anything but Aleut or Russian, so what I learned came mostly through gestures." He looked at Dina again, but she shook her head.

"They seem to be nearly starved, living on dried salmon and what they can dredge up from the sea. I can see the hunting fleet has gone, for most of the town's residents are women."

"Gone?" asked Lightner. "Don't they hunt here?"

"This area's hunted out. Every year they must go farther and farther to find seal and otter."

"What about trade?" asked Becker.

"Banner, the man in charge, shakes his head, but then asks for food. I gather they can't offer a banquet, and we certainly can't feed two hundred people out of the ship's stores. Would there be any objection if I took Lady Dina ashore? See if she can make out anything more?"

Lightner rose from the cask where he sat. He was so short he could very nearly stand erect in the cabin.

"Lady Dina knows only the Russian from the drawing room," he said pointedly. "I can't see how that can help. And if the ragged men ashore should try to seize her, we'd have a battle on our hands. I shouldn't trust any of them, I don't believe, sir."

"They could hold her for ransom, demand all our food," said Becker.

"There's a Russian woman here," said Savage, "Banner's wife, and Anna Grigoryevna. We could ask them to be present at a meeting."

A mutter went around the cabin that Dina could not identify as affirmative or negative.

"Take her," said Mr. Becker finally. "If she's willing to go. But with a guard."

"Lady Dina?" asked Savage, looking at her from the corner of his eye.

"If I might be of help, certainly."

"Mr. Becker, issue guns to six of the largest men. Mr. Loti will go as captain of the guard. Lady Dina, I suggest you dress as elegantly as your wardrobe allows."

Dina put on the best of her two gowns, one that had been dark blue but was now faded from repeated washings in seawater. She folded the ragged edge of her silk scarf, where she had drawn out the threads, toward the inside, arranged it over her head and shoulders. Nothing could be done about her boots, the ones she had worn on the night of her escape. They had been sewn back together twice.

What title should she give herself among these people? In Russia a daughter held the same title as her mother, so she would be a countess. Savage would introduce her. She must speak to him about it before they landed. Would he think her vain, demanding to be called *comtesse?*

"I don't care what he thinks," she muttered to herself. He was a nasty brute. She wondered if he introduced himself as *comte,* which he had every right to do in the Russian world.

He awaited her at the railing. She held out her hand to delay entering the boat.

"Are these people impressed by rank, sir?" She remembered to add the title of respect only at the final moment. He grinned at her, letting her know he'd sensed the instant of hesitation.

"Very much so, *comtesse.* Had you wondered how I would introduce you?"

"Yes," she said. "Do you call yourself *comte?*"

"No. Dealing with Baranov is touchy business. He has no grandiose titles, so it's best to be plain Captain Savage. His naval officers all come from the aristocracy and give him no end of trouble, parading their titles of prince and count before him and claiming precedence."

He offered his arm for the descent down the swinging rope ladder into the heaving boat. It was the first time she'd touched him since she'd unconsciously grasped him after the terrifying nightmare.

"Do you always make your decisions so they conform to what is good for business?" she asked when they were both seated. The sailors fended off from the *Pearl Stallion,* unshipped their oars. The boat rode low in the water with the added weight of six large sailors and their muskets. Dina was delighted to see that Charley was one of her guards.

"Exactly. What's good for business is right. Not exactly the attitude of the *ton,* is it?"

"No. You must find the hostesses of Calcutta very amusing in their preoccupation with rank."

"I do indeed. Although being able to claim rank is very convenient in dealing with the Company."

As the boat neared the shore, Dina could see the buildings more clearly. Nearly all were in a state of dilapidation. The men lining the shore wore leggings and long shirts made of fur and skins, except for several priests in black robes. From what she could see, not one woman was there to welcome her. The six armed sailors jumped into the shallow water and waded ashore while the oarsmen pulled the boat far enough up the shingle that the passengers wearing shoes could step off the bow onto dry land. Mr. Loti barked an order, and the sailors formed a rough square. Savage shoved her into position, surrounded by the armed men.

"Comtesse Endine Wilmount," he announced grandly, removing his own hat with a flourish. The assembled crowd raised their fur hats and bowed, some very grandly, some awkwardly. The crowd ambled toward one of the larger buildings, Dina still surrounded by her honor guard. Examining the people more closely, she saw many *were* women, but dressed exactly like the men in leggings and long shirts.

They entered a large room lighted with torches and furnished with great variety: large carved chairs, rough-hewn benches, some tables of splintery planks and others of polished wood that must have come from some Russian cabinetmaker. She was shown to one of the largest of the chairs.

"Deputy Governor Ivan Banner," said Savage. The Russian was dressed in a combination of European clothing and the skin and fur of the rest of the population.

"Dohbree v'yehcher," said Dina graciously. *Good evening*. The words brought a torrent of speech from the man, who obviously expected her to be fluent in his language. She waved her hands to make him stop. She held her thumb and forefinger very close together and searched her mind for the Russian word for *a little.* The word escaped her.

Her host beckoned to someone across the room. He was instantly joined by a woman in European clothes in a style so antique Dina could not remember when they might have been in fashion. The man embarked on a flowery speech, which included the word *Comtesse* and ended with the name Banner, so Dina concluded this woman was his wife.

"Lady Banner," she said, bowing her head and hoping that was the proper title for the woman. She hadn't the slightest idea how to start, for she'd never learned any business terms in Russian.

Lady Banner spoke at some length, sorrow on her face. Dina understood one word. *Chay.* Tea. She leaned toward Savage, but before she could speak to him, another word sprang from the chain of indecipherable language. *Sakhar.* Sugar.

"I think she's apologizing because they have no tea to offer us. Or sugar."

Banner pulled his wife aside rather roughly and reclaimed the conversation. More and more people drifted in, and the room filled with the stench of unwashed bodies and wet fur. Banner's convoluted sentences flowed about her like a kind of music. Tea again, sugar, and *muka*. Flour. *Muka* and *lotka*.

"They seem to have no flour, for he's asked about the ship and flour in the same breath."

"Ask him if they'll trade for pig iron. I think they use iron to pay their native hunters."

"I don't know the word for pig iron. It never came up in my conversations with the Russian ambassador's daughter," she said wryly.

"Tinware? Pots and pans?" Dina shook her head.

"Cloth?" Dina racked her brain. She had most certainly talked about fashions with the ambassador's daughter.

"Sholk?" she asked. "Silk?"

"No, woolens and cottons."

Banner interrupted them. *"Sholk, nyet,"* he said sternly. From the next rapid sentence she caught *zapreshchenni*. Forbidden.

"He says, I think, that they need official permission to trade for things like silk, that trade with foreigners for such things is forbidden."

"But they'd trade for food?" asked Savage with concern. Dina replayed Banner's last statement in her mind and tried to decipher which word meant trade. *Targovlya?*

"Find out for certain where Baranov is," Savage muttered.

"His Excellency Baranov?" inquired Dina obediently. *"Gdye?"*

"Ah!" exclaimed Banner. *"Novoarkhangelsk."* He mimed shooting and warfare. "Boom, boom."

"New Archangel? Do you know where that is?" Dina asked Savage.

"Never heard of it. They gestured south when I asked about Baranov, so I'd assumed Sitka. Maybe they have a new settlement."

"*Sitka*," agreed Banner, nodding. "*Novoarkhangelsk, Sitka*..." The two words were followed by a voluminous flow of language she did not understand, but Savage bent forward, his hand upon her arm.

"He said *Kolash*. That's what they call the Indians around Sitka. Ask him if the Kolash were defeated."

"We didn't talk much about war, either," she said out of the corner of her mouth. But she asked, "Kolash?" and mimed someone falling over.

The crowd laughed in agreement and applauded. A native man came forward and began an elaborate pantomime, obviously describing the retaking of Sitka. His performance gave Dina a chance to lean back and relax. Trying to speak a language one had only played with, and that years ago, was exhausting business.

Women near the doorway got to their feet; Dina's first impression was that they wanted a better view of the mime dance going on in front of her. When others in the hall rose to their feet, she turned to Savage.

"What's going on?" Before he could reply, she saw the woman, tall, regal, dressed in a combination of silk and furs. She had the dark skin of a native, but the air of someone accustomed to command. Two children held her hands, a boy of about six or seven and a younger girl. The girl was stunning, combining the best elements of Russian blood and the blood of the native people.

Banner barked a command at the performer, who stepped back and bowed toward the Indian woman. Banner escorted her to Dina. She did not curtsy, but nodded her head. Who was this woman? Someone they all respected, certainly.

"Anna Grigoryevna," whispered Savage in her ear.

"Who?" The name gave no hint of the Indian woman's status, except to indicate that her father was someone named Grigor.

"Anna Grigoryevna," repeated Banner. *"Comtesse..."*

Savage stepped forward to rescue him. *"Comtesse Endine Wilmount."*

Dina rose to her feet. She nodded to the unknown Indian woman. Whoever she was, she was respected here, and to insult a person of prominence wouldn't help Savage's efforts to trade. Dina returned to her chair.

The woman pushed the boy forward. "Antipatr Aleksandrovich," she said. Then the girl. "Irina Aleksandrovna." Both children took Dina's hand; the boy bowed, the girl curtsied. With a gesture, the woman recalled the mime, who picked up where he'd left off. The woman did not take a seat, but stood off to the side, alone except for her children.

Dina kept her face calm, but clenched her fists in anger. Why hadn't Savage told her? Aleksandrovich. The son of Aleksandr. Baranov, of course. The woman was not his wife, but his native mistress. There was no Lady Baranov. Savage expected her to receive this woman, be polite to her. Never in her life had she associated with a woman from the shadow world of the demi-rep.

"I'm not sure we can learn anything else here," said Dina under her breath, making sure Savage heard. At that very moment, the performer marched sternly across the room, his right arm raised. Suddenly he bent over in agony, clutching his arm. The crowd roared, "Aleksandr!"

"Was Baranov killed?" Dina asked in alarm, then realized she had spoken in English and no one but Savage understood her. She leaned toward Madame Banner.

"Baranov? *Adarovye?* Baranov's health?" She pointed at her own arm.

The woman made an elaborate, sad statement, then ended with another string of words in a happy tone.

"I believe he was wounded but has recovered," said Dina to Savage.

"Thank God!" exclaimed Savage.

She sat through two more dances, then leaned toward Madame Banner, laid the back of her hand on her forehead to show weariness.

"*Spat, lotka,*" she said.

The entertainment stopped immediately, as if their hosts had been waiting for her signal to end the party. Outside, her guard waited. Savage offered Dina his arm and together they marched to the boat, still drawn up on the gravelly shore. She neither looked at nor spoke to him. She sat in the boat, staring straight ahead, boiling with resentment at the awkward position in which he had placed her. She shook off his proffered hand and climbed the ladder alone, taking the arm of Lieutenant Becker when she reached the level of the deck. The main cabin would be the best place for the confrontation, so she strode across the deck, head high, until the confines of the hatch forced her to bend down. Savage was close behind her.

"Close the door," she ordered when he stuck his head in. If he thought the meeting of the officers was going to continue before she'd had her say, he was mistaken.

"Why did you do that to me?" she demanded imperiously. "You said Baranov's lady. There's no Madame Baranov in America."

"No, she's called Anna Grigoryevna."

"But you didn't tell me that. What if I've insulted her? I had no idea who she was." Her voice had risen, but she didn't even glance at the skylight. Let them all hear her. "How am I supposed to greet a Russian governor's kept woman? His native mistress?" she hissed.

"She's treated with respect. I believe she's a princess among her own people. I suppose you behaved perfectly well."

"A princess! Why didn't you tell me? All I did was nod to her. I might have insulted her."

Savage took two steps, all that was necessary to close the gap between them. Ruddiness had overcome his tan; his complexion resembled that of the natives on shore. Dina waited for his anger, wondered if he would lash out at her for baiting him. Hoped, in a way, that he would. He was a brute, and she would show him up for what he was. He reached for her hand.

"I'm sorry, *comtesse,*" he said softly. "I don't make a very good courtier, do I? I should have told you."

He bent back her hand, turned it over and laid his lips on her palm. They burned through her flesh, and her blood pumped the heat around her body.

"Forgive me. I believe you handled the affair very nicely." Dina relaxed her frown, but didn't lose control, didn't let her emotions show.through her cool exterior. He gestured toward the bench, sat beside her after she was seated.

"What do you think he said?" he asked.

"Baranov is in Sitka, which they recaptured just a short time ago. He was wounded in the fight to recapture the place. Is it a town, or a trading post?"

"It was a fort called Saint Michael."

"It's something called New Archangel now. Banner is afraid to trade for anything but food, because the officials forbid it."

"Yes. The trading last year was illegal, but they were desperate for the supplies. What shall we do?"

"Baranov is reestablishing this settlement on Sitka, I suppose. Perhaps he needs pig iron and pots and pans. Shouldn't you discuss this with the rest of the officers?"

"No. You're sufficient for a council of state." He rose, stooped under the deck beams, smiling down at her. "Thank you for your advice. The wind's right—we're weighing anchor and heading for Sitka. And would you please check Lightner's figures on our bearing?"

Chapter Ten

Dina waited in the main cabin until the four sailors had arranged themselves respectfully outside the door. She handed her books, quills and ink to Charley, then joined the men in the climb to the deck. Their progress on the stairs was rather ragged, but once on deck she walked amidships in state.

Her regal escort in Pavlovsk had led Charley to believe such adulation was her due, and he insisted she be similarly accompanied when she came on deck to conduct the lessons. He walked ahead, carrying her things as if they were orb and scepter. Dina glimpsed Savage, his lips quivering in a suppressed grin. If he laughed, she'd never forgive him.

A crate had been provided as her seat, and her pupils clustered about it, each equipped with a bit of sanded wood and a charred stick from the galley. Charley and two men who had some sketchy reading ability sat to one side, with Hampton's Bible. They were halfway through Genesis, but she insisted they listen to the beginners' lessons daily, as a review.

She led her class through the letters, watching as each made the marks on his improvised slate. They held up their boards and together spoke the sound of a letter, then wiped the charcoal away and wrote another. A few eyes glanced upward, over her head, then returned to their work with redoubled effort. Dina sensed that someone was standing behind her, and knew it was Savage. He had every right to be there, for this was his crew. He was quite correct when he said a good captain knew everything going on aboard his ship. But she wished he would stand where she could see him. Was he making fun of her?

She looked at the men before her. No one laughed; no one so much as smiled.

"The next letter is *S*," she said clearly. "It is the beginning of—" She stopped. It is the beginning of Savage, she thought. No other example came into her mind.

"Sail," suggested Charley softly.

"Sail," she repeated. She pointed upward, to the expanse of white, taut in the Pacific breezes. "Sail."

"Sail," repeated the eighteen men sitting cross-legged in front of her.

"Sail," said Charley, who then wrote the word on his board and displayed it to the men. Using him as an assistant saved her from dirtying herself with charcoal.

She went through the rest of the alphabet automatically, every nerve in her body aware of Savage's presence behind her. There must not, could not, be anything between them. Except that more and more often his nearness filled her with a warmth that suggested fulfillment, completion. A feeling that had nothing to do with fear. And often, in the middle of the night, when she heard the watch being changed, she recalled the nightmare and the comfort of his arms. Strangely comfortable, when at that very moment she should have fled in fear of him.

"Now we shall have our readers perform," she said, turning around to face the captain. "I have them all three reading the same thing, because, although Charley's the best, some of the things in the Bible are mysteries to him. Lambs and wine and wheat."

Charley pushed his companions into place before their captain and their teacher. He had very definite ideas of formal procedure, which Dina presumed came from his experiences as the son of a powerful man. Charley pointed out the starting place to his companions, and looked at

Savage with some apprehension, as if he would be blamed if the other two failed to perform well.

"And Jacob loved Rachel, and said, I will serve thee seven years for Rachel thy younger daughter," read the first man strongly. Dina suspected Charley had helped him with the verse and he was actually reciting from memory. The book was passed to the next man.

"And—" he hesitated at the unfamiliar name "—Laban said, It is better that I give her to thee, than that I should give her to another man—abide with me." He had some problems with *abide,* but eventually got the word out.

Charlie took the book, turned to Savage and read proudly. "And Jacob served seven years for Rachel, and they seemed unto him but a few days, for the love he had to her."

"Very good," said Savage. "Very good. Your school's going very well, I see. Now what do you do?"

"Charley and his friends go through the next three verses of the Bible, and I give them help if they need it. And the men who have learned the most letters help those who have learned the fewest. I believe teaching is the best road to learning, so they teach each other."

"Go ahead, go ahead. Don't let me stop you."

She paired off the men, the best with the slowest, constantly aware of his eyes upon her. The men settled down, heads bent over their boards, their hands black with repeated erasings of the charcoal.

"Lady Dina, what is this word?" asked one of the readers hesitantly.

"*Beguiled.* It means to trick, to make someone believe something that's not true. Why are you reading this? I said the next three verses. You're reading ahead."

"We couldn't wait. We want to know what happens," protested the other. "Look, this man, Laban, he told Jacob he could have Rachel, the girl he loved, and then on the wedding night put her sister in the room."

"Not believe," said Charley stoutly. He stopped, wrinkled his brow and thought through what he intended to say, so that his English would be as nearly perfect as possible before his teacher and captain. "I not believe it. Man in love with girl, he not be fooled. Man know—" he moved his hands over the body of an imaginary woman "—shape and blood of girl he love." He dismissed the story with a wave of his hand. "I not believe it."

"But it's in the Bible," protested one of his comrades.

"Seven years it say," said Charley, poking his finger at the previous verse. "Man can love girl seven years, maybe all years till dead, but not love her and not know girl from sister when he on top!"

"You're a pagan," said the other man heatedly. He turned to Savage. "It's in the Bible, and that makes it true, doesn't it?"

"Maybe Leah and Rachel were very much alike," suggested Savage, who managed to change an incipient smile into a look of great thoughtfulness. "Or perhaps in those days the women were kept away from the men, in a harem sort of place, so Jacob had never really been close..."

"Then how he know he love?" challenged Charley. "Man don't love girl just see. Love girl touch, have fun with."

Dina's face burned, and she knew her cheeks flamed red. She knew exactly what Charley meant by "fun," and the only man she'd ever come close to having "fun" with stood beside her.

"Why don't you finish reading the story? Maybe that will explain it. I'm taking your teacher to see the figurehead."

She had no way to avoid walking beside him to the bow of the ship, for he had not issued an invitation. He'd given an order.

"You've never been this far forward on the ship?"

"No. You know where I've been. Wherever you let me go."

"I didn't know if I could trust you. Now I know I can."

"Trust me with what?"

"With the men. I worded that incorrectly. I didn't know if I could trust the men with you."

"What's changed?"

"They respect you. Charley thinks you're some kind of queen at home. He asked Loti if they shouldn't make a fan for you. In the Pacific islands, a fan is a sign of nobility. If any man dares to touch you, Charley will throw him overboard. After he tears him apart, I suspect."

They stood leaning over the bow, before them the flowing mane of the brilliant horse. Dina saw for the first time that the gemlike color was achieved by small plates of iridescent shell fastened to the wooden base. Here and there the wood peeked through, where plates had torn away.

"Who does this work?" she asked. "It's beautiful."

"The young sailor named Hine. An American. He was apprenticed to a jeweler until he ran away to sea. Two years ago he suggested that the ship should be decorated with a real pearl stallion, not simply a wooden carving. As soon as we're anchored in a calm harbor, he'll make the repairs. Storms always take away a few of the plates."

"Why a pearl stallion? Why not your name, or *Savage* something?"

"The pearl stallion is a symbol of love and affection, at least to me."

"A strange symbol," she mused. "A stallion usually represents strength, or domination." She did not speak the rest aloud. The symbol of a virile man, who might possess any woman he wanted. A fit symbol for the man who stood beside her, who towered over nearly everyone on board, who ruled his universe with an iron hand.

"After I was born, one of the things my father gave my mother was a brooch, in the shape of a horse, because she was fond of horses. It was set with pearls."

"I see," she said, wondering if she really did.

"She sold it so she'd have the money to pay the local curate to be my tutor. Without that, I'd have grown up ignorant. Mother couldn't read and write, so after I'd learned my letters, I taught her, and my sister."

"Your father was wicked," she exclaimed. "Truly wicked, to leave a son without education."

"No, not wicked. Just frightened that he'd lose his place in society. It was bad enough that he'd married a chambermaid. He had to keep her shut away, out of everyone's sight. To pay any heed to her, or her children, that made him seem weak. He had behaved in a way that violated everything the *ton* found acceptable. The expectations of others cause all of us to do terrible things."

"Like with Anna Grigoryevna? The governor won't take her home with him when he returns to Russia, will he?"

"I don't know, but I doubt it. He'd need a great deal of courage to return to Saint Petersburg with an Indian woman and two half-breed children. I don't think love extends that far."

"Jacob served seven years."

"Do you believe that?" he asked with amusement.

"No. No one loves for that long. Jacob had some other reason for wanting Rachel, and called it love. Maybe she had a fortune. I suspect love is a temporary madness," she said.

"Between men and women, love is often a fantasy engendered in the loins," he said. "But then, I promised you I'd not bring that subject up between us."

"Thank you. Charley's not so considerate of my feelings, as you saw just a few minutes ago."

"But you handled yourself very well. No fainting fit, no sinking to the deck, no swooning. And you're getting so tan, your blushes are hardly noticeable. You'll get accustomed to the islanders. They're very matter of fact."

"So your father loved your mother just so long as it was convenient?" she asked, to move the conversation away from her blushes.

"Yes, although I'm not sure it was ever convenient. He was in a panic to be sure of an heir."

"My parents, I've been told, had a love match. It shocked many people, because she was not of his class. By the time I came along, there was nothing but hate. Perhaps," she said with sudden inspiration, "you're right. Jacob didn't really know Rachel. She stayed in the women's quarters. He loved a fantasy, not the woman, so the love might last for seven years...."

"Fourteen. Remember, he had to serve another seven years to get her after Leah was foisted off on him."

"If you read the rest of the story, after he has Rachel, he gets angry with her because she doesn't bear children. So in reality, the love didn't last once he got her," she said with finality.

"So we can only love fantasies?"

"Perhaps."

"Charley would disagree with you. He said men only love women they...know well."

"Then we're safe," she said archly. "Charley is a dear, and quite intelligent. He may well be right."

"How much mathematics do you know?" he asked suddenly.

"Mathematics?" she asked in surprise, not seeing the connection between their theoretical discussion of love and the concreteness of addition and subtraction.

"Yes. You obviously studied it. How much?"

"My brother had a tutor, and I studied with him. We went partway into trigonometry before my father...died."

"I want you to start a mathematics class. Teach the midshipmen, Barber and Loti."

"But that's Lightner's duty. I can't keep challenging his position."

"You don't have a choice. I give the orders and they're carried out. Lightner is not teaching the boys, but confusing them. He's afraid to teach them for fear they'll soon know everything he does. You'll start a mathematics class for Barber and Loti, and Charley, as well. I'm going to make him a master's mate. You had best get back to your class. I've interrupted you enough."

She watched his back as he headed aft. He had no coat on. His canvas trousers stretched on flat buttocks as he walked. His shirt was slightly too small across his powerful shoulders. Some part of her body yearned after him, stretched out in an elongated emotion, straining across the deck.

The ship glided amid a myriad of islands, each dark with pine forests. For days they had waited off the coast while fog enshrouded the edge of the continent. Now the sun shone so brightly Dina could feel its reflected heat rise from the deck. She moved into a spot shaded by the mizzen sail. She was not disappointed by her first sight of New Archangel, because she had schooled herself not to expect too much. It would not be a city. It would be a rough frontier settlement.

Savage ordered the anchor dropped long before the ship was near the fort. He and every other officer who possessed a glass scanned the shore. Just as at Pavlovsk, small boats pulled away from the shore and headed for the ship.

Dina wondered if she would be going ashore to serve as interpreter. Her Russian, so scanty, was a bit better now, because she had used her spare time to record, in her diary, every word she could remember. She had practiced the phrases she'd once known: *How beautiful your dress is. I'm honored by your request. You flatter me.* None of them very useful under the circumstances, but at least saying the words reminded her of how the language sounded.

Savage ordered a boat over the side, came on deck in his gold-trimmed coat without looking at her. He was going ashore alone, except for the oarsmen.

A rocky promontory jutted out into the bay, and on its top rose a fort made of planks. From a tall staff flew a flag bearing the double-headed eagle of imperial Russia. Below the fort, on the slope of the hill, a huge building stretched down to the waterfront. Away from the hill, low buildings of planks and logs were scattered, stopping abruptly at the line of dark forest. The forest looked like a fortress itself, a wall made up of trees as straight as columns.

Here and there, smoke rose from chimneys and open fires. Dina noticed a crowd of men working around a partially completed building. The sounds of their hammers and axes came across the water, completely separated from their movements. A man's arm would rise, the ax would drop. Several seconds later, the thud of the blow would be heard on the ship.

When the ship first came into view, the shore had been crowded with people. Now many drifted back to their work, but some still remained to greet the foreign captain. Dina found it hard to tell men from women, since both wore skin leggings and long shirts, but she had concluded that many of those left on the shore were women, because a number of children clustered about.

The crew labored under Becker's direction, hoisting empty water barrels onto the deck. The supply they had taken on in Sumatra was nearly gone, and the rest of the journey, in tropical seas, required that they leave with every barrel full.

It was evening, but the sun was still riding high, when Dina saw the captain's boat put off from shore. Mr. Becker met him as he climbed on deck. Every officer was on deck, eager to hear what had passed between the captain and Baranov. Savage looked around, studied the clustered water barrels.

"Very good, Mr. Becker. We'll take on water and wood tomorrow."

He went below, every eye following him, every face showing disappointment at his silence. Dina, frustrated by the lack of information, went to her cabin and closed the door. It was stuffy, but dark, which couldn't be said of the deck at any hour of the day in this northern latitude.

"Lady Dina," said Kranz's voice softly through the door.

"Yes."

"The captain would like to see you in the main cabin."

Another conference with the officers, she thought, heaving herself off her bunk so suddenly she hit her head on the beams. She picked up her shawl, then remembered how hot the cabin got when packed with six or seven men and left it behind. She stopped in the doorway, surprised. Savage sat alone in the twilight, his head in his hands. When he heard her enter, he straightened up, but did not attempt to rise.

"Come in." He patted the bench beside him. "Sit down. I need to talk to someone." Dina took her seat, not where he had indicated, but twelve inches beyond.

"Baranov won't trade furs for anything but food."

She had no idea what he expected of her, so she kept silent.

"What would you suggest?" he asked suddenly.

"I believe, sir," she said slowly, "I'm the wrong person to ask. Your crew, your officers, have sailed these waters with you. You should consult with—"

"I don't want to consult with the officers. I want to know what you think."

"I know nothing about this place. I suppose you should go someplace and get food. Is it so terribly important that you get the furs?" she asked.

"Yes. That's the only thing the Chinese want. They'd laugh at my cotton and wool and tin pans."

"So that's how you've done it!" she marveled. "Uncle and Captain Freemantle couldn't figure it out."

"That's how I've done it, but not this time. This winter the settlement here was in desperate circumstances, worse than in Pavlovsk. Nearly eight hundred people, hardly any supplies at all. Hundreds got scurvy—they made beer from pinecones to cure it. They've got fish, meat from seals and walrus. They want bread."

"Would the Sandwich Islanders buy the cotton and tin pans?" Dina asked hesitantly, afraid of showing her ignorance. "You said we'd go there to get supplies. Couldn't we get food there for these people?"

"They want flour, bread. The Sandwich Islanders don't raise grain."

"Who in this part of the world does raise wheat?" she asked innocently. "Anyone?"

"The Spanish. In California."

"Then we must go to them...."

"Britain is at war with Spain," Savage reminded her. "And the Spanish have laws forbidding their colonists to trade with foreigners."

"So do the Russians, but they seem to be willing to wink at the authorities when they need something. Why shouldn't the Spanish?"

"The Spanish have warships in the Pacific. The Russians don't. We'd risk getting the *Pearl Stallion* shot up, maybe sunk."

"Go back to India, get a new cargo," she said, a bit frustrated by his rejection of all her ideas. "Go trade the pots and pans for food and come back."

"That loses an entire season. An entire voyage without profit. The crew and officers sign on expecting a prosperous year. We'd arrive in India with nothing."

"They take that risk when they join you," she snapped.

"Indeed they do. But the responsibility's mine."

"And you don't want to disappoint them?"

"Of course not. But that's why I must talk this over with you. Everyone else on board would advise a course of action that gives us a chance to pull the cakes from the fire. You're not involved, so you can assess the risks more clearly. What would you do if you were me?"

"I'd have never left home," she said, following the words with a bitter laugh.

"Yes, you would have. You're more daring than you think."

"I'd try to find someplace to trade the things we have, and get food. Are there any Americans about? They raise grain."

"On the other side of the continent," he said sardonically. "Shall we go seeking the Northwest Passage?"

"Don't make fun of me," she retorted. "I mean American ships. Don't they carry that sort of thing?"

"Why should they want to trade with me? They make their own cloth and tin pans. They come out here for the same reason I do—furs."

"Then," she said with great patience, "to pull the cakes from the fire, you must get close to the flame. You go to California. Have you been there before?"

"Before we went to war with Spain. In California we'd have to watch very carefully, try to find out immediately if any Spanish naval ships are about."

"Do the Spanish keep an army there?"

"Not an army. A few soldiers, scattered here and there, and from what I saw, most of them worry more about eventually getting land of their own than they do about the defense of the colony. Most of the crops are raised by missionary priests and the Indians they've converted."

"Would they trade with us without letting the authorities know?" He gave a thoughtful mumble through his pursed lips. His lips reminded her of those of a man getting ready to steal a kiss. Except that Savage's kisses were made with his mouth open—assaultive kisses, designed as preliminary to other things, not as the end in themselves.

"Do you speak Spanish?" he asked.

"No. You?"

"Very little. Fortunately, Hampton does, from his time traveling in the West Indies. Perhaps," he continued thoughtfully, "we could avoid Monterey, the capital, and put in someplace else. Get our trading done before the governor finds out. There's a harbor north of Monterey, but I've never sailed into it. Hard to find, but according to Americans I've met in the Sandwich Islands, the most magnificent in the world."

"The Americans go there?"

"Yes, the Boston ships, they're called here in the Pacific."

"If the Americans find it possible to trade, the Spanish in California aren't very strict about obeying their own laws."

"Spain isn't at war with America."

"Perhaps we aren't, either. It's been months since we've heard any news from home. We may be at war with Russia, for all we know."

"True."

"And even if there's a war, that's in Europe, and shouldn't have much to do with us out here. If people need cotton cloth or tin pots or pig iron, I'd think they'd look the other way and take it."

"You, my dear, are a practical woman. That's the way you'd do things, if you ran a colony. I don't even know who the governor of California is, or whether he's from Spain or Mexico. He may be a native of California, which would make things easier. A courtier, who's looking to make his way up in the world, is more careful to obey every law coming from Madrid."

"There's just as much chance that a courtier would be trying to gain a fortune out of his governorship, and would be willing to trade with you so long as a large part of the profits end up in his pockets."

"As I said, you're a practical woman. Shall we go to California?"

"Or go back to Calcutta with your tail between your legs?"

"A stallion doesn't put his tail between his legs," he told her. "He fights."

"So you were going to do this anyway? Why did you bother to ask me?"

"Talking to a wise woman is the best way to straighten out one's thoughts. When the idea first crossed my mind, it seemed absolutely insane. I needed it to come from someone else, so that I'd see all the consequences."

"That's something I need to learn," she said. "All my life I've jumped ahead without considering where I was really going. I came aboard the *Pearl Stallion* supposing you were bound for England. I just assumed that's where you'd be going, without thinking, or bothering to find out."

"That's not a good example," he told her. "You were in a pretty spot of bother, and needed to act fast. You actually made a very good choice. Where do you suppose your uncle thinks you disappeared to?"

"I've wondered, and I hate that they're probably worried, especially Aunt Lily and Emily. I keep telling myself they've figured it out by now and know I'm with you."

"What they think is that you became crazed from that fever you pretended to have. Or have you forgotten the desperate illness that made it impossible for you to hear Freemantle's proposal? They think you wandered off into the countryside. You perhaps fell into the river and drowned. You may have ended up dying in a field and been eaten by tigers."

"E...ah!" exclaimed Dina, shivering.

"You may have been seized by natives who saw your value and spirited you to the north, where they sold you to some powerful man. By now you've learned to share his bed and are with his child."

"I'll kill myself," she threatened.

"Please don't. Then again, you may have been recognized as you crept away, and they may know quite well where you are. Freemantle would no doubt go to great lengths to recover the beautiful woman who was to have become his wife. He's probably talked to all the boatmen on the river, and the ones who brought you to the ship may remember the young sailor with golden hair. You stole your uncle's clothes, and perhaps he missed them immediately the next morning."

"I rather doubt that."

"They may even think I abducted you, that you share more than my rum and pickled beef."

"One thing's for certain, they can't possibly suspect what I'm really doing. Uncle George said I hadn't the qualifications to be a governess, and now I'm teaching nearly twenty men to read. And studying mathematics with two midshipmen and a South Sea islander who confuses me with Queen Charlotte."

"Remember, too, my dear, they cannot believe you live comfortably on a ship with more than fifty men, without carnal contact. No matter what you say when you return, they'll not believe that. Plan your life around that fact, even though it's a lie. We all have to live with the past others ascribe to us. That will be the past you have to bear, and you must face it bravely."

"As you carry the burden of your mother?"

"My mother is not my burden. The burden is what others think she must have been. The elite of England assume she was an inferior creature, a servant, stupid and without human emotions. They presume these elements were passed to me in the womb, so I'm less than my peers. What would your friends in London think of Charley?"

"That he's a savage, who will remain a savage inside, no matter what he learns or does."

"And what is Charley? To you?"

"One of the finest gentlemen I've ever met."

"Even though when he first came to your cabin he planned to kill you?"

"Yes. He's a gentleman because he changed his mind. I think a true gentleman is always ready to change, when he's faced with something new that contradicts what he's believed before."

He moved restlessly, and his body slid closer to hers.

"I hope I can fulfill your expectations of a gentleman. When you told me he'd been in your room, I was enveloped in a storm, in an emotion I never dreamed I'd ever feel—crazed jealousy. I'm as guilty as your friends of judging Charley. At that moment I thought he was a primitive who couldn't control himself. I thought he'd ravished you." He shook his head, admitting some new truth to himself. "No, that's not what I feared. My fear was that you'd welcomed him. The idea that you would reject me but accept him burned a hole in my mind, and in that insanity I mistreated you. I've changed now, learned something. Will you forgive me?"

Dina glanced up at the skylight and was relieved to find it closed. His words stunned her. Would he be jealous of any man who might have her? And did his confession mean that he still wanted her, in the way he'd wanted her at the Allinsons so many months ago?

We're on our way back to Calcutta, she reassured herself. *In a few months the* Pearl Stallion *will sail into the Hooghly. All I have to do is keep my distance from him and I'll be safe and whole.*

California! she remembered, and dug her fingers into her legs in despair. Weeks sailing south, then back north; weeks, perhaps months, that she'd not counted on. She should not be here, should not have enjoyed so much the pleasure of talking to him alone. She should not look at him on the deck out of the corner of her eye, admiring the strength of his legs, the grace of his body. She must insist that others join them for meals, lest his hand reach under the table for her, as it had done before. Lest his touch condemn her body to an irresistible acceptance.

"I must get back to my mathematics," she said weakly. "I stay just one lesson ahead of the young men."

"Thank you for helping me," he said.

She ran to her cabin, threw herself across her bunk. Was this how it felt to desire a man? How could she possibly want a man to perform the disgusting act of sex? She could almost feel Savage's hand upon her thigh, his fingers pressed against her back, his mouth engrossing hers. A powerful spasm claimed her entire body.

I fought him that night, but I wanted him.

Before that night in Calcutta, she had never once been drawn into the sensual world. With shock she realized that the exquisite pain she had experienced in his arms was physical desire. And the source of that desire was Savage.

She lay on her back and fantasized that he came in, removed her clothes, lay on top of her. Charley called it "fun." Could it possibly be fun to have a man, a man like Savage, possess one?

Had Anna Grigoryevna felt this desire before she yielded to the governor? Had she plunged ahead, knowing the end to which she would come, unable to reject the Russian ruler because her body burned for him?

If she accepted Savage, would the satiation of her body make up for the future, when she'd be passed from man to man? Would she learn to enjoy that life, as the harlot of Calcutta's elite?

She sat up in alarm. Savage was jealous of any other man. He'd not let her be passed from secretary to councilman. He had abused her because he suspected she had accepted Charley, not because she had challenged his power on the ship. If she gave in to Savage, became his mistress, perhaps he would demand that she serve him forever. That she remain his possession, as thoroughly as the *Pearl Stallion* was his.

She imagined her life with him on the *Pearl Stallion.* Would she share the bunk in his cabin, or would he come to her whenever he felt the overpowering urge to use her? In England, when he finally had his fortune? He'd find a wealthy merchant's daughter for his wife, a woman who brought gold to his purse.

There were women in London not spoken of in mixed company. Women who lived in fine rooms, paid for by their wealthy lovers. That was what she would be, his mistress, and he would come to her, rouse the storm within her, bring her satisfaction. He would surround her with the things his wealth could buy. Perhaps, when his wife was in the country, he'd take her to the theater, to salons. And everywhere they went, the whispers would be the same: Savage's whore.

Until he grew to hate her. Until the beauty he saw in her ended in childbirth. Would he acknowledge the children he gave her?

She remembered women on the streets of London, ragged women, trailed by pinched-faced children. Had any of them been the beauty of three seasons? Were any of them daughters of earls? Had they, too, felt the burning compulsion to yield to a man, without thinking of the consequences?

I've got to think ahead, she told herself sternly. *I must think of the results of my actions, not just for now, but for years in the future. I must not, must not, give Savage any hint of my feelings.*

Chapter Eleven

The fog cleared suddenly, as if the ship had sailed through a gauzy gray stage curtain into the limelight. The land to the east was nothing more than an undulating line. Dina stared ahead, strained her eyes, but could not discern the promised break in that barren skyline.

"Trees!" yelled Charley from the foretop. Savage ran forward, scrambled up the rigging.

"How can they think to see one particular tree at this distance?" Dina asked Hampton, who stood beside her.

"It's not one tree, but a mountainside covered with them. The American captains say they sail along the coast until they can see these trees, so tall, they assured me, they must be the tallest in the world. Sail directly toward them, and you find the mouth to the harbor."

Savage slid down the ropes, yelling orders as he came. The sailors rushed to alter the set of the sails, the helmsman turned the wheel. They were sailing directly toward the shore.

Charley's voice rang out once more, assuring those on the deck that he could see the passage through the mountains. The *Pearl Stallion* plunged ahead, her life depending upon his promise. Savage climbed the mizzen rigging, clung by his left arm, his glass tight to his right eye. His body twisted with the heave of the ship; Dina's body responded with its own leap of hope. She beat down the sensation resolutely, turned away and refused to look at the long, strong legs braced above her.

Slowly the outreaching hills closed about them, and finally even those on deck could see the narrow strait; beyond, still miles in the distance, the trees stood like the pillars of the sky. Savage descended from the rigging, his last lengthy step bringing him uncomfortably close to her. He barked quick commands as the rough water in the channel buffeted the ship. Above them, on the hills to starboard, they saw men running, spreading the news of a ship in the offing.

"They've spotted us over there," remarked Mr. Becker. "It has the appearance of a fort."

"We'll stay out of cannon range," said Savage.

Dina examined the gray wall on the point of the hill. She searched for the slit that would betray the battery, watched for the puff of smoke, the first warning that the men on the heights had unlimbered their cannon. Nothing happened, beyond a great commotion among the soldiers visible on the roof of the fort. Eventually one climbed upon the wall. Even from this distance she could see the speaking trumpet in his hand. His shout carried over the water.

"What's he saying, Dr. Hampton?" asked Savage.

"He's ordering us to anchor under the fort."

"Tell him yes. Proceed, Mr. Becker, until we're in calmer waters and out of cannon range. You there, Mr. Barber, get some of the men milling about, as if they don't know what they're doing."

Barber set a number of sailors running to the bow, then had them aimlessly climb the rigging, while several more amidships picked up the carefully flemished ends of ropes and pretended to be altering the set of the sails. In the meantime Hampton mounted the starboard rigging, cupped his hands about his mouth, and shouted over and over again, *"Sí, señor! Sí, señor!"*

Soldiers ran along the shore, keeping up with the ship. They continued to shout and wave their hands in great agitation.

"They're asking, 'What ship is that? Where are you from?' " reported Hampton. "Shall I tell them Boston?"

"Don't reply," said Savage. "We must keep them uncertain until the last minute. And I shouldn't like to be found out in a lie."

The soldiers on foot were joined by a dozen men on horseback. The sunlight glinted from muskets and from at least one drawn sword. One of the riders seemed a bit out of place, for he wore the brown robes of a priest.

"They're demanding our surrender, sir," said Hampton.

"I believe we passed the battery before they got the cannon loaded," said Becker. "I think I spotted it on this side of the fort."

"We'll anchor here," said Savage. "Mr. Barber, load the forward and aft cannon with grapeshot, and let no one aboard. I'm going ashore."

"Do you think that's wise, sir?" asked Becker.

"We can't make trades by hiding behind our guns," snapped Savage. "We've little choice now but to go ahead with our plans. Either they have compassion for the plight of the Russians, or they don't. Lady Dina, are you prepared to accompany me?"

She stepped forward, clad in her oft-repaired blue dress and silk scarf. Her boots had been liberally patched with canvas, but the repair was not immediately obvious, since Charley had painted them black. If she kept them well tucked under her skirts, no one would ever guess.

She could not avoid sitting beside Savage in the small boat, for otherwise she would be in the way of the men at the oars. She drew the scarf about her shoulders, laughed inwardly at herself for supposing such a fragile shield could defend her against a man like Savage.

"Let's hope the commandant of this fort is as gallant toward ladies as most Spaniards," he said lightly. "Else we may be in a pickle barrel a bit too steep to climb out of."

"You'll be the one in the pickle barrel," she said, trying to speak as casually as he did. Her heart pounded in her throat. "I shouldn't have any trouble making a good match among the soldiers. I'll become a lady of this country. Do you suppose the governor's married?"

"Yes, and probably left his wife behind in Vera Cruz or Mexico City. You've resisted being a kept woman so far. I'd recommend it here, also."

His grin was interrupted by a jerk as the boat grounded on the sloping beach. The sailors sprang out and pulled it upon the sand. Savage gestured for Hampton to leave the boat first.

The man with the drawn sword rode at the head of the soldiers. He yelled. It must have been a command to halt, for the horses stopped abruptly. The leader dismounted and ran down the slope, the sound of his jangling spurs audible above his shouted Spanish.

"He wants to know where we're from and our business here," said Hampton.

Savage stepped away from the crowd of sailors and made an elegant bow in the direction of the agitated officer. The sun glistened off the gold braid of both men. Dina noted with dismay that the Spaniard quite outshone Savage in gold braid, for it decorated not only the front of his coat, but the seams, as well.

"Captain Saurage," Savage said, "of the *Pearl Stallion*." He pointed to the ship. "Hampton, tell him we're a British merchant ship, on a voyage of mercy. And introduce Her Ladyship."

Hampton stepped forward, bowed grandly and made the speech they had rehearsed during the long days of planning. Dina didn't understand the rapid Spanish, but she heard him say, *"Doña Endine Wilmount."* The mention of her name and title brought the officer up short. His gold braid was tarnished, Dina noted as he came closer. It was not bullion, but plated brass. He would see the gold on Savage's coat was real, and be impressed.

"Don Luis de Arguello," said the commander of the troop to her. He bowed with a courtly grace that seemed a bit out of place on the dry, barren hillside. There was not

one structure in sight, barring a few poles to tie small boats to. No population moved upon the hillsides, except the soldiers.

Dina made a curtsy, on the assumption that the Spanish might be impressed with excessive politeness.

"We're to go to the fort," said Hampton after Don Luis had spoken at some length. "There seems to be someone there who outranks him, so perhaps he's merely a deputy."

The Spaniard provided Savage with a horse by demoting one of his troop to foot soldier. Hampton was forced to walk. Dina saw from the officer's gestures that she would be boosted up behind one of the soldiers. There was nothing to be done except stand still as the man put his hands about her waist and lifted her onto the rump of the horse. Her tattered boots stuck out, and it was impossible to conceal them.

The little troop set off, climbing the hill by way of a sandy trail that wound through scrubby bushes. The farther they went, the colder and damper the air became, until, as they approached the fort, Dina felt the cutting edge of the wind and saw fog roll like sea billows across the hills between them and the ocean. Without a pillion, every lift of the horse's rump beat upon her, so she was happy when Don Luis ordered a halt before a low whitewashed building.

They were ushered into a large room. In the center was a long, roughly built table. At the opposite end, a few sticks burned in a brazier. On either side of this fire sat men clad in the ornate uniforms of the Spanish military. Only one stood when the strangers entered, but both looked rather astonished when they glimpsed her.

The man on the left, who stayed seated, was small and elderly. His fine white hair made a halo about his head, and his shoulders were bent from either fatigue or the effects of age, or perhaps both. His right foot was propped upon a stool.

The other man was much younger, no more than thirty-five or forty, taller than average, but short when compared to Savage. When he turned toward Dina, she gasped in surprise. She laid her fingers upon her lips as the introductions were being made.

"His Excellency Don Jose de Arillaga."

"The governor of the two Californias," Hampton muttered out of the corner of his mouth. What was he doing here? The capital was in Monterey.

Dina made her deep bow to the governor, then stared again at the younger man. He, of course, didn't recognize her, a beauty of London, in a ragged gown and with a scarf over her head. It had been several years. Perhaps she'd changed too much, her complexion ruined by India and exposure to the sea air.

"Captain Don Anson Saurage," said Hampton. "Doña Endine Wilmount." The Spaniard raised a quizzing glass to study her, his increasing astonishment apparent in the sudden erectness of his shoulders and the lift of his head.

"Don Miguel Villamonte y Cortes," said the grandee, without waiting for a formal introduction. He bowed to Savage. "Doña Endina needs no introduction. We have danced together in London," he added in perfect English.

Savage glared at Dina; his expression asked for an accounting of this untoward occurrence. She gave a slight shrug of her shoulders and hoped he realized she was as shocked and surprised as he.

Don Miguel spoke, and servants appeared with two chairs. He said something to Hampton, who reluctantly edged toward the door.

"Wine shall be brought," Don Miguel said. "Please explain this strange mission that brings an English captain and a lovely Englishwoman to our shores."

"We thank you for your kind attention," said Savage. "We should not have come except for the gravest of emergencies."

Don Miguel bowed in acknowledgment, leaving the floor to Savage. At that moment a servant arrived with an earthen jug borne on a crude wooden tray, along with an assortment of finely cut crystal glasses. The interruption called forth another round of flattering pleasantries, then a toast to His Most Catholic Majesty. Dina watched Savage closely, wondering how long he intended to string out the courtesies before stating the reason for their visit.

"We should like to know what brings you to California," said Don Miguel finally, with a bluntness negating all the flowery words that had gone before. Savage began his rehearsed speech, describing the plight of the Russians in Sitka, exaggerating points that he knew could not be checked at some later date.

"We have come for no other reason than this," he said sincerely. "I sail on my own account, not as an emissary of my king or government. The *Pearl Stallion* is not a harbinger of British warships beyond the horizon. The visit, if you would prefer, can go unreported to my government." The corollary—"And you shall not have to report it, either"—remained unspoken, but obvious.

The two Spaniards began a conversation in their own language, Don Miguel keeping his eyes on the guests, not the governor. He thinks we might understand Spanish, thought Dina, and is watching for our reactions to what they say. She glanced at Savage, saw that his face was relaxed and noncommittal.

"The governor," Don Miguel finally translated, "says he can do nothing. He should long since have put you under arrest and seized your ship, but his great sympathy for your errand leads him to be generous." Don Miguel lifted the jug and refilled Dina's glass. The local wine was excellent, but she knew she must not drink more. She took the opportunity to speak to him personally.

"How strange that we should meet here," she said, "halfway round the world."

"Far different from where I last saw you. How do you come to be on this ship?"

"Captain Saurage has very kindly offered me passage home, after I was stranded, quite against my will, in India. And you? This is a great distance from the Spanish legation in London."

"His Majesty expressly asked me to make a tour of the outlying provinces of Mexico. The war in Europe gives him concern for the borders of our empire."

"How wise," said Savage. "The very thing my country failed to do in North America, and that neglect ended with the loss of our colonies there." Dina admired the way Savage seized the opportunity to flatter the Spanish and to call attention to the failures of his own country. What terrible luck that the governor and Don Miguel should be here in this isolated place, not at the capital in Monterey.

"I cannot believe that you would not have compassion for human beings who are dying for want of food," said Savage, to return the conversation to the subject at hand. Don Miguel translated, and then the governor shook his white locks and spoke at some length.

"He says we may be at war with Russia. One never knows these things immediately. And Spain is most certainly at war with the British."

"Tell him Spain may not be at war with Britain. One never knows of peace immediately, either."

Savage's remark, translated by Don Miguel, brought a pause in the governor's oration. Savage eyed Dina, and she knew he expected her to make her speech.

"My lord, Your Excellency, would you hear a poor lady who is unaccustomed to speaking before men, a lady who hesitates to thrust herself into the matters of war and peace and the negotiations between nations? In Russian America I have seen women and children who are desperate for food. Food that you might furnish, and our ship carries the means to pay you." She lowered her eyes, listening to Don Miguel's rapid translation. Savage surreptitiously kicked her in the shin.

"I saw a child," she continued hastily, "who lay still, nothing moving but his eyes, but those eyes begged for assistance. May I tell you of this child? He is the son of an American who was trapped by the terrible winter in Sitka, the son of a Boston merchant," she added significantly, since she knew they patronized the occasional Boston ship for some of their goods. "The father gave his own food to provide for his son, but the sacrifice was in vain, for the man died, and now his son lies close to death. We may already be too late," she added in a low voice, shaking her head in sorrow.

She wondered if the governor would believe this invented tale. She watched his eyes while Don Miguel translated. The old man's mouth opened slightly, and for a moment Dina thought he had been moved to grant their wish. Then his mouth closed, but a tremor remained on his lips.

"I beg of you, sir, Captain Don Anson Saurage is willing to sacrifice his cargo in return for food for these people. He's a merchant, who sails the seas for profit, but he has been so distressed by the situation in Russian America, he'll empty his ship upon your shore once he's assured of your willingness to provide food."

Dina thought that a nice touch. It wouldn't be trading with the enemy at all. Just charity, and a pile of manufactured goods for the taking laid upon the beach.

"She has begged of me so eloquently," said Savage, with rather more drama than she thought necessary, "that I finally had to yield to her importunities. It will cost me gravely, but she assures me I lay up stores in heaven by the act."

Don Miguel smiled sardonically, and Dina knew Savage had gone too far with that remark about heaven. The conversation between Don Miguel and the governor lengthened, leaving her uncertain whether further pleas would be useful. Finally Don Miguel turned to Savage and lifted his glass.

"His Excellency says you are to return to your ship. He will make some decision tomorrow. Until then, neither you nor your men are permitted onshore. His Excellency is committing a grave breach of imperial law by allowing you to stay within this harbor."

No horses were furnished for the return trip to the beach, and Dina interpreted this as a lack of respect for her and

Savage. Hampton, who had been exiled from the negotiations, trudged along with them. By the time they reached the boat Dina was exhausted and her boots were full of sand. Life on board the *Pearl Stallion* did not provide enough exercise. She must ask Savage for permission to walk on deck for an hour or two each day.

One of the men guarding the boat yelled a warning when he sighted the returning captain, and two sailors came running from behind a few stunted bushes growing above the shore. Dina saw movement in the brush. The sailors pushed the boat off the beach. She looked back and saw a woman standing on the sand, gazing wistfully after her retreating clients.

"It's amazing how quickly the scent of money draws the women," said Savage. "So there's some sort of settlement about here."

"A few miles south on this peninsula," said Hampton. "One of the establishments built by the priests to educate and convert the Indians. There's at least one more at the south end of the bay."

Once on board, Savage ordered all the officers to the main cabin. A strong wind had risen that kicked up white caps across the great bay and made sitting on the open deck uncomfortable.

"Well?" asked Lightner impatiently.

"We'd counted on finding a local official who would take the risk of illegal trading in order to gain a great profit. Our misfortune is that the governor of the province is here, not at his capital. And he has a visitor from Madrid with him."

The men groaned.

"But the governor said neither yes nor no," continued Savage. "Lady Dina was very eloquent in her plea. I kept my eyes on him when the translation was made, and I thought he showed some pity."

"But this fellow from Madrid," said Becker. "The governor can't possibly skirt the law with him around."

"The gentleman said nothing one way or the other. And while this official presence may make our job more difficult, there's the possibility it could have the opposite effect. He's acquainted with Lady Dina. How, Your Ladyship?"

All eyes turned to her, and Dina wondered how she might explain the sort of acquaintance made on a London dance floor to these solid, practical men. "Two...no, three years ago, he was attached in some way to the Spanish legation in London, before the war came between England and Spain. He attended many of the same balls and parties I did, and we danced together on several occasions. Beyond that, I don't know the man."

"Whose palm can be crossed?" asked Becker bluntly. "The governor's?"

"I doubt the governor can be bribed," said Savage. "He's an elderly man who seems beyond the age when he might hope to return to Europe a wealthy man. He'll end his days in California. Hampton?" he asked. "Did you learn anything?"

"I sat with the soldiers in their barracks," he said. "The ones who'd been on the beach knew I understood their language, so they were careful what they said in front of me. But eventually they got used to my presence. They're expecting a frigate to come up the coast from Mexico. She hasn't called yet this summer, and they're concerned for her safety. The Boston ships have not put in an appearance on the coast this season, but everyone's anxious for them to come. One of the soldiers was angry at our arrival, because his leave had been canceled as a consequence. He'd planned to go across the bay to visit a young woman, which means there must be Spanish settlements around this bay."

"Every man on deck tonight," ordered Savage. "Muskets and pikes all around, but no boarding netting. That would give them the idea we don't trust them."

"Captain," said Hampton, "you know the soldier who wanted to visit his sweetheart across the bay? Just before we left, he managed to whisper to me, ask me if I could get him some needles to take to his girl."

Savage smiled broadly. "This man, is he a simple soldier, or..."

"He's a sergeant," said Hampton.

Savage slapped his thighs with a resounding smack. "And where did you arrange to meet him?"

"He'll be out on that point tonight, and show a light. He called it Rincón, the corner."

"Make sure the boat's left tethered to the anchor chain, so no one onshore observes one being put over the side. Wait until the moon's down, no matter when he makes his light. Take him a bit of cloth, too. A man must impress his sweetheart," said Savage, laughing.

As the men left the cabin, Savage laid his hand upon Dina's arm. When they were alone, he extinguished the lantern, and the darkness enveloped them. "Dark nights are a pleasure after those infernally long days up north," he said. "Leads a man to keep on working when he should be in his bunk."

"Yes. I've been able to sleep again since we've come south." Just enough light filtered through the stern windows to show him approaching the spot where she sat.

"What do you know of Don Miguel? You know more than you said."

"If you're concerned about my past, he meant nothing to me at the time, and means nothing to me now," she said loftily. A heavy silence ensued that lasted for several moments. Perhaps she had offended him by making a reference to his jealousy.

"I don't know much about him," she continued, "but I suspect several things."

"Anything that might be useful to us?"

"When he was in London, he spent most of his time with heiresses, so I stood no chance. I heard gossip that he was seeking a wealthy English wife. He paid a great deal of attention to Miss Amelia Strawn..."

"Who is now my sister-in-law," said Savage wryly.

"Yes. Her father was not willing to pay the same price to marry her to a Spanish grandee as he was to buy her the title of countess."

"A wise decision, I presume, although wouldn't the lady have been better satisfied with Don Miguel's strutting masculinity than with my brother's frailty?"

"You promised not to raise the specter of sex between us, but continue to do so," she accused.

"So I do. You lead me to it, you're so beautiful. And I'm lonely, for since leaving Sitka, you've avoided me."

"Yes."

"Why?"

"I...I've been busy. The mathematics classes take so much time, I have to study..."

"Liar. You're afraid."

"Yes," she admitted quickly, to disarm him and end the discussion. "We were talking about Don Miguel. He's still in need of money, I believe."

"How did you come to that conclusion?"

"His left epaulet has been repaired."

"That may simply be due to the difficulties of reaching California. There's probably a shortage of gold-bullion epaulets in the province."

"It has been repaired twice, and one of the repairs is not recent. The second one covers the first, except for one corner."

"Brilliant girl. I hope you've developed some scheme to make your own way upon your return to England."

"Why should that concern you now?" she asked in astonishment.

"Because you've just demonstrated your unsuitability for marriage. You're too observant. You would notice stray black hairs, even though your husband took care to wear a dark waistcoat. You'd see that the mud on his boots came from the alley behind the theater where he admired a young actress. You'd smell attar of Oud upon his shoulders, when the only scent you use is lavender. Oh, I've very nearly strayed to the forbidden subject, although you're the one who has led me there."

"It's always the woman who's to blame?"

"We men are very weak. Our minds circle upon one subject, even when duty calls to battle, or to make an illegal trade with the Californians."

"So what's our next step?"

"Between us, or in the matter at hand?"

"In the matter of getting food from these people," she said angrily. "There's nothing between us."

"You're mistaken. There's much between us. I'm coming to depend upon you."

"Then cease, for I'll not be here any longer than necessary."

He sighed the wretched sigh of a forlorn lover. Dina hoped his was a pose, for she was not certain how she would handle his advances, here in the cool dark of the cabin.

"Much depends upon the Spaniards' next move," he said seriously. "If we're contacted by Don Miguel first, it may indicate that he wants to make some arrangement. Then again, we might receive a peremptory order to depart from the governor tomorrow morning, or wake to find the Spanish frigate blocking our way out of the bay. I hope not the last, for I'd not look forward to spending the next few years in a Spanish prison, or losing the *Pearl Stallion.*"

"What do you make of the soldier's arrangement with Hampton?" she asked. "Could it be a trap? Would they capture our surgeon and hold him hostage for our good behavior?"

"Possibly, but I doubt it. The man wants something to win his lady's heart, and needles seems a strange request. Inventing a trap, a man would have asked for something romantic—silk, perhaps, or tea."

"If that's true, it betters your chances of selling the cargo."

"Betters *our* chances, my dear Doña Endina. You're in this deeply."

"More deeply than I could ever have imagined. If needles are scarce, what about tin pots and pans and basins. Perhaps you should send a gift to the commandant of the fort. Are there any suitable gifts on board for the governor and Don Miguel?"

"I never travel without an assortment of gifts, and the things I'd planned for Baranov should do even for someone as grand as Don Miguel. They'll be sent off at first light."

"It's against my nature to beg, Captain, but might I ask for a few yards of the cloth before it's bartered away to the Californians? My gowns have all but fallen apart."

"From what we've seen so far, I don't think this place can furnish you with a modiste, or a milliner."

"I'll manage the sewing myself," Dina said proudly.

Chapter Twelve

In the morning Dina found the ship wrapped in layers of mist and fog. Water dripped from the furled sails, slid down the lines and formed ever-changing patterns on the deck as the ship heaved easily in the small swells of the bay. Mr. Becker stood aft, his eyes on the shore.

"Good morning, Lady Dina," he said formally. He rarely spoke to her, seldom gave her more than a morning greeting.

"Good morning, Mr. Becker." She was aching to know if anyone had arrived from the fort.

"The captain?" she asked hesitantly.

"Has gone ashore. With Dr. Hampton," he said.

"Someone came?"

"The priest from the mission across the sand hills."

Dina's heart fell. She'd been so certain Don Miguel would be waiting in the morning twilight, ready to make some arrangement that would give him control of the cargo. Could the Spanish frigate be hiding nearby? Had the Spanish already made Savage a captive? With her captain gone ashore, could the *Pearl Stallion*'s crew fight off an attack?

The clunk of oars came through the fog, but it was several minutes before the boat materialized. Dina leaned over the railing, hoping to see Savage returning, but the boat contained only the oarsman. The moment he was on board, he ran to the quarterdeck, handed a slip of paper to Mr.

Becker, then turned to Dina and gave her a similar note. The large letters read:

> Lady Dina, We are to dine with the commandant and his family. You will come ashore to meet us.

No signature, but the slashing black letters could have been written by only one person. They reminded her of the man—tall, dark, bold.

She wished she might dress with some care, but her second dress, of shadowed lavender, was in worse shape than the blue one. She had no choice but to wear exactly what she had worn the day before. She smiled wryly when she put the dress on, recalling the woman of only a year past, who had refused to wear a gown more than once during the season.

It *would* be possible to live on one hundred pounds a year, she realized. Perhaps she could sell her journal to some printer in London. Even twenty or thirty pounds would be of great assistance. Then what? A journal about the provincial town where she would make her home would have no market value at all. But a novel, she thought. She'd read enough of them. She would write one.

She went so far as to imagine the title page: *A Journal of a Voyage to Russian America, Spanish California, and the Sandwich Islands.* Her name would not appear, of course. *By a Lady.* That would give an air of propriety; demonstrate that she was not seeking notoriety. The men and women who frequented the salons would know, of course.

She combed her wavy hair. Soon she'd have to devise a way to get it under control, for it had grown out some since she'd left Calcutta. For now she simply brushed it back behind her ears and covered it with the tattered silk scarf.

When she climbed back on deck, the fog had cleared enough for her to see the shore. No one waited there, but a bustle of excitement permeated the ship. Some of the men came on deck prepared to go ashore. Their pigtails had been renewed, and most had put on clean shirts and trousers. They were obviously expecting to find some women waiting for them, Dina knew, and she smiled at the disappointment they'd experience when they stood on the empty, sandy beach. Then she remembered the woman in the bushes. Nature's urges would be resolved, somehow.

A group of horsemen came into view, and she instantly recognized Savage and Hampton, accompanied by a priest. They led a horse with an empty saddle that she supposed was meant for her.

She joined the sailors in the ship's boat. The closer they came to shore, the more unsettled Dina felt. The saddle was not designed for a woman. Where was she expected to ride? Her concern must have been plain on her face, for as he helped her from the boat, Savage pointed out the arrangement.

"There's a scarf hanging from the horn for your right foot. It's the best we could arrange."

He helped her mount. Dina wrapped her right leg around the saddle horn, and Savage shortened the stirrup for her left. While not exactly steady, Dina decided she could ride the few miles to the fort without falling off.

The Arguello family had gathered to welcome the visitors, and the elegance of the women made Dina blush, aware of her dowdy apparel. They wore brightly colored dresses, fashioned not as complete gowns but in two pieces, a bodice and a flounced skirt. The sashes around their waists were tied on the side and hung nearly to the bottoms of their skirts. The fringed ends sparkled with beads and bangles. Dr. Hampton translated their greetings and introduced her to the three women, Señora Arguello and two daughters, both in their teens. There was no time for feminine conversation, for the men arrived immediately—the governor, Don Miguel and the commandant.

The table service reflected the same mixture of European gentility and provincial poverty Dina had noticed the day before. Silver bowls stood beside roughly carved platters. Wine was poured from crude earthenware pots into elegant glassware.

Don Miguel served as Dina's dinner companion, but she did not receive a great deal of his attention, because he spent much of his time translating the conversations of the governor, the commandant and Savage. She ate silently—a soup of beef with tiny dumplings, and a dish of beef and vegetables cooked together, intensely flavored with peppers, onion and garlic. The bread was unfamiliar, very thin rounds of dough that bore the marks of the hot surface upon which they had been cooked. Señora Arguello, she noticed, did not bother with spoon or fork, but simply rolled the bread into a tube and scooped up the food from her plate.

"California," said Don Miguel, translating the governor's remarks, "is very precious to His Majesty. The English and Russians must look to their safety when they intrude into these territories."

"But the Americans?" protested Savage.

After translation, the governor thought for a moment, then spoke to Don Miguel while looking at Savage.

"Truly, we must be aware of the Americans," said Don Miguel, "but we do not go to war with them. Since Bonaparte so falsely sold Louisiana, a territory that historically belongs to Spain, to the Americans, we will be on our guard even against the Boston ships."

"But you trade with them?" questioned Savage, pressing the point. "Does your law apply to all nations, or just to some?"

"We have been forced to make accommodations occasionally," said Don Miguel. His voice did not convey the sad resignation with which the governor had uttered the words in Spanish. "The war in Europe makes it more and more difficult for the authorities in Mexico to furnish us the supplies we need."

Dina studied Don Miguel, trying to look beyond the unemotional words of the translator. He seemed totally indifferent to the governor's confession of illegal trading, and repeated it without evidence of approval or disapproval. If her suspicions about him were correct, sometime during the afternoon he would make a sly reference to a bargain, and if he made it to her, she must be ready to arrange a meeting between him and Savage.

The dinner ended with fruits preserved in honey. Watching the women move about the room, Dina decided their costumes were immensely practical. There was no need to wash the entire garment if dirt spotted the skirt or bodice. Their skirts did not brush the floor, but ended slightly above the toes of their slippers. By adding or subtracting flounces, Dina saw, the garments might be made very suitable for life aboard ship. When the company left the table, she abandoned Don Miguel and found Dr. Hampton.

"Could you please tell the ladies I admire their clothes?" she requested. After he had translated, she continued: "I'm very much in need of new garments, and would like to learn to make some after their fashion."

This remark brought cries of delight. Their rapid Spanish tumbled over Hampton's attempts at translation, but gradually she learned she was being invited to stay with the family. Hampton went to fetch Savage as Dina was embraced by three excited women.

"I believe they will help me make myself some new clothes," she told him. "If you could spare me some of the cloth, I'll pay you when we reach Calcutta." My uncle will owe me quite a sum from my allowance, she thought.

"We'll settle in Calcutta. What do you need?"

Hampton made a list in his tiny pocket diary and volunteered to return to the ship. Dina found herself escorted to a private area of the house, to view the more elegant pieces of the *señora*'s wardrobe. Through gestures, she made the women understand that she needed practical garments, not bodices of velvet and flounces of lace. But her hands strayed to a large shawl of creamy Chinese silk, heavily embroidered with peonies in shades of pink and rose. "I shall get one in China," Dina said, knowing no one understood her.

Finally an ox cart arrived at the door, laden with enough fabric to make three wardrobes. The driver handed Dina a note.

"Give the more elegant pieces to Doña Arguello and her daughters. Thus do we bribe the fair sex to break down the intransigence of the other."

The *señora* gasped as the bundles were unwrapped, and when Dina handed her a length of cloth of gold and showed her with gestures that it was hers to keep, the woman had to sit down. Dina appeased the envious daughters with velvets.

Where had these come from? Savage had admitted to having a stock of cotton and wool, but not these beautiful things. At the bottom of the box were packets of pins and needles, hanks of thread and silken embroidery floss.

Servants were called in to join the sewing circle. Needles flew, and Dina found it difficult to watch all the operations: the sewing, the measuring and the cutting of the fabric for her skirts and petticoats.

The sewing was interrupted by a servant who passed small glasses of a sweet liqueur. Under the influence of the alcohol, the speed of the needles declined, and so did the conversation, making it possible for Dina to pick up a few words in the few hours remaining before sunset.

By the time of the evening meal, Dina was dressed in a blue bodice over a bell-shaped skirt of darker blue. Her inadequate petticoats were filled out by some from her hostess's wardrobe. She felt properly dressed, and was certain she could duplicate the outfit herself, once she was back on board the *Pearl Stallion.*

The meal consisted of more flat bread, beans, and some boiled vegetables Dina did not recognize.

"Has your day been pleasant?" inquired Don Miguel. After hours of hearing nothing but Spanish, she had to think a moment before she was able to answer in English.

"Lovely. It's pleasant to be off the ship for a day. And yours?" She hoped he would give some hint about his negotiations with Savage.

"I rode down the peninsula," he said. "A great whale was sighted in the surf, although by the time I arrived it had moved away from the shore and seemed of a mind to rejoin its fellows in the deep."

He hadn't been with Savage at all? She wondered where the captain and Hampton had gone.

As the sky darkened, she realized they intended for her to spend the night. At first she resisted, but as fog rolled in, she decided she would rather stay in the warm adobe than walk or ride to the shore in the chilly wind. The bed was a rather crude affair, nothing more than a wooden frame with rawhide stretched between the sidepieces. But the sheets over the grass-filled mattress were of linen, and the plump feather pillows were covered with linen edged in lace. For the first time in months, she lay in a bed that did not swing with the motion of the sea.

She had enjoyed her day immensely. With the Señora and Señoritas Arguello there was no need to justify her past, even if she had known the words to explain. Life with Aunt Lily and Emily, she now realized, had been a constant strain. Perhaps these California women thought her very strange, a woman who traveled alone on a ship full of men, but they were gracious enough not to speak of it. Or let it affect the way they treated her.

She drifted into sleep, but woke within an hour. The bed and house were rooted to the ground. She had spent too many nights lulled to sleep by the eternal motion of the sea. How long would it take, once she was home in England, before she no longer thought of the ocean, before the *Pearl Stallion* became nothing but a subject for hilarious tales in salons? How long before the memory of Savage no longer caused a flush on her skin and a contraction in her belly?

The next day, a crowd of men, and half a dozen women, appeared for the midday meal. She found no chance to speak to Savage, although he nodded at her and smiled at her new blue dress. She looked forward to talking to him at the dining table, but instead she was ushered into a smaller room where she, the Arguello women and the other female guests dined separately. Something, obviously, had to be done to draw Don Miguel into the open. Savage, she knew, had made no contact with him during the morning, for she and the other women had sat happily in the sunshine, plying their needles, while Don Miguel saddled and experimented with a variety of horses in the nearby paddock.

After finishing their meal, the women joined the men in the large dining room. To Dina's surprise, two musicians, one with a guitar, another with a violin, played in the corner, and the sweet liqueur of the afternoon before was passed around. An older gentleman, wearing a gold sash, approached Señora Arguello and offered his hand while moving his feet in time with the music. The *señora* stood, went to the center of the room, lifted her full skirts to the side, turned twice in the measure of a dance, then went back to her chair.

The man approached the older women one by one. Dina watched with trepidation, knowing her turn would come eventually. She followed the ritual as well as she could, and was rewarded with applause.

Once the dancing became general, Dina found herself opposite nearly all of the men at one time or another. A few more women appeared, and the line of the minuet became longer. The orchestra grew, too, with the addition of another violin.

Dina looked down the line of dancers as she turned on her partner's arm. Savage had one of the *señoritas* as his partner, and his smile was flirtatious. Dina's heart skipped a beat as she remembered that smile from another dance. The girl dropped her eyes, but not in modesty. She displayed her lashes with great skill, then looked at the captain again in adoration.

Instead of doing something productive, Savage is flirting with a child, she thought angrily. She sought out Don Miguel. She lowered her lashes, then looked up at him and smiled a gentle, seductive smile. She'd take matters into her own hands.

"Are you enjoying yourself, Doña Endina?" asked Don Miguel.

"Very much. I haven't danced since Calcutta."

"You miss your bright life in England?"

"Very much. As soon as we return to Calcutta, I'm sailing to England." But not back to my bright life, she thought.

After the dancing, a supper was laid in a smaller room to the side. The dancers crowded about the table; they scooped up beans and stewed beef with the flat bread, drank wine, and flirted. Don Miguel drew Dina aside.

"Would you like to see the moonlight on the water?" he whispered. "The moon has come up, and is most beautiful."

"I would love to," she replied. A breath of fresh air would not be amiss, and this might be the moment when Don Miguel would betray his interest in dabbling in trade. Working through her would be the most discreet way of handling it.

They walked across the hard-packed plaza in the center of the adobe buildings. Don Miguel led her beyond the cluster of buildings and the noise of the crowd.

The moonlight formed a band of silver across the bay. Dina gasped, for the *Pearl Stallion* lay in that shining ribbon. Her hull and masts were defined against the glowing water, a ship of jet sailing in a sea of quicksilver. As they stepped to the edge of a sandy hill, a gust of wind caught them. Dina shivered in the blast, and wished she had a shawl.

Don Miguel leaned over her. "You are cold. There is a small hut just a few feet from here. There we may observe the moon, but retreat from the wind."

The moon made deep shadows on the ground, and she followed his guidance as they dropped down the hill. The last whispers of noise from the houses above dropped away, and only the sigh of the wind in the low bushes caught her ear. A small square shape loomed before them.

Don Miguel pushed aside a cowhide hanging over the opening. As he had promised, a small window faced the bay, and through it the moon flooded the tiny room with light. Dina stepped toward the window, but his arm restrained her, pulled her backward and against him. His arms encircled her; she cried out as he forced her body against his own, one hand pressing on her stomach to tighten the fit of her hips against his.

"Do not bother to scream, little English one," he said. "No one will hear you."

She paid no heed to his advice, but shrieked as loudly as she could. She pushed against him, trying to force their bodies apart as he turned her in his arms, but he simply laughed. He placed his face against hers, tried to kiss her, but she lowered her head and butted him in the chest.

One twist of his arm, and she was on the floor, sitting stupidly with her legs sticking out from under her skirts. He dropped upon her before she had the presence of mind to jump up and make for the door; he forced her shoulders onto the floor. It was damp and cold beneath her.

"Bastard!" she shouted in his ear. "You damned bastard!" She writhed beneath him, making it impossible for him to control her. When his hands held her shoulders, she hit at him with clenched fists. When he grabbed her hands, she twisted away from him and kicked at his groin. He sat on her stomach, letting her struggle proceed, dodging her fists, laughing.

"It will happen, little one. Why exhaust yourself?"

She answered by pulling her knees up and rolling over, almost spilling him onto the floor. She heard her new dress rip in the struggle. He had something that felt like rawhide around her left wrist. He sprawled his body on top of hers and worked her left arm around until it touched what appeared to be a table leg.

She screamed as the rawhide strip tightened, then pounded on his back with her right fist. If he tied her, there was nothing she could do to protect herself. With her left hand secured, he wrestled for the right one. She thrust her arm beneath her body, but he pulled it free and looped rawhide about it. The cord cut tightly into her wrist. She sobbed when he pulled her right arm out at full length, trussed it so that her upper body was immobilized. She kicked out at him with her feet. Don Miguel moved to her side, out of range of her legs, and sat back on his haunches. The moonlight shone upon him, as if a lantern hung over his head.

"Are you comfortable, little one?" he asked sardonically. "I would have preferred not to do this, but you will not be still."

She snarled at him, out of breath from her struggles. She could see that he was opening his breeches. When the front flap hung loose, his hands went under her skirt, under the petticoats, and pushed them upward until she felt the cold ground with her bare thighs. She kicked him; he grabbed her ankles and spread them apart.

Dina's frustrated right hand flailed at the spot where the rawhide tied her down. She jerked at her right hand and felt a slight movement. Whatever held her, it was not solidly planted.

She had to do something, for Don Miguel's hands were sliding upward, grasping her knees, then her thighs. She tried to kick him, but her legs were too far apart, and he was slowly moving up, up between them. Her thighs trembled under his cold fingers. This must be what it felt like to be possessed by the devil.

She clutched frantically at whatever held her right hand. Her fingers closed upon a shaft of rough wood. Just then, his body lowered upon hers, and she felt the length of him between her thighs.

"You should feel sorrow for me," he said. "I am staying in a house with three women, and not one is available to me."

With one determined heave, she swung her weighted right arm, which had been strengthened by the days of hefting the sextant. She had no chance to plan the arc of her blow, but in an instant he was gone from her, lying on his side on the floor of the hut. She gazed stupidly at her right hand, now resting on the left side of her body. Her wrist was tied to a strange, heavy hammer, the head of which had been pecked from stone. She dragged the right hand to the table leg and loosened the knots that bound her. Don Miguel took one shuddering breath. She thought about hitting him again, but he lay still. She scrambled to her feet, grasped the hammer, shoved the heavy hide aside and stepped into the brilliant moonlight.

Which way to go? The ship still lay in the moon's glowing path, which looked for all the world like a road she could walk upon, run upon, to the refuge of the *Pearl Stallion.* She stumbled straight down the hill, straight toward that brilliant road, paying no attention to the bushes that grasped at her skirts.

"Lady Dina!" someone cried. She sobbed with relief. It was Hampton. She staggered in the direction of the voice, saw three silhouettes, one of them Savage's.

"Dina?" asked Savage. "What are you doing out here?"

"Don Miguel," she said, and wished her voice was normal. How could she possibly explain? "I killed him." She struggled to hold up her right arm, lifted it with her left to show the hammer still tied at the wrist. A snarl, like that of a wounded animal defending its young, encompassed her.

"Where he?" It was Charley.

"Charley. Hampton," said Savage, his voice hard and calm. "Take her back to the ship."

"Untie this thing from my wrist," she begged. "Take it back to that hut. Some worker will miss it."

Savage's big fingers struggled with the tight knots. He finally took the rawhide strip in his teeth and wrenched the thing apart.

"Get her to the ship," he ordered. She walked between Hampton and Charley, concentrating on making her feet touch the ground with each step. Moisture ran down her thighs. Could it be blood? How? She'd murdered him before he had a chance to finish.

Murder! Her dreadful peril rose up to meet her like a wall. Not just her own danger, but the danger she'd created for everyone on the ship. She'd murdered Don Miguel, crushed his skull. What would happen to the trade Savage needed to make? The ship? The crew? She moaned in distress when they lifted her into the boat and rowed her to the *Pearl Stallion*.

Hampton guided her steps down the companionway, and she realized he planned to take her to his domain on the orlop. He'd undress her, treat her bruises, and he'd know what had happened.

"My cabin," she begged.

"I should see how much you're hurt, Lady Dina," he said soothingly.

"No. I'll take care of myself."

Chapter Thirteen

Dina sat on her bunk, her back against the bulkhead, her legs drawn up protectively. She had washed herself and found, not blood, but a smear of moisture on her thighs. Her wrists hurt where Don Miguel had bound her; her rump, where she had landed when he threw her to the floor, ached, and she was certain it was bruised. She still shook with fright, but she was, oddly enough, very satisfied. A man had finally tried to do what she'd dreaded for years, but he'd paid for it. And so would any other man who tried. I shouldn't have let Savage take the hammer back, she thought. But it would have been an awkward weapon to carry about.

She dreaded the moment when Savage would return and confront her with what she'd cost him. He'd be terribly angry. No trade could possibly be arranged now. In fact, he would have to leave as soon as possible, sail the *Pearl Stallion* out of the harbor before the governor and commandant found Don Miguel's body. Would he leave her behind to face the consequences of her murder? She hoped all the crew members were close by, so that no one would be abandoned in the hurried departure.

She waited for the knock, the voice of Kranz or some other member of the crew telling her the captain wanted to see her in the main cabin. Prepared as she was, she jumped in fright when the knock came, heavy and leaden against the planks of the door.

"Yes," she croaked. Then "Yes," again, more loudly.

No answer, no request. Savage opened the door and stooped beneath the frame. He hung the lantern he carried upon the hook in the beam, pulled the door closed and joined her on the bunk. The ropes by which it was suspended creaked in protest at the weight.

"We'll have this matter out here, where we're not so likely to be overheard."

She drew her legs up closer to her chest, hugging her knees.

"What in the circles of Satan possessed you to go out with that Spaniard?" he hissed. His voice contained all the threat of a serpent ready to pounce. There was no way to retreat from him, for he filled the tiny space, a dark bulk magnified by the flickering light.

"He asked me to see the moon come up across the bay," she replied weakly.

"You're the most inept flirt the *ton* has ever produced," he said. "By God! Don't you know Spanish women may flirt, but always in public? They're never alone with a man. By accepting his invitation, with no companion, you proved you were willing."

"I knew him in England," she said stoutly. "He never tried such a thing in London."

"Because he knows that to live in Rome one does as the Romans. But we're no longer in London, just in case you haven't noticed," he said sarcastically. "You're in his territory now, and he had every reason to expect you to be pliant and accommodating."

"I did it for you!" she shouted, determined to resist his sarcasm, while deeply ashamed of what she had done.

"For me?" His eyebrows, that single dark band across his forehead, separated and raised. "You think perhaps now I'll ask you to marry me, since another man found you so attractive he tried to rape you. At least I'm assured he means nothing to you—" he sneered "—since you've not inquired after his condition."

"Condition?" she squealed in surprise. "I didn't kill him?"

"Gave him a very large lump on the head, but no, so far he's with us. I don't believe he remembers exactly how it happened."

"Doesn't remember?" she gasped. "Doesn't remember he tied me up?"

"It will all come back to him, in a few days. We can hope he'll be excessively ashamed of himself, and feel he got the punishment he deserved, but I doubt our hopes will be realized. His kind think women exist for his uses."

Dina felt a great weight melt from her shoulders. She hadn't killed Don Miguel. But the weight was replaced by a growing lump of fear, knotted in her chest.

"More likely he'll have me arrested for attacking him," she said shakily.

"No, he won't. First, because you're not leaving the ship again. You're confined to the *Pearl Stallion,* for I can't risk having you divert more wind from my sails. Second, he won't say a thing about the affair, because no man likes to admit to having failed at ravishment, particularly when the woman slammed a stone hammer into the side of his head. I suppose he didn't think you were strong enough to lift the thing."

"I wouldn't have been strong enough a few months ago. Taking noon bearings..."

"Saved you from rape. I'm pleased that somehow I, at one or two removes, am responsible for your deliverance," he said with elaborate irony.

"I went because I was trying to get something started with Don Miguel," she protested.

"If you wanted to get something started with Don Miguel, you succeeded very smartly!" He laughed his belly laugh and tossed back his head.

"I mean about the trade," she said in irritation. She itched to slap him, but she knew all too well his strength, and had experienced what happened when it was combined with anger. "I've been watching, and for two days nothing has been done. Yesterday Don Miguel went down the peninsula to see a whale, and this morning he rode horses, while you—"

"Am making the arrangements," he said bluntly.

"What arrangements?"

"For the trade. It will go very smoothly, if you just keep your graceful hands to your sewing and leave the rest to men who know what they're doing. Don Miguel's death would have made things very difficult, if not impossible. Your effort to draw him out did me no favor.

"You don't know the rules, so you should not play the game." He was using his quarterdeck voice. "Henceforth, whenever we're in port, you're confined to the ship, unless I request your presence ashore."

"I nearly ruined things, didn't I?" she whispered.

"Yes. While you were of some use in Pavlovsk, you are a great deal in the way here."

Dina hated the fact that her eyes overflowed; she felt a tear run down each cheek. She had so wanted to be of help.

"But then, Don Miguel is a very poor excuse for a man," he said soberly, shaking his head. "No wonder Miss Strawn had no use for him. You would, quite probably, have found him unpleasant, no matter what the circumstances. I, on the other hand..."

"You expected me to yield to you!" she shrieked, the memory of the evening at the Allinsons clearer than that of the one she had just experienced. "You laughed at me!"

"And I let you go. Please do remember that. I let you go without needing a whack on the head to convince me."

"And I thank you," she whispered, unwillingly. "I'm sorry I very nearly ruined everything." She sat upright suddenly. "What do you mean, the arrangements are being made? You haven't seen Don Miguel, except this evening."

"They progress without the interference of the Spanish dandy. Everything will be handled through the padres at the mission."

"The priests?" she cried.

"Yes. It seems they're the Californians most vocal in their criticism of the government restrictions on trade. They have hundreds of converts to feed and clothe, but very little opportunity to exchange the fruits of their labor for things from the outside. They tempt the native inhabitants of California into their establishments with promises of trinkets, but the trinkets are very scarce."

"And the governor? And Don Miguel?"

"Will look the other way. Technically, I shall give the entire cargo to the mission fathers as a donation. They, in return, will fill the *Pearl Stallion* with wheat and beans and strange-looking vegetables, as a gesture of goodwill toward their Russian brothers."

"Why didn't you tell me?" she exclaimed. "I'd never have gotten myself involved with Don Miguel if I'd known!"

"You've been busy with your wardrobe," he said. "The proper interest of a woman, I suppose. But dresses are not too practical aboard a ship. I thought you were certainly safe in the company of the commandant's women. It never occurred to me that you'd foolishly expose yourself to the kind of danger you did."

"How did you know I was with him?" she asked suddenly.

"Charley saw the two of you go, and when you disappeared over the sand hills, he came to get me."

"Thank you. But I managed to get away myself, and didn't need you," she said proudly.

"Indeed you did. Where were you planning to make your retreat?"

"Back here. Back to the ship."

"The *Pearl Stallion* is your safe haven?" he asked.

"I suppose so," she said in wonder. "She was my refuge in Calcutta, and here I felt just the same."

"No feeling about the captain, then?" he asked, grinning. "Captain Savage is not the calm harbor you sail to?"

"The ship," she said firmly.

"I've made your excuses to Señor and Señora Arguello. You will stay on board—"

"Because you can't trust me." She completed his words bitterly.

"That, and because I don't trust Don Miguel, once he recalls who so soundly thrashed him about the ears. Some men, once defeated by a woman in such matters, are more determined than ever to complete their plans, in any way possible."

"Could you please see that my things are brought back to the ship? I'll get some sewing done."

He took the lantern, leaving her to the dark and to the growing pain in her backside. Thank heavens! Don Miguel wasn't dead, and she wasn't a murderess.

"I taught him a lesson he'll not forget," she snarled to herself. Or at least, would not if he ever recalled what had happened.

She dozed sitting up, but did not really sleep. Whenever she sank into a moment's deep repose, troubling dreams stalked the edge of her consciousness and she jerked awake.

Dina sat in a hammock chair in the stern, watching and listening to the efforts of the crew as they unloaded the ship, bale by bale, chest by chest. A few small boats came out from the shore to help carry the cargo, each transporting a strange load of its own. Coarse bags of grain, baskets of melons, earthenware jars, that might contain anything from beans to wine.

The days passed in a regularity of fog and sunshine. The mornings were warm and delightful. The sun drove away the low clouds, and she could sit on deck, pleasuring in a slight breeze. Later a cold wind drove her into the main cabin, and with it came the enveloping fog.

The noon observations were taken faithfully each day, much to her amusement, for the ship did not stray by more than a few yards. But she dutifully joined in with the officers, and daily thanked the sextant for the strength it had given her arms.

Most days she sat and sewed and thought, for her experience had given her much to think about. Not about the hurts, which vanished in a few days. But about the ship, and the affection she had for it, and its captain, who had insinuated that he would be more than willing to be her refuge in time of crisis. The more she considered the situation, the more she had to admit that Savage might be her shelter. As he had rudely pointed out, he had not violated her, but had allowed her to leave when she was in his power.

So perhaps she could trust him, more than any other man. Ever since that horrible night when he flew at her in anger and jealousy, Savage had been considerate, sometimes even gentle. He had spoken to her harshly after her encounter with Don Miguel, but he might have done worse. She didn't resent being confined on the ship. In fact, the thought of facing Don Miguel made her stomach queasy, and she was glad a quarter mile of sea stood between her and that possibility.

The shadow of the mizzen sail crossed her work as the sun moved. The shadow darkened suddenly.

"Hold out your hands," Savage ordered.

Dina dropped her sewing and obeyed. Whatever he held was completely concealed in his huge fist. He grasped her hand and closed her fingers around something round, waxy, slightly rough.

"An orange!" she cried.

"Small, but an orange nonetheless."

"I haven't had any fruit since..." She racked her brain trying to remember the last meal when there had been a bit of pineapple.

"Since we left the China Sea," he said.

"You look pleased with yourself," she said playfully, in answer to the smile that wreathed his face.

"The cargo is unloaded down to the pig iron."

"And when will that be taken out?"

"I've decided to keep it until we reach the Sandwich Islands. If I give it to the Californians, I'd have to take on rocks as ballast. On the islands I may be able to buy sandalwood to take its place."

"Why sandalwood?"

"It's one of the few things the Chinese will accept. Sandalwood and furs. All we must do is get out of this place whole and we have prospects of a cargo of both furs and sandalwood, the best possible."

"Aren't you worried about the Spanish frigate?" she asked hesitantly.

"Hampton's friend, the man who wanted needles for his sweetheart, told Hampton the frigate always lands first in Monterey. A messenger rides from Monterey to the fort here, to warn them they'll have company in a few weeks. In return for a bit of red silk, the good soldier is going to warn us as well."

Dina looked toward the shore, at the gangs of sailors wrestling bags and boxes into small boats.

"And the sailors? Are they staying close enough that we can leave quickly?"

"No one goes farther than the mission, which is about three miles away. The place has taken on something of the air of a fair since we've arrived. Families from the south have come to look over the goods we've brought, as well as hauling up carts full of food to trade for it. The news is spreading fast."

"And I suppose the sailors have added their own sort of gaiety to the affair," she said sardonically.

"Naturally."

His pleasantries nearly overcame her good sense, and she was close to asking him if he'd found a woman for himself. One glance at his face—his mouth a straight, thin line, a muscle working in his jaw—made her swallow the words.

Savage lay in his bunk and made himself think about the puzzle of the California weather. How could the nights be so chilly here, in the depths of summer, in a southern latitude? The explanation must lie in the configuration of the land, which drew in the fogs of the sea.

He shivered under his blankets, and not just from the cold. Were the Californians playing him for a fool? Waiting, delaying the loading of the ship, until the frigate came? Hampton had not spoken to the sergeant for two days, and when he inquired about the man, he'd been told he had gone south. If he was not at the fort, how would he warn them the frigate was on its way?

Savage listened to the sounds the ship made, swaying gently at anchor. Perhaps he should pull out at first light. Leave the last few cartloads of provisions on shore. The wind whispered faintly in the standing rigging, and the ship moved. He struck a flint and steel and lighted a candle, looked at the compass on the beam over his head. The breeze was from the south. He forced himself to extinguish the candle and lie down again. Fretting himself into a fever would not help at all.

A suggestion of voices whispered over the water. The men camped onshore were talking. They must have been awakened by a scavenger trying to get at the food that had come down late in the evening on two ox carts. A faint creak from the other side of the bulkhead told him Dina had turned over in her sleep. The sound brought unwelcome thoughts of her, and he tried again to make his brain concentrate on the puzzle of the California climate.

The distant sound of oars being unshipped, a splash as the oarsman let them drop in the water, brought him out of his bunk. He pulled on his jacket and boots, the only things he'd taken off when he came down to sleep. No one should be about in a boat at this time of night. Ten men were ashore, including Lightner, as the officer, and Charley.

Savage made no effort to be silent in the companionway, which he took two steps at a time. He arrived on the deck so quickly the boat was less than halfway to the ship. "What's going on?" he demanded of Loti, without ceremony.

"Don't know, sir. Can't hardly see, the moon not up. But something woke the men onshore, for I heard talking."

Savage paced twice across the deck, knowing it was useless to do anything until the sailors in the boat reported. The problem might be simple. Perhaps some of the men had run off to the mission against orders. Perhaps they found it impossible to sleep because of the rats and sand fleas. His heart pounded, because he knew it was nothing simple. Only a major problem would cause them to send a boat. He prayed that Charley was one of the oarsmen, for the big islander could move a boat faster across the water than anyone else aboard.

He laid his hand upon the cannon that stopped his progress. The bronze was damp and cold. He forced himself to stand still for several seconds, then turned to face the shore once more. He could make out Charley's shape in the starlight, the bend of his back as he strained at the oars. The boat pulled around the ship and came up against the side out of sight of land. Something was wrong to demand such secrecy, and Savage's heart bounded into his throat.

The man who scrambled up the side wore the leather jacket of the common soldiers at the fort. His legs, clad in light-colored breeches, were visible in the starlight as they swung over the gunwales. They seemed disembodied, separate from the dark torso.

"Señor Capitán," he began.

"Go down and get Hampton," Savage ordered and Loti dropped through the hatch in a rush. Everyone on the ship knew the significance of a secret visit from a Spanish soldier. Savage leaned over the railing until he could see Charley in the dark boat on the dark water.

"What's happened?"

"Soldier, he come running, point to ship, look mighty afraid."

Of course, Charley couldn't tell him anything more. He didn't understand Spanish. Hampton scrambled onto the deck wearing a white nightshirt which reflected the starlight, leaving his head and hands part of the shadows.

"Is this your friendly sergeant?" Savage asked, pointing to the Californian.

"No." Hampton turned to the soldier and spoke to him, releasing a long volley of Spanish from the man. Hampton did nothing but nod to keep the one-sided conversation going at full gallop. Finally he waved the man into silence.

"The frigate is in Monterey," Hampton translated. "The governor left a message with the commander at Monterey to send the ship here immediately. Don Luis suspected the sergeant had turned traitor, for he foolishly showed off the scarlet silk I gave him. They've locked him up. This man says we've got to leave immediately, for the frigate will be here tomorrow, the next day at the latest."

"Why did he come to warn us?" asked Savage suspiciously. What might the Californians gain by having the *Pearl Stallion* leave now, in a rush? A few hundred pounds of flour?

Hampton spoke to the soldier. The Spaniard drew himself up with dignity, as someone does when he has been insulted. Savage noticed that a grimace, as of pain, accompanied the movement. The soldier stripped off his coat, threw it to the deck. His face twisted and his teeth clenched as he lifted his arms to draw his rough shirt over his head.

The man's back was furrowed, gray in the starlight. When Loti raised a lantern, Savage saw the blood where the lash had dug into the flesh. The man spoke a few determined words.

"He wants to come with us," translated Hampton.

"Get him below, where he can't cause any trouble, and tell every man on board to get on deck, quietly," said Savage to Hampton. "Quietly," he repeated. A thousand thoughts chased one another around his head. Another bad consequence of flogging. A man who has been flogged may betray you.

"Mr. Loti," Savage said slowly and thoughtfully, "go back with Charley, find out what's still on the beach. Put everything that must come aboard in a pile close to the landing. None of the provisions. Put any grain, flour or wine in a second pile. We'll bring them out if we have time."

Becker stood at his elbow. "Mr. Becker, trouble onshore. Get every boat in the water."

Savage walked to the quarterdeck, but could see nothing on shore except the looming sand hills. Lightner had had the good sense not to strike a light and warn the sentries at the fort that the shore party had been roused. Watching the sand run through the glass under the binnacle light, Savage made himself concentrate on how he was going to get the ship out of the enclosed harbor.

How soon would the moon come up? Not until an hour or so before dawn, and then only a poor sliver of a thing. He looked east, and was pleased to see no brightness over the distant mountains. A faint splash of oars warned of the approach of a boat.

"Captain," called Loti in a hoarse whisper. Savage leaned over the side to see his shadow in the dim light.

"Everything's in the boats, including all the wheat, and two tuns of wine."

"Good. The men?"

"Only two left onshore. I'll get them next trip." Already men were heaving the heavy sacks onto the deck.

"C-Captain," Loti stammered. His face was turned upward and caught the starlight. "Something else wrong."

"Yes." Savage's heart skipped a beat. Everything that might have gone wrong danced through his mind.

"Mr. Lightner ain't there."

"What?" yelled Savage. He gripped the rail and leaned over even farther, risking getting hit by a sack of wheat. He moderated his voice. If one of the men had yelled like that, he would have sent him below.

"Where's he gone? Does anyone know?" he asked in a calmer voice.

"Don't know. He told Charley he'd be back before moonrise."

"Before moonrise, we'd better be out of this harbor," snapped Savage. "As soon as you can, send someone out here who knows the whole story. He must have told someone where he was going and why."

The next boat brought three men and a load of the big orange gourds the Californians called *colache.* The men took great delight in tossing them from the boat to the deck, where other men caught them.

"Where's Lightner?" he growled at the first man on deck.

"At the mission. Said he'd be back before moonrise."

"What's he doing at the mission? I ordered everyone to stay at the landing place."

"Woman," said the sailor starkly. "Lightner's well-nigh gone mad over a woman there. Says she's the best thing he's had since he was a lad in Scotland."

"When did he leave?"

"Just before dark."

"Hell!"

Another boat appeared out of the darkness.

"Get aboard," he ordered, remembering to speak quietly and calmly. "We're weighing anchor in a few minutes."

He looked up at the feathered vane hanging in the rigging. Just enough breeze to get out of the harbor, and, thank God, it stayed in the south.

"Sir," said a voice at his elbow. He looked down at the top of Loti's head. "Are we going to leave Mr. Lightner?"

"Yes. There's no time to wait for him."

"I'll go get him."

"Do you know where he is in the mission?"

"No, sir. But I can look . . ."

"Search through dozens of rooms, and rouse everyone so they can warn the fort we're bidding them adieu? Lightner disobeyed orders."

"But, sir, who's to be navigator, if not Mr. Lightner?"

"That's my concern, Mr. Loti. You see to those men swinging in the boat."

"Who's to be navigator?" he muttered to himself. He very nearly sent someone down to wake her, but his spirit rebelled. Hell could freeze, but he'd not have that woman free to roam his ship, in a position to give orders to his men, standing on the deck in a skirt that caught the wind and plastered against . . .

It was his first thought of Dina since he'd come on deck, and he congratulated himself that he was not so far gone that he couldn't concentrate in an emergency. She should, of course, be warned of what was happening. He looked about, but everyone was quietly working, preparing to set sail.

She opened the door on the first knock, dressed, so she must have been awake for some time.

"What's going on?"

"We're leaving immediately. The frigate's in Monterey."

"But I thought—"

"I don't have time to explain now. Stay here. The cannons at the fort will fire on us as we round the point. If it gets bad, go down to Dr. Hampton on the orlop."

"Is it because of what I did?" she cried in anguish.

Was it? His mind raced through the possibilities, and at the same time his arm, acting almost independently, reached out to her, wrapped about her waist, pulled her close to him.

"No. They were planning all along to betray us, lull us into thinking we were safe, just waiting until the frigate came."

He patted her head with his hand, reassuring her. "It has nothing to do with you, what you did to Don Miguel."

When she didn't reply, he released her, except for her hand. Thoughtlessly, without considering his previous orders, he dragged her on deck, not quite understanding why he needed her there. She should stay in her cabin, or in the orlop.

"Boats secured, sir," said Loti, the moment Savage's head emerged through the hatch. "All aboard, except for Mr. Lightner."

"Up anchor, quietly. No chant."

"Lightner?" The sound of her voice enclosed him, breathless.

He kept his fingers crossed, out of sight, until the click of the ratchets came faster and faster. Thank heavens, the anchor wasn't fouled. Should he put on all the sail she could carry, and get out as fast as possible? Or raise just enough to give her motion through the water, hoping no one at the fort would spot the ghost ship until it was too late?

The commandant was no fool. The cannon were already loaded, and someone had been stationed to keep watch, in case the quarry tried to escape.

"Everything she can carry, Mr. Becker," he ordered. The sails glowed in the dim light, instantaneously changing the ship from passive to active.

While his mind paid strict heed to the ship and the men who stood awaiting his orders, some part of him watched her. She stood out of the way, at the same time carefully observing the quiet scrambling of the men about their duties. She smiled when the *Pearl Stallion* came before the wind and the great square sails were shaken free. She stepped forward and turned the glass when the last grain of sand had run its course.

She did not flinch when the shore batteries flashed in the midst of the black hillside, nor did she cower waiting for the impact of the balls. From that first flash, only one came aboard, putting a hole in the foresail. Of the second flash, no result was seen at all.

The horizon to the east glowed, and the crescent moon topped the undulating skyline, outlining the gigantic trees. He wondered if Lightner had reached the beach, and what he thought as he regarded the silvery bay, empty except for the crude boats of the Californians.

"Sail ho!" screamed someone from the maintop.

To the south, visible from the deck, were the topsails of the Spaniard, an evil glow in the faint moonlight. He drove the *Pearl Stallion* before the wind, depending on her sleek hull and the spread of her sails to outdistance the enemy. Three hours before noon, the threatening white spot sank below the horizon. They drove on, to put distance between them.

He turned, for the first time, to observe the deck, crowded with every soul on board. Loti and Barber stood quietly with their instruments. Becker watched the last grains of sand fall from the top of the glass and announced noon. The woman he had once thought only superficially attractive, the woman he loved, stood on the quarterdeck. She lifted the sextant. The blue gown she wore had short sleeves, with flounces dropping to her elbows. As her arms came up, the flounces fell away and he saw the strength of her fine muscles.

By damn! he thought joyfully. Don Miguel had taken on the wrong woman. He'd tried to dip himself into her for a taste, but she'd given him back a bitter draught. The Spanish bastard must still be nursing a headache, Savage thought happily.

"Lady Dina, set a course to pick up the North Pacific trades," he ordered. She looked at him, puzzled, pleading for help. He joined her in the main cabin, stood close as he explained the impossibility of sailing straight up the coast of North America and reaching the northwest coast with any degree of safety and certainty.

In one strangely long instant, he almost took her in his arms, almost spoke of how much he appreciated her intelligence and loyalty. He could trust her, and she would learn.

More important, when that moment passed, he knew he was strong enough to resist the temptation of her until his love vanished, as a pleasant fragrance might vanish, dissipating into the atmosphere.

"The navigator draws three shares of the profits from the voyage," he said gruffly.

Chapter Fourteen

Dina finally gave up in frustration and dismissed her class. Few of the men could concentrate with the black islands bordering New Archangel in view. Even the story of Sampson and Delilah held no attraction for her best readers, and the slower ones had long since lost interest in the plight of the Hebrews in Egypt.

Except for Radgni, the former shipyard worker, who glowered as he read of Pharaoh's tyranny. Dina feared he equated the story with the plight of his own India, systematically falling under the power of the British.

She had voiced her concerns to Savage. "Should I allow him to read about the Hebrews and their rebellion against the Egyptians? I'm afraid it rouses his resentment against the British in India."

"Of course they resent us," he had said with a dismissive wave of his hand. "And they'll rise up and throw us out someday, without needing inspiration from the story of Exodus."

Most of her days were taken up with teaching the Californian to speak and read English. Martin Alejandro, she had learned through days of halting conversation, had been accused of a crime in Mexico—a crime he insisted he had not committed. As a result, he had become a soldier and been sent to the northern frontier.

Her students carefully wrapped the Bibles borrowed from more literate crew members in canvas bags and returned them to the hammocks of their owners. Back on deck, they lined the railing, chattering like monkeys. Dina joined the officers on the quarterdeck. Savage acknowledged her presence with his eyes and nothing else. Since California, the relations between them had been of the coolest. He spoke to her only out of necessity, and she copied her mood from his. Polite, but not familiar. The relationship appropriate between a captain and one of his officers. One of his lesser officers. The lowest of those who stood on the quarterdeck. She wore one of the new gowns she'd made since they left California. She felt his glare, his disapproval of her new costumes, but she felt more comfortable appearing before the crew in skirts.

"Lady Dina." His voice brought her forward, out of her reverie.

"Are the manifests complete?"

"Yes, sir," she said firmly. The loading in California had been hasty and erratic. With Mr. Becker's help, she had inventoried the entire cargo and made three copies of the list, copies carefully stowed on a shelf beneath the chart table.

"Do you know German?"

"No, sir."

"Unfortunate. Baranov speaks only Russian and German. You'll come ashore with me. Bring the lists, and a book to take notes. I'll translate what I want you to write down."

"Yes, sir."

New Archangel was now in view. Human figures ran along the shore, men rushed down the hill, deserting half-completed buildings. At the boom of a cannon, Dina jumped, almost tumbled into Mr. Barber's arms. Savage saw her sudden fright and grinned.

"No hostile intentions now, Lady Dina. We're being welcomed."

In the weeks since the *Pearl Stallion* was last in port, the residents of New Archangel had been busy. New buildings stood where before there had been nothing but the dark wall of the forest. A stubby wharf stuck into the harbor.

Savage brought the ship quite close to it before he ordered the anchor dropped.

In her cabin, Dina put on a small bonnet she had fashioned from scraps of fabric left over from her dress. She had formed roses from the remnants of the silk scarf, and she flattered herself that the creation might be found acceptable in London. Before she had gathered up the manifest and a notebook from the main cabin, she heard the boat being lowered into the water. Savage was wasting no time in starting his negotiations with Baranov.

The crowd onshore continued to grow, and from her perspective in the small boat, nearly level with the water, they seemed threatening. Calls carried over the water, and she heard the question.

"*Pishcha?* Food?"

"They're asking if we've brought food, sir," she said to Savage.

He cupped his hands about his mouth and shouted at the crowd. They cheered, the roar echoing around the harbor, off the wall of forest. A group of men cleared a spot for the boat to land, for the crowd surged forward as if the tiny boat carried the cargo they desired.

In the center of the cleared spot stood a short man, thickly built. He wore a cap of fur, and his clothes were of skins. His hands were gnarled, the knuckles swollen with work, and his face was lined from exposure to the elements. Every other resident of New Archangel stepped aside as he walked toward Savage, his hands extended in greeting.

"*Mein gros freund!*" he exclaimed.

Dina struggled to keep her face under control. This shabby, aging creature was Aleksandr Baranov? The lord of Russian America? The man for whom the beautiful Anna had sacrificed herself?

"Comtesse Endine Wilmount," said Savage. Dina hastily extended her hand to the man and dipped into a low curtsy. She was taller than he. "His Excellency Aleksandr Baranov."

They were escorted into a room much like the one she had seen in Pavlovsk, except not so luxuriously furnished. The tables and chairs were rough, and had obviously been made on the spot, from trees cut as the land was cleared. She had nothing to do except sit quietly as the two men talked in a language she did not understand, except for the oaths. Savage's German was studded with an occasional curse in English, seemingly uttered with the best of intentions. An occasional Russian word strayed into Baranov's speech. Savage demanded the manifests; she furnished them.

The negotiations seemed to progress, for Baranov removed his hat occasionally and scratched his bald head, deep in thought. He finally slammed his hand down on the table; Savage did likewise. Both men smiled at her, which she found confusing. Had they been making some bargain that involved her?

"Go to the boat," said Savage out of the corner of his mouth. "Tell the men to return to the ship and collect the dishes the cook's preparing for the feast. Furthermore, half the crew may come ashore, but they must be warned not to eat anything here except fish, of which there seems to be a surfeit. We must not deplete their food supplies."

"Yes, sir," she said, and left the room after making a curtsy in the direction of Baranov.

I'm one of the crew, she thought happily as she walked to the wharf. *He would never before have trusted me with such a message, but things have changed.* She remembered that things had changed because poor Mr. Lightner had been abandoned in California, and she wondered for a moment how he was managing to survive in that enemy land. But even thoughts of Lightner couldn't dampen the delight she found in Savage's new regard for her. And in her new regard for herself. When she returned to the meeting hall, Baranov had disappeared. Savage grinned at her.

"Open the book," he commanded. Dina fumbled for her pencil.

"Eight thousand pelts," he said, almost furtively, "one quarter sea otter. The rest fox, wolf and seal, but we haven't settled the proportion yet. It will go our way. He wants our cargo badly, for some of the Russians have scurvy, despite pinecone beer."

She wrote frantically. "He wants everything we can spare, even salt beef and pork. Get Barber or Loti, whichever's left on board, to go through the barrels and figure out how much we need for the voyage to the Sandwich Islands. We'll give him all the fruit we picked up in California, for the islands can furnish us with a multitude more at practically no cost."

She made notes in a rapid shorthand. Did he expect her to take these orders to the ship immediately, or after the evening meal? Then she remembered that the Russians didn't include women in their feasting.

"Baranov has asked me to spend the night ashore, so you must convey my orders. Tomorrow morning, the whole crew at work emptying the ship. Tell Becker to put a small crew on refilling the water barrels and getting firewood. Tomorrow afternoon, the second half of the men can go ashore." She scurried to complete the notes.

"Anything else, sir?"

"Yes. As part of the bargain, I've agreed to come back next summer, with food. By the way, you have an otter skin. I told Baranov he must give you one, above what he's giving in trade. I explained that you are a fine lady of London society, and when you appear with a cloak trimmed with sea otter, it will start such a fashion he can ship the pelts to England, not struggle with the Chinese market."

"Thank you, sir. Was that what the table-slamming was about?"

"Yes."

Dina stood up to go.

"Where are you going? There's no need here to change for dinner," he said with amusement.

"I hadn't thought I would be included," she confessed.

"Yes, indeed. Baranov has three young naval cadets, all of noble family, in residence. They would be greatly disappointed if you were absent from the table. And you look quite stylish. Have I told you how much I like your California gowns?"

"No. I had supposed you didn't favor them."

"I do. Particularly the blue one. It goes with your eyes."

Their conversation was interrupted—quite fortunately, Dina thought—by Baranov, who returned dressed in antique black pantaloons and a faded coat that had once also been black. He had assumed a wig to cover his baldness, but the tattered thing would not stay on his head, so he held it in place with a white scarf tied under his chin. Dina's chest vibrated with suppressed giggles as she was escorted to the table by one of the young naval officers. The one of highest rank, she presumed.

The dinner table conversation was a bedlam of languages, English between herself and Savage, German between Savage and Baranov, and Russian among Baranov, the young cadets, and two other men whose occupations she had been unable to determine. She spoke her halting Russian to Baranov and her young companion, turned to Savage to translate from Russian to German to English when the conversation went beyond her limited vocabulary.

She ignored a second, muttered conversation among the three cadets. Witticisms in French, every phrase a sneering insult to Baranov. "*Le paysan, le mendiant.*" The peasant, the beggar.

Baranov signaled for Savage's attention, and spoke to him at some length.

"His Excellency inquires if you might be willing to become a resident of New Archangel," Savage relayed to Dina. "He has a child, a daughter..."

"Irina," said Dina, remembering the beautiful child who had curtsied to her in Pavlovsk.

Baranov beamed. "*Da. Irina.*"

"He would like to bring Anna Grigoryevna and both his children to New Archangel as soon as suitable accommodations have been built. He needs a governess, especially for the girl, for he desires that she grow up as an accomplished young lady. He fears he will insult you with the offer, but I assured him you had been seeking profitable employment of an honorable nature."

Dina could not have been more surprised if Baranov had asked for her hand in marriage. Several seconds elapsed before she collected her wits.

"You do not have to answer immediately," said Savage soberly. "We shall be here several days. But you might have worse offers."

"Tell him," said Dina slowly, "that I shall consider it. But that I must fulfill my obligations to you while the ship is in port, since you have so kindly trusted me with much of your writing and record keeping."

Savage translated her remarks to Baranov, who nodded seriously. The wig slid back and forth under its restraining scarf. One of the young gentlemen laughed derisively. A whispered French phrase floated past her ear. Dina sat erect, unable to breathe for the tight anger in her breast. One of the cadets had said, "It will not happen, for the captain will not give up the ship's whore."

She turned, glared into the three young faces. Every one of the three men blanched, clearly only now realizing she understood French. One tried to conceal his guilt under a sneering laugh, another bit his lower lip, and the third, the young man next to her, drew away.

When she spoke, she made each word distinct. "The crew of the *Pearl Stallion* is made up of gentlemen, down to and including the cook's boy. Which is more than can be said for the company at this table."

"Dina?" said Savage softly. His eyes asked her what had happened to call forth the angry tone.

"One of our companions misspoke," she said pleasantly, "and I corrected him."

"I wouldn't know," said Savage. "I never learned the language."

"His Excellency, does he understand French?" she asked, smiling.

"No."

"Then we shall cease using French at this table," she said, turning to the three cadets. "A gentleman finds no need to conceal his remarks within a language others at the table do not comprehend."

The conversation revived, mostly without any contributions from the cadets. Dina waited long enough that her departure could not be blamed on the hasty words, then excused herself. Savage walked with her to the wharf and the boat waiting for her there. Laughter and singing echoed throughout the village, and everywhere she looked she saw crew members hanging on the arms of brown-skinned women.

"What passed between you and the young nobility?" Savage asked.

Dina gave him a brief summary of the French conversation.

"Now that he knows you speak French, Baranov will be more insistent that you remain as governess for his daughter and son. He may offer you three, four times the salary you could command in England."

Dina shivered.

"I should not keep you standing here," he said apologetically. "The air is cold."

"I didn't shiver with the cold," she said stoutly, "but at the prospect of living in New Archangel, with the eternal company of Russian naval cadets who think the nobility of their birth gives them the right to come proud over others. People who are their superiors in all things except birth."

"You are of that nobility," he reminded her.

"So are you," she retorted.

"But I was never taught it," he said.

"I believe," she said seriously, "you may be one of the fortunate ones of our class."

She conveyed Savage's orders to the officers on board, then retired to her cabin. The long northern days were passing, and darkness crept into the bay, making it necessary to light lanterns. Dina carried one to her cabin, but soon put it out and lay in the darkness. Everything was working out very well; she should feel elated at Savage's success, for three shares of the profits were to be hers. Yet her spirit tossed with unease. She went back over the conversation to see what could possibly be making her unhappy. The behavior of the cadets was not enough to account for the dismal shadow oppressing her heart. She thought of the walk back to the boat, the dark women, the sailors.

In a flash she understood why Savage had so happily stayed on shore tonight. Baranov would offer him more than a bed. Under the sheets and the counterpane, a woman awaited the pearl stallion. She clasped her hands to her breast.

"It's none of my concern," she whispered. "I don't care what he does." But the ache in her thumping heart told her otherwise.

The *Pearl Stallion* danced over the long swells of the Pacific. Savage clung to the mizzen rigging, and Dina, so well had she practiced her resistance, felt no impulse to stare up at him.

"Lady Dina!" he called happily. "Come up! You must see this!" Dina looked doubtfully at the lines he expected her to climb. It would be difficult in a calm harbor, but at sea?

"Mr. Loti, help her," Savage ordered.

She'd never before climbed off the deck. She kicked off her makeshift boots and, with the young man's assistance, fit her stockinged feet over the rat lines. The men below would see up her skirts, she thought, but she was already on her way up, and to retreat now would give the men cause to laugh at their navigator.

"Don't look down," cautioned Mr. Loti beneath her. "Look up, to the place you intend to go."

She focused her eyes on Savage, moved her right hand and foot at the same time, grasped tightly with fingers and toes, moved her left. Savage was closer by eight inches. She glanced down, then jerked her head up, frightened by the distance to the deck.

"Come on!" cried Savage, gesturing with one hand and clasping his glass with the other. He held on to the rigging with his legs alone. She kept her eyes on him as she lifted herself another few inches, then a few more. His canvas trousers pulled tight over his thighs; his knees bent with the roll of the ship, pulling the fabric even tighter. Two more steps upward, and his hand was reaching down to help her.

She curled her feet around the ropes and leaned into the slope of the rigging.

"Safe?" he asked, and she nodded. He moved across the rigging until his body pressed against hers, forming a support for her. She leaned into him.

"Look," he commanded, thrusting the glass toward her.

"I can't let go," she protested.

"Of course you can. I'm holding you. Look, look where we're going."

She raised her head to the southwest and saw, jutting up from the sea, mountains and foaming clouds rising to the top of the heavens. The mountains were green-black against the rich sky, and none of them larger than a man's hand.

"I thought the Sandwich Islands would be larger," she said with disappointment.

"Plenty large enough for what we need. Here, look through the glass. I'll hold you." At the same time he thrust the glass into her right hand, he lifted his leg across her, so that she was pressed tightly into the ropes. She found it possible to release her hands and raise the heavy glass to the distant islands. A drum throbbed inside her, centered low, where his thigh pressed.

The mountains sprang closer, and she saw the black and green now as distinct tones. The sea around the mountains glittered, not like jewels, which only reflect light, but with a light of its own. And this light was absorbed into the mountains, so that they glowed with the black-and-green light of magical jet and emeralds. Suddenly she found the name of these islands too prosaic, too bland and English. It might do to call the dots on the map the Sandwich Islands, but the reality must have another name.

"What do the people who live on these islands call them?"

"Owyhee."

The drumbeat below her waistline sped up, lifted to her heart. The word became the sensation.

"Say it," he commanded.

"O-wy-hee," she said unwillingly. The syllables seemed an acceptance of his closeness.

"And there is only one word of their language you need know. *Aloha*. Say it."

"A-lo-ha," she repeated. "But what does it mean?"

"It means hello, it means goodbye and we are sorry to see you go. It means we are friends, welcome, go in peace. And it means I love you."

"A very useful phrase," she said wryly, wishing he hadn't taught her the word while he had his leg draped about her.

"All you need to know."

"I should think that could be very dangerous. What if someone should think I said hello, when I really meant to say goodbye?" And how does one say I do not love you? she wondered.

"The movements of the body and the tone of voice help determine the meaning," he said. "You'll soon learn. You learn everything very quickly."

"I should like to go down now," she said, as the drumming pounded in her ears. "We'll be able to see the mountains from the deck very soon, won't we?"

"Very soon. Before nightfall, we'll be in the harbor of Honolulu."

"What strange names!"

"And these people think London and Plymouth are very strange names. It's all a matter of perspective."

She agreed with him so that he would let her go.

Savage was rueful that he was proved wrong, for the wind changed and they did not make Honolulu harbor until the following morning. Three ships were anchored in the snug bay, each one with the gaudy flag of the United States flapping lazily from some line in its rigging. One glance told him they were whalers. He examined the thatched huts on the shoreline, but saw no movement.

"Where's the harbormaster?" asked Mr. Becker impatiently.

"Where are the women?" asked Barber.

A man climbed down the side of the nearest American whaling ship, into a small boat, which he proceeded to row to the *Pearl Stallion.* Savage went to the railing to welcome him.

"Captain Harley, of *Carly's Prize,* out of Salem," he said by way of introduction, gesturing toward the ship he'd just left. "You be a Britisher," he said, looking up at the flag at the mizzenmast.

Savage introduced himself and agreed that, yes, he did hail from Britain.

"Hope you're not in great need, for the king has laid *kapu* on all British ships."

For a moment, Savage thought his blood had turned to ice water. Six days' food left in the ship, and King Kamehameha had forbidden any trade with British ships? He flexed his fingers to make sure they still worked.

"Why?" he asked with exaggerated calm. "What did Great Britain do to the King?"

"Why, one of your countrymen came in here not past a fortnight ago, acted all high-and-mighty, and in front of the Britisher who sometimes translates for the king made some jest about the king of the Calabash Islands. The toady went back to his master with the story, and the ship was ordered to clear out."

"And he takes revenge on the rest of us, for one man's insult?"

"Well, the fellow wasn't done. He went on to Kauai and made some rash promises to the king of that island, about helping him invade Kamehameha's territories."

"Good God! I hope someone had the good sense to sink the bastard," snapped Savage. Posturing martinets who tried to overawe local rulers were the bane of every trader's existence. Insulting the local people was no way to conduct business.

"He sailed away. Perhaps he got provisions from Kauai. Which you may have to do."

"I've traded with the king before, and nothing but good feelings between us," said Savage, hoping that would still hold true.

"What were you planning on trading with the king?" asked the American slyly. Savage saw the path the conversation was taking. This captain wanted to sound him out, see if a three-way trade would be to his profit. No choice but to be honest, for the thing might have to be done that way.

"No trade. Cash. Gold coin."

The American murmured in appreciation. "Where ye bound?" he asked, a bit more openly.

"Calcutta," said Savage.

"Where ye been?" Savage decided the conversation was delving a bit too deeply into the *Pearl Stallion*'s itinerary. A judicious lie was in order.

"California," he said sharply. "This is a scientific expedition, nine months out of England."

"Scientists, are ye?" said the American. Savage edged him toward the railing. "Well, now, if you can't convince the king of the noble nature of your calling, you're welcome aboard at any time. Name's Harley. Remember that. On good terms with Mr. Young, who's close to the king."

Savage watched the American row himself back to *Carly's Prize*. He dared not reveal his distaste for the man.

He might be forced to depend upon him to get enough food to last until they reached Canton.

"*Kapu,*" said Becker with a low whistle. "Damned bad luck."

"Couldn't be worse," agreed Savage, walking back to the quarterdeck. He glanced around the circle of his officers. Everyone looked worried, except Dina, who looked confused.

"*Kapu,* Lady Dina, means forbidden. The king has forbidden trade with British ships. What are our alternatives?"

"Buy from the Americans," said Becker bitterly. "They'll charge double and triple, but I can't see any other way."

"The American captain mentioned another island," suggested Dina. "How far is it? Could we get food there?"

"Possibly, but the two kings are at war. If we patronize the king of Kauai, we risk the enmity of Kamehameha. He's the more powerful of the two, and next year could find him in control of all the islands. What would we do then, when we call to resupply?"

"Captain, there's some confusion on shore," pointed out Mr. Loti. Every glass on deck was instantly trained on the thatched huts at the head of a short wharf.

"The king," said Savage. "I believe our worries are over. He never can resist selling for hard cash." He looked around the ship. "Get everything not needed at this moment below decks."

Men and officers dashed about, stowing every bit of portable equipment. Savage stepped across the deck to Dina's side.

"King Kamehameha looks upon anything he sees as his by right. Some careless ships have lost a great part of their cargo by leaving it visible on deck when the king came aboard."

"He's coming aboard?" asked Dina.

"Yes. Do you want to see the greatest king in the Pacific?" Savage handed her his glass. "After you look, perhaps that glass had better go to my cabin. It's the best one I've ever owned, and I'd hate to lose it."

He watched Dina's face eagerly as she stared toward the shore. Her mouth opened in surprise.

"Which is the king?" she asked.

"The tallest one."

"But—" she sputtered. "He's— He's—"

"Nearly naked," agreed Savage. "Now you understand why some British captain made slighting remarks about him. Don't underestimate his power, just because he comes out with a bit of cloth wrapped about his hips."

Savage glanced back toward the shore. A canoe pulled away from the wharf, but it contained only one man besides the paddler.

"I don't like this," he said suddenly. "Usually the king comes out in considerable style."

By this time the entire crew was on deck or hanging in the rigging to observe the royal presence and hear what the royal representative would say. Savage wished his conversation could be a little less public, but the crew had as much at stake as he did. The man who scrambled up the side had on a pair of ragged pantaloons. Hope surged in Savage's heart, because he knew the man. He was not dealing with a stranger.

"Mr. Young. How fine to see you again this year."

"*Aloha* to you, Captain. A bit of unpleasantness. Perhaps you've heard, for I saw that Captain Harley paid you a visit."

"Indeed. But it can't have anything to do with the *Pearl Stallion*, surely. We've had very pleasant relations with the king in the past, and our trading will be on the same basis as before. Cash," he added significantly. It would do no harm to remind them that he paid in gold.

"The king commands you ashore," said Young. "All your officers are welcome, but the crew must stay on board until some agreement is reached."

"I understand." Savage looked over the crowd on the quarterdeck. Everyone would want to come, of course.

"Mr. Barber, you are in command until we return." The boy's face fell. The disappointment would be a good lesson in self-discipline. Savage had overheard Loti teaching Barber how to say, "I would like to make love with you," in Hawaiian.

"Dr. Hampton, would you care to accompany us? Lady Dina, I think you'll find something ashore to enter in your journal."

The boat was quite full without the addition of two oarsmen, so Loti joined Charley at the rowing. Savage sat facing the shore, studying the crowd that gathered around the king wherever he went. Many women lazed about the thatched huts in various stages of undress, their heads and bosoms decorated with flowers. They were waiting for the king to give permission for them to receive the sailors. At the edge of the water, in a separate group, stood three large women wrapped in fabric printed with geometric patterns.

"See the three ladies?" He pointed them out to Dina. "They're the king's wives."

At that moment, the three made some decision, gestured to a servant standing behind them. The servant took the wrappings from all three, and the women plunged naked into the surf. Dina gasped so loudly that practically everyone on the boat heard her.

"Fine material for your journal," he said lightly. She nodded, but did not look at him, did not take her eyes from the performance on shore.

Once they were on the beach, Savage gestured for the rest to stay behind him as he walked into the thatched building. There were no walls, so the king had a full view of the ship's company as they approached him from the shore. Savage entered into the shadow where the king sat majestically on a sea chest. Mr. Young, whose powerful young rower had outdistanced their boat by several lengths, was already standing next to his sovereign. Savage stopped at the entrance to the building, bowed, then advanced toward the king, stopped and bowed again.

"The king says you may bring in your officers," said Young. Savage turned and waved his hand. Everyone made the proper obeisances; Lady Dina dipped into a full court bow, the silk roses on her hat almost touching the ground. Her hair was getting quite long, Savage noted, and hung from beneath her bonnet, over her shoulders.

"You may introduce your officers to the king," said Young.

He met most of them last year, thought Savage, but he complied, starting with Mr. Becker, as befitted his rank. "Lady Endine Wilmount," he said as he ended the recital. "Navigator."

The king spoke to Young at some length in the musical language of the islands.

"The king says he has never seen a lady from over the sea as an officer on a ship," said Young, and the courtier's voice revealed that he'd never heard of such a thing, either.

"Lady Dina is quite accomplished. Perhaps you might tell the king that she was born to a noble father in England."

Young translated. The king stood up; it was an act Savage always found intimidating, since King Kamehameha was one of the few men he'd ever met who was far taller than himself. Kamehameha walked around the group of foreigners. They moved closer to one another, unconsciously, under the examination of the monarch. The king spoke to Young.

"The king asks, do you wish to trade?"

"I wish to buy food, pork, yams, taro, fruit, anything his people might wish to sell. And I'll pay cash."

The king and the translator spent several moments in conversation. Young's face grew troubled.

"His Majesty the king...he will agree to do business, except..." The Englishman's voice trailed off, and the strain in his face let Savage know the price for the food was going to be exceptionally high.

"Except what?" asked Savage impatiently.

Young pointed at Dina. The king's arm came up at the same moment, pointing in the same direction.

"You will give the king the noblewoman whose hair is like Pele's."

Savage's eyes no longer focused. Everything swam about through the air, as if the shore and sea had changed places, and a film the color of blood covered that confused world in scarlet. Give Dina to the king? He'd not given her to some anonymous ruler in Sumatra. Giving her directly to this man, knowing the actuality of the loins possessing her, that would be worse, ten times worse!

My God! I love her!

"No!" he roared, his voice thundering, along with the pulse of blood in his ears.

The king sat down on his sea-chest throne and laughed uproariously. He's laughing at me, laughing because he's upset me, thought Savage, but the understanding did not stop the raging of his heart. He struggled to bring his anger under control.

The king and the courtier talked, the king smiling.

"The king does not want her forever, Captain," Young explained. "Just for the time when you'll be loading your ship. He says, your men lie with the women of the islands. Why is it of such great moment that he should enjoy a woman of your land when you bring her here?"

"No." Savage choked the word out. He could hardly speak. He bowed stiffly, turned around and waved at the group behind him to leave. Only when his arm went up did he notice that his hand was clenched in a fist.

Chapter Fifteen

"The women are quite unhappy," said Captain Harley, who sat with Savage on the quarterdeck of the *Pearl Stallion.* Dina, in the main cabin with the skylight fully open to admit the fragrant breeze, heard every word that passed between the two men.

"They were ready to swim out to meet you, but the king's orders forbid it, seeing as how you're a Britisher."

"Every man in this ship counted on several days ashore to rest and recover," said Savage. "We've had a very tiring voyage. What's the situation on the island of Kauai?"

"Still under the control of its own king. Kamehameha's last invasion was a failure."

"Is Kamehameha still intent on conquering the island?"

"He seems to be, but the plague last year killed off most of his generals, not to speak of hundreds of other people on this island. The king himself was very ill, and I think he blames the deaths on the anger of his heathen gods. He must believe his failure in the conquest of Kauai angered them, for he's recently bought himself a ship with another invasion in mind. His workmen are kept busy building a fleet of canoes to make the crossing."

"But immediate invasion?"

"No. Not that anyone suspects."

"War would be a foolish thing," said Savage. "The islands are the center for Pacific trade. Both kings should think of that before they plunge into fighting. The religious men of California are in favor of opening that province to foreign trade. If they get their way, the Sandwich Islands would have competition in supplying the Pacific traders and whalers."

Dina heard the clink of glass upon glass. Savage was pouring more California wine for the American.

"California," repeated Captain Harley. "How do you find affairs in California?"

"I was in port there only briefly, for an emergency. I had no chance to travel away from the harbor."

"Well treated?" asked Captain Harley.

"Moderately. They were anxious to keep me in port until their armed frigate came up from Mexico, but I escaped the trap. I believe England and Spain are still at war, so they were completely within their rights to try to capture this ship."

"I hope President Jefferson keeps us out of the European confusion. War is never good for trade," said the American profoundly. "Not in the Atlantic or the Pacific." He pursed his lips, as if undecided, then spoke again. "Do you go to Kauai to reprovision?"

"I haven't made up my mind," said Savage.

"Keep my offer in mind."

"If Kamehameha should find out you're selling me food, he might order you out of his harbor."

"Aye, that is a concern, but I've already restocked and am homeward bound."

"Could you get a message to shore for me?" asked Savage.

"Yes."

"Ask the harbormaster to request of the king permission for my crew to go ashore. Just for a few hours."

"The women, and the men who profit from them, will put pressure on the king to grant your wish. They're losing money, with your men being off-limits. Might be possible," mused Captain Harley.

"My men would appreciate it," said Savage.

"I'll go now," said Harley. His booted footsteps reverberated through the decking, into the lower cabins. "It'll take some time to get the message to Kamehameha, for he went back to his home at Waikiki. Maybe by evening."

Dina heard the American captain climb down from the deck, then heard the splash of his oars in the water. From the stern windows, she could see him, rowing toward the thatched huts on the beach.

Did men feel the need for women so frightfully, that the urge took precedence over hunger? In the weeks since leaving California, she had taken over more and more of the ship's accounts, and she knew what was in the hold. Barely enough food to last another week; on short rations, perhaps two. Yet Savage would let precious days go by while the men went ashore to frolic with the women.

Lightner had not been able to resist a woman at the mission. His carnal desire had led him to disobey orders, and now he was trapped in California. The governor and Don Miguel had probably put him in prison when they discovered he'd been left behind. Was a man's need for sex stronger than the fear of imprisonment?

Sex dominates men's lives, she thought regretfully. They'll violate every principle they pretend to live by when they want to put themselves into a woman. The king of the Sandwich Islands, who should think of nothing but the good of his people, is willing to let down the barriers against trade, barriers he himself erected, if Savage will turn me over to him. She closed her eyes and bit her lower lip at the recollection of that awful moment when the huge king had pointed at her, when the English translator had made the demand. She had felt as if she would melt into the ground. Her legs had lost their strength. Had Savage noticed she barely made it back to the boat? Her feet had moved only out of habit. She'd thought of nothing but regaining the shelter of the *Pearl Stallion*.

Here she was safe from the demands of that giant. Savage would not turn her over to the king. His rejection of the demand had been so violent, she was certain he had insulted the king. He would not leave her in Sumatra; he would not give her to that horrible man.

But what would they do about food?

I should thank Savage, she thought. *I must let him know how much I appreciate the care and kindness he's given me, how comfortable I've come to feel on this ship. Everyone, from the captain to the newest sailor, treats me with respect and honor. What can I do for Savage, for the crew, to repay their kindness?*

The dark knowledge of what she could do descended like a suffocating curtain. A black veil wound about her. It was horrible, frightening—and plain. She herself could break the stalemate, get food for the voyage to China. But the thought of that dusky king made her legs weak.

"Mr. Becker, all hands," said Savage's voice above her head.

She climbed the companionway slowly, strength renewing itself in her body as she made up her mind. She walked aft to the quarterdeck proudly, knowing she held the solution to the dilemma in her hands. All it would take was courage, and she could not be cowardly before these men. They had done so much for her. She had a responsibility to the *Pearl Stallion.*

The sun set in a rush behind the steep mountains, and in the twilight the crew crowded the deck, drawing straws to see which ones would be the first to go ashore. When a man laughed and cheered, everyone knew his straw had been long. Once the process was complete, Savage waved everyone to silence.

"Remember, back here at sunup, and if you can slip food aboard, all the better. Put a few pieces of fruit, at least, in your shirts. Let the women feed you, all you can eat. Mr. Becker and Mr. Barber may go ashore. Mr. Loti will stay on board with me."

Mr. Loti did not suppress his groan of disappointment, and Savage laughed at the young man. Dina took the opportunity to step forward.

"May I go ashore, too, sir?"

His startled glance told her he hadn't even considered that she might want to go ashore. He stammered, then pinched his lips together to close off the sound. Finally he nodded.

"Don't wander. Stay close by. I can't see what harm could come to you." He stepped toward her and leaned down to whisper in her ear.

"You're aware of why the men are going ashore, aren't you? Every bush and tree will conceal a loving couple, and I cannot protect you from the sight."

"I know," she said. "But this may be my only chance to see the island."

"Not far," he repeated.

The boats were already being lowered, the sailors pouring over the side to fill them. Dina waited until she saw Mr. Becker enter a boat and joined him.

"Does the king live nearby?" she asked him casually.

"No. The king lives on the shore, about two miles east. At a place called Waikiki. Some people call it a palace, but last year I walked the miles to see it. His palace is just more grass houses, like the ones here. Perhaps bigger. With more elaborate decorations. Ugly heathen gods carved from wood."

The road was obvious, a dusty flat track leading toward the rising moon, which was not quite full. The sea glistened silver, but she did not notice. She closed her mind so that she would not turn around, run back to the protection of the ship. Her legs trembled so much that at times she could barely put one foot in front of another.

The encounter with Don Miguel was horrible, she told herself, because he overpowered me and I couldn't resist. It will be different with this king, because I'm going of my own volition. She imagined the man upon her, as Don Miguel had been, and suddenly realized the flaw in her reasoning. By offering herself, she bound herself as thoroughly as Don Miguel had done. Once she walked into the presence of the king, she had to accept whatever he chose to do. Pride would make retreat unthinkable.

Dina stopped by the roadside to control the nausea that cramped her stomach. The king had said just so long as the ship was being loaded, she reminded herself. And Savage will hurry, knowing that I hate what the king will ask of me. She clenched her hands into fists and walked on. She found it difficult to keep reminding herself that she owed this to the *Pearl Stallion.*

She eyed each cluster of thatched houses, but saw nothing that matched Becker's description. Certainly the king lived in something better than these hovels? How big would the palace of a savage king be? The glint of torches let her know when she had arrived. The light flickered on tall wooden carvings, upon elaborate ridgepoles that jutted far beyond the steep roofs they supported.

No one stopped her progress. She walked among the huge thatched houses, waiting to be noticed, looking curiously through open doorways to find which contained the king. Dogs and pigs rooted around in the moonlight, searching for scraps of food. Someone chanted quietly in the language of the islands, and Dina had a sudden fear that there would be no one about to translate for her. She would not know the king's intentions in advance; she could only accept what he chose to do to her. She turned to flee.

Shouts, men running, and she froze in her tracks. Dark, half-naked figures surrounded her, eyed her, but made no move to touch her.

"What are you doing here?" said a voice in English. It was not Young, but a different man, shorter, who spoke with the accents of America. The group of men parted to let the unknown white man through.

"I am Lady Dina Wilmount," she said firmly, "of the ship *Pearl Stallion,* and I need to see the king."

"Why?" The man did not react at all to her title, nor did he offer the least courtesy. He did not invite her inside, he did not offer her any kind of seat. He kept her standing in the dusty passageway between two grass houses.

"I will explain my reason for being here to the king."

"You're the woman from the British ship," he said.

"Yes."

"The king made a request of Captain Savage, and the captain denied him in a most insulting way. The king does not look with favor upon the captain."

"And I've come to repair that discourtesy."

"It would be better if the captain came himself."

So it would be, she thought, but Captain Savage is not one to turn a woman over to any man, king or not.

"I've come to beg the king to forgive Captain Savage's outburst. Englishmen have different notions about what is proper between men and women."

The man laughed, said something in the language of the islands to the men surrounding her. They burst into laughter. Her statement must seem ridiculous to them, when, at this moment, half the crew of the *Pearl Stallion* were with island women.

"Come," said the American. Dina followed him deeper into the maze of buildings. "Wait here," he ordered.

From inside the largest house, she heard a familiar voice, that of the king. Her resolution wavered. She steeled herself, gritted her teeth. It could not possibly be as frightening as what Don Miguel had done, except that it might last for several days. How often would he make her do it? The American came toward her, now in bright torchlight, now in flickering shadows.

"The king will see you."

Dina followed him toward the huge house, trying to remember the ceremonies Savage had followed when he appeared before the monarch. As she entered the door she stopped, dropped a deep curtsy. When she rose, a shocking tableau greeted her eyes. The king lay stretched out upon a pile of mats, naked. A young woman knelt beside him, massaging his stomach. Trays of food were on the floor to one side of the king, and on the other side sat Mr. Young, clad in nothing but a loincloth, holding a sheaf of papers from which he seemed to be reading.

"The king wishes to know what you're doing here," said Young, beckoning her forward. Dina walked toward the monarch, then remembered that Savage had bowed twice, so she made another deep curtsy. She had rehearsed her speech all the way from the harbor.

"I have come to offer myself to the King, who requested my presence. He must forgive Captain Savage, who acted most hastily in rejecting the king's request. I beg the king to forgive him, because Captain Savage has been under great duress for some weeks." Young waved to her to stop speaking, turned to the king and translated. The king grunted under the pressure of the massage. When Young signaled, Dina spoke again.

"The king understands the burdens of power, and the captain has worked under the same burdens. He overcame many difficulties to take food to the Russians in North America. They were starving, and he gave most of the ship's food to them, to help them in their distress."

Young spoke to the king, who waved the naked girl away and sat up. Dina lowered her eyes, not only out of respect for the king, but also to avoid seeing his long, bulky body, now turned fully toward her. The conversation between the two men continued for some time. She stood motionless, hardly daring to breathe. This was much harder than being presented at court. With Queen Charlotte, you knew exactly what was going to happen, that within a few minutes the daunting affair would be over. This king could keep her standing here all night.

"Has Captain Savage brought you to His Majesty?" Young asked suddenly.

"No," said Dina. "I've come myself, as His Majesty requested."

"The captain did not accompany you to Waikiki?"

"No."

"Does the captain know you're here?"

"No."

Young turned away from her and spoke to the king. The monarch concluded the conversation very rapidly, waved his hand.

"You may go," said Young.

Dina raised her head.

"Go?" The king lay back on the mats, and the young woman knelt beside him. Young rose.

"Come away with me," he said shortly.

Dina dropped another curtsy to the king, who paid not the slightest attention, and backed into the shadows, confused by what had passed.

"But he wanted me," she protested. "He asked Captain Savage for me."

"He does not want you in the way you think. You're too pale and too thin, although he is enchanted by your hair."

"Then why did he ask the captain—"

"The King wished to humble the proud Englishman. He has learned from the Americans, who sometimes bring their wives on their voyages, that white men cling most stubbornly to their women. They do not understand even the most common courtesy, that women are shared with men of great nobility. His Majesty intended nothing but to humiliate the captain, make him give up his woman in the sight of his crew and the Americans. His Majesty desired to show the British his great power."

"That's all he wanted? To shame Captain Savage?"

"To shame the British, in revenge for the insult he suffered at the hands of the other captain."

"Then he brings shame upon himself," said Dina sternly. "A great man, a king, does not take other women. He should be an example to his subjects, an example of morality by living a moral life himself."

"And do the rulers of England never take other men's wives?" asked Young sardonically.

"King George has lived most blamelessly," protested Dina. "He and the queen are examples of the greatest fidelity."

"And the Prince of Wales—he does not toy with other men's women?" Dina knew she was growing red, and hoped this renegade Englishman did not notice it in the torchlight. She had avoided balls and country weeks where the prince would be present, for his behavior with the married ladies was shocking. She hung her head.

"The prince is gossiped about, certainly," she admitted.

"He acts as a great ruler should act," said Young, "in no way different from His Majesty King Kamehameha. The prince sees a woman he desires, he makes the request, and it is done, because it is an honor both to the woman and to her man. So His Majesty may ask for any woman on these islands."

"That's bar—" she began, then swallowed her words. She must not insult these people. The lives of every member of the crew of the *Pearl Stallion* depended on the king's being appeased. "We must buy food," she began meekly. "If Captain Savage comes humbly to the king, if he gives me to the king, would he give permission—"

"The captain had his chance to please His Majesty at the time the king made his request. Now that you've come here in this fashion, I doubt Savage could gain favor by making the most humble offer, for by coming yourself, you've shown yourself to be disobedient and willful. The captain refused His Majesty's request when it would have been appropriate, and the moment is past."

I've done it again, thought Dina in horror. *I've spoiled any chance that Savage can please the king. I should have convinced him to bring me here. But how might I have done that?*

"You've come a great distance. Are you hungry?" asked Young. "Perhaps you'd like to meet the queens, and their servants can bring you food. I'll explain that you are *ali'i,* a noble lady in your own country."

"Thank you," she said humbly.

The noble lady, introduced as Queen Kaahumanu, paid absolutely no attention to Dina. She, too, was receiving a massage and lay completely naked on a mat. The only sounds were her grunts and groans of pleasure.

Food was brought. Dina recognized fish, meat and fruit, and made her selections from these dishes. The fruit tasted like ambrosia upon her tongue. Since leaving Sitka, she had eaten nothing but biscuit and salt beef, with a weekly serving of pudding with dried apples and a dose of lemon juice.

She became accustomed to the silence, so much so that she jumped when the queen finally spoke. From behind her came Young's voice, speaking to Her Majesty.

"I have told Her Majesty that you are a noble lady from far away. She wishes to know the name of your mother."

"My mother was the countess of Cairnlea." The translation was made.

"Where does your mother live?"

"She died many years ago. When I was twelve years old."

After Young spoke, the queen made noises of sympathy, and her face showed grief and sorrow.

"And your father?"

"The earl of Cairnlea. He died a few years ago."

The queen was exceedingly sympathetic, and Dina noted with amazement that tears rolled down her cheeks.

"Her Majesty feels great sorrow for your ladyship. She hopes the love of your husband, Captain Savage, helps you face your grief, being alone without your parents."

"Captain Savage is not my husband. He's a very good friend, who's helping me return to my home."

Now the queen's face showed great surprise.

"Her Majesty asks, where is your husband?"

"Tell Her Majesty I have no husband."

The translation was followed by a long, voluble speech from the queen. She gestured for Dina to join her on the mat.

"You must lie next to her," explained Young, who still maintained his distance, standing near the door.

Dina did as she was told and approached the Queen, who patted the mat in a universal gesture of invitation. Dina felt rather foolish, stretching herself out beside the fat, bare woman.

"Her Majesty asks how many children you have."

"None," replied Dina, mystified that her unmarried state had not eliminated the possibility of children. Then she remembered the women waiting on the beach, and decided that the Sandwich Islanders accepted children, any children, more heartily than the English did.

The queen now patted Dina's back in sympathy; tears overflowed her eyes, and she murmured words of comfort.

"Her Majesty says you are too thin, which must account for the fact that you have no husband and have had no children." While Young spoke, the queen clapped her hands. A servant entered the house and moved the tray of food closer to Dina's hands. "Her Majesty suggests you must eat more."

Dina helped herself to more of the fruit.

"Tell Her Majesty thank you very much for the food. We have had no fruit on the ship since we left Russian America." She ate gluttonously as the conversation went on around her.

"Her Majesty suggests that you learn to keep still, for moving too much causes one to lose flesh."

"I have very little opportunity to be still on the ship," Dina replied. "I must keep up with my duties, as well as keeping my clothes clean and in repair."

The queen reacted with shock when Young translated.

"Her Majesty says those things should be left to your slaves." Dina twisted to see Young's face and saw the shadow of a smile at one corner of his mouth. "I have explained to Her Majesty that you have no slaves, but perhaps you have a servant."

"No, I have no servant."

The queen now proceeded to poke and prod Dina's body, and spoke with a tone of protest.

"Her Majesty is very concerned that you're so thin. She wonders if you wouldn't like to stay with her until the *Pearl Stallion* calls again at Honolulu. She would make sure you were nicely fat by then, and Captain Savage would most certainly make you his wife."

Dina repressed her amusement at this curious notion, and at the same time conceived a way she might make use of the queen's sympathy. Would it be possible for the queen to overcome the king's *kapu?*

"Please tell Her Majesty that I should become nicely fat on the ship, except that we've been very short of food. Tell her we left nearly all our food with the Russians at Sitka, because they were starving. We left it behind willingly, because we thought we would be able to reprovision with the help of His Most Gracious Majesty."

Young smiled at her before he began the translation. *He knows precisely what I'm doing,* thought Dina. A long conversation ensued between the courtier and the queen. Dina held her breath, wondering if the ploy might work. How much influence did this one queen have over the king? After all, there were two more women with the same title.

"I have explained the unfortunate situation of the *Pearl Stallion* to Her Majesty. She says Captain Savage made a great mistake in not granting His Majesty's request. You would have found His Majesty most...enjoyable company, and perhaps he would have got a child upon you, so you would not be alone in the world." Young plainly enjoyed making his translation, for he eyed her with mocking amusement.

"Yes," said Dina, agreeing heartily, nodding so that the queen would see. "Please explain to her that I am not Savage's woman, that he did not feel it was within his power to grant the request. He is not my husband, and is not the man to give me to another. I have an uncle in India, and another in England, who make these decisions for me. They would be very angry with Savage if he had preempted their rights."

Another long delay, as Young and the queen talked.

"Her Majesty will speak to the king and convince him to take you into his household. She's certain he did not understand that you are not Savage's woman, that the captain could not give you away. But since you offer yourself to His Majesty..."

Dina reared up on her elbows, appalled by the turn the audience was taking. If things kept on in this direction, she'd end up trapped in this ridiculous royal court for a year or more.

"Please explain to the queen that I must return to my home. My uncle, and his wife, my aunt, and a cousin, they don't know where I am. They must be terribly worried...." Dina made her lips tremble, assumed a tragic expression, and was delighted when she forced a tear from her eye.

"And tell her, to return me to my family, the *Pearl Stallion* must buy food. We cannot sail for India until we have food. And perhaps you could explain that if I arrive in India so terribly thin..." She didn't have a chance to finish. Young was already making the appeal to the queen. And, she was glad to see, he kept his face straight.

The queen's litter rode on the shoulders of eight sturdy men. Dina felt exceedingly foolish reclining on the thing, but Young had pointed out that the queen would be most distressed if she walked back to the harbor. Exercise of that kind caused thinness, he explained.

"Will she speak to the king?" asked Dina anxiously. Several baskets and parcels were heaped beside her on the litter, so she would have adequate food for the morning.

"She will speak to him," said Young.

"And will he be moved?"

"You could have no better ambassador," said Young. "Queen Kaahumanu is not the highest-ranking of the queens, but she is the most loved. The wife of his heart. She will appeal to his great generosity by pointing out your plight. She'll explain that you cannot win the man you love until you have become plump and comely."

"She believes I'm in love?" asked Dina in surprise. "I said nothing of the kind."

"Her Majesty is most perceptive of the feelings of others. She always knows when any of her ladies have cast their feelings toward a man. She is most moved by your love for Captain Savage, and weeps for you, that in your present condition he does not return it. She will explain this to the king."

"Savage!" she said, too loudly and with too much shock. She lowered both her voice and her eyes. "Tell the queen she knows me well, and that I thank her for everything she's done for me. Perhaps Captain Savage will thank her, also," she added, a bit cynically.

"The queen could speak to Captain Savage. A man can learn to love a woman, knowing in time she will please him."

Dina bit her lip. "You say His Majesty loves the Queen. How long have they been . . . married?" Was that the right term to use for the connection of these people?

"Many, many years," said Young. "Long before I came to the islands. There were years when they quarreled and separated, but both were unhappy. It was Captain Vancouver who brought them back together, and reunited them in love."

"Captain Vancouver," she exclaimed. "But he was in these waters a decade, or more, ago."

"I believe it has been that long," said Young.

Dina rode back to the harbor on the shoulders of the servants of the queen. Physically she returned in a regal state, but emotionally she was as uncertain and confused as a young serving girl. She prayed the queen would not send a message to Savage. What would he think if he received a royal communication on the advisability of marriage? Dina knew exactly what he'd think. He'd assume she'd spoken to the queen about her need for a husband, that her choice was Savage.

She did hope the queen's appeal to her husband bore fruit, quite literally. If the king gave in on that point, perhaps it wouldn't become necessary to tell Savage why she'd gone to the royal enclosure in the first place. She remembered only too well his reaction to the barest hint of physical involvement with Charley. How would he react if he was to find out she'd offered herself to Kamehameha?

She should have asked Young to keep quiet about that. It must remain a secret. The trotting bearers came within view of the harbor. She saw the *Pearl Stallion* in the moonlight, a ghostly ship in the flat light. The ship, a dark silhouette, became the man. She had to tell him the truth. She dared not keep secrets from him, because it was upon him they all depended.

She jumped down from the litter when it was deposited near the cluster of grass huts by the water's edge. The servants carried the food to the shore, where the ship's boats were pulled onto the beach.

"Dina?" asked Savage's voice from the shadows of one of the houses. He stepped into the moonlight, and she saw several sailors behind him.

"Yes."

"Where have you been? Hampton came ashore and didn't find you. We've been worried."

"May we go to the ship before I tell you where I've been?" she asked. "I'd rather not speak in front of these men," she whispered.

He led her to one of the boats pulled up on the coral sand. When the queen's servants saw which boat he intended to take back to the ship, they rapidly loaded all the food parcels into it, leaving barely enough room for Dina and Savage to squeeze onto the rear thwart. One of the sailors shoved things aside and took the oars.

He was very close to her, and there would have been no way to escape him if she had wanted to. His arm crept about her waist, his fingers pressed against her side, kneaded her through the bodice of her California dress. He's relieved that I've returned, she thought. He's been worried.

Once on the ship, they sat close together, aft of the mizzen mast, and spoke in low voices.

"You intended to buy food by giving yourself to the king?" he asked in amazement.

"Yes, but he didn't want me. He never wanted me, but simply intended to disgrace you. To shame you. In retaliation for the insult of the other captain."

His fingers touched her hair, and she did not pull away.

"Do you think the queen will be of any help?"

"Mr. Young says she will be. That the king loves her best of all, that she will convince him."

"When you went, you were frightened?" he asked gently.

"Yes."

"It was a generous sacrifice," he said.

"I told you the truth. The king didn't want me. He sent me away. There was no sacrifice."

"I was not speaking of anything the king did. I was speaking of what you did, overcoming your fear in that way."

"I didn't overcome it. I shook the whole time I stood before him."

"You've been very brave. Most Englishwomen would have run, screaming, if the king of the Sandwich Islands pointed at them and demanded they come to him. You did not. You stood before him with dignity, and perhaps solved our rather serious dilemma."

He kissed her gently on the forehead.

"Morning is coming," he pointed out. "The sky's already quite light in the east. Perhaps you'd like to spend some time in your bed."

"Yes." She went to her cabin, left the door open so that the deliciously fragrant air would circulate about her. It had been necessary to tell Savage everything, but there was one part of the night that Dina would not share with him. She was in love with the Honorable Anson Saurage, Captain Savage. The knowledge had been passed to her by a woman who had loved one man for many, many years.

Was it possible for an Englishwoman, or an Englishman, to love in that way? Or was that possible only here, in these islands, where a queen wept for a stranger's misfortunes? In this place where the word for love fell from everyone's lips with a multitude of meanings, reminding them constantly that love intertwined with all things?

Chapter Sixteen

Savage worked at the makeshift desk in his cabin, taking advantage of the smooth sea to bring the ship's log up to date. He preferred to write at the chart table, but Dina was there, making fair copies of the manifest. He dared not interrupt her, for last evening at sunset the lookout had seen the southern tip of Formosa. They were now in the South China Sea, with Macao and the trading factories of Canton but a few days away.

He thought with pleasure of flashing that manifest before the hong merchant, seeing the man struggle to keep his face noncommittal when he noted the number of otter skins in the cargo, the sandalwood in the hold. Savage thought of Dina, her eyes wide, at her first sight of Macao, her thrill at the bustle of the factories in Canton.

No, he couldn't take her there. European women were forbidden in the factory district. She must stay on the ship at Whampoa. He would have to go to the factories alone, and the degree of his swift disappointment at the thought surprised him.

His body, sitting at rest, was aware of her presence nearby, and the longing distracted his mind from his business. More and more often at night, he could not suppress the knowledge that she lay but a few feet away, on the other side of the bulkhead. The two months since leaving the Sandwich Islands had been difficult, and he counted his good luck that they had made a rapid passage.

His sensual unrest was caused, he was certain, by his continence on the islands. After the king rejected Dina, he'd had no choice but to show his own strength of character. Kamehameha's gibe about Europeans and Americans taking island women, but not allowing islanders access to their own, had fortified him against the lovely, flower-bedecked beauties on the shore. Within a week of leaving the island, he'd regretted his sacrifice, for every night his desire for the woman beyond the wall burned hotter. He had expected his longing for her to cool, her attraction to lessen. Instead, it grew stronger with each passing day.

"I'll have Chinese women in Canton," he muttered. He would sink into them, again and again, satiate himself. Then two more months, perhaps less, and the *Pearl Stallion* would sail into the Hooghly.

The cabin was growing stuffy, for the morning sun beat upon the deck close overhead. He lifted from his stool enough to open the skylight. A soft mixture of voices sifted through the opening from the men on deck.

I went down into the garden of nuts to see the fruits of the valley, and to see whether the vine flourished, and the pomegranates budded.

Charley and his friends were at their reading lessons.

What a change Dina had made in the ship! Not one man but could read a bit, now. Barber and Loti were so skilled in mathematics, they could find a position accurately, and Charley had nearly caught up with them. With a small crew, it was convenient to have several people capable of doing any one job. Perhaps he should have her start teaching mathematics to all the crew, so that no one would be mystified by the sextant and charts.

Then he remembered that she would be leaving within a few weeks. After they reached Calcutta, he would see her onto an Indiaman bound for England. His thoughts were interrupted by a new voice, and a new topic, from overhead.

How beautiful are thy feet with shoes, O prince's daughter! The joints of thy thighs are like jewels, the work of the hands of a cunning workman.

Shoes! Perhaps someone in Macao could make her some shoes. He hated to see her in the clumsy boots made on board ship. She didn't seem to mind, however. How she'd changed! The fashionable lady of the *ton* in dresses after the design of California! And made with her own hands. Her ivory skin tanned to brown by the sun of the tropics...

Yesterday, he had nearly reached out to touch her brown cheek, had checked his hand at the very last moment.

Thy navel is like a round goblet, which wanteth not liquor; thy belly is like an heap of wheat set about with lilies.

He dropped the quill and stared at the skylight. What in the devil were those men reading?

Thy two breasts are like two young roes that are twins.

The Song of Solomon. He did not want to hear any more. But this was their reading time, and their only book was the Bible; could he send them away without everyone knowing the phrases upset him?

How fair and how pleasant art thou, O love, for delights!

He groaned and tried to return to his work. Twenty-two degrees north latitude, he sighted a Spanish trading ship, obviously bound for the Philippines.

This thy stature is like to a palm tree, and thy breasts to clusters of grapes.

The reader's voice grew husky with desire. Some other man on the ship was ready for the lovely women of China.

I said, I will go up to the palm tree, I will take hold of the boughs thereof: now also thy breasts shall be as clusters of the vine, and the smell of thy nose like apples.

Savage sprang up and poked his head through the skylight. "Charley, take your men someplace else to read. I'm trying to get some work done, for God's sake!"

He had to get some exercise, walk off the rising desire within him. He snatched open the door, stepped into the main cabin. Dina sat at the chart table, but not working. Her head was lowered, and her hands were in tight fists in her lap.

The skylight was open. The crazy men had frightened her, with all their talk of climbing palm trees. He threw himself out the door, up onto the deck. He paced the width of the quarterdeck, but there was not space enough to relieve the pressure building inside him. He strode all the way to the bowsprit and leaned over to see the figurehead lift against the glorious green water of the South China Sea.

A studious voice wafted around him, borne upon the wind.

Many waters cannot quench love, neither can the floods drown it.

The figurehead dipped below a wave, emerged streaming foam. Savage grasped the railing. He did not want that to be true. Love must be dissolved, evaporated. Else it would destroy everything he worked for; love would destroy his future.

"A city!" exclaimed Dina, staring across the half mile of water separating them from Macao. She stared hungrily at the town. The morning sun glinted on the windows of buildings three and four stories high. It reflected from the towers of the cathedral and the walls of the fortress on the highest point of the peninsula.

"Do we stay here?" she asked.

"No. We go on up the river, to Whampoa Island. We anchor there, take smaller ships to Canton, where the trades are made."

How she'd love to walk among these houses, see women in European clothes, eat properly cooked dinners on china, with silver knives and forks. She glanced at Savage; his eyes devoured her, as they had so often in the past few days. She tried to hide her disappointment.

"We cannot," he said, explaining unnecessarily. "Our cargo's too precious, and too many of these junks—" he swept his hand around the horizon, indicating the Chinese ships "—are close to being pirates. We get our trading done as quickly as possible, get the furs off-loaded and on their way to Canton."

Dina nodded and appreciated that he took the time to explain, instead of simply giving orders. Now she understood the impossibility of stopping at Macao, and her desire to see the town was mollified.

As they sailed up the estuary of the Pearl River, the view changed, the hills retreating from the water to hang in the hazy distance. Along the shore, the land seemed barely higher than the water. It was green, divided into small fields of waving, unripened rice. An occasional building jutted against the skyline, the roofs gracefully curved in the manner of the Orient. Finally, near sunset, she saw numerous European ships anchored close in to an island. Huge ships of the East India Company, the bulky trading ships of the Dutch, two-masted brigs flying the Stars and Stripes of the United States. Some of the American ships were so small, she wondered that they had made it across the ocean.

Here, amid the crowd of ships, the *Pearl Stallion* anchored. Dina waited, but nothing seemed to happen. At every other port, Savage had ordered a boat out and had gone ashore, but now he stood, like every other member of the crew, staring toward the shore. A boat put off from a wharf and headed toward the ship. Savage walked across the deck to where Dina stood.

"Do you still have any of your sailor clothes?" he asked as he came up behind her.

"Yes."

"Go change. It's just as well that the hong merchant doesn't know we have a woman aboard. I'll want you in the main cabin. Don't say anything during the meeting, but take down what's said."

Dina heard the boat come alongside, heard someone climb onto the deck. She slipped into the cabin, and found Kranz laying out a selection of food.

"The Chinee expect something to eat, and tea," he said. "No business without eating." Dina made herself comfortable in the corner of the cabin, where the padded bench extended beyond the stern windows.

Savage paid absolutely no attention to her when he gestured the Chinaman into the cabin. He offered sugar cakes, poured tea. Dina raised her pencil, but found she could not understand a thing the hong merchant said. Finally she picked out one word.

"Furs?"

"A few," said Savage negligently. He offered the man more to eat.

Half an hour elapsed before Savage rose, went into his private cabin and returned with a bundle. He shoved aside the trays of food, placed a seal skin and a fox skin on the table. The merchant made sniffing sounds. Savage dipped back into the canvas-wrapped bundle.

The black otter skin gleamed in the beams of sunlight slanting through the stern windows. The merchant hissed on an indrawn breath. He turned away, as if he hadn't seen the beautiful thing. He studied the cabin, looked at the poverty of the tiny space, curled his lips in a sneer. Savage sat down, flashed a tiny smile at Dina, picked up his own teacup.

The silence lay heavy, each man waiting for the other, the merchant very obviously trying to decide what to offer for the cargo. He tumbled the carefully written manifest to the deck, and Dina noticed that his fingers trembled ever so slightly. One of the bejeweled hands drifted to the otter skin, caressed the fur.

"T'irty dollah," he said, shaking his head, as if he had offered an outrageous price for something of second quality.

Savage laughed. Dina furiously wrote the offer in her book, listening for Savage's counteroffer. He said nothing. Minutes passed.

"T'irty-fi'," said the merchant.

Savage leaned back against the stern windows and twisted his head to look across the anchorage.

"In London, ladies are beginning to trim their cloaks with fur. Sometimes, if the cloak is to be worn in the winter, they line the entire thing with fur. The Chinese have taught us nice lessons in fashion. London women not only desire silk, they delight in the opulence of furs."

The merchant sucked in his breath, said something Dina did not understand.

"My friend, the king of the Sandwich Islands," continued Savage casually, "was most generous to this ship. His men brought us canoes filled with sandalwood, which we loaded for ballast. He gave us many gifts, and filled our hold with food. I have sufficient provisions to make Calcutta."

The merchant stood up—he could stand completely erect beneath the beams, Dina noted—and bowed. Savage escorted him to the deck, and Dina heard him descend to his boat.

"Come up, Lady Dina!" Savage shouted down the skylight.

Savage, Becker, Hampton, Barber and Loti were gathered aft.

"So what did you think of our merchant friend?" Savage asked.

"He would attract every eye at Almack's," she said grimly, thinking of his elegant silk robe and hat, his jewels. "But nothing has been settled."

"A great deal has been settled. He knows what I won't accept for otter skins, he was very impressed with the quality, and he knows we can sail away and leave him with nothing for his trouble. He suggested we could not obtain provisions until the cargo is released."

"Is that why you remarked upon the generosity of Kamehameha?" she asked.

"Yes. And, further, I gave him a hint that furs could be sold profitably in London. Tomorrow, or the next day, or next week, he'll be back, with a more reasonable offer. But things take time in China."

* * *

In less than a week, Dina wrote in her book the terms of the agreement between Savage and the placid-faced merchant. The crew divided itself into halves, so that they could enjoy time ashore. Small sailing sampans moved beside the *Pearl Stallion,* and the bales of furs were heaved out of the hold.

Dina stayed out of the way, but kept her journal at hand. She made sketches of the sampans, the merchants in their silk robes. She was making a pencil sketch of a junk toiling down the river against the wind when she found Savage standing next to her.

"Tomorrow you'll go upriver with me. As my secretary."

"But you said women aren't allowed!" Her heart skipped in anticipation. How wonderful, if her book could describe Canton! It would create a sensation in England that she, a European woman, had actually been in Canton!

"I'd feel better with you along. You know what's been taken from the hold, you can write fast enough to keep up with me, and you'll be able to check my figuring."

"What must I take?"

"The detailed manifests, a book to take notes in."

"Then we won't be gone more than one day?"

"It takes nearly all day to get there. Whatever you need for a day or two. And bind up your breasts."

"What?"

"I don't want any suspicion that you're anything other than my ship's secretary, a rather young boy. Bind up your breasts. Be ready at first light."

Dina tossed on her bunk, unable to sleep in her anticipation of the adventure. She sprang up at the first soft rap at her door. Dressing took longer than normal, since she had to wrap a length of soft muslin about her breasts. Savage waited on the deck, his sturdy figure outlined by the faintest light. Only a suggestion of gray on the eastern horizon showed that it was indeed morning.

Charley waited in the smallest of the ship's boats. His huge arms dragged on the oars, and they made an almost silent passage through the anchored ships. They drew near a small vessel whose strange outlines were visible against the morning sky. Dina had become accustomed to the unbroken flush deck of the *Pearl Stallion.* The boat that would take them upriver had raised decks both front and back.

"Hello, Savage," said the man who welcomed them at the side. "Good to see you again. Prosperous voyage?"

"Fair," drawled Savage. Dina stood behind him respectfully, clutching the bundles Charley handed up from the boat.

"Good wind this morning," said the captain. "We'll make a quick passage to the factories."

Savage went below, into the small cabin, and Dina followed him. The place stank of fish and sour humanity.

"I think," he said, wrinkling his nose, "that we'll find the deck a more pleasant place to be." Dina nodded and followed him back up on deck. She found a place to stow the bundles under a rusting cannon, then sank down on the deck, propped against them. Other men came aboard, obviously captains who were, like Savage, arranging their homeward-bound cargo. The crew raised the anchor and the triangular sails.

She had intended to sleep, leaning against her bundles, but the morning sun displayed a scene so fantastic she did nothing but stand at the railing and drink it in. Junks and sampans sailed upriver alongside them, and others came downstream, beating against the onshore wind. Again and again islands divided the river into channels. Vessels of all kinds separated and came together in a quiet dance, weaving together, then apart, as their captains chose different routes.

The autumn sun had set and twilight had descended upon the river before the boat drew against a wharf. Beyond, she could see a row of buildings, three and four stories high. The factories. They made an unbroken wall for an eighth of a mile along the river. Savage led her into a courtyard in front of the largest of the mansions. The flag of Great Britain fluttered on a pole before it.

Dinner was served by Chinese servants in a huge dining room. The head of the table was occupied by the resident agents, ship captains, and pursers from those ships whose captains did not handle the business arrangements themselves. Dina found herself at the foot of the table, surrounded by clerks, most of them Portuguese from Macao. When they questioned her, she gave brief answers in a low voice, and hoped they thought Savage's young secretary simply shy. After dinner, Savage beckoned to her.

"Come," he said quietly. She followed him up a narrowing flight of stairs, down a hall. He opened a heavy door, left it open while he struggled with flint and steel to light a candle on a table.

By the flickering light, she saw the dim reaches of a large room, a curtained bed in one corner, a cold fireplace, a table and chairs, and a thick rolled mat leaning against the wall near the fireplace. On the table were the bundles they had brought with them on the boat.

"Our room," he said shortly.

"Our room?" she asked, aware that there was more than a little shock in the two words.

"The factory is crowded right now, the beginning of the trading season for tea. I didn't think you'd care to spend the night in a dormitory full of sailors. Get your notebook and the manifests. Mr. Harrowburn will be here soon.

"My secretary, Wilmount," said Savage casually, "will take notes on the conversation, if you have no objection." Mr. Harrowburn didn't even nod in her direction. Savage turned to Dina. "The accounts?" he asked. She drew the papers from the leather folder she had carried under her arm all the way from Whampoa. Harrowburn turned his attention to the list of furs that the *Pearl Stallion* had sent to the warehouse.

"Two thousand otter?" he asked, unbelieving.

"Twenty-four hundred, actually, but four hundred are from the south, and not so valuable. Close to six thousand fox, wolf and seal. Plus the sandalwood."

"How did you pry sandalwood out of that old ruffian in the Sandwich Islands?" asked Harrowburn.

"I have a friend at court," said Savage, following the statement with a laugh, as if he'd made a jest.

"What are you looking for to take in return?"

"Antique porcelains, and if they are not available, modern. Only complete dining sets, unless you can furnish me with spectacular pieces. Just enough chinaware to serve as ballast, to replace the sandalwood."

"I'll see what's available."

Dina made her notes in rapid slashes, in a code only she could read.

"Get me all the silk you can find, both fabric and threads," Savage said. "Are embroidered shawls with fringe available?"

Dina's head came up, but Savage didn't so much as glance at her.

She was exhausted from the long day and her sleepless night. Twice she lost the train of the conversation as her head nodded. The value of the cargo astonished her. The otter skins had brought forty American dollars each, more than eight British pounds. Savage spoke of thousands of pounds' worth of silk, of porcelain.

"Fill out the manifest with whatever's on hand, for I don't want to be long in port. I must be in Calcutta early in the year." Mr. Harrowburn nodded, made a few notes of his own.

"Do you plan on staying here long?" the man asked.

"No. I'll be returning to the ship tomorrow. I trust you'll let me know what you've found for me." After Mr. Harrowburn left, Savage slumped in a chair by the fireplace.

"We leave tomorrow?" Dina asked.

"It's too dangerous to stay. One day I can get away with having you here. Longer than that, the hong merchants may find out, and all their goodwill would vanish. The factors here are not mystified by your sex, by the way. Women have been smuggled in before."

"Why aren't women allowed in Canton?"

"The Chinese fear the Europeans and Americans will become firmly planted here if they're allowed to bring their women. Which, considering the history of Europeans in other parts of the world, is probably correct. You're not planning to publish your journal under your own name, I suppose?"

"No. Of course not."

"Perhaps you could change the name of the ship and the captain, just in case a copy of it ever surfaces in China."

"I shall, if that would be of help to you. So you intend to remain in the China trade?"

"At least one more year. After all, I did make a promise to Baranov. He's depending on the *Pearl Stallion* returning with its hold full of food. And even if I decide to return to England, I've a good crew who can take the ship around the world without me. And perhaps I'll buy another ship or two. Barber and Loti will soon be fit to command. The younger ones can take over the sailing, and I'll not cause myself a permanent stoop from crouching under low decks."

He stood up, grabbed the roll of matting, spread it out on the floor.

"You can have the bed," he said.

"Not at all," she said sternly. "You're the captain. I'm the secretary. Making you share your room is punishment enough. I'll take the floor, since you've saved me from an attic full of men."

Savage laughed, and blew out the candle. She heard the bed creak as he climbed in. How much was he going to undress? She sat on the mat for a moment before pulling off her boots, and nothing else. There was one woolen blanket. She pulled it up high beneath her chin. The binding about her breasts was uncomfortable. She sat up once more, raised her shirt and unwound the strip of muslin.

She lay still, mentally calculating the value of the cargo Savage would be taking back to Calcutta in the *Pearl Stallion.* What, she wondered, would be the worth of three shares? Sleep caught her before she'd inventoried even the silk.

The corridor was cold, and the stone floor beneath her feet uneven. She should not be here.

Dina resisted the dream. She did not want to remember what happened at Moreton. She must get back to the ship, she thought.

The scream was thin, rising to a peak, then cut off. She stood paralyzed.

She was dreaming. She'd wake up. She struggled to get out of the cold corridor, but her feet did not move. Her father looked at her, saw her. He would force her to watch the whole horrible thing, then he would kill her, too.

Dina clasped her hands tightly over her mouth, watched the fair body writhe under the blows of the heavy cane, and listened to her mother's screams. The shrieks filled her head, she struggled against the paralysis holding her, a paralysis that, as she surfaced into wakefulness, became tighter and more concrete.

"Dina, Dina," he whispered. "It's a dream. Nothing has happened."

She was in his arms, struggling against his strength.

"Nothing will hurt you, Dina. You're safe here with me. Nothing evil has happened. It was all a dream."

"He killed her!" she gasped.

Savage's hand smoothed back her hair.

"It was but a dream, Dina. No one has been killed."

"He killed her," she insisted. "My father. He killed my mother. I saw him do it."

His arms tightened around her, drew her so close she felt the beating of his heart through the linen shirt. She leaned into the comfort of him.

"Oh, my dearest," he whispered. "My very dearest."

She lifted her arms and twined them about his neck. She was safe, for the first time in her life. Savage was her protector, and would care for her.

"He didn't know I saw him beat her. He threw her down the stairwell, then told everyone she had leaped over in a fit of madness."

She clutched at him, clinging to him as the only solid being in her quaking world.

"It will not happen to you," he said soothingly. "You'll be loved, no one will hurt you in such a way."

"But he loved her once," she moaned. She curled herself more tightly against him, hoping she could sink into his strong arms and never emerge.

"I love you," she whispered. "I do love you, Savage."

The answer came, more of a dream than the dream had been.

"I love you, my lady. God! How much I love you."

Only then did her mind absorb the fact that they sat on a thin mat, on the floor of a room in the British factory in Canton. The room did not sway with the swells of the ocean, but stayed very still, and only the agitation of their breasts created the illusion of motion.

"Will you call me by my name?" he asked. "There are few people in the world to call me Anson."

"I love you, Anson," she said, lifting her hand to touch his jaw. It was rough with a day's growth of beard, and it seemed she could sense the dark color with her fingers. He eased her down upon the mat, then stretched out beside her, thrust his arm beneath her head so that she rested in the notch of his shoulder.

"How long did it last?" he inquired gently. "How long did they love one another?"

"I don't know. A few years, perhaps."

"Longer than the love my mother enjoyed," he said. "How long shall we love one another?"

"I don't know. At the moment I feel as if I've loved you forever, as far back as the past can reach."

"The only direction with meaning is the future," he said. "Do you see into the future?" He lifted himself to hang above her, his body supported by his arms. Her heart pounded in her throat, and she found she could barely speak.

"No." She lifted her arms and embraced him, drawing him as close as his stiff elbows allowed. "But we have tonight. Tonight we are sure of our love."

He moaned. One of his hands explored under her shirt, discovered her breasts free and full. The fingers that touched her were solidified flame. Any thought of resistance evaporated in the heat he generated. He turned her on her side, so that he might cradle her breasts equally in his firm palms.

"Dina," he whispered hoarsely, "I want to put my lips on your breasts, I want to kiss you deeply. So deeply my passion will awaken yours. But if I do these things, I'll not be able to stop until it's done completely. Will you yield that to me? I'll not force you to it, but I should like to know now, before we go farther."

Complete love? She focused her mind on the place he desired, where he intended to enter her.

"I shall not hurt you," he muttered, as if reading her thoughts.

She reached toward his hips to open his clothing, to show him the full scope of her own arching desire. He had nothing on but his shirt. Her hands touched smooth flesh, sensed the underlying strength of muscle. He moved, thrust his sexual rod into her hands. Without thought, she grasped him, ran her hands the length of the shaft that would violate her. No, not violate. Fill her, fill the void, end the ache, complete the mating that had begun so long ago, with his lips upon her palm, under a flapping punkah. She cried out as his tongue touched each of her nipples in turn, delicately.

"Promise of better to come," he said, and she heard the smile in his voice. "Let me undress you, so I may kiss you everywhere."

His lips followed the cloth he tugged away, her breasts, her shoulders, her hips, her thighs. His mouth found her sensual center, and she cried out in both pleasure and surprise at the unexpected delight. He lifted her into a dome of blue, where she was surrounded by an intensity of color, like the tropical skies, the island ocean. The rich azure penetrated her, flowed into her where he gently, slowly, spread her body to accommodate his fullness.

She thrust upward to speed the full connection, felt his mass complete its task, his loins pressed firmly against hers. His body weighed upon her, restricted her movement and her breath, but she felt no fear. The sapphire dome encompassed them, sank inward until it pressed them together, merging their bodies into one. He moved upon her, inside her, moaned as she moaned, thrust pleasure deeply within her. She was taken unawares when the pure blue world fell apart in a rain of white fire.

Her loins, her abdomen, her thighs, were in the center of the flame, and he was the fire, burning into her, over and over, crying out above her as he reveled in the same exquisite torture.

Savage rolled onto his side, bringing her with him. He dared not put his weight upon her, with nothing beneath them but the thin mat. On a feather bed, he'd do it, collapse upon her body, for he knew some women found great pleasure in it after the turmoil of sex.

He kept his hand tight against her buttocks, so that the sensual connection would not be immediately broken. She still moaned, called his name. How wonderful, that she had never used his given name until tonight, for now, whenever she said it, it would recall the sexual tension in her belly, the relief brought by the ultimate touch of him.

That touch was dying, and he hated to see it go. Within her, madly swollen, he had reached a height greater than he had ever before known. He had given her her first time, her virgin sex, and he had brought her to blossom like an experienced woman. And, he thought in wonder, for me it is also the first time. The first time I've made love to a woman I truly love.

He released her hips, and their bodies separated. He drew her against him, and she relaxed there, a spent bird in the haven of the nest. Her fingers sought him with a fragile caresses of thanks.

"My dearest," he whispered. "You have given me great happiness."

"Thank you," she said. "I did not know."

"What didn't you know?"

"That love was of two parts. The way I love you on the ship. Respect, adoration. . . ." Her voice trailed off in her embarrassment. She had yet to learn to speak easily of sex.

"And this? The combining of bodies in the way of beasts? You didn't know it could be part of love?"

"No. And it is not the way of beasts. It is the way of lovers, I believe."

"It is indeed the way of lovers," he said heartily. "For all eternity it's been so. 'I am my beloved's, and his desire is toward me,'" he quoted, recalling the frightening day when Charley had read the words so casually on the deck above his head.

There would only be tonight. His fingers traced the rise of her full hips. She sighed at the pleasure of the touch. He grazed her nipples with his palms, delighted in their hardening, in the shiver that seized her body. He would bring her again to readiness, for he was already there.

Chapter Seventeen

Love came between them, a heavy curtain weighted with the fear of where the emotion might lead. When he sat in the main cabin, Dina busied herself in her own. On deck, she carefully placed herself on the opposite side from the captain.

There could be nothing between them on the ship. He had made that quite plain. In the cruel light of day, she wanted nothing more to happen, no matter how much her body strained toward his. From that night in Canton until the day when her monthly flow came, she had lived in terror that he might have put a child in her. If that had happened, she would have had no choice but Sir Hall and his friends. Now, when they reached Calcutta, she would go to an East Indiaman, one bound for England.

She had filled up the pages of her journal, and rather than ask him for another, she now wrote up and down, across each filled page. She made no note of what had happened in Canton, except to draw a meteoric star in the narrow margin. The image was not necessary for recollection. During the days, it hovered at the edge of consciousness; at night, his union filled her anew. Sometimes she heard him on the other side of the bulkhead, and the sound brought a flash of desire.

He would not marry her, of that she was certain. She brought him no fortune, and a wife would stand in the way of the revenge he had planned for the ladies of the *ton*.

Only once in the six weeks' voyage did Savage call her into the main cabin and speak to her alone, and that just a few days before they were to arrive in Calcutta. She obeyed the summons with misgivings. He did not, as usual, pat the bench beside him to invite her to sit, but gestured toward the stool before the chart table. She perched with her back pressed tightly against the lip of the table.

"I should like to ask you a favor, to be done for me in London," he said.

"Anything I can do for you will be a welcome task," she said sincerely.

"I'll give you a note to my banker. Please select a London house for me to purchase or, if there are none to purchase, to lease. I no longer know what prices homes in London's better areas command, so I shall trust your judgment about values. I should like it to be in Mayfair."

"Park Lane?"

"Preferably, and one large enough for a wife and family. Suitable, also, for rather expansive entertainment. Until I return, you'll live there and see to its proper decoration. At least you'll stay there until you've made other arrangements for yourself."

"Until I've found a husband, you mean?"

"Yes, I suppose that's what I mean," he said warily. "I'll order my banker to furnish sufficient funds for its upkeep, and such work as is necessary to make it acceptable."

"I'm sorry, but I cannot," she said firmly.

"Why not?" he asked in astonishment. "It's quite a simple request, and well within your talents, I would suppose."

"You yourself have said everyone will assume I'm your mistress. For me to superintend the purchase of your house will only verify the gossip. What will people think?"

"I don't give a damn what people think. I want to know you're living in a suitable place. I can't throw you back into the maws of London without making some provision for you. Your share of profits from the voyage will be somewhere between four and five hundred pounds. With that invested properly, and your allowance, you should be able to live in London—not luxuriously, but in comfort, so long as you needn't pay for your own shelter."

"This is all quite unnecessary. I have no intention of living in London, but in some rural village, where my expenses will be completely covered by my allowance. I must thank you for this past year's lessons. I now know how little I really need to be very content."

"But I intend to return to London," he countered. "You must have my house ready for me. Within a year, two years at the most, I'll reestablish myself in England."

"Is this part of your revenge?" she asked in a low voice. "Does this house play a part in bringing your brother to his knees?"

"Everything I do leads toward that end," he retorted. "With the profits from this voyage, my fortune appears made. One more journey, and that only because of my promise to Baranov, then the *Pearl Stallion* anchors in the Pool and I see London Bridge again. And then I bring justice to bear."

"Justice?" she exclaimed. "You think it justice to shame your brother?" In a flash, she realized what part the house would play, and it had little to do with Lord Valmont. The courting of the young women of the *ton.* He would need an elegant place to entertain their mamas, to make them envy his wealth, overlook his background.

"You told me once what you planned to do to the women of the *ton,* and I'll not be a part of it. If you want revenge upon society, you'll do it yourself, without my help."

"I don't know what you're talking about," he said. "I'll need a fine house in town. I'm asking you to see to having it arranged. I've not requested that you cry it about that I'm hunting for a wife."

"But you've asked me to flaunt your wealth in the most obvious of ways, and at the expense of any reputation I may have left. Regardless of what people believe when they hear my story of the past year, living in your house, they'll call me your mistress."

"Perhaps, if I return with the same pain in my heart that I carry now, that's what you'll be," he said harshly.

"No," she said emphatically. "I told you a year ago what I wanted. Marriage. I know how completely impossible that is between us. To carry out your revenge, you must be able to offer the temptation of your hand and your wealth. I'll not be there to see it. I think perhaps I'll seek out a cottage in the Cotswolds, for I've always enjoyed seeing the sheep upon the hills. . . ."

"You'll live in my house, in town," he said, making the statement a command.

"You can command me, Captain, in anything relating to this ship and my duties within her. You cannot command my life, unless you see fit to make an honorable union. I thank you most gratefully for everything you've done for me during the past year. I thank you for not ravishing me when you had the opportunity, I thank you for not dumping me into the arms of Sir Hall, for letting me stay on the *Pearl Stallion,* for not abandoning me in Sumatra, for refusing to give me to the king of the Sandwich Islands, for letting me teach the men to read and learn the skills I'll need in my new life.

"I am not so grateful, however, that I'll be a part of your vicious intentions. You must find someone else to be the instrument of your revenge."

He shifted uneasily upon the padded bench, gazed out the stern windows at the white wake the ship left behind in the green sea.

"What if, when I return, love has not died?" he asked quietly.

"Cherish it if you wish. Clasp it to your bosom. But I shall not, for love held closely in that way is as deadly as the asp was to the queen of Egypt. I'm glad I've grown to love you, for I never had loved before, and I feared it. Now I know that I'm stronger than love, that I can leave it behind."

Savage got up and went to the door of the cabin. He turned, and his tight, bleak face made her cry out.

"I wish I had your faith in my own abilities," he said, so softly she barely heard him. "You've made the correct decision. Perhaps this is my first step in learning to hate you. Hate's the only thing that could possibly conquer what I feel for you right now."

Dina fled to her own cabin, barricaded the door with her bag. She flung herself on her bunk and let the tears come. If he had stayed one second longer, if his bleak, unhappy face had confronted her for one more instant, she would have gone to him. She would have embraced him, kissed him, begged to be allowed to caress away his displeasure and sadness.

The oblique light of early morning cast long shadows across the flat brown landscape bordering the Hooghly. The thickets of bamboo were lost in their own immense shadows. Everything upright—a temple, a man walking beside the river, the bullock carts toiling toward Calcutta—was made small by the length of its shadow.

The *Pearl Stallion*'s shadow traveled before her and off to the side. Dina stood so that she could see the span of charcoal gray the ship created upon the brown waters. Even this close to the ocean, the river stank, and the smell seemed less offensive if she did not see the color of its filth.

Savage stood on the other side of the deck. Since their last conversation, all communications between them had ceased, except for words needed to operate the ship. Dina looked forward to the breaking of the last tie, Savage's arrangements for her passage to England. No, there was a second thing. He would bring her the news she dreaded to hear. What had happened in the shipyard? Uncle George might be in prison, or perhaps have been sent back to England in chains for trial. What had happened to Aunt Lily and Emily?

And if nothing had transpired, if Uncle George and Captain Freemantle were still carrying out their schemes, she must stay well out of their way. A year on the *Pearl Stallion* had made her a partisan of Savage's, regardless of the ill feelings that divided them at the moment. She, like the rest of the crew, had very nearly been a victim of Freemantle's trick with the water barrels. She would choose Savage over Freemantle, if it came to a battle in which she must take sides.

The sun swung slowly upward until it was high overhead. Dina retreated to the shadow of the mizzen sail before the anchorage came into view. Before the hulls of the ships were visible Dr. Hampton was cheering from his perch in the mainmast, waving his hat.

"The *Red Hawk*'s anchored just beyond that Indiaman!" he shouted toward the deck, as if everyone on board would share in his joy. Dina's stomach lurched in sick worry that Miss Hawkins might not be aboard the ship, that all that was awaiting the doctor was a letter, telling of her marriage months ago to some worthy of Charleston, South Carolina.

"We'll see if we can't find a berth nearby!" shouted Savage. He grinned upward, amused by the happiness of his friend. Dina prayed fervently that Savage's love would be weaker than that of the doctor, who had carried Miss Hawkins in his heart for four years. But then, the doctor was an American, and she suspected they were given to more sentimentality than Englishmen.

The anchors ran out, splashing the filthy water upward, fouling the ship almost to the gunwales. Dina scanned the Indiamen lying at anchor, hoped one of them was leaving for England within the next day or two. The heat was oppressive, breathless, and she longed to be at sea.

Signal flags ran up, announcing to the shore the ship's identity, as if a hundred glasses on the beach had not already picked out the glittering figurehead and the sleek black hull. The official signals had barely hit the deck when another series, directed at the *Red Hawk*, soared. Dr. Hampton clung to the ratlines, a glass clapped to his eye.

"She's there, I can see her!" Hampton shouted.

Dina breathed a great, audible sigh of relief.

"It's a great relief, is it not?" said a sardonic voice beside her. She whirled on Savage, who had come noiselessly near her.

"I had worried," she said flatly.

"Poor foolish man," said Savage, a sneer in his words. "To believe so faithfully in love."

"Indeed."

Their conversation was interrupted by flags from the *Red Hawk*. Figures were seen going down the side of the American vessel, and two of them wore skirts.

Dina turned away from the reunion of the lovers, for the sight of Hampton's arms outstretched toward the dark-haired girl made her own body yearn for the massive one standing silently by the railing. She glimpsed Savage, and saw his mouth tight, his body stiff, as he, too, she guessed, resisted the appealing call of the expressions of love.

He greeted Captain and Mrs. Hawkins politely, then introduced his officers, which forced Dina to venture away from her retreat behind the mizzenmast. The American captain was short and stout, his wife dainty. Savage invited everyone below, where Kranz spread out wine, tea and cakes. Dina hung back to take her proper place at the rear of the group. Captain Hawkins thrust Hampton and his daughter ahead of him, offered his wife his arm. The two of them smiled, looked at the adoring couple before them, laughed at some private amusement. For one instant, Captain Hawkins's lips brushed the corner of his wife's mouth. Dina saw the gesture, the glow in the man's eyes. The woman's hand grasped her husband's arm in a barely noticed tightening.

An uncomfortable fluidity possessed Dina. There was something in the man's eyes that she had seen before, the day King Kamehameha came to the ship and announced he was yielding to his queen's entreaties, furnishing provisions to the *Pearl Stallion*. Had she just never noticed that glance between husband and wife before? Or had she never before met two people who had remained in love?

Dina found she was unable to avoid sneaking glances at the lovers—not the young ones, but the elder couple. Worse, she saw that Savage was also captivated by the gentle regard radiating between the captain and his wife. It was to be expected that Hampton and his Laura would have eyes only for one another. It was quite another thing for Captain Hawkins to gently touch his wife's fingers when she handed him a cup of tea. And for her to respond to the touch with a fleeting smile designed only for him.

Dina took a glass of wine, but was unable to drink it. She did not want to believe in the love that flaunted itself so unselfconsciously before her.

"I shall have to leave you under the care of Lieutenant Becker," announced Savage, "for I must report immediately to the harbormaster, as well as make arrangements for refitting in the shipyard."

"I wish you good luck," said Captain Hawkins genially. "But I suppose you, with a connection to the East India Company, do not have the problems we've encountered in dealing with the shipyard." Savage, who had started to rise, sank back onto his seat.

"What problems?" he asked, the note of concern plain in his voice.

"We'd expected to buy a few extra spars and some cordage here in Calcutta. Dealing with Captain Freemantle, who's in charge of the shipyard, has been difficult."

Savage's brows rose and separated, Becker's face tightened, and Hampton drew his eyes away from his intended long enough to shoot a troubled glance at Dina.

"He's more than once suggested we might receive quicker service if we were willing to pay certain premiums for ship's stores," continued the captain. "I suppose that's what it will come to in the end."

"And these stores would come through some other agency than the shipyard?" asked Savage with curiosity.

"Yes. I've hesitated, naturally, fearing perhaps he simply wants to pull a foreigner into an illegal scheme, which might end in the seizing of the *Red Hawk*. It would be wiser, perhaps, to make our way to some eastern port and find what we need there."

Savage stood, as much as he was able, with determination.

"Have as little to do with Freemantle as possible," he said curtly. "His nemesis has arrived." He walked out, leaving Captain Hawkins staring after him in amazement.

Night fell, but none of the crew left the deck. The ship's work—what was necessary in port—was done, but often heads lifted to gaze toward the wharf, where the ship's boat rocked gently and the oarsmen loafed against the pilings. It was quite late when a cluster of lanterns on the wharf illuminated the boat pulling away. It disappeared on the dark waters, then materialized alongside the *Pearl Stallion*.

Dina watched the huge shadow heave itself upon the deck, repressed the surge of warmth that threatened to overwhelm her. I hope he has made the arrangements for me, she thought, so I can leave and never see him again. I love him so much, and I am so close to throwing myself to disaster in his arms.

"Prices are high," announced Savage happily. "We shall complete a prosperous voyage." The crew cheered, but he raised his hand in the lanternlight and stilled them.

"We start unloading tomorrow at first light. After that's done, while the ship is being refitted, we'll all have our time ashore. Officers will join me in the main cabin."

Every space below decks was stifling, the main cabin more than anyplace else, because it was filled with sweating men. Dina took the stool by the chart table to avoid joining Savage on the bench.

"Lord Mornington is gone, left several months ago, when his replacement as governor-general arrived," began Savage.

"And his replacement is—?" asked Becker.

"*Was* Lord Cornwallis. He lasted but two months, before he died on a trip upriver. The temporary governor-general is Sir John Barlow. I know very little of him, and he knows less of me. As you probably assumed from Hawkins's revelation, nothing has been done toward an investigation of the shipyard. Sir Hall Allinson did not see fit to study such a serious allegation while Lord Mornington was here, for fear he would cast a shadow upon His Lordship's final months in command. He had no time to raise the matter with Cornwallis, and since Sir John is in a tenuous, temporary position, Sir Hall hesitates to take any action upon a single accusation."

"So Freemantle is still bleeding the shipyard of goods, which he sells for his own profit," said Becker bitterly.

"So it seems. I went to Sir John, insisted upon seeing him, although he did not particularly appreciate giving up his evening ride. He protested that the shipyard ledgers are reviewed regularly, but I pointed out Mason's part in the scheme, and he saw how, with the cooperation of the head clerk, theft might be hidden. I laid before him the fraud of our water, suggested the avenues which an investigation should take." He turned to Becker. "He wishes to see you tomorrow morning, to hear your account of what transpired when you were in the shipyard. You might suggest that he use Captain Hawkins as a tempting bait, to catch Freemantle in his profitable activities."

"A good idea. Freemantle wouldn't suspect a foreigner of being in league with the governor-general to catch him."

"Now, gentlemen, good night, and sleep well, with the assurance that within a week we'll divide stunning profits. I wish to speak privately to Lady Dina." The men trailed out, not to their cabins, but to the cooler reaches of the deck.

"Your absence was, for several days, a great mystery," said Savage without any polite preliminaries. "Your aunt and uncle thought you had wandered away in a feverish haze."

"And then?"

"Your cousin inventoried your clothing and realized some items were missing. Your uncle seems to have discovered the theft of his sailor suit, which he had planned to preserve for use at the next costume ball."

"And they supposed I was with you?"

"Exactly. Your behavior led them to believe you were infatuated with me since you disappeared on the night of the *Pearl Stallion*'s sailing. It was really no surprise to anyone this morning when their glasses revealed a figure in skirts. Sir Hall was quite ribald in his remarks, and would welcome you at his house even yet tonight. Would you care to go?"

"Good God! No!"

"The *Northern Star* will weigh anchor within a few days, bound for England. I've reserved a cabin for you."

"Thank you."

"The captain is willing for you to come aboard immediately, if you'll restrict yourself to your cabin and stay out of the way of the preparations. I assured him you were quite familiar with life on shipboard."

"Does he need a navigator?" asked Dina ruefully.

"I don't believe so," said Savage. He crossed his legs and groaned. "But the *Pearl Stallion* does, damn it! A navigator and a surgeon, lost all at once!"

"There must be many men who would be willing to ship with you."

"Many, but whether or not they're skilled doesn't always become apparent until we're well out to sea. Think of Lightner's incompetence."

"I often," said Dina softly, "think of Lightner, and what may have happened to him in California. We abandoned him with the enemy, and they may have had no mercy for him."

"He disobeyed orders," said Savage shortly, but Dina saw his strong white teeth come together and his lips pull back. He shifted his weight, patted the bench and beckoned to her.

"Come here, Lady Dina."

She obeyed his order, but did not sit exactly where his hand had indicated.

"Will you alter your mind about the house? Will you become my agent to find a London residence?"

"No."

"Will you then grant me one favor?"

"Not if the favor is to find a house where you may entertain and seduce women, only to abandon them."

"No, this favor is quite different. Will you wait for me?"

"Wait for you? Wait for you to do what?"

"Return to England. Will you forgo any marriage until I return?"

"I see no reason why I should make that promise," she said in astonishment. "You'll not marry me. I have no fortune. I've already passed up many chances, and to pass by others, at my age, would be unreasonable."

"Dina, I love you. I'm uncertain that I shall stop loving you, and perhaps when I return to England—"

"You'd be willing to overlook my lack of fortune? Has Hampton lured you into the belief that love is eternal?" She laughed derisively, until she noticed the serious eyes and the set mouth.

"Do you never think upon the night in Canton?" he whispered.

He moved so quickly, she had no time to escape his arms, his mouth. He covered her face with kisses, his hands spread upon the curve of her hips. While her mind told her to resist, her body betrayed her. She sank into the pleasure of his love, cupped her hands about his face and returned his kisses, joining their lips in hot anticipation. He was the one who withdrew from the embrace, pushed her away.

"I shall see to your transport to the *Northern Star* tomorrow morning," he said curtly, "before we begin the unloading. You'll carry a draft upon my agent in London, who will see to getting you your money from the voyage." He went to the door of his own cabin, then turned.

"Remember, Dina. I love you. I always before believed love was temporary, but now I'm not so certain."

"The skeptic has been converted?" she asked archly.

"No, but led to doubt his own wisdom. And you?"

"Love frightens me. It is such joy, was such a joy with you, there is certainly nothing to do but fall from such heights. Remember, I saw what that fall does to a woman."

"Miss Hawkins's parents—they have not seemed to fall."

"So you noticed that, too," she said.

"I did see it, and the presence of that affection sent shivers to my boot soles. What if love doesn't fail? What if it maintains itself, and we are left to face the same profound feeling months, years, decades, after its inception?"

"It is quite more likely," she said stoutly, "that love is nothing but a fool's paradise. I have seen many people who pretended to love, and I have heard husbands whisper terms of endearment into the ears of jades, while their wives sat in neighboring rooms, praising the permanence of their devotion."

"Have your things ready for the morning," he said sadly. "You'll be taken to the *Northern Star* at first light."

He disappeared into his cabin. Dina sat quietly, studying the play of lanternlight on the small waves of the Hooghly. She had not thought about it, until now, but her terror at the touch of a man had disappeared. When had it happened? Sometime between that dreadful night in California and the trip with Savage—with Anson—up the Pearl River, her mind and body had shifted from one side of the great circle to another, and remained there. She wanted to feel again his fingers lifting her breasts and molding them to his pleasure, the tentative stroke of his tongue upon her nipples, and the culminating pressure of their merging bodies.

So many things had happened to bring about the change within her. She recalled the drifting pain, her utter dismay, when Charley had stood before her and read, with seeming innocence:

As the apple tree among the trees of the wood, so is my beloved among the sons. I sat down under his shadow with great delight, and his fruit was sweet to my taste. He brought me to the banqueting house, and his banner over me was love.

"His left hand is under my head, and his right hand doth embrace me," she whispered.

She crept to the door of Savage's cabin, tried to hear the soft pulse of his breath within.

"I lay down under his shadow with great delight, and his fruit was sweet to my taste," she whispered. There was no response from beyond the door.

Chapter Eighteen

From the deck of the *Northern Star,* Dina watched specks move about on the *Pearl Stallion,* on the deck, in the rigging. Whenever she was allowed out of her cabin, she leaned against the rail, watching the launches receive the boxes and bales of goods from the *Pearl Stallion*'s hold. Boats rowed from the ship to the shore, and one morning she was delighted to spy two bulky figures disembarking onto the wharf—Charley and Savage.

What business did he have onshore? She fancied him visiting the governor-general. More likely he was arranging for the cargo of food the ship would carry to Russian America. Would he dance at a ball, where her aunt and uncle would see him? Dine at the table of a secretary or a councilman?

The thought that he might go to a woman tortured her. She imagined him sampling the young women who had come to Calcutta during the past year, women more cooperative in dispensing their favors than she had been. Laughing, giggling, crying out in passion upon the silver-draped couch in the screened veranda. She moaned and fled to her cabin.

The cabin was twice the size of the niche she had occupied on the *Pearl Stallion,* yet each morning when she awoke she wished desperately to be back on that cramped ship. There she had been part of the crew. Here, on this vast Indiaman, she was alone, without even a friendly glance from the overworked officers. And crew members dropped their eyes and hustled past, not daring even to look at her.

She worked on rewriting her diary, transcribing it into the new journal Savage had given her as a parting gift. She had sunk so deeply into her memories that the knock at the door suggested, for a moment, that she was on the *Pearl Stallion*, with Savage only a few inches away, beyond the nearest bulkhead. The illusion vanished when she heard the strange voice.

"Your Ladyship, you have a visitor."

A new jump in the speed of her heart. Savage. Who else would come to see her? She jerked open the door. She hardly recognized her uncle. He was very thin, his face narrow and gray. His shoulders sagged.

"You might at least have let us know you were here, even if you cannot find it in your heart to stay with us until this ship sails," he said in a weak accusation, condemning her even as her greetings died on her lips.

"I had not expected you to want me as a guest," she said. "I was afraid my reputation had not survived a year on a trading ship."

"Nor has it," he snapped. "When we realized what you'd done, we prayed you might not survive the voyage, rather than return here with no prospects at all."

"My prospects in Calcutta are the same as they were before I left."

"If you had trusted my protection, you need not have feared such disgrace," her uncle said. "Unless, that is, your unnatural desires lead you in that direction. You might have married Captain Freemantle."

"I had no inclination to be married to that vicious man."

"Vicious? How dare you speak so of him, after spending a year with a man who flaunts his unnatural lusts in public!"

"A man whose restraint and kindness have given me hope for the future."

He studied her for several moments, looking through the top half of his eyes to compensate for the stoop of his body.

A year of thievery had taken its toll, and Uncle George showed the burden of an ever-increasing threat of apprehension. Dina debated inwardly. Should she tell him Savage had gone to Sir John Barlow? That Barlow had interviewed Becker and was personally peeling back the layers of falsification?

No. Let him enjoy these last days, as much as he might, until the scandal overcame him.

"Lily asks me to invite you to dine with us today," Uncle George said, his tone changing to one of cautious friendship. "Emily wants very much to see you before you leave. She married Mr. Porter soon after you ran off, and is expecting her child any day."

"A child!" exclaimed Dina.

"Yes. She lives a truly respectable life. Your escapade went hard with her, and for a while she despaired of gaining a marriage proposal, since you shamed us so in throwing yourself at Captain Saurage."

"Could she visit me here?" asked Dina with caution.

"Emily is very near her time."

Dina nodded. Asking a woman heavy with child to make such a journey was unreasonable.

"I can come for only a short time. I would have to arrange for the ship's boat to take me ashore and wait until I returned. I cannot dine with you, but will be pleased to visit. Could you send the landau?"

"Most happily. You must not expect Lily to ride down to welcome you, and to be seen with you in public."

"Of course not," Dina said wryly.

Loti came racing down the narrow street, almost running into Savage in his haste.

"He's coming!" he gasped.

"Spread out," said Savage, gesturing to the crowd of sailors. "Don't let him pass."

The sailors had barely taken their position as a living barricade across the street when the curricle and its two matched grays rounded the corner. Captain Freemantle made no effort to stop.

"Out of the way, you scum!" Freemantle screamed, wrestling with the reins to control the nervous animals.

Savage walked to the side of the open coach. "I wanted to see you, Captain, and thought perhaps you wouldn't accept an invitation to visit me on the *Pearl Stallion.*"

"Why shouldn't I visit you on your ugly ship?"

"I'm sorry." Savage bowed with elaborate irony. "I'd supposed you might hesitate, since we were likely to be ghosts. All of us died of dreadful thirst in the middle of the Pacific, didn't we?"

"I don't know what you're talking about."

"But Sir John Barlow does. Sir John Barlow knows everything. How long now, Captain, before the soldiers arrive, and you never see your beautiful horses again?"

Freemantle jerked the whip from its socket and lashed violently at Savage. Savage raised his hand, took the blow across his palm and closed his hand around the whip. Freemantle tugged at it, but it did not come free.

"Such behavior is not polite, Captain. I should challenge you."

"I don't fight the bastards of servants!" shouted Freemantle, jerking on the whip.

"I merely desire to inform you that your days of freedom are numbered," said Savage pleasantly, "so you might better plan the hours of life you have left before the prison doors close. This morning you had some dealings with the American captain, I believe."

"My business is mine alone. If the vile American spoke to you, he did so out of turn, and betrays his low origins."

"Oh, but it was not to me he spoke, it was to an assistant of Sir John Barlow. I thought you might find it useful to know you were observed."

Freemantle blanched beneath his tan. He dropped the captured whip and grasped the reins with both hands.

"Observed?"

"Yes. Captain Hawkins was the bait. The trap will spring soon."

"Why are you telling me this? You're lying, trying to frighten me. You have no reason to warn me of anything."

"But I do, because I demand my revenge, and the frightened rage in your eyes gives me some solace."

Freemantle's face tightened. He wheeled about, as if he heard the sound of marching soldiers.

"No. They're not coming now. Their dalliance pleases me, for every minute they delay is a minute of terror for you. Terror like that I felt when I learned what was in my water barrels." Savage handed back the whip politely. "Go now, Captain, and enjoy your last hours of freedom."

Freemantle grabbed the whip, struck down viciously, but Savage stepped out of the way, laughing.

"Let me get on my way," Freemantle snarled thickly.

"Certainly. But first—" Savage walked to the wheel of the curricle, lowered his voice "—I thought you might like to know about the beautiful woman you intended to make your wife. She is indeed beautiful, in every way. She moans when a man's hands touch her. She returns kisses with great passion. When I came to her, her hips lifted, willingly, inviting me within."

"You bastard!" screamed Freemantle, lashing out with the whip at random. Savage danced away from him nimbly. "You filthy bastard, you scrubwoman's bastard!"

The whip landed full upon the back of one of the horses. It reared, screaming, then sprang, dragging its companion with it. The line of sailors parted to let the curricle through. Savage relished his triumph, his hands on his hips as he watched the retreating figure. His delight in the man's terror crystallized in his gut, then rose as a mammoth bubble of laughter. He threw his head back and roared, spread out his hand and let the blood from the slash across the palm drip upon the road.

The house had not changed. The same airless rooms, the same bulky, cheap furniture brought from England. Aunt

Lily stared at her for a moment, her face a mask of fear, the glow of madness in her eyes. She dropped her head, as if she knew her terrible secret might be read there. Emily's stocky body was swollen with her pregnancy, but in contrast to her aunt's, her face showed nothing but contentment. The servant brought tea and cakes.

"Dear Dina," said Emily. "We were so worried about you. Until I realized you had taken some of your frocks, we feared you had fallen into the river."

"I'm sorry I caused you concern," said Dina sincerely. "But you must understand—" she turned to her uncle "—I could not stand the idea of marrying Freemantle. And Sir Hall, I'm sure, intended to turn me into one of the women who serve him, and that I could not bear."

"How exactly did you get out of the house without anyone hearing?" asked Uncle George.

"I changed into your sailor clothes, climbed the banyan tree and dropped over the wall."

"The banyan tree!" exclaimed her aunt, her voice rising to a shriek.

"Be quiet, Lily," said her uncle. "And did Saurage help you get on his ship?"

"No, I crept aboard while everyone was busy loading fruit and vegetables. I hid in a sleeping cabin until we were far out to sea. Captain Saurage intended to send me back on the first Indiaman we met, but then I discovered his destination, and he made me come with him."

"You should know, Lady Endine," said her uncle proudly, "that very soon I shall have a significant investment in a trading vessel. I, and some other investors, already have the ship hired. You might tell me, in confidence, where you sailed with Captain Saurage."

While her uncle spoke, Dina looked at her aunt. Madness. Madness that came from terror. And the banyan tree? Could she discover what was so horrifying about the banyan tree?

"Do you know, Uncle George, that the very day I met Captain Saurage, that afternoon, I heard you and Captain

Freemantle talking in the garden? I was hiding beneath the *banyan tree.*" She laid stress upon the final two words.

Her aunt shrieked, her clenched fists pressed against her mouth.

"The banyan tree. She knows what's beneath the banyan tree!" she shrieked.

"Shut up, Lily!" shouted Uncle George. He sprang up and tugged the woman from her chair. "Perhaps you should go to your room and rest."

"No. I know what you did. I know what you put beneath the banyan tree!" The woman struggled with the strength of the insane, threw her husband away from her. Emily heaved herself from the couch to come to her aunt's aid, but Aunt Lily escaped her, plastered herself against the door, screaming.

"The banyan tree! The banyan tree!"

"Mason, let me in," came an excited voice from the other side of the door. Aunt Lily staggered away, staring at the door as if it were dripping blood. Freemantle burst into the room.

"My God! Mason, they know! The bargain with the American this morning—" His eyes fell upon Dina. "You! You foul whore! What are you doing here?" His hand shot out and grasped her arm with such force he hurt her. "You'll come with me to the ship. We'll leave immediately, and you'll do for me what you did with Savage. And then I'll throw you into the sea, you bitch."

"You can't take the ship, Captain," said George, his voice pleading. "There's no crew yet, and the provisions aren't—"

"I'll take the men from the shipyard. They'll serve me as well in one place as the other."

"But the trading license has yet to be issued. Sir John...." Her uncle's gray face turned white and his fear spilled forth in frantic, sputtering words. "You won't leave...me here...to suffer alone? It wasn't my idea...in the beginning. It wasn't my idea!"

"You won't mind prison, Mason. And I'll share the wealth with you, because this whore will tell me where Savage has been. Won't you?" he said shaking Dina.

She clenched her teeth to keep them from chattering. "No," she said with sudden determination. "I won't tell you anything."

"Where?" he shouted. He held her at arm's length, and she was twisting away, searching for a path to safety, when his right fist slammed into the side of her face. She lost her footing and, for an instant, her sense of where she was. Freemantle pulled her to her feet. "Where?"

Uncle George offered no help. She must free herself and get away from the house. Dina swung her body, a pendulum from the point where his hand crushed her arm. She swung back with her full force, throwing herself against him. He had been slightly off balance, so her blow sent him sprawling, but also carried her with him, into a wavering world.

Someone shrieked. Her hands and knees felt the scratch of the sisal mat, and she could smell its dust and mold. She watched a strange dance of polished boots, moving in time to curses and screams. Then a cry of agony, hardly human, ending in ghastly moans.

"Where?" asked a thick voice above her. But she would never tell him. She struggled to her hands and knees, trying to grasp the black boot and pull him to the floor. A crushing blow against her side, then pain, deep, into her heart. She knew the black boot was drawn back, ready to kick again. He would kill her, and she hadn't told Anson the truth.

Anson would never know how deeply she loved him. That she would indeed wait for him. Would have waited for him, except now she was dead, and there was no opportunity.

"Where? Where? Where?" raged Freemantle's voice. Turmoil and noise surrounded her, as if everything in the room had fallen down at once. She could not fill her lungs, and her mind spun, fell into a vortex of diminishing light.

She grasped at one last vision, Savage high in the mizzen rigging, looking down at her, smiling. Then came a black mist.

Someone knelt over her, and she automatically raised her arms above her head to fend off the coming blow.

"Dina. I'm here. I'll take care of you."

He lifted her; the pain caused by the pressure of his arms was more than she could bear, and she cried out, struggled to be let down. She had one glimpse of the disordered room, Emily's bulky body on the floor, her arms clutching randomly for help. Beyond was a brown form, grotesquely impaled upon a length of steel that caught the sunlight and reflected it into her eyes. And blood. A beautiful pool of spreading crimson.

"Charley!" Savage yelled. He thrust her into other arms. "Get her to the ship. Send someone to the *Red Hawk* to get Hampton. She's hurt."

There was something she had to tell him. It hurt to open her mouth.

"Anson," she begged. He leaned over her.

"Something terrible has happened. Something terrible about the banyan tree—" She stopped. It hurt too much to talk.

"I'll see to it. Charley will take care of you."

"No." There was something else. Savage's face leaned close. His expression of unbelieving shock told her the truth about the bodies on the floor, about his feelings for her.

"Anson," she whispered.

"Yes."

"I'll wait for you. I do love you."

She yielded to Charley's firm grasp, tried to stifle her moans as his strength pressed her bruised flesh against his body. When he handed her into a boat, she groaned at the pain the transfer caused. She was conscious enough to see the board lowered over the side of the ship, to be aware that she must not struggle against the ropes, but allow herself to be tied to it, then lifted over the gunwales.

Then the gentle motion of a ship at anchor, the rhythmic sway of her bunk, and the peace that came with the assurance that she was safely aboard the *Pearl Stallion. I will never leave again, ever,* some part of her mind resolved. *There is nothing ashore but pain and tragedy.*

Dr. Hampton's face came in and out of focus. Someone bound her chest, so tightly she protested. Then a cup at her lips. The motion of the ship became the gentle rock of a cradle, and near her a rough voice murmured words of consolation and love.

Dina first appraised the world with her ears. The faint creaks of the ship at anchor in the Hooghly; the quiet breathing of another person in the cabin with her. She opened her eyes. She was not in her own cabin, for the compass on the deck beam above pointed steadily north. Her head ached dreadfully. She tried to raise her hand to her face, but found she could not move it. Her heart pounded, and the memory of Don Miguel binding her hands surfaced in her disordered brain. She struggled upward, saw Savage's dark eyes, and his broad hand holding tightly to hers. He sat on the deck beside the bunk.

"Hush," he whispered. "You're hurt. Stay quiet."

She sank back against the pillows, flexed her fingers against his to show her obedience. Her heart slowed, and she relaxed in the cocoon of his protection. His hand stroked her hair back from her forehead. So many times he had used the gesture to calm her, to strengthen her, to show his love.

"Do you remember what happened?" he asked.

"I went to see Emily, for she's going to have a baby." The left side of her lips didn't seem to move, and her speech sounded like that of an invalid.

"Do you remember who did this to you?"

"Freemantle."

"I must not make you talk," he said. His lips brushed her cheek. "But I had to be certain you did not suppose I had struck you."

"I should never have thought that."

"You did once. You dreamed I hurt you."

"Long ago," she protested weakly.

He clasped her hand so tightly, the pain of it overcame the other pains.

"I did this to you, Dina," he moaned. "Please forgive me, for I did do this to you."

"I remember," she protested. "It was Freemantle."

"But I drove Freemantle to it. I met him on the street. I taunted him, told him that within hours he'd be arrested. I wanted to see the fear in his eyes. I wanted to see him rush about, trying to find safety. I wanted him to feel the panic I felt when I dumped that first barrel of vile water." His voice sank, the words coming in agonized clusters, as if he were plunging a dagger into his own breast, time after time. "I told him...the beautiful woman he desired for his wife...had been in my bed. I boasted...that you had come to me willingly." He moaned, unable to continue, then plunged ahead resolutely with the confession. "I wanted my revenge...drove him into a frenzy, without thinking of what, in that rage, he might do to you."

She twisted her head on the pillow, stared at his anguished face.

"I should not have gone to see Emily," she said. "I should have known something like this would happen. But I so wanted to see her before the baby came."

Her last view of her uncle's house rose behind her eyes: Emily, moaning on the floor.

"What happened to Emily?" she asked in alarm, lifting herself up on her elbows, almost screaming at the pain the sudden movement caused. He rose, pushed her back against the bunk.

"Hampton says you must stay quiet."

"What happened to Emily?" she persisted.

"She tried to stop Freemantle. He hit her, kicked her."

"The baby?"

"I don't know. She's being cared for by her friends." He stifled another small moan, but it had been sufficient to betray his grief and regret.

"Uncle George? Where is he?"

"My dear, don't speak. You must rest."

"Someone was killed. There was so much blood. Uncle George?"

"Yes," he said unwillingly. "He tried to distract Freemantle in his rage. Pull him away from you and Emily, I suppose. Freemantle drew his sword and drove it through him."

"Who came?" she whispered, trying not to move her lips "I thought I was dead. Who came and saved me? What were you doing there?"

"The soldiers, from the governor-general. I followed them, to have the pleasure of seeing Freemantle and George Mason led off to prison. Yesterday morning they made a sale of ship's stores to Captain Hawkins, without suspecting it was a trap."

"Aunt Lily?" she asked in despair.

"She's using your cabin on the *Northern Star,* going back to England. I believe she has relatives who will care for her."

He clasped her hand, caressed her palm with his fingers. She returned the gesture, found it soothing, distracting her attention from the agony of her body. His fingers strayed from her hand to her arm. They created a gentle pressure, supporting her, keeping her from descending completely into an abyss of despair.

"She's mad," she said simply. "Something has driven her mad."

"Much has happened since we sailed away a year ago. A clerk at the shipyard discovered the fraud in your uncle's bookkeeping. They killed him, buried him under your uncle's banyan tree. Seeing the crime, knowing the body was in her garden, destroyed your aunt's mind."

Dina closed her eyes and tried to likewise shut her mind, blot out the whirlwind of catastrophes about her. She felt

Savage's lips touch her cheek, brush the right corner of her mouth.

"I thought it best that your aunt go back to England. Perhaps there she has a chance to recover. To forget what happened in India."

"I shall never forget," she murmured, opening her eyes to see him.

"Nor will I." He smiled unexpectedly. "It has been a dreadful shock, to fall in love with one of those awful women who come to India to find husbands." She tried to return the smile, but it hurt, so she lifted her hand and traced the line of his lips. "Rest, and try to sleep. Someone will be near you. There's nothing to fear."

She closed her eyes obediently, secure in the confines of the *Pearl Stallion.*

Chapter Nineteen

"I should like to get up," said Dina. "I'm very tired of staying in bed."

"You're to stay in bed for another week," said Dr. Hampton, who gave Savage a sidelong glance, as if enlisting an ally. "I would not have approved this arrangement if I'd known," he said, looking at the hammock slung aft of the mizzenmast, "but now that's it's done, I suppose it would be cruel to send her below again."

"It gets dreadfully hot in the cabins," said Savage, by way of justifying bringing Dina on deck.

"Change the wrapping about her chest every day, to keep the ribs in place. It must be clean, every day. Otherwise, there's nothing to be done except let her recover. Two or three weeks, and she might risk setting off for England. If you do—" he addressed Dina "—take several long pieces of muslin to tie yourself into your bunk during rough weather. Falling or being tossed about could reinjure your ribs." He looked across her body at Savage.

"If the *Red Hawk* were going by the Cape of Good Hope, I'd suggest to Captain Hawkins that we take her home, or at least as far as the African settlements, where the weather's cooler. But he insists it's easier sailing west to east by way of Cape Horn."

"I'm sorry to see you go," said Dina, "but I'm sure you're anxious to return home."

"Tomorrow?" asked Savage.

"When the wind sets right, the captain says. You'll come to Charleston when you order your next ship from an American shipyard? You'll come visit us?"

"Yes. In two or three years, when Barber and Loti are ready to take over command."

Hampton lifted Dina's hand in his own, bowed over it and kissed her fingers.

"And you must come to visit us, too. Don't be in a great hurry to leave Calcutta." He glanced at Savage, but continued to address her. "You should take time for a leisurely recovery. Perhaps some friends ashore..."

Savage nodded sharply, drew Hampton away, amidships, where they talked in low voices. Dina threw off the blanket that Savage had tucked about her against the cool of the morning. The sun, despite the sail rigged to give her shade, promised another blistering day. Only the lightest breeze whispered in the ropes.

The afternoon was almost gone before she heard Savage's boots on the deck, opened her eyes to find him standing beside her.

"Asleep?" he asked.

"No. Just resting. It seems that's all I can do for the present."

"Resting is what you're expected to do. The *Pearl Stallion* will be taken to the shipyard day after tomorrow. I've found a house where you'll be cared for."

"I can go stay with Emily."

"No, you cannot. Mrs. Porter is not well."

Dina pushed herself upright, but quickly regretted the motion. Every change of position brought shooting pains.

"Not well?" she asked as the pain subsided. "What are you keeping from me?"

"Lie down."

"I'll lie down and be still when you tell me the truth."

"I was told that Freemantle was kicking you, and Emily attempted to restrain him. He turned on her. As a result of his blows her travail came upon her. For a day, her life was despaired of, but she's recovering."

"And the child?"

"A boy. A great lusty boy."

Dina reached out her arms to him, begging for comfort. He took her hands in his. She lay still, her eyes unfocused.

"Everyone who's kin to me comes to such a disastrous end," she mused. "There's no one left but Uncle Leonard and Emily."

Savage tightened his grip on her hands. Did the gesture mean anything? Was he offering himself to take the place of those she had lost? He loosened his grip, but retained her hands in his, relaxed and untroubled. The sun had dropped so its rays found their way beneath the sail. He moved his body to shade her face. A faint noise attracted his attention, but Dina could not see who stood beyond the mast.

"Yes, Mr. Becker."

"Sir, the men have asked me to speak to you."

Dina twisted her head and saw, amidships, the entire crew standing, expectant.

"Is something wrong?" asked Savage with sudden concern.

"The men are doubtful about the applicants for the position of navigator. They've asked me to request of you—" Becker cleared his throat "—that Lady Dina stay in that position, sir."

Savage took a step away from her side. "It's impossible."

"They say they trust her, for she does not give herself airs about her knowledge, but spreads it about happily. And does not pretend to know what she does not."

Savage spun around and stared down at Dina, his jaw thrust out in shock and surprise. Then he turned back to Becker.

"No," he muttered, so quietly she barely heard him. "They don't understand. No." The crew had drawn closer.

"No," he said in a louder voice. "She's going to England as soon as she's recovered." The men did not retreat, in fact pressed closer and stared at him, as if the intensity of their eyes might make him change his mind.

"My God!" he shouted. "You're men. Don't you understand? Every night, she's only inches away from me, and I burn to bring her to me. I've spent a year in the hell of resisting that lust." His voice rose to a shout. "In Canton, though, I betrayed everything I'd promised you.... I'll not have her aboard!"

He almost ran to the hatch, as if fleeing a great threat. He made one step downward, then turned to the crew.

"Don't you understand?" he shouted. "I love her!"

He threw himself off the deck, his boots thundering on the companionway. Dina lay stiff, appalled at the public confession. The tension of her muscles made her chest hurt; the pain circled as if drawn with a knife. She closed her eyes. The whisper of bare feet on the deck told her the stunned crew had retreated to the bow. How would it go, between captain and crew, now that they knew? She thought of rolling out of the hammock and crawling down to her own cabin, but at the last moment remembered the space was no longer hers. Mr. Becker had reclaimed it. There was nothing to do but stay where she was, to let Savage work out his rage and pain below, alone.

Her heart ached for him, for his confusion, for the guilt he felt about her injuries. But there was also a warm glow that went some way toward mitigating the pain in her heart. The crew wanted her back. How she would love to be back! Savage would not allow it, but the fact that they had asked for her would keep her company, all the way to England. She lay quite still to keep the aches in her chest contained, and reveled in the delight of what had just happened. The men liked her, trusted her, and wanted her back. Their petition would stand in her memory all her life, and give her hope that the future held some happiness for her, after all.

She had learned so much from them, from the *Pearl Stallion*.

She would not return to the trivial patterns she had lived by before, but would seek something more substantial. A small cottage in a village no longer terrified her. In some country town, she could do what she had done here, and win respect and love. She would never again pretend to wealth, or to knowledge she did not have, but she could offer what she did possess to others. She envisioned a circle of rosy-cheeked children, children who had no chance to go to school, no chance to learn even the simplest lessons. She would teach them to read, to add and subtract. She would buy a few books, and they could come to her cottage to glimpse a world beyond their village.

She would not waste money on dressmakers, but would make her own frocks. Her food, her furnishings, all would be very simple. And she would be content to wait through the years, wait for Savage to, perhaps, come for her. She could not force his decision, but he might yet come for her.

She thought of his drawn face, the pain of his final words, the public declaration of his love, drawn from him as a knife from a wound. She turned herself slowly in the hammock so that the pain did not flash through her chest. She was only a few feet from the open skylight.

"Anson," she said quietly. "Come here. I wish to speak to you."

She waited for several minutes, then heard faint footsteps. He stood over her, contained, unemotional, stiffly correct.

"I'm sorry I said such things in your hearing," he began. "It was a most unsuitable performance, and I apologize. I blackened the reputation of—"

"You spoke only the truth."

"To say such things in front of you, about you, when you're unwell and in pain..."

"Please, after I've gone, tell the men I'm most flattered by their request. It shall be a pleasant memory, for all of my life."

He pulled a stool next to her hammock, sat down, took her hand, caressed it sedately with the tips of his fingers. The darkness crept about them; it was no more complete than the silence between them. Stars twinkled overhead, and in the east a brilliant fireball streaked across the sky for an instant.

"I believe," he said finally, a trace of his old spirit in his voice, "that a mutiny is being conducted forward."

Dina opened her eyes, saw his face by the light of the lantern hanging above them in the rigging. The light created dark shadows around his nose, made his eyes deep wells. But he looked strangely content, for a captain whose crew was in rebellion.

"A mutiny?"

"Yes. None of the crew has gone ashore for the night, and there's quite a bit of talking and arguing."

"Mr. Becker will bring it under control."

"Mr. Becker seems to be part of it," he said wryly. "I believe it has something to do with finding a new navigator."

"You'll find someone," she said. "And if you don't, Charley knows quite enough. Have you considered Charley?"

"Yes. I may settle on him. But he talks of going home soon, and if he should abandon me in Macao, I'd be left to search again."

Three lanterns floated the length of the deck, like disembodied spirits. They drew near, clustered about her and Savage. The mutineers had come to some conclusion, for in the pools of light she saw serious, determined faces. Charley stepped forward without hesitation and faced Savage.

"We have a petition for you," he said clearly, proudly, each word of his correct English distinct.

Savage bowed his head. She noticed the nervous contraction of a muscle above his ear, a faint shadow changing from dark to light, but when he looked up at Charley, his face was resigned and serene.

"I'll accept your petition, but I won't say I'll grant it."

Charley bowed, extended his hand to another man, who gave him a scroll. Charley unrolled it with all the dignity of one of His Majesty's heralds. A sailor raised a lantern high to light the paper.

"Hear this, all ye people upon the *Pearl Stallion,* all low and high, all rich and poor..."

"'Tisn't many of us poor after this voyage," muttered a crewman standing behind him. Charley shot him a look of disgust.

"...for we lay before his High Mightiness, the captain, this our plea."

Savage's serenity vanished, turned to astonishment, his mouth opened slightly in surprise.

"For we have said unto him, think not of others, but give honor to the daughter of the great lord, the woman who guided us from the perils of California, the woman who opened the eyes and ears of the ignorant..."

Savage's mouth twitched slightly. He was fighting a grin. Dina found it hurt a great deal to keep her laughter bottled up in her bruised chest. Charley, acquainted only with the Bible as written English, had cast his petition, as a matter of course, in the cadences and wording of the Psalms.

"But he says, this woman has ravished my heart," continued Charley, "and must be sent away, else I shall dishonor her. She shall return to her own people. So, we say to him, whisper to her, 'O daughter, consider, and incline thine ear, forget also thine own people, and thy father's house,' for if he should say thus to her, she will forget her own people, and cling to him in love."

The incipient grin on Savage's lips disappeared. Shadows flickered on his throat as he gulped.

"And no man on this ship will say, 'This is wrong.' No man will say, 'The Captain lies with a woman, why should we not have women for our own?' For the daughter of a lord is as glorious as the queen in gold of Ophir, and she should not lie alone, for then she is barren. And her father's spirit is cast out by her barrenness. But only a man of like glory, the son of a lord, should lie with her, should end her barrenness."

It was Dina's turn to feel uncomfortable. They wanted her to have a baby? What in the world would she do with a baby on board a ship?

"And we see the captain is sick with love. We do beseech you, Mighty Captain, take her to yourself, like the stallion takes the mare upon the mountain, like the hart takes the doe, and end your sickness. We shall rejoice that she gives you pleasure and comfort, and shall not complain of our weary state."

He handed the paper to Savage with a flourish, who winced as if the very touch of the manuscript caused him pain.

"I believe," he said seriously, "that the lady must also be consulted. Under English law, you cannot give her to me without her consent."

The men withdrew a few feet and whispered among themselves.

"Yes," Charley said finally. "Lady Dina may say yes or no, also." He bowed. "We beg her pardon we did not address our plea to her, as well."

Savage handed her the paper.

"Careful of the pins. I pricked myself," he muttered.

No paper large enough had been available, so they had pinned three sheets together. Below the dramatic petition was the signature of every man aboard the ship. Dina's eyes filled when she saw them. Not one man had made his mark, but each had written his name according to his rank, from "Lt. Edw. Becker," down to "S. Radgni" and "Martin Alejandro." Her tears spilled over, and she turned her face aside so that they would not see now the message affected her. She stiffened to end the emotional reaction, for crying made her chest hurt.

"I believe," said Savage after clearing his throat, "I should speak to Her Ladyship alone. It's not customary for a lady to make such a decision with an audience."

After a bit of muttering and consultation, the crew withdrew amidships.

"I don't believe any captain ever received a more eloquent petition," he began. "But it's for you to decide."

"What am I to decide?" she asked. "The petition was addressed to you. What are you offering me?"

He sat on the stool, his elbows on his knees, his head in his hands. His shoulders slumped. The moment of his decision was plain, for he stood erect, his head brushing the sail rigged overhead. He smiled down at her, then bent over and kissed her quickly, avoiding the left side of her mouth.

"Will you be my wife?"

So long she had waited to hear the words! A year ago, waiting in fear and panic, knowing she must accept without wanting to. In Canton, in despair, fearing what her passionate body might lead her to. She reached out to him. He grasped her hands, turned them over, leaned down and placed a kiss upon each palm.

"What of your revenge upon the *ton?*" she asked. "You can't have both that and me."

"Revenge is not so simple as it seems. I have much less taste for it today then I did a few weeks ago."

"And your brother? Will your new resolve extend to him?"

"I pray he lives happily, and if he has a son, I'll offer him the same courtesy I hope he'll offer mine."

"Then you've taken Charley's plea to heart, and will end my barren state?" she asked, a sparkle of laughter edging into her voice.

"Charley's right. The spirit of the Cairnlea's survives only in you. Perhaps, if we have a son, some of my friends in the Company in London could prevail upon the king to create him anew the earl of Cairnlea."

"That's of no significance," she said, surprised at her own quick certainty. "I'd rather my son were a sturdy, honest captain of a trading ship, than live the life my father and brother did. A title and wealth can so easily lead a man into dissolution."

He leaned down and kissed her. "So? What shall the answer be? Shall Lady Dina be the wife of Anson Saurage and navigate the *Pearl Stallion* once more to Russian America?"

"I think yes. But the marriage contract has yet to be negotiated. I remain Lady Dina, and I still get three shares of the profits, and it's mine to do with as I wish."

He laughed the deep, rich laugh that had frightened and captivated her so long ago. "I once told Hampton you were only interested in titles and money. It seems I'm right."

"Yes. Particularly when I earn them."

"I think I'll give you everything," he said playfully. "For what I'll demand from you, you'll deserve more than just three shares."

"When do the demands start?" she whispered when he leaned over to claim a kiss.

"Tonight. No—as soon as you're well. I'll not cause you pain."

He picked up the petition from where it had fallen on the deck, walked forward.

"Her Ladyship agrees to the terms of the petition...and so do I," he announced. "We've decided it would be best if we were wed."

The cheers flooded around Dina's ears, and men clustered about her hammock, thanking her. Savage fought against the crowd to return to her side, but every man extended a hand to delay him. Either Barber or Loti opened the signal locker, for two red flares shot skyward and exploded into crimson lilies against the velvet black. Dina noticed Savage talking, gesturing to Kranz, before he came to her, scooped her out of the hammock.

Chapter Twenty

"Forward, all of you!" Savage roared at the crew. Dina, in his arms, felt the rise and fall of his chest. "If I find anyone aft of the mainmast, unless his duty brings him here, I'll send him ashore. Her Ladyship needs her rest." Dina laughed into his shirt, anticipating the night stretching before them, anticipating no rest at all.

Savage's order was greeted with applause, a shout of approval, and a general flight to the bow of the ship, leaving the way open for him to carry her below. A lantern hung in the stuffy main cabin, and a sullen breeze drifted occasionally through the open stern windows.

"Can you stand if I put you down?"

"Yes."

He lowered her feet to the deck, keeping his hands about her waist. She wavered, bent beneath the beams.

"Just long enough for me to get you undressed," he whispered. Two straw-filled mats lay side by side on the deck. So that was what he had requested of Kranz! He unbuttoned the loose silk gown, pushed it off her shoulders, then pulled her shift over her head, keeping it carefully away from her bruised face. Nothing was left but the wide muslin bandage that bound her chest. He guided her to the mats and supported her as she lay down.

He blew out the candle in the tin lantern. She knew from the sounds in the darkness that he was removing his own clothes. By the time he came to her, her eyes had adjusted to the darkness and she saw the lines of his magnificent body as he knelt beside her.

"Nothing tonight," he said, "except the certainty that nothing will ever come between us."

"Indeed? You'll leave your wife unloved?" She felt in the darkness for his hands, drew one to her and placed it over her breasts.

"There's a great difficulty we must discuss," he said, his fingers searching for and finding her nipple. "I don't know how we'll get married. March is nearly here. Ten days, two weeks at the most, and we must be under way, if we're to meet Baranov by midsummer. There's no time to post the banns."

"The men brought us together tonight. Tomorrow, they can marry us."

"No, Dina. Our marriage must be legally done. There can never be any question raised about your position, that you are my wife. I want no gossip that you're a kept woman, pulled from the Calcutta dung heap." His fingers traced circles about the fullness of her breasts. She enclosed his erotic shaft in her hands.

"It is legal. It's the Quaker way. My mother and father were married so. We write our promises to one another, read them before the crew, they sign as witnesses, each one a guarantor of our pledge to one another. In England, the government and church must accept the legality of a Quaker marriage."

He dropped beside her, thrust his left arm beneath her, rested his right hand on her mound. Then his fingers slid between her thighs, fondled the expectant flesh. She lay quiet, still, relaxed, letting him nurture her sensuality without heightening her breathing. She spread her legs, admired his control. The brush of his hands down the length of her thighs felt no stronger than the touch of a warm breeze.

He did not rouse her to raging passion, which would have caused her pain, but enveloped her in caring. She felt her own wetness, and when she lifted her hand to once more clasp his organ, he, too, was moist. Within this calm, unhurried love, their bodies had grown ready for one another. He shifted her, very tenderly, to her side, lay behind her, and the tip of his erection spread her opening without entering.

"Dina, if I had come to you this way a year ago, without frightening you, would you have yielded to me?"

"A year ago it would not have been possible. The very sight of you, the very thought of a man ready for a woman, sent me into panic."

"What's changed? What changed in Canton?"

"Love, I suppose. Knowing I could trust you. And... what happened in California. I learned I could resist, protect myself."

"Lie still," he said, rearranging her body, stroking her back and hips until her breath came in slow, shallow gulps. He settled more deeply within her, bringing with him a fathomless sense of reconciliation, of perfect union. His fingers held her hips firmly, he withdrew from her, pressed in slowly.

"What if Don Miguel had succeeded?" she asked. "How might you have felt about me?"

"I have never agreed with the generality of men over the value of a maidenhead. What I treasure is a woman who finds the same joy I do in the act of coming together."

"What if I had found pleasure in him?" she persisted.

"Don't ask," he muttered, his fingers tightening, pressing to her bones. "When I think of what I did to you, because of a silly suspicion..." He kissed the back of her neck. "I hope jealousy never again seizes me in that way, but I find I cannot be sure. Will you promise not to test my resolve? To be faithful in this way?"

"And you? Can you give me the same promise?"

He raised himself slightly, and her flesh parted easily as he extended the reach of his shaft to its ultimate depth.

"I can give you the same promise," he said firmly.

"Then tomorrow we'll say it to one another in public, and it shall be so for the rest of our lives."

His fingers found her mound, stimulated her lightly as he moved within her. Her body became translucent liquid, a pool intended for his submersion. A pebble fell from a great height, and the ripples spread from the point of his touch, a rhythmic sequence of internal caresses. She lay quite still, wondering at the sensation, so like, yet so different from, the passion he had excited within her in Canton. His slow, gentle thrusts ended with a sharp penetration, then another and another, a bellow of welcome relief, and the heat of his seed filled her.

When his cries ceased, when he lay still behind her, the ripples echoed back through her body, until their sensual passion was consumed within the great heaving ocean of love.

Dina paced across the veranda of the house that had been her home for the past ten days. She was sure she could walk to the wharf without any difficulty, but Savage had insisted she wait for the sedan chair. *I'm quite well,* she said to herself, *and he's treating me like a child who can't make decisions.* But, she had to admit, she enjoyed being cosseted and protected, and she had seen the extent of his concern over the past days.

His concern . . . and the physical expression of his love, which had become more and more intense as her body mended. She shoved the recollection away from her, for the smallest reminder of his sexual skills caused a tightening, her body preparing for a new round of lovemaking.

A crowd of sailors ran down the street, the sedan chair bouncing in their hands. Her husband ran beside them. The mob skidded to a breathless stop in front of the house.

"Radgni's coming with a barrow to carry your things to the ship," he said. "Climb in." She accepted one of the many proffered hands, climbed into the chair, felt it lifted by a dozen men.

"Have you thought of anything else you need? Tomorrow's the last day we can take supplies aboard."

"Nothing...except...several yards of muslin. White muslin."

"I'll have one of the men see to it. Wouldn't want you to exhaust your supply of petticoats."

He laughed, making gentle fun of her insistence that she wear skirts on board ship. The muslin wasn't for petticoats, but she would not tell him. At least not for a while.

"Now, come and see your new home," he said, once they were on board.

"New home?" He led her down the companionway. The main cabin looked no different, but when he opened the door of his sleeping cabin, it was as if the ship had been rebuilt. The bulkhead between her tiny space and his had been knocked out, making a cabin at least seven feet wide and ten feet long. The bunk hanging from the beams was huge, as large as any bed on land. The canvas curtain that had covered his coats—the curtain behind which she had taken her refuge—was gone, replaced by one of green silk with gold threads woven through it. Two sea chests stood in front of the drapery. A chair, a real chair, occupied one corner, and another sat before the writing shelf. On the far bulkhead, a frame had been built, and within it nestled a tin basin. Above was a looking glass with a carved frame.

"It's beautiful!"

"Now, you must rest here, for the water boy is coming out, and I'm going to be busy." He knelt before her and removed her slippers, then grasped her ankles and lifted her legs onto the bed. "I'll send someone ashore for your muslin."

She lay on her back, staring up at the compass. It was really too soon to be certain, but her monthly time should have come two or three days ago. And the voyage might last eight, ten months, even a year, so she must be prepared. Would muslin be enough? Perhaps blankets? No, she decided, relaxing gratefully in the motion of the ship. She'd wrap the child in her silk shawl.

* * *

"Look, downriver. An Indiaman," remarked Savage. All Dina could see in the early-morning light was the pile of sails, like a cluster of white cloud catching the sun.

"A good wind for him," said Savage from across the folding table. "Bad for us." He was impatient to be gone, she knew. Three days they had lain, ready to weigh anchor, but trapped in Calcutta by the foul wind from the sea.

The Indiaman drew nearer. Savage studied her closely. Dina tried to see what he was seeing, the set of her sails, the angle of her decks. What did the ship tell him?

"The wind isn't quite so strong this morning," he mused. "Perhaps it's preparing to change."

He walked away from her to better observe the newcomer as it glided past and anchored a quarter mile beyond the *Pearl Stallion*. It carried mail from England. Letters not more than six months old. There would be none for her, for six months ago Uncle Leonard had received the first news of her flight. This Indiaman probably carried letters from Uncle Leonard to Uncle George, letters discussing the disposition of her jewelry, warning George not to take her back if she reappeared in Calcutta, for Leonard would not want his own daughter corrupted by the presence of his whorish niece. How long before he learned of his brother's death? Of Freemantle's fate?

Within a week, Freemantle would ascend the scaffold built on the waterfront, only a mile from where the *Pearl Stallion* floated. In the presence of every curious Englishman and Indian, he would be dropped into eternity, as payment for the murder of the clerk and George Mason. Except for his rage and the thrust of his blade, George Mason would be standing on the scaffold beside him.

Footsteps close by, a sound she knew and looked forward to hearing.

"At least," he said, "we'll get late news from England before we sail."

"Do you expect something?" she asked curiously.

"No. There's never anything for me, except business."

"Mail, sir," said Becker's voice behind them. He laid a thick packet on the table.

Savage picked up the canvas envelope without looking at it. His eyes were focused upon the feathered vane in the rigging. It betrayed a new variation in the breeze, a light air blowing occasionally at right angles to the river. He drew a knife from his boot and slit the stitches in the canvas, glanced again at the vane.

He thinks the wind is changing, thought Dina gratefully. By nightfall, we'll be out of this heat, on the ocean.

The papers crackled when he unfolded them, casually, his eyes darting from the letters, to the vane, to Becker, who distributed mail to the sailors. Dina watched him, for the pleasure it gave her. For the small triumphs she felt when she guessed what he was thinking.

His face changed, and the fingers of one hand covered his mouth as if to stifle a gasp. He would have grown pale if his dark skin had permitted it. His eyes focused solely upon the letter now. He folded it with a sudden crunch, shoved it back into the canvas envelope.

"Come below," he ordered curtly.

She followed him down the companionway, her busy mind attempting to sort out the possibilities. What could be in the letter to disturb him so much? Had his brother done something in England to affect his standing with the Company? Might Lord Mornington, now in England, have betrayed his trust, had his license been withdrawn? He thrust the packet into her hands, lowered the skylight and slammed the door behind her to shut them in.

"My lord," began the letter, in elegant script.

She looked into his troubled eyes.

"Edwin is dead—" his voice trembled "—and Amelia gave him no child."

Edwin? Edwin Saurage, the earl of Valmont. No. The intelligence curled like smoke through her brain. She was looking at the earl of Valmont. She studied the letter, its date. Six months ago, more than six months. When they were sailing from New Archangel into the Pacific, his brother had drawn his final breath. In Canton, when she first lay with him, even then he'd been Lord Valmont. In another world, he had been accepted as Lord Valmont.

The sounds of that other world pounded in her ears, visions of it flashed behind her eyes. The pushing mamas, displaying their daughters before the titles and wealth they wished them to acquire by marriage. Right now, in that world, the season had begun, the gossip was circulating: The new Lord Valmont was wealthy, handsome, without a wife.

He could have his choice. The daughters of dukes and marquesses—even, perhaps, a daughter of the king—would be willing to be his countess.

The fragility of the parchment she had so carefully folded and placed in her sea chest came home to her. "I shall love you forever," they had both declared. No matter how many witnesses signed it, did it truly bind him? Her hand dropped instinctively to her stomach.

"You can now have any woman you want," she whispered.

"What?"

"In London, right now, the *ton* will fawn over Lord Valmont. Any woman you see . . . Our marriage is very informal."

"Informal?" he asked, and she saw the puzzled squint of his eyes, the drawing together of the slash of brow. "What are you talking about?"

"If you wish to be released from it, I cannot stand in your way." She knew two tears had started their paths down her cheeks, and resented them. Resented her too-easy descent into weeping emotionalism. "You can marry great wealth and great prestige."

"Informal? Is that what you think of our marriage?" he said, rather too loudly. Even with the skylight shut, the remark would have carried on deck.

"I simply mean to say, if you should want to be released, do not go to the law. I'll—"

"Informal! By heaven, everyone on this ship heard what we said. It's written in the log of the *Pearl Stallion.* You saw me put it down. Informal! Do you think to go back on something that every man—"

"Anson, please, don't shout. I love you, I want to be your wife, but if this changes things..."

"It changes nothing." He stamped a foot impatiently, with more than a touch of anger. "It changes nothing! In fact, you'll be quiet about it. That's an order! For this voyage, at least, I'll still be Captain Savage, not some bloody snuff-taking aristocrat. No one's to hear a thing about it. What would Baranov say, if he knew I had a title?"

"The crew will certainly hear, onshore."

"There's to be no more shore time. The wind's changing. By evening we'll be sailing down the Hooghly. You'll not mention this. You're still Lady Dina, not Lady Valmont, do you understand? You'll be Lady Valmont when I give permission." He spoke roughly.

"I'm very proud to be Lady Dina. I worked for that title."

His face relaxed into a broad smile, a smile that pulled her toward him as certainly as his strong arm.

"Nothing. Say nothing. But this voyage will end in a different way. From Canton, we'll sail to England. Would you like to try Cape Horn? I've never sailed it, and Captain Hawkins said from west to east—"

"It's the easiest way," she said, completing his thought. Would they be back to England in time? She looked directly into his black eyes, dark depths into which she had long since cast herself. "What you have before you, the title and estates of the Valmonts, isn't it also the easiest way?"

"No. Once, when I was much younger, I wished to be Lord Valmont. Now the thought terrifies me. I can't conceive of a life so slow and patterned. So walled about with tradition and formality."

"You'll be a most unusual lord," she said, raising her face to his and standing on her toes. He leaned down for a kiss, just as the ship swung on her anchor cables.

"The wind," he whispered before their lips touched. "It's changing." He turned away, ran up on deck, two steps at a time.

Dina followed more slowly, stood aft, out of the way, watching the lifting of the anchors, the setting of the triangular sails that would catch the quartering wind and send them down the Hooghly. She watched the last buildings of Calcutta disappear in the distance. She would probably never see the town again. Russian America, the Sandwich Islands. What would the queen think, when she saw her still thin, but with a child on the way? Her pregnancy would be obvious by then.

Canton, Cape Horn, England.

A child. Anson's son, engendered in one of those ecstatic nights in Calcutta, when he had taught her the varieties of passion. Or such varieties as a woman with three broken ribs could perform.

The Cairnleas were gone, the male line was dead. That would not happen to the Valmonts, she resolved. That line would continue through her, and through the love her dear Savage gave her.

The first rolling waves of the Bay of Bengal carried the *Pearl Stallion* upward in a graceful arc. She pressed her fingers against the rigging, counting the months until the child would arrive.

"December." She mouthed the one world quietly.

He was beside her, and he laid his hand upon her busy fingers.

"December what?" he asked curiously. "What will happen in December?"

She had promised never to keep anything from him. But in this case . . . Calcutta was still too close for comfort, the wind still right for him to sail back and leave her, with the best of intentions, in some trusted woman's care.

"I was just wondering. Will we be in England by Christmas?"

"That depends on the winds and the skill of our navigation." He threw back his head, laughed at her, at the sky, at the wind, at the joy of once more being at sea.

"Lady Dina," he said in his voice of the quarterdeck. "Please set a course to the strait. I believe on this wind we can reach the North Channel."

* * * * *